TIGHT LIES

TED DENTON

BLOODHOUND
— BOOKS —

www.bloodhoundbooks.com

Print ISBN 978-1-914614-11-8

For anyone who ever just got back up and went at it again.
For MJP. Always.
For the service men and women who choose to risk their lives, intent on making our world a better place. Heroes all.
...and for a once in a lifetime dog...

FOREWORD

The author takes no responsibility for the validity of factual research conducted during the writing of this book. Please note that there is no insinuation that the British government and its officers nor the PGA European Golf Tour, its employees, players, caddies, sponsors or agents are in any way or have ever been corrupt. There is no deliberate intention to relate Russian criminality to the oil and gas industry, to sport or to politics except for solely creative purposes. References to real companies such British Petroleum are only used to add corporate authenticity within the book around the subject matter and there is no insinuation that they are or ever have been involved in any political or commercial corruption. Rublex Corporation is an entirely fictional entity with no reference to any existing or previous organisation.

INTRODUCTION

In the sport of golf, a 'tight lie' is deemed to be the position (or lie) in which one's ball has come to rest either upon bare dirt, very short grass, or where there is very little grass beneath the ball. This often makes the connection between the club head and golf ball harder to strike cleanly and therefore the outcome of the intended shot is harder to execute with accuracy.

Tight – (adjective): difficult to deal with or get out of; experiencing a feeling of constriction.

Lie – (noun): a resting position; a false statement made with deliberate intent to deceive; a falsehood.

1

Occupying the back corner of some cheap dive of a bar with a chipped tumbler of Bourbon for company, I sat chewing on a splintered match. The place was a dark rancid hole. To tell the truth I looked just about bad enough to fit right in. Hell, the regulars hadn't even looked at me twice with my three-day old stubble and oil-stained checked shirt. None of the usual lingering stares at the thick white scar which scores its way up from my neck, petering out across my left cheek.

I scanned the bar at leisure. An old scab-ridden whore, skin ravaged from too much sun and cigarette smoke, was staggering on skinny legs encased in tattered pantyhose. She wobbled between two time-worn men, labourers or mechanics with nothing waiting for them back home most likely, each slouched upon a solitary barstool yet connected by a shared silence and a bottle of Tequila. She was bothering them for drinks, hoping to turn a quick trick in the stinking alleyway behind the building.

The desperate scene played out in front of an ox of a man who was tending bar. Heavyset with broad rounded shoulders, his greasy black hair hung down to a protruding stomach. He sported a vibrant short-sleeved Hawaiian shirt, fashion appearing starkly in contrast with the dismal surroundings and his pockmarked, humourless face. The shirt stretched over a pair of massive ham-like arms and lay unbuttoned to the navel, displaying an unseemly mat of tangled black chest hair.

The barkeep's neck and chest were covered in heavy patterns of green and blue tattoo ink and to cap it all off he was missing most of his front teeth. I didn't see this guy making front page of the local tourist board's promotional brochure anytime soon.

Took a swallow of Bourbon. Chased it with a couple of painkillers. Savoured the burn as the action played out in front of me. The whore cackling with laughter. Two spindly, decrepit drunks squabbling at a table to the side of the bar. They began to scrabble at each other, knocking down chairs as they tore at shirts and faces with grubby fingernails, breaking glasses and spilling drinks as they went. Nobody seemed to notice. Ox surveyed the saloon bar with not so much as a raised eyebrow, polishing a grimy glass with a dirty rag. Above him hung an oversized pickaxe handle mounted on a couple of rusted masonry nails. A scrawl of thick black marker pen beneath announced: 'The Peacemaker'. I smiled to myself. My time spent within the murkier elements of the British armed forces had instilled a twisted appreciation of a man who took pride in his work.

The door banged open. A stream of light flooded the barroom as a couple entered. My focus heightened. A rat-faced man with sinewy arms led the way, his blond ponytail trailing down a cracked leather waistcoat. He dragged a young Mexican girl by her upper arm. She was petite and dressed up like a child's 'cowgirl doll' in tight denim Daisy Duke cut-offs, ankle boots and midriff revealing tank top.

She squirmed in the man's rough grasp. He threw her down at a nearby table and gestured to the barkeep for service. Ox duly appeared with two bottles of beer, still soaked from the cool of the fridge. He set them on the table. Retreated. The blond guy took a long swig of beer, sparked a Marlboro Red from a battered Zippo lighter and inhaled. This was plainly not an establishment which concerned itself with pandering to the ubiquitous American anti-smoking laws. The man reached across the table and grabbed a fistful of the young girl's hair. She was sixteen at the most but showed a whole lot of living in those pretty brown eyes. He pulled her forward across the table kissing her roughly on the mouth. A bony hand thrust itself down the front of her tank top. He laughed and pushed her back into her chair, a crumpled and frightened mess trying to play the grown-up woman. I watched from across the bar, jaw clenched in anger. And through force of habit found myself tracing my thumbnail down the deep scar on my face. Scoring it deeper. Partly seeking reassurance from the familiar contours, partly working it to ensure its permanence as my defining mark. I drained the glass, sat back, inhaling slow and deep to hold my rage in check. I studied the bar. No one else seemed to care. Another biker mistreating his girl – just part of the fabric of the place. I closed my eyes in resignation and breathed. The fickle lens of my mind's eye transported me so vividly back to my service within the Regiment. A time where respect was earned through action and deed. A life governed by a much-needed structure which had, at that time, brought order to my worthless life. There was a time, way back in Hereford, England, when the name Captain Tom Hunter, youngest commander of A Troop or any of the four squadrons of 22nd Special Air Service Regiment of the Regular Army, had been spoken with pride, even held up as an example for fellow soldiers to emulate.

I thought about my life now and how things had changed.

~

A fist slamming into a table and the sound of shattering glass snapped my attention back to the here and now. The blond biker had the tiny Latina girl by the arm again and was forcing her to her knees under the table. She was sobbing. He leant back chuckling, one hand on his beer and the other on the top of her head as she reluctantly busied herself in an attempt to pleasure him. Moments later he was holding his drink over the girl's bobbing head, pouring splashes of beer down on top of her. Feeding her humiliation. The sound jarred me. A painful memory, not buried deep enough, came bubbling over. That was enough.

I stood, scanning the bar for overt threats. The rest of the punters continued about their business. Ox was leaning forward, meaty forearms resting on the bar, smirking as he enjoyed the show.

I staggered across the bar in feigned inebriation, as if solely intent on ordering yet another drink. Nearing the couple, I took two quick steps forward and kicked the edge of the table forcefully into the chest of the unsuspecting biker. The impact smashed him backwards off his chair, onto the floor. I flew after him and, pushing the girl aside, stamped down on the knee joint of his flailing leg. Pulled the table off, held it up and over him. Shouted at the girl to stand. The biker was screaming out in pain, hands groping at the shattered kneecap. Going nowhere fast. Without pause I slammed the table's sharp edge downward into his windpipe.

I glanced up to see the huge bartender, moving faster than his corpulent body belied, wielding The Peacemaker in both hands. It scythed towards my head. I dived sideways as the weapon collided with the table, cracking the top in two.

4

Momentum slid me into a cluster of three older guys; all long greasy grey hair and tasselled leather jackets.

One of these men pulled me from the floor by my hair, striking me hard in the temple, scrambling my senses. The Ox was coming for more, swinging The Peacemaker with gusto like he was batting out the ninth inning for the Dodgers. I stooped and, reaching into my boot, pulled out the eight-inch hunting knife strapped inside. Thrust out wildly into the armpit of my mature assailant and twisted. It was enough to free me from his grip and I lurched forward again pulling out my Beretta.

'Stay the hell where you are!' I shouted in general at the bar, spinning and pointing the gun towards the motley crew assembled at ringside. 'Nobody move and we are out of here. Gone. If so much as a goddam finger reaches for a gun I swear I will shoot it the hell off.'

Ox stood still. Breathing hard, sweat pouring off his fat acne-scarred face. His expression was contorted with rage. The Peacemaker rested inside his meaty double-handed grip, making him look like an oversized tennis player. All he needed was a headband. 'You've killed him, man,' he howled, glancing at the biker sprawled on the floor of the bar. 'He's not moving. You're dead, you son of a bitch. I'll lose my licence for this. I promise you are finished, punk!'

I inched back, covering the bar evenly with the barrel of the Beretta as I moved. I reached the young girl who was crying and shaking. 'You cool?' I said, stealing a glance towards her mascara-streaked face. She nodded. Taking her wrist, I continued to edge backward together until we reached the door. We piled through into the sunlight; a cacophony of cursing and shouting behind us.

'Who are you? Where are we going? What the hell is going on, man? You killed my boyfriend, asshole,' she cried, tears streaming down her pretty face.

'Listen, I don't know how a nice girl like you got caught up in all this but from where I was sitting it didn't look like you were having much fun. Your parents hired me to get you away from that bastard. It's a done deal. My car's down the next street. You're coming with me and we've gotta run. NOW!'

We turned the corner on the block as a throng of people rushed out onto the street behind us, followed by the throaty punch of motorbike engines gunning. I was damn near dragging the girl off her feet and, by the time we reached the car, she was missing a boot. The beaten-up rusting red jalopy was specifically picked for the job so as not to stand out in this low rent gang-infested neighbourhood in Bell, the predominantly Hispanic suburb of Los Angeles. Right then I wished I'd gone for speed over style.

I ripped open the unlocked car door and pushed the skinny brown girl onto the seat. Jumped into the driver seat, twisting the key in the ignition. On the second time of asking it spluttered into life. Over the pop and crackle of it backfiring I shouted across, 'Consuela – there's a blonde wig in the bag at your feet. Put it on.'

'What? Like no way. This is all just so crazy, man.' Her tiny fists were balled up tight in her lap. I could swear she was pouting.

'Connie, put that dumb wig on!' an urgent hiss as I swivelled my neck around me, checking for action on the streets. 'We've got to get out of here. We're dead if they catch up with us. Do it now!'

Scowling, she pulled on the wig. It was thick and heavy with platinum blonde curls. I threw on a baseball cap with shades kept ready in the dash box. Rolling down the window halfway, I stuck an elbow out and casually slid the vehicle into the road. We weren't going to outrun anyone in this thing, so we'd have to bluff our way clear. We approached the intersection. A screech of tyres as two leather clad bikers pulled out sharply, skidding into the path of a fast-moving blue Ford pickup running in the opposite direction. One of the hogs bailed onto its side in the effort to stop. It slid under the wheels of the truck, the rider's leg trapped underneath. The pickup driver, moustached, sporting an unwashed mullet and wearing the apparently obligatory checked flannel shirt, threw open his door, hollering and gesticulating wildly at the pair. The fallen biker rose to his feet, wiped his bloodied mouth on the back of his hand. As if watching a well-rehearsed synchronised dance, he pulled out his handgun at the identical moment that his wingman and mirror image did so too. With a point to make they began pumping holes into the side panelling of the sky-blue Ford, tearing the metal apart.

This was the perfect opportunity for us to slip away unnoticed. I threw the jalopy in reverse and backed up down the street. Spun the vehicle in a neat skid, flipped into a side street, and put my foot on the gas, leaving nothing behind us but dust.

Twenty clear minutes on the freeway passed in silence as we threaded out of town, most of which saw Connie sitting with the blonde wig on her lap and a sorry pout on her face. I punched some numbers into my cell phone. 'Mr Rodriguez, I've got your daughter. She's safe and well,' I said, grinning over at Connie. The girl's instant response was to wrinkle up her nose and dart her little pink tongue out at me. 'We're ready to make the drop as arranged, Mr Rodriguez. See you in an hour and you can take it from there.'

2

SPAIN. EUROPEAN TOUR: DAY ONE.

Daniel splashed cold water on his face and exhaled. He ran wet fingers through his floppy blond hair. Looking in the mirror, he straightened his collar and forced a smile. He could barely believe he was here. This was it. The door was ajar to a new world of infinite possibility.

Peering around he absorbed the alien opulence of an apparently endless washroom; what had just been a simple door to the toilet leading off from the lobby in the Bayfield Mandarin Hotel. He was greeted by a classic example of traditional Spanish finery and an unmitigated deployment of wealth: gold-plated mirrors, marble tops adorned with carefully folded pristine woollen washcloths, glass bottles of exotic looking oils and thick white creams. The setting only served to exaggerate the long distance he already felt from England and the life he'd grown up in. The dreary hometown on the outskirts of Sheffield, from which he had left at dawn in a battered taxi that very same morning. Waving to his parents standing at the doorstep in their pyjamas against a backdrop of cold, swirling drizzle.

The meeting had taken place barely five weeks ago now. And time seemed to have jumped forward since, because now he was actually here. Daniel had been working as an intern in a small publishing house in Sheffield – a business still clinging to the fading success of the single celebrated author they had ever been lucky enough to represent. 'The Ego', as he was referred to somewhat churlishly, had delivered them a bestseller. A clever and well-regarded spy thriller. The book was a well-researched, technical and refreshing view on modern espionage. For its time. That 'The Ego' hadn't yet managed to deliver the much vaunted and overpromised sequel meant that things had moved on apace with the subject matter. There were doubts, from those that knew him, whether he would be able to keep up. It was the cause of serious consternation and turmoil amongst the partners in the business. The significant advance he'd already been paid was having a deleterious effect on company cash flow and the whole situation snagged intemperately on an increasingly fractious and frayed working atmosphere. If Daniel had been asked to sum up his working environment in just one word, he may well have selected toxic as the descriptor.

He'd studied computer science at Sheffield University before taking forensic accountancy as a vocational option to satisfy his father. He'd mixed this in with modules in sports science and investigative journalism to satisfy his own wider interests. Living at home to save money in line with cautious parental advice, rather than studying elsewhere in the country, had stifled any possible claim to genuine independence. Only two of his classmates who came through comprehensive school with him had secured a coveted place in higher education. It wasn't hard to envy their shared flat, succession of drunken escapades and tales of daring-do documented via an endless stream of social media updates. Still, surviving his parents and keeping sane for twenty-one years was, he considered, quite an achievement in itself, albeit one that might not generate as much attention from girls on an Insta feed. Daniel had been blessed with an overprotective mother and a down-to-earth, no-nonsense father whose life mission was to preserve as much money as possible for some future, but as yet unspecified, purpose. They were both sticklers for the rules and shared an irrational fear of any form of lawbreaking, however moderate or necessary it may be. On one occasion, the curtains had been kept drawn and the milk left on the doorstep for a week to maintain the pretence that the family were abroad, having returned to their vehicle some six minutes after a car parking ticket had expired, albeit unnoticed. Despite the cruel caricatures, Daniel knew they were good people. Good ordinary people who wanted the best for their only child. Irrespective, it was still depressing to see his entire future life sketched out far in front of him. Being forced to share his parents' lives was a slow and torturous death. In his mind he knew he was destined for more.

He had met Silvio working at the publishing business. A portly, permanently tanned, silver-haired gentleman of Italian heritage with a predilection for snugly fitting waistcoats, brown buckled brogues, and long, indulgent lunches. He didn't work for the company, happening instead to rent a desk there in order to conduct his own business, the mainstay of which was to sell sports content for media consumption across books, magazines, television, and online. He came and went as he pleased with an easy smile and never concerned himself, it seemed, with the bitter undercurrent of resentment emanating from the morose publishing staff whose building he shared. He'd noticed Daniel busying himself around the office and, when the boy had shown a keen interest in some of the sports content across his desk, he'd decided to indulge him. When the deal came together, it all happened so fast. Silvio had contacts in golf, an opportunity on the European Tour, and a tie-up with an American sports agency to cement. They had some talented up-and-coming southern hemisphere players currently living in London. There was no one to manage them in Europe as they weren't yet ready to progress to the US PGA Tour, typically considered the hardest to win playing privileges upon. In order to secure the gig, the plan was that Silvio would create the illusion of having a ready-made team. Daniel could be moulded quickly to fit that remit and no one at the American sports agency would be any the wiser. They'd already worked with Silvio and he had the solution they needed. Daniel got an exciting opportunity he would grab with both hands. Everyone wins.

Five short weeks and a crash course in the beautiful intricacies of professional golf later, here he was. Like plenty of boys, he supposed, Daniel had enjoyed sports at school above academic lessons. He was a naturally gifted sportsman, tall, rangy and athletic with good hand-eye co-ordination. In preparation of the new career, he'd hacked a golf ball round the local pitch and putt track to half decent effect, heralding his father's advice and foregoing the unnecessary expense of a single lesson.

Now he stood in the washroom of the Bayfield Mandarin Hotel in the Valencia region of south-eastern Spain at the start of a prestigious European Tour event. He needed to front up and blend in to take this opportunity. Play it cool and make it happen, he told himself. *Would anyone spot that he just didn't belong*, he wondered. Daniel Ratchet, Player Manager to some of the hottest young guns competing to win this week's European Tour event, who feels like everyone is looking at him. As if he stands out a blinking mile. A kid who got lucky by meeting an old man in the right place at the right time. Daniel Ratchet, with just one chance to make it work. No turning back.

The door to the washroom swung open. Two swarthy middle-aged guys filed in wearing well-filled matching white polo shirts, navy shorts and long white socks pulled up to the knees. They chatted animatedly in Spanish. Daniel, no longer alone with his thoughts, nodded a greeting, dried his hands, and exited back out into the hotel. The place was a hive of activity, buzzing with glamorous, well-dressed, sun-kissed people. Players, denoted by their heavily logoed caps, crowded around a free-standing noticeboard. An olive-skinned girl in a crisply pressed uniform stood next to it answering questions. A large antique desk stood dominating the space, behind which an unsmiling leather-skinned matron in her mid-fifties sat addressing the impatient queue of players. Notes were being entered into a large binder. Her streaky blonde ponytail was scraped tightly back from her forehead exposing deeply etched lines worn into the strong features of a handsome Germanic face. The scene was the epitome of no-nonsense, diligent efficiency and the brusque tones with which she addressed the players showed that she meant business.

Daniel joined the back of the throng and studied the noticeboard. The pairings for the first round of the event were listed sequentially by tee-off time. These were strict minute-by-minute timings which could not be missed, on pain of disqualification, by even a few seconds. Daniel's role as Player Manager was specifically to look after two promising young guys from the Crown Sports stable, Aaron and François. Australian and South African respectively. Noting the piercing stare directed towards him from the older of the two women, presumably for loitering and obstructing the view of the board, he double-checked relevant tee-times for his guys and made a mental note, before slipping away.

Growing up as an only child, Daniel was quite used to spending time alone. He'd break free of the house at any given opportunity, seeking to escape the predictable monotony of family routine by setting out on long distance country runs. Out through the town and into the undulating greenery beyond, leaving the quiet terrace and its cul-de-sac behind. What he felt now though was a different type of isolation. Here he was surrounded by people teaming through the clubhouse. It left him feeling awkward, like something might stand out about the way he was dressed or that he was somehow perpetually in the way.

Silvio had warned him of course. 'Don't be put off when you get out on Tour. There's a lot of what they call "etiquette" in golf. It's a game for the rich made up of endless rules. So, what do you expect, eh? You can either feel part of it or not. A smart boy like you will learn soon enough and until then just keep your head down, your mouth shut, and try to look the part.' He'd lay his hands on Daniel's shoulders in an avuncular manner as he issued his nuggets of advice. 'People will typically assume you are what you say you are until you prove otherwise. Life on Tour is a bubble. Just a week will feel like months have passed. It's intense and addictive and you'll wonder at times if you can even survive it, although you'll soon realise, my friend, that it's a world you can't live without!' He'd finish the pep talks with one of his beaming benevolent smiles.

Daniel approached the security guard and flashed the cherished metallic Tour money clip, which served as an all-access pass for approved Tour personnel and players. He entered the spacious restaurant reserved for those involved in that week's tournament. There were small clusters of players and officials gathered at the various tables. Eating. Chatting. Studying charts of the course. A few he recognised from the television or their picture profiles in the Tour handbook, but most he didn't. To his left, a gleaming glass wall looked out onto the luscious green course with imposing mountains beyond that traced the curvature of the building. The entire right-hand wall of the room was pinned by long tables adorned in starched white tablecloths. They shouldered a regal spread of buffet-style platters and servers. A wide range of hot and cold food had been laid out in deep trays, accompanied by stacks of sparkling crockery. Two moustached waiters ladled generous portions from the silver slavers. Daniel selected a small helping of rice and chicken with a warm bread roll. Having missed breakfast in his rush to catch the flight, and with his nerves persuading his stomach against a plastic-wrapped aeroplane sandwich, he could certainly have eaten more. Not an untypical situation given that growing up he would often be teased for a prodigious appetite and a set of hollow legs. Somehow the current situation didn't become an overladen plate.

Daniel found an empty table in a corner and sat, watching intently, taking everything in. People came and went. There were some obvious cliques, players of the same nationality or age grouping together. He could hear raucous laughter from a gang of three South African players. A cluster of serious looking blond Nordic types, perhaps Swedes or Danes, played artistically with forks through their food, speaking in deep tones about their practice rounds and current challenges in their game. In an attempt to look preoccupied, Daniel took out a card of the course and toyed with memorising the layout of the holes and their yardages. It made little sense. Swirls, icons, and tiny numbers peppered the pocket-sized chart. He tried to glean what he could. Although more pertinent material for the players than their agents and particularly more so for the caddies, he needed something convincing he could regurgitate at an appropriate moment in conversation which might otherwise expose him as a total golf-fraud. There was so much to all this. Daniel wiped his brow. He was way out of his depth and drowning fast.

'Mind if we sit here?'

Daniel looked up into the friendly brown eyes of a heavily muscled, sandy-haired German guy in a tight-fitting polo shirt which looked as if it could have been painted on.

'No, please. Be my guest. Er... I'm Daniel,' he said, adding quickly, 'from Crown Sports.' Part introduction, part explanation.

'Hi, Daniel,' came a cheerful voice from behind the broad shoulders of the German. 'This is Michael and I'm Matilda.' A slender, smiling vision in a white T-shirt and tailored blue shorts.

She placed a bowl of salad onto the table in front of her, followed by two toned, bronzed legs slipped under it. They looked like the perfect couple. A wholesome advertisement for the human race itself, or least an endorsement for some high-end luxury Swiss spa. He pictured them feeding each other muesli at sunrise whilst practising complex yoga moves.

Glad of the enforced company and conscious that he stood out being the only person eating alone, Daniel pushed his course chart aside and began engaging the pair.

'Busy week, isn't it?'

'Mmm, yes,' Michael replied between mouthfuls of a thick slab of bloodied steak that Daniel eyed with pangs of envy. 'For us, always busy. Lots of the guys need fixing up in the truck.'

'The truck?' Daniel replied carefully, not wanting to show himself up so soon.

'Yeah, the physio truck – we're the treatment team – don't tell me you're the only one who hasn't used us yet?' giggled Matilda in a gentle Swedish accent.

'Ah right, I'm new out here actually,' blustered Daniel by way of apology. 'But I'm sure my guys have worked with you before. Do you happen to know Aaron Crower and François Steine?'

'Of course!' Matilda shot a glance at Michael and leaned in conspiratorially. 'Aaron is a perfectionist who likes to be pampered. He uses his maximum quota of stretching and massage sessions before and after every round. I guess François sees using the truck as a sign of weakness or something. He could slip a disc out there and would still rather soldier on than get any help.'

Michael flashed a knowing smile and looked down at the table, shaking his head.

'We work together to get to know all the guys' exact training routines, areas of their bodies that are prone to weakness, and everything required to get them ticking like clockwork. Each player is very different,' said the German.

'You must have great memories. That's a lot to keep on top of,' keened Daniel, set on making a positive impression.

Michael pulled out a slim white USB memory stick from his pocket and tapped it against the side of his head. 'Yeah. Great memory, us Germans,' he grinned. 'I keep everything on this. All the bio-stats on every player you could want. I keep it with me everywhere; it just plugs straight into any device, even a smartphone, and you're good to go. So, I don't need to be so smart myself after all you see!'

Daniel felt foolish again but then Michael was smiling at him good-naturedly and, before he was able to change the subject, a French player with heavy stubble and a slightly disgusted look on his face tapped the big German physio on the shoulder. Explaining that he had an early tee time in the morning he insisted that he be slotted in for urgent treatment to fix a tightening in his calf muscle. Michael looked first at Matilda and then at Daniel with raised eyebrows before pushing his plate of half-eaten steak out in front of him, easing his massive frame up out of the chair. Holding an arm out in front magnanimously, he invited the Frenchman to lead the way from the restaurant, longingly staring over his shoulder at the uneaten food with a comic look of exasperation.

'Is that always how it is?' Daniel asked. Matilda smiled. An open and easy smile. Daniel was suddenly aware of how beautiful she was. 'It's how it always is with Michael. He can't do enough for the players and they take advantage, you know?'

'And what about you?' Daniel retorted, a smile playing around his lips.

'No one takes advantage of me, I can quite assure you,' she replied, her perfectly manicured blonde eyebrows arched above a challenging blue-eyed stare.

'Oh, that's not what I meant at all. Sorry, it's just that, well, are you as dedicated to the job as Michael is? You must work together closely as a team I suppose. I bet it's hard work with so many guys on Tour and a new event every week?'

'I can assure you that there's no choice but having to work closely when you spend all day together in a sixty-foot truck crammed with all our equipment. We even have to share the same email address, so no escape – even in cyber space! But, hey, you get used to it. The Tour is my life and Michael's a sweetheart. Guess what? I finally realised my ambition to travel to Russia and spend six years studying business at the famous Stockholm School of Economics in St Petersburg, only to end up with no job and a bunch of student loans. I was very lucky to get the job out here and now I don't know anything else I suppose.' She paused before checking herself. Daniel watched as she skewered a piece of crispy salad with her fork. 'And you?' she said. 'You must be one of these hotshot player agents then.'

Another challenge. She speared a crouton and crunched it between pearly white teeth. It clearly amused her to see how easy it was to put her new acquaintance on the back foot.

He felt himself blush. Was it embarrassment, or perhaps a little pride at the reference to his new job? His eyes dropped to his plate of uneaten and rapidly cooling chicken. 'I'd hardly say that. I don't even feel like I know what I'm doing most of the time.'

And then their eyes met. Matilda snorted in surprise. 'Well now that makes a change! Usually, you know-it-all agents out here are all the same. Pumped up full of testosterone, confidence and swagger. It's quite sweet to hear you asking for help.'

'Thanks, I think,' said Daniel. 'I'm not sure I was asking for help though, was I?'

'It's quite okay, Mr Hotshot,' she replied, reaching forward from across the table and displaying an elegantly presented diamond on her ring finger as she squeezed his hand. 'I'm sure we can make sure that you don't get too lost out here.' Again, that sweet infectious giggle.

And with that, her salad barely touched and the conversation apparently over, she eased out of her chair. Daniel watched the gentle roll of her hips as she glided smoothly through the maze of tables out of the restaurant. It was several moments after she had left that he finally felt himself exhale.

3

ENGLAND. LONDON. WHITEHALL.

'Your meeting with Boris Golich is scheduled for 4pm, sir,' a stiff young man announced in an impeccable rendition of the Queen's English. The grey-haired civil servant, encased in perfectly creased dark pinstripe, sat deep in thought. The office, just off the corner of Whitehall, was small yet smartly presented. He barely acknowledged the aide as the bulky folder was presented. 'Everything you require to know about the co-funded gas exploration deal is within, sir. Please don't hesitate to enquire if there's anything further I can assist with.'

The phone on his desk rang and, after watching it rattle in its cradle for a little longer than was polite, Derek Hemmings, who had been staring wistfully out of his rain-streaked window, moved hesitantly toward it, took a deep breath and answered. It was the call that he'd been dreading since arriving that morning at the refined environs of the Foreign Office. Andy Bartholomew was on the line. Derek's senior counterpart at the Department of Trade and Industry was a short, balding, pugnacious Scot whose name was pronounced in the manner in which one might clear unwanted phlegm from the back of one's throat.

'Right, the pressure's really on this time, Hemmings,' he snorted. 'We can't afford another screw up on the seismic scale of the trade visas for cash debacle. There are seven thousand British jobs on the hook for this gas operation in the Falklands. Boris Golich's Rublex Corporation is co-funding the operation and will be piping gas into Europe with a big fat BP badge on it. And in case you missed that, old man, the B in BP stands for British.'

'Thank you for the insightful synopsis as ever, Andy,' Derek responded coldly. 'Forgive me that I don't share in your unfounded ebullience, but my consternation is simply thus. I'm due to meet with Boris Golich at sixteen hundred hours today. However rich and powerful he may be and with whomever he may now be friends, the man is purported to have a rather unsavoury past. I'm not really sure that the British government should be working with him at all. Job creation programme or not, I'm afraid.'

'Not your concern, pal. BP has agreed terms. We're shutting out the Americans on this one. The Prime Minister has ratified it. It is as they say...' he paused for dramatic effect, inhaled, then exhaling as he spoke his punch line, '...a done deal.' The 'A' was pronounced 'hay'. Derek shuddered.

'Then what do you need me for, pray tell? Surely I don't need to be dragged into this viper's nest at all if everybody is seemingly so keen to work with this gangster?'

'Do as you're told, Hemmings. Your department is there to dot the i's and cross the t's. Can you manage that, son? Don't mess it up this time and do not come back without a signed agreement. I hope that's clear.'

'All I'm saying is that it would be illegal and in contravention of our manifold international trade and energy undertakings, to say the least, for Great Britain to enter into a long-term and far-reaching commercial partnership with a criminal organisation. This relationship requires pipelines to be laid across several international borders. The geopolitical implications will be huge and could place global trade relations at significant risk.'

'Criminal organisation?' spat Andy. 'Show me some proof of that then, pal. There's nothing criminal about Rublex and you know it. They might be an aggressive, high-growth corporation but that's no crime. And they've capital to invest with the UK. That's been a serious rarity in recent times. You do remember the bloody recession, don't you? Do you remember the sodding Brexit farce? How about global economic shrinkage due to the pandemic? Need I go on? Besides, the Americans had their chance to partner in the exploration on the Falklands with us and they wouldn't put their money where their mouth is. Without developing that territory for all its rich natural fossil energy, Maggie's war would have been in vain. Tumbledown would never have happened, Hemmings. We should have left it to the bloody Argentinians if we followed your view of the world. Is that what you would have wanted?' A rhetorical question. He continued unabated. 'You're pathetic. Rublex Corporation is our only option to make this deal happen and deliver economic growth to Britain. If we don't take this opportunity, the Chinese will step in to finance the deal with Rublex. Golich has acquired the exploration rights in the international waters. That tie-up will leave Britain out in the cold.' Derek squirmed in his seat, shifting from buttock to buttock. 'They'll build an offshore infrastructure platform to house thousands of Argentinian workers, instead of Brits, and enjoy the proceeds of what's rightfully ours. I'm sure you find all that just fine and dandy, don't you, Hemmings?'

'It's a fine argument in the grand scheme of things,' he conceded, 'but I'm still uncomfortable, Andy.'

The abrasive Scot sensed the older man's resolve weakening. He decided to change tack, display some contrition. 'Listen, Derek, we both know what these things are like, don't we? Both of our departments need to work together on this one. For Christ's sake, we all need a big win, you know that. Some good news to put out in the media for once is much called for. You play golf, don't you, pal? What's your handicap playing off these days?' Andy swished his Montblanc pen through the air for his own amusement, pleased with himself for his new line of approach on the phone. He continued, 'Well, Rublex sponsors the European Tour now. Those guys are squeaky clean. They're a trusted corporate brand right across Europe and all over the world. Boris Golich has invested millions in the game personally. Which gangster have you ever come across that plays golf? It's a gentleman's game, Derek. I should bloody know, it was us Scots who invented it! When you meet, just talk to him about birdies or ostriches or eagles or whatever you lot are into.'

Derek hung up and stared out of the window. He watched a child in brightly coloured Wellington boots stamping with glee in the rain puddles below; the expression of fun and freedom felt so far removed from his own gloomy outlook. He'd seemingly risen as far as he could within the department, his appointment to Senior Executive Officer his last promotion just over five years ago. His retirement was planned for seven months' time at the end of the year. His forty-third year in service of Queen and Country, an honour he had taken most seriously for the main part of his adult life. Of course, for some time now, he'd noticed the rise of a younger, more aggressive breed of political animal superseding him. Career politicians and slick, ambitious civil servants drunk on power, skilled at lobbying in the shadows and hungry for success. Less concerned it seemed with the responsibility of long-term judicious governance but led moreover by avarice for political headlines and personal glory. He lacked the energy and bite anymore to stand up to the Andy Bartholomews of this job. Quite simply, Derek was weary of the posturing, the personal positioning and one-upmanship that came with the brief.

4

Two days and a hangover from hell later, I sat in a sports bar at LAX waiting for my flight back to Europe. Hunched over a frothy glass of beer and a roast beef sandwich, cursing my aching joints. The phone buzzed. I opened the text to find an encrypted message flashing for urgent attention. I grimaced. Complexity was The Hand of God's chosen method of communication. Frowning, I jotted down the letters and numbers of the code on a beer mat in front of me and duly added the sum of my birth date to the total numbers. After assigning a numerical value to the letters by their position in the alphabet, I added them together and multiplied the two sums. There was a reason I never played Sudoku and this was it. I found using code an unnecessary and frustrating process. There'd been times when I'd simply been too wasted to calculate the code out and respond in good time. I once asked a girl lying next to me in bed to do the sums. I think it freaked her out a little for a one-night stand. But Charles insisted on security at all times and if I wanted the number to the current secure phone then there was only one way of figuring it out.

I headed to the back of the bar and punched the long

number into the neglected payphone. Another of Hand's frustrating rules: Never make contact on your mobile unless there is no other choice. Charles answered on the second ring, his voice bright and polished. Imposing.

'Thomas, dear boy, I gather everything was a success.' It wasn't a question.

'Yeah, all sorted and full payment on its way from Mr Rodriguez. Although I gotta say, in my opinion, I think Daddy's going to struggle trying to keep that that little firecracker under control.'

'Enough with the family psychoanalysis, Hunter, that's not your concern.' He waited a beat before continuing with a grave undercurrent in his voice, 'Now listen up, Tom. We've got a problem I'm afraid.'

'What's happened?'

'A comrade, a gentleman I served alongside in the forces by the name of Bob Wallace, has been in touch. He believes there's been a kidnapping or something worse in Spain. He's got no proof, but a sports agent he knows has vanished, gone for two days and nights unaccounted for.'

'Come on, Charles, the bloke's probably stopped out with some saucy señorita for the night and is getting the ride of his life. This isn't our area. Besides you know after a job I like to kick back a little, take some time out. Get a little crazy.'

'We need to act. The clock is ticking. Bob Wallace wouldn't reach out unless this was critical. He mentioned that this chap had uncovered information regarding alleged fixing on the professional golf tour. Had data stored on a tablet. Sounds volatile. He'll pay the Unit's fees and your bonus for bringing the Target back alive himself, out of his share of a recent win bonus earned from one of the golfers he coaches. Of course the costs are discounted on account of our history in the Forces together.' I pumped another few coins into the phone and picked at the peeling paint on the wall with my thumbnail.

'Tom, right now we're in the golden period,' Hand continued. 'You know as well as I do that if we don't get onto his trail within eighty hours of the snatch, then our chances of finding him again will be diminished by over a hundred and fifty per cent.' I sighed, nodding in resignation to myself.

'I want you on this now. Ella will send you the relevant mission information and full briefing notes to your phone in encrypted files. When you land, please liaise with Mickey to pick up fresh unmarked weaponry and ammunition on the ground, again Ella will send you the co-ordinates.' I rapped my knuckles against the metal box, seeing my next few weeks of planned partying evaporating before me.

'Take this seriously, Tom, and make sure you bring this lad back. His life is now in our hands.'

I hung up and scratched the stubble on my chin. The Rodriguez girl was the seventh job that we'd completed together as this discreet self-contained Unit which was available for private hire. We'd been put together by The Hand of God after his official retirement from the mob. He'd tracked me down in a Guatemalan squat two years before where I was using crystal meth and too much dirty cocaine, earning money from bare-knuckle fights and shaking down dealers for their ill-gotten gains. He found me at rock bottom in a world of pain, and once again Hand had to save me from myself. Now our system was strong. Charles found the jobs and negotiated the payments. Mickey, a tenacious, life-hardened cockney, worked ahead of us on the ground and set up vehicles, weaponry, communications – anything we needed to make a job run smooth. He was a tough little bastard; the best I'd ever worked with. If he said it would be there and your life depended on it, you could always bet on Mick.

Another on the team was Phil Manning, a big affable guy, with a ready laugh and as reliable as they come. He was a dedicated family man, married for what seemed like forever to his childhood sweetheart, Leanne, and doting father to three little girls. He'd trained in the Marines. When he'd been injured in combat in Afghanistan, Leanne had insisted that he pack in the job. The Army was all Phil had known and he'd struggled to hold down a normal civilian job. Cash-strapped and needing to put food on the table, a mate had put him on the radar of Charles Hand. Kidnap rescue seemed like a compromise to Leanne. Phil could keep his sanity and she hoped it meant he wouldn't be shot at day in day out, or so she thought. He was a solid man to have beside you in a firefight. We'd been teamed on a few jobs and our styles seemed to complement each other. I could kick in doors and crack some skulls whilst Phil had our backs.

There were a few other guys on call, who came in and out of the crew. All ex-military and usually prior acquainted with The Hand of God's maverick leadership style. Sadly, we'd lost some good men during the seven jobs that we'd taken on so far. It never seemed to work out easy.

Then there was Ella, a bright and pretty brunette, whom Charles had enlisted as researcher and operations hub manager back at our London base. Rumours abounded that she'd been completing a PhD in Military History when they met. Charles had been delivering a guest lecture on the effective strategies of guerrilla warfare. She was fascinated by his battlefield and covert operations experience spanning every continent of the world. When he finally confided in her about the new private Unit and our ambitions, she was intrigued and determined to participate in any way which was welcome. Yes, Ella with the big brown eyes, those large heavy breasts, and a wickedly flirtatious smile. Regardless of how she had ended up with the team, she had certainly added a different dimension to HQ and could sure run rings around me when it came to smarts.

Of course, then there was me. Tom Hunter. The nothing to live for, the no job too dirty, self-abuse junkie. I'd been described as leaving a wanton trail of destruction wherever I went. And as a man for whom heavy violence and the darkness of killing comes with unnerving delight. There might have been a ring of truth to some of that.

I stood over the phone tracing a lazy thumb down the tract of my scar. I reflected on the conversation. Charles Hand had brought me back from the dead at least three times. So far. I owed him everything and now he had made it clear that he needed me to step up for this job. The call had been unequivocal. Forget about taking time off, a young man's life was in the balance. Tom Hunter was back in play.

5

The relentless sun beat down, burning through an endless canvas of azure sky. A solitary wisp of cloud flirted with the apex of the sprawl of rugged red mountains, providing a dramatic backdrop to the golf range. The only sound to be heard was the swish of metronomic golf swings and the pop of golf balls being drilled across the range. Daniel exchanged a flash of his Tour money clip for a courteous nod from a smartly dressed Spanish attendant who unclipped the white rope dividing the players and coaches from the spectators. It was perhaps the first time he'd been on the receiving end of this type of deference and Daniel was starting to think that he could get used to it. As he stepped onto the range the thump of his heartbeat picked up. He didn't recognise anyone. Panic rose in his throat. It was if a massive searchlight was now trained directly upon him, highlighting his every sound and movement. His mind drifted to a story recounted by Silvio of a spectator's phone going off on the backswing of one of the more famously bad-tempered stalwarts of the game during a competitive round. Said player had thrown his club to the ground and crossed the ropes to scream in the face of the unwitting spectator who was now fumbling frantically in his pocket to silence his ridiculous sounding ringtone. Needless to say, the guy didn't take the call. Daniel checked his mobile was off for the fourth time. Then subtly checked the fly on his trousers was zipped for good measure.

A line of immaculately dressed golfers each stood in their own space next to a stacked pyramid of dazzling new white balls. Huge golf bags emblazoned with the player's name in heavy stitching were set slightly behind. Some were striking balls, deeply focused on their own rhythm. Others worked with a swing coach who stood behind them, holding the shaft of the club at the top of their backswing, tweaking angles to reset by tiny margins. Some golfers were chatting away to their caddies, who polished club heads with furious industry or fished inside one of the manifold deep pockets of the golf bags searching for rangefinders, pitch forks or other tools of their trade. A few refreshed themselves with cool drinks from one of the number of smart, squat well-stocked fridges which adorned the range. Daniel noted three or four well-groomed guys in reflective sunglasses pacing up and down behind the line of players. Sometimes hunkering down to watch a swing, sometimes moving forward and having a quiet word in the ear of a certain player. The casual swap of a joke, the touch of an arm. These guys were the real deal. Established golf agents or player managers as some called themselves. Confident. Natural. With an overt hint of arrogance, Daniel observed.

'Jeppe's swinging beautifully today, don't ya think?' came a broad Scottish brogue from behind him; delivered as a statement of fact. Daniel swung around to face a short stocky man in his late sixties, wearing a tatty navy-blue flat cap. A thick hand-rolled cigarette was clamped between his teeth. He continued uninvited, 'Ay, the kid's in the groove for sure. I think he could be tough to beat this week, that one.'

'Yeah, I think you might be spot on there.' Daniel smiled back in response. He had no idea which golfer the man was referring to and, following twenty minutes of intense study of the players on the range, had noticed no discernible differences between the lot of them.

'Mark my words, sonny. Jeppe's the one to watch this week. My boy Stephen's coming along too, got him releasing the club head nice and smooth now, after a fashion.' He nodded down the line to the end of the range where a tall languid figure in yellow set his knees and fixed a perfect acute angle between his spine and the backs of his long legs.

'You're Stephen's coach then?' Daniel enquired, deciding he needed to take risks which might expose his ignorance if he was ever going to learn anything.

'Ay and I've worked with a bunch of the boys out here over the years. This is my twenty-fourth year on the Tour and you could say I've seen most things come and go.'

'That's incredible,' gushed Daniel. 'You must have seen a few changes over the years, I bet.'

'Just more assholes than ever,' came the deadpan retort.

Daniel faked a short nervous laugh, uncertain if the old coach was even joking. 'Really? Why's that then?' he asked.

'More money and distractions getting in the way of the game. Golf used to be the last bastion of fair play, I'm just not so sure about that anymore.' And with that the old coach threw the brownish yellow stub of his beleaguered cigarette onto the grass and shuffled off towards the end of the range. Daniel considered that the stooping gait could be a deliberate coping mechanism against years of chronic back pain.

He was grateful for the interaction which had buoyed his confidence. He had been starting to feel a little like the oddball in the playground who no one wanted to talk to. Alone with his thoughts again he noticed that his forearms were starting to burn from the attentions of the unforgiving Spanish sun and cursed himself for neglecting to wear sunscreen. Aaron or François were nowhere to be spotted on the range. It was important that he met with them and introduced himself before the event kicked off the next morning. Grabbing an ice-cold bottle of water from the fridge at the back of the range, Daniel made it his mission to track them down. Striding with purpose back through the ropes he cut a straight line for the clubhouse. At least he could try to look as if he knew where he was headed.

It was no surprise to find that the changing rooms of the clubhouse affixed to the hotel were anything other than sumptuous. There wasn't much of a frame of reference for comparison, but they were more luxurious than, say, any fancy bar he'd previously stepped foot in and a different scale altogether to the musty leather and chestnut wood office of Mr Pembridge, the managing director of the insurance firm where his father had toiled for the last thirty-six years.

The blue and gold motifs patterning the elegant marble floors drew the eye up to thick piles of freshly laundered fluffy white towels lying folded on polished wooden benches. The immense lockers themselves had doors made up of single pieces of heavy mahogany, each carved with an intricate coat of arms. Two dark-skinned men in starched white tunics, pressed trousers and white deck shoes busied themselves with carrying armfuls of towels, wiping vast glistening mirrors and polishing gold taps.

A shirtless fat man was picking at the dried mud on the bottom of a pair of expensive-looking golf shoes. The mud was flaking all over the marble floor, scattering under lockers and benches alike. An anxious attendant hovered nearby. The man carried on oblivious, working the wooden golf tee around his spikes while humming a jaunty tune to himself. A massive hairy belly flopped over the brim of his shorts, completely obscuring any belt. He was in his late forties with closely cropped black hair speckled with patches of salt and pepper. His fat, creased face sported a rasp of greying stubble.

'What are you looking at, sunbeam?' he said out of nowhere in an unexpectedly high pitched Liverpudlian accent, now looking hard at Daniel with beady eyes.

'Sorry, excuse me. I'm, er, looking for a couple of players actually,' said Daniel, taken aback.

'And you are, mate?' came the response, scathing and immediate.

'Oh, I'm Daniel Ratchet, an agent with Crown Sports. Have you seen Aaron Crower or François Steine by any chance?'

'No, Danny, I haven't. I'm Jeppe Ossgren's bagman here and he's the only bloody player I need to worry about.'

'All right then. Thanks. Nice meeting you,' Daniel murmured as he turned on his heel, chastened by the whole experience. He'd been seduced by the refined setting and hadn't been expecting an awkward confrontation.

'No problem, sunbeam,' came the sing-song call from behind him.

Daniel stopped and checked himself. *To hell with it*, he thought. 'So, er, Jeppe's swinging beautifully today, isn't he? He's in the groove for sure. I think he could be tough to beat this week.'

Silence. Then after a few moments, 'Yeah you're dead right there, mate. You've seen something there, you know. He's got the bit between his teeth. We're due for a big cheque this week.'

'Well, good luck, mate,' said Daniel pleased for having got away with positioning himself as an expert.

'Hey, sunbeam,' came the voice behind him. 'You know what? You'll probably find Aaron in the physio truck getting stretched into shape before his early round tomorrow. And François just came off the course from a practice round so he will most likely be grabbing a shower at the hotel before he heads out to eat early with the other Saffas.'

'Great. Thanks very much,' Daniel answered. With that the exchange was over and the burly caddy was back to scraping golf shoes again, humming away to himself and paying no attention to anyone or anything.

Feeling a bit more comfortable with the situation, Daniel strolled back out towards the sunshine. He drained his bottle of water, depositing the empty packaging in a litter bin before threading his way along the paved walkway up to the massive free-standing trailer truck which served as the Tour's mobile physiotherapy service. The door was wide open and he hauled himself up the little metal steps, poking his head inside. The internal space was much bigger than expected. To the right, a self-contained office with soft seating, a coffee table, whiteboard and drinks dispenser. The main central space contained a weights machine with all manner of levers and pulleys dangling over inbuilt plastic seats. To his left, two massage tables were bolted to a hard plastic floor. Beyond this were compact medical cabinets holding a stainless-steel washbasin and flanked by wall-to-ceiling cupboards. Matilda was leaning over the half-naked torso of a man lying face down on a towel. She was extending the guy's arm out ahead of him and rotating the shoulder as if simulating a swimming stroke.

'Excuse me,' Daniel said in a low voice, conscious of startling anyone.

'Oh hello, hotshot,' Matilda answered as if it was the most natural thing in the world glancing up from her exertions of kneading the tired knotted muscles of the golfer below her.

'I was hoping to find Aaron Crower here.'

'You found him, mate,' came a relaxed voice emanating from the hole at the head of the massage table.

'Oh, hey Aaron. It's Daniel Ratchet, from Crown Sports. We met briefly in London a few weeks back after you had secured your Tour card.'

'Ah yes, my fellow new boy out here,' replied Aaron thoughtfully, now sitting up and rubbing the suntanned shoulder which Matilda had been working. 'How are you finding life on Tour then?' he continued. 'Not such a bad way to make a living, is it?'

'Not at all!' Daniel admitted. 'Just wanted to make sure you had everything you needed before play tomorrow?'

'Good on yer. Well, I'm out freaking early unfortunately but it should give me a fair crack before the wind picks up in the afternoon.' He slowly rotated his wrist one way and then the other, studying the movement. 'I've been having a tinker and could do with a new thicker grip on the wand and a wedge adjustment to fifty-two degrees. That's one and a half wraps of grip tape by the way, not two, in case you were thinking about getting carried away.' He looked directly at Daniel, unsmiling. 'Go and see the boys in the Callaway van to get it fixed up for me, will yer, mate? Andy, my caddy, has got the sticks. Oh, and a new box of Pro Vis will work a treat too.'

'No problem, Aaron, I'm on it, I'll pick that up with Andy for tomorrow. Have a great round,' said Daniel, frantically repeating what he had just been told over in his head.

'On yer, mate,' came the muffled response as Aaron pushed his face back into the massage table and Matilda began working the knots in his back.

Daniel edged his way out of the truck, hoping to catch Matilda's eye as he left. He was rewarded. She glanced up from her work on him with a coy flicker of a smile.

Kicking his way along the neatly paved walkway behind the

hotel complex, Daniel felt a surge of energy welling up inside him. He was thinking about Matilda of course. This was coming together nicely. Was it possible an incredible girl like that could be into him? How could that be if she was engaged? It was probably something he should steer well clear of. Not that he hadn't always done pretty well with girls. A diffident charm and boyish good looks made him sought-after boyfriend material at a comprehensive school filled with testosterone pumped bad lads, gamers or football obsessives who either saw girls as a type of property to be used and disrespected or as a necessary inconvenience. He was dragged from his daydreams by the sudden impact of a huge German hand slapping him on the back.

'Can't keep away from Matilda, I see,' boomed Michael, shaking his head and smiling. 'Just like all the rest.'

Daniel froze, unable to think of a quick response. *This is really awkward*, he thought. *Matilda may have said that it was claustrophobic working with Michael but that's no excuse to be paying too much attention to another man's fiancée. Even worse to get busted doing so by the man himself. Still, despite calling it out, Michael seems to be really quite relaxed about it and she seems to know what she's doing. The ball's very much in her court. I guess I'll go along for the ride and see what happens.*

He play-punched Michael on the arm and grinned at him in response. Then sloped away to find Aaron's caddy, a myriad of unanswered questions swirling around his head.

Andy Sharples was evidently a stylish man. He'd come into caddying fairly late by conventional standards but, by all accounts, was highly regarded amongst his peers. He was renowned for his meticulous preparation and thorough care of whichever golfer, on whichever Tour, he was working.

Randy Hughes, the infamous larger than life founder and Chief Executive Officer of Crown Sports could be considered, amongst several more unpleasant things, as a man of guile. His business dealings were deliberately centred on North America for financial reasons alone. He dabbled in big-time boxing, UFC, NASCAR, and in managing US PGA Tour golfers. Crown Sports did very well out of it too. They put together some of the very highest value and most creative sponsorship and promotional deals for those individuals, assets and events which they'd come to represent. Randy's contact book was legendary. It included Hollywood celebrities, leading sportspeople, and leaders from their fields in the worlds of finance, business and crime. His prodigious energies were focused where the big money was and, where golf was concerned, he viewed the European Tour as merely a stopgap for young players to learn their trade before they progressed up to the 'major leagues' in the U S of A to play for the big bucks. Aaron Crower and François Steine fell into this bracket. The opportunity for Silvio and Daniel, therefore, was one of mutual convenience. It meant Randy could keep control of his young international rising stars and earn out of them without the hassle and expense of having to set up a European satellite office. His philosophy was that talent is a commodity to be traded, which requires a measure of nurturing and a good deal of control to maximise profitability. He'd wanted to match the precociously talented Aaron Crower with a steady experienced hand who could filter through the right kind of messages as he plotted his first full season in the sport. Andy Sharples knew the nuances of the game at the professional level. He was the perfect choice to help a new boy on Tour to make good game management decisions and keep his head in pressure situations. With very little persuasion, except of the dollar bill variety, Andy had, at Randy's direction, ditched his last employer in the middle of his pre-tournament preparation to make himself available for the rising star.

Daniel approached the cluster of caddies. They were sitting together on cheap plastic chairs nestled behind the enclave of massive golf equipment trucks parked at the back of the main hotel complex. Something struck him instantly. Andy was dressed, and seemed to hold himself differently to the rest of them. More like a player than a bagman he noted. Lean, with a neat black quiff and perfectly crafted goatee. His clothing was comparatively expensive and impeccably turned out. While the others in the group played a hand of cards, Andy smoked a long, thin cigarette and pondered over a small black pocketbook. As he neared the group from behind, Daniel noted the pages were filled with endless lists of unintelligible numbers and letters. But by this stage in the day, weary and bewildered enough, he'd given up expecting things to make natural sense. Recognising Andy from the description he'd picked up, Daniel addressed him directly.

'Andy, hi. Daniel Ratchet from Crown Sports. How you doing?' Offered in the soft northern lilt he'd worked so hard to dilute.

The group stopped talking amongst themselves almost as one. Backs straightened. Sets of surly expressions fixed back at him, both quizzical and inconvenienced.

'A pleasure...' replied the caddy slowly, putting on a slim pair of square sunglasses to avoid squinting into the orange sun which was setting over Daniel's shoulder. He offered his handshake with a half-hearted nonchalance.

'I wondered if you could help me out. Aaron's got some requests for tomorrow regarding his clubs and I wanted to get them sorted.'

'Looking after the sticks is my domain. It's not a problem.'

He was economical with his words, seeming to avoid unnecessary use of language. It helped create an aura of self-confidence.

'Right. So, the wand needs a new grip and he wants his wedge tweaked to fifty-two degrees and a new box of Pro Vis.' Daniel repeated the list verbatim, hurriedly unburdening himself of the detail which sounded like technical specifications from an engineering manual as he spoke it aloud. Somehow the perception washed over him that he was now standing with the cool kids smoking behind the bike sheds in school, wanting to be accepted by the gang. 'Is this something you can help with, Andy?'

'I've already taken care of it.' Andy sighed, flicking his eyes back at the group who eyed Daniel with a measure of passive aggression. 'We discussed it on the range and the guys in the van have worked their magic.'

Daniel visibly relaxed, glad the conversation didn't warrant a more detailed interrogation on the specifications in case he was asked to interpret what Aaron had wanted. 'You're a star. Thanks so much.' He smiled.

'You the new Jerry McGuire round here then?' Andy followed this with a staged throaty chuckle, which served as an invitation for the whole group to laugh openly.

'Not sure about that, but I am managing the Crown Sports stable out here now. I've heard you're a steady influence, Andy, helping Aaron to get some good consistency out of his rounds and scores. Helping him to keep his head in check when the pressure's on.' Daniel had ignored the jibe and was wondering if and how he should exert himself at the right moment. He'd been apprised of the apparent pecking order on the Tour by Silvio. Agents thought of themselves up near the top of the food chain with the players and the caddies, although, in reality, more helpful to the player in shooting a good score on the course, were viewed more like the hired help. Caddies, of course, felt the reverse was true, that they were the insightful shamans of the game and the moneymen were nothing but vultures.

'It's working well,' responded Andy. 'You should put your money where your mouth is and back that scoring consistency with your wallet.' He waggled the pocketbook at him. 'Billy Boy tells me you think you know a thing or two about who's got game. Given you're such an expert I'll give you odds against who you reckon is going to place this week.'

'I'll have to get back to you on that. I'm running about a bit right now so can't stay and chat I'm afraid.' *Don't get into a discussion on player form*, Daniel chided himself. He turned to leave and the moment passed.

'Listen, Dan,' soothed Andy after him in an accentless voice which he couldn't place. 'Some of the caddies and Tour staff are going for a few drinks tonight and you're welcome to join us.' He left a deliberate pause. 'Unless you've got something better planned, that is?' The quick glance towards the assembled card players, whom Daniel considered to be more interested in heckling than gambling, was rewarded with a selection of smirks in response.

Daniel rattled through his options. A night alone in his room in front of some boring movie repeat found on cable TV, after an uncomfortable dinner for one in the posh hotel restaurant. Or the chance to grab a few beers and ingratiate himself with the people who seemed to really know how this place worked, even if they did seem a tough bunch to crack. He had to begin getting to know people and this was as good a place to start as any. He was in.

'Sounds good. Where and when?'

'Excellent,' replied Andy in a disinterested drawl, already returning his attention back to the pages of his notebook. 'Meet us in Muldoon's Irish bar in the town centre about eight-ish.'

He didn't look up as Daniel left.

'I think I really like him, Michael,' said Matilda, cupping her hands around a steaming mug of green tea. Michael offered a toothy grin as he stacked bandages and bottles inside one of the storage units in the truck.

'Nothing I haven't heard before, my sweet Matilda. We both know you seem to have a thing for the agents out here.'

'Stop it!' She giggled. 'He's different. One of the good guys.'

'He does seem a little more innocent, that's for sure.'

'I feel like he needs protecting, Michael. I want to give him a chance. I want to help him find his feet out here. What d'you think?' She swivelled in her chair to face him directly.

'Well, if you really want my opinion, I agree that he seems to be someone you could trust and he's certainly interested in you! You should follow your heart if you really like him. But treat him gently. If he is serious about you, he won't get over you quickly.'

'I'm glad you like him too, Michael. That's important to me. You're the closest thing to family I have out here.' She beamed up at the giant German.

He stepped towards her and gave his response. A simple, gentle kiss placed upon her angled blonde head. Both his blessing and a signal that the conversation was done.

6

I grabbed a few hours of well-earned sleep on the fourteen-hour flight to Spain from LAX. Ella had worked some magic and managed to change my schedule without undue delay. The muscles in my shoulders and arms ached from a few nights of sleeping rough. I'd crashed in the back of the old jalopy as I had staked out the movements of the Target and her captor prior to the take down in the bar. The aeroplane seat slid back and reclined. Ella always booked business class for overnight flights on jobs so the team were rested and ready for action. Right now it felt like luxury. In the scheme of things, flying was probably when I managed to rest the most. There wasn't much else to do. A few stares were already being thrown my way. Nothing I wasn't used to. Not only was I dressed differently to the other passengers in this section of the cabin but after the exertions of the previous few hours I was also well aware that I stank. I pulled the sleeping mask down over my eyes and could hear disaffected murmurings around me as I started to drift away. Memories of how far I had come on my journey to be here now, travelling the world, amongst these well-to-do folks, danced into my dreamlike thoughts.

I'd enlisted in the mob at sixteen and despite being, to quote the Sergeant Major, 'an angry, feral, under-educated toerag', managed to haul my way upward inside a rapid couple of years. There, I tasted motivation that I hadn't dreamed existed following an unceremonious expulsion from the school that I'd barely attended in the preceding few years. School was a waste of time for a kid like me. Authority was just a line to be crossed. The way I saw it, I wasn't interested in learning and the teaching staff were too jaded or too exhausted to make me. Mine was once described by an army psychologist, intent on ticking a box on his neatly compiled form, as an 'unsettled childhood'. I got caught up in some bad situations. Some I got away with. Some, much to the chagrin and disdain of both my caseworker and the police, I didn't. Trouble always had a knack of being able to find me and I bowled through my teenage years with a cavalier confidence born of early physical development allied to raw natural strength. It led to a lot of confrontation and more than my fair share of notorious and bloody fights with the older gangs which haunted our neighbourhood. When the time came for me to get out, the army had been recommended as the only viable chance I stood to start afresh. To see a bit of the world. The truth is, back then, I had no idea that the one thing I'd display any given talent at was also the one thing I'd end up battling a compelling compulsion towards. Killing.

That was how it began. I was too young and arrogant when I signed up as a squaddie in the Royal Fusiliers infantry regiment. Like many of us, I was treated like crap. And then beasted regularly to try and break my spirit. One cold grey afternoon, spitting with icy rain on the bleak expanses of Exmoor, it had got too much. I'd flipped out. Broken the jaw of the cruel, supercilious, privately educated, didn't-know-his-arse-from-his-elbow senior officer in charge. It had felt good at the time. The two weeks in solitary following, not so much. In the aftermath of the enquiry, I was offered a deal. Face a dishonourable discharge or be assigned to a new platoon in the regiment, to be run as a separate unit under its own auspices. The small group was put together under the supervision of the apparently soon-to-be retiring Major Charles Hand. A man who came to be known by those who served with him simply as 'The Hand of God'. I was still just a boy.

We were trained like athletes and disciplined like prisoners. Put through hours of intense physical endurance and multi-form combat training daily. Hand took us to the very edge of our anatomical limitations. My mate, Steve, a tough kid from a council estate in Bolton, also hand-picked to be in our elite team, was running next to me on an ultra-marathon across the moors one night when his ankle just snapped. Nothing touched him. He didn't trip. The bone had simply been put under so much pressure that it had nothing left. Steve was stretchered away and we never heard of him again. He was presumably kicked out of the mob on the basis of his previous misdemeanours. I don't get the psychology behind it but somehow I responded to Hand. I thrived in that challenging environment. There was nothing good waiting for me back home, so the choice was to drown or learn to swim.

Over time, I grew up. Learned respect and I learned discipline. I learned how to fight. And I learned that killing came naturally to me. Unnervingly so.

And I was promoted. I was trusted and given my own tactical team to lead. Our extreme environment exposed us to torture, unauthorised killing and unspeakable war crimes which would never be written as a part of history. Crimes that would never see the inside of any court of law. And it was only the start.

The long sleep had replenished me. I was woken by the plane bumping onto the hot Spanish tarmac before pulling to its final halt. I always travelled as light as possible. Usually just the clothes on my back, cash and a phone. Weapons would be collected from Mickey once we got into theatre and the job was primed. Fresh clothing could be picked up if needed and as we rolled. I made my way into the terminal, swapping grins with couple of stewardesses on my way past. It reminded me of how long it had been since I'd had any sort of date. Talk about work-life balance.

The requirement at hand now was simple: familiarise myself with the mission brief and Target background. Set up the rendezvous with Mickey, who had no doubt already arrived from London a few hours in advance to start putting things in motion. After that it was going to be a long drive to the golf resort and I was impatient to get going. With time to kill, I ordered a double espresso from a quaint independent coffee shop inside the terminal building. It was good to see the little guy holding their position against the mighty global coffee brands; rebuffing their indefatigable quest for global domination. Better coffee too. And that was something I knew something about following my spell in Guatemala. I'd have hooked myself up to an intravenous drip of the stuff if I could.

I pulled out my phone, opened the application. Punched in an access code to download the case files. As smart, analytical and detailed orientated as she was, Ella Philips, our administrative manager and expert researcher, was also a fun, quirky individual. It was no secret that I would have liked to get to know her a little better, in every sense. The pressure of the jobs and a few different time zones hadn't seemed to allow for that. Yet. It felt like she was the human glue that held the guys together in the Unit. She was always fussing over us, especially me. I suppose someone had to. The Hand of God had found a real gem with Ella, that's for sure. A valuable resource, she had gotten me out of some tight scrapes in theatre through providing live intel on a Target or serving up some GPS co-ordinates to deliver an innovative escape route in the nick of time. I smiled at the screen as I was reminded of another of her traits. The woman had a PhD in military history. That, coupled with an irreverent humorous streak and unnerving sense of occasion, inspired her to surprise the team with resonant historical quotations throughout a job. As the data file loaded before me, a quote in italics swirled across my screen:

There are four columns marching on Madrid and yet a fifth within.

I recognised the quote as from the Spanish fascist General Franco. It was both a reference to the country origin of this job and a warning of the insidious nature of war where enemies and allies may not be as easily identifiable as they would first appear. The demarcations of allegiance can be blurred more often than at first appearance. *Duly noted, Ella*, I thought and busied myself with digesting her report and the background to the job which included a detailed set of mugshots and personal profiles highlighting individuals I may need to recognise and interrogate at this professional golf tour event. I also committed to memory the co-ordinates of where to meet Mickey in a couple of hours, a little outside the city.

I sucked the final dark coffee grounds into my mouth, running the grit between my teeth. Ordered a second double espresso with a nod of the head. My mind drifted back to previous visits to Spain. Vacations. A fairly typical story of a bunch of boozed up British lads in their early twenties letting their hair down. Except in our case we were probably worse than anything the tabloids might have conjured.

Take a gang of highly revved up squaddies who had been deliberately kept away from women and alcohol for months at a time whilst training intensely. Those few breaks we got to decompress were pretty messy affairs as you might imagine: lots of drinking, lots of fighting, lots of shagging, and a few instances that seemed to involve the lot together. On a rare occasion when we'd hired a car instead of motorbikes, we'd saved cash and opted for the cheapest box with four wheels that we could fit our gear into. I pictured the tiny Ford Fiesta with an engine so small it could barely make it up the hills, even in second gear. I can still hear the sound of my crew, squeezed into the back, howling and crying with laughter like braying donkeys as I bounced on my arse behind the steering wheel as if bucking a set of reins. It was a comic sight; the jolting and overloaded motor struggling to make it up the incline as local families stared and pointed in disbelief from the sidewalk.

I wouldn't be hampered for speed like that this time round. With the clock ticking, I approached the car rental desk, deciding that a top-of-the-line Range Rover would do the job. Cost would be no issue this time as I handed over the Unit's credit card. The transport is a gift from The Hand of God.

7

Admiring the image displayed back at him in the full-length mirror of the fifth-floor hotel room, Daniel nodded with approval. He'd showered, then shaved with care. Selected a black short-sleeved shirt with blood red trim, dark blue jeans and black leather belt. Boots which sported a slight Cuban heel added further to his natural height of just over six foot. He'd caught some colour in his face from today's sun and could see that his wavy blond hair was picking up some lighter notes already. He smiled. Back in Sheffield with his mates, he'd definitely be heading out on the pull tonight.

The room that Crown Sports had booked was beautiful. The bed was vast with a solid wooden frame and carved headboard. Everything seemed to be operated by a remote control that opened and closed the window blinds and patio doors, operated the massive wall-mounted plasma TV screen and changed the lighting and air conditioning with so many permutations that it would be a challenge to set it the same way twice. The bathroom was done out in marble with a large corner bath punctured with Jacuzzi jets and a walk-in shower so big it even had lighting controls, music speakers, and a seat. The balcony was decked out with a simple white wooden table and chairs. It overlooked one of the hotel's shimmering swimming pools. Inviting blue water surrounded with greenery and palm trees. Daniel sat out on the balcony dripping wet after his shower, drinking a cold beer from the minibar, an act in itself that might have induced a minor aneurism in his father. *The mark-up they put on those drinks is nothing short of criminal, lad. It's how they get you!* He cast his mind over the day, the amazing hotel, the new way of life, the vibrant characters and various nationalities he had met already. And yes, of course, Matilda. He closed his eyes and hoped that she might be there tonight.

When he arrived at the bar just after eight o'clock the party was already in full swing. The place was heaving. Squeezing his way through the throng of bodies, Daniel scanned around him for any recognisable faces. He waited at the bar for an eternity as a succession of attractive girls got served before him. With a beer duly secured at last he pushed back through the chaos into an outdoor area at the back. It was cooler outside but poorly lit.

A pretty girl in a red T-shirt and sarong that barely covered her ample bottom was dancing on a table, waving a bottle of tequila. People were standing around talking and laughing. Some were jumping up and down in unison to the raucous beat of the music. Daniel caught sight of Andy waving from a table at the back and threaded through a group of lobster pink sunburnt tourists clinking beer bottles and passing around a jug of sangria. There were twelve guys sitting together. Aside from Andy, Daniel recognised four others from the caddy card game behind the equipment trucks and the belligerent fat Liverpudlian from the locker room. It was he who greeted Daniel first, clearly the worse for wear.

'Hey, sunbeam, come over here and give Billy Boy a kiss,' he cooed, crashing his massive elbow into the ribs of the man sitting next to him and laughing.

'Settle down, Billy,' said Andy, deftly pulling an empty chair from under the table of the couple behind him without asking and swinging it round in a single motion beside him. Daniel sat and Andy, dressed in white linen, made him feel welcome, complimenting him on his shirt and watch, before making the introductions. They were all caddies except for one who represented the bottled water company, responsible for keeping the fridges on the range and the tournament tee-off areas replenished. Daniel forgot the names almost as soon as they'd been given.

The night wore on and the table heaved under the increasing weight of empty glasses and discarded bottles. The jokes and banter seemed to grow in proportional volume. Daniel got into the swing of things. He held his own both in the rapid consumption of alcohol and the quick-fire conversation. He even managed to avoid getting caught giving any strong opinions on players or the golf course which would expose him for being the inexperienced fraud he felt. Sean, a twenty-three-year-old ginger skinhead from Glasgow, was lining up a long row of grubby looking shot glasses and loosely pouring a stream of some indeterminable liquid into them from a bottle which he held unsteadily a foot or so above. And he was making a total mess of it too. Daniel was relaxed. He was coming to equate these guys more with the earthy Sheffield blue-collar workers he'd known so well, as opposed to the polished perma-tanned multi-millionaire golf professionals he'd watched being interviewed on TV. Despite his new-found pretentions of grandeur, the reality was that this was probably more his speed.

The only person keeping any semblance of sobriety and control around the table was Andy Sharples, regardless of the regular replenishment of his glass from a personal bottle of expensive looking vodka, fetched discreetly from an inside jacket pocket. As Billy Boy returned to the subject of his 'miserable bitch-of-an-ex-wife', pounding the table with a meaty fist, spilling drinks asunder while bemoaning the fact she keeps screwing him over for more alimony, Andy pulled Daniel to one side and enquired, with a single arched eyebrow, if there was anything the new boy needed to know about life on Tour.

'You guys do this all the time?' Daniel questioned.

'What's that bullshit expression?' Andy pondered, lighting one of his long slender cigarettes. 'Ah yes. Work hard, play hard! Well, as you can see, Danny, you could say out here that life's a ball – a golf ball!'

'But don't you all have to get up early to be on the course and play in the morning?' Daniel asked earnestly.

'Don't be soft. It's Aaron and the rest of the pros who have to be sharp tomorrow. The guys you see here have all done the hard work earlier in the week.' He waved his hand around him towards the table. 'We've walked the course, we've studied the yardages. Our hard work's done. If your man makes the weekend it's quids-in and we're laughing. If he misses the cut, then we don't get a fat bonus but we still get our wages so who cares? We usually hit a strip club or tap up some whores depending on the city and where we have to be next week.' One of the group howled at the mention and began to simulate sex with the table.

'Don't some of the guys bring their wives on the Tour though?' asked Daniel, intrigued. He noticed that, like the others, he too was becoming increasingly intoxicated as time wore on.

'Schoolboy error if you ask me, Danny. Besides, it's easy to spot the players who got married before they made it on Tour from those who got hitched afterwards. Right, lads?' Sniggers from the table.

'Yeah,' chimed in a cheeky mixed-race cockney, known ubiquitously as Razor on account of not being the sharpest. 'The wives after they made it big are about three shades blonder with a double-D cup!' He emitted a hyena-like cackle at his own joke.

Flushed with the apparent success of his wisecrack and now seriously slurring his words, he continued, 'Tell him, Andy. He'll find out soon enough. It's the caddies who pull the strings out here. We're the ones who really run the show. Right, boys?'

From out of nowhere, Andy suddenly lurched to his left, grabbed Razor by his throat and flung him backwards off his chair and onto the ground behind him. 'When are you going to learn, you dumb mongrel? You keep your mouth shut until I tell you otherwise. Get it?' Andy leered down at his prey as he pinned Razor to the floor by his neck. The rapid sudden violence of movement made Daniel's head spin and by the time he'd recovered and considered whether he should perhaps intervene or move somewhere safer himself, Sean was helping Razor to his feet, Andy was back in his chair smoking, looking completely unruffled and the party had picked back up again. And then Billy Boy was standing on his chair clapping and conducting a choir of drunken Danish guys in football shirts. Sean was leading Daniel over to take his turn on the row of shots and the whole incident simply blurred into the long tapestry of the evening.

8

At ten to four in the afternoon, the gleaming black Mercedes pulled to a smooth stop in front of the alabaster pillars of a St James's Square gentleman's club. Rain splattered on the windscreen of the car, drumming an erratic, hypnotic rhythm. Derek sighed and stuffed the manila folder deep into his suit jacket to protect it from the wet. A portly, heavy-jowled man in the standard Club uniform of long black overcoat, replete with black felt bowler hat, stepped forward and opened the passenger side door, offering the protection of a wide umbrella as he did. Hemmings trotted up the steps and sidled inside into the familiar surroundings of The East India Devonshire Sports and Public Schools Club. He nodded at the wiry Italian butler, thinning hair scraped back over his forehead. The greeting in response was warm. 'It's a pleasure to see you again, Mr Hemmings. If you please, sir, your guest is waiting for you in the Ladies' Drawing Room.'

Derek grimaced. The irony of holding a meeting with this dirty Russian gangster within the refined, elegant surroundings of the Ladies' Drawing Room was not lost on him. Being a privately owned, members-only club the establishment retained

53

strict rules on the entry of and usage by ladies. It may be unfashionable and antiquated in this day and age but Derek respected the traditions and felt they represented a sanctuary of order in a hectic, all-access, politically-correct world. Ladies weren't permitted in the bars, the Library, Smoking Room (the lighting of cigars in the club was now sadly no longer permitted but the name of the room endured in glorious defiance) or even the Dining Room at lunchtime. To enjoy lunch at the club a lady must be accompanied as a guest of a gentleman member in the Luncheon Room only. The Ladies' Drawing Room represented a refined environment in which to entertain female guests away from the main rooms, so as not to impinge on the relaxation or important matters of discussion and debate among the other members. It was the very room where, on 21 June 1815, The Prince Regent (later George IV) first heard the news of the English army's victory at Waterloo. Major Henry Percy, aide-de-camp to the triumphant Duke of Wellington, interrupted the dinner party to present four captured French eagles and the Duke's victory dispatch. Today it lay empty, reserved exclusively for Derek's important meeting.

Hemmings trudged up the stairs with heavy feet, stopping outside the set of tall, delicately hand-painted wooden doors. His knock was hesitant, to his instant annoyance for having already ceding the psychological advantage of the meeting before it had even begun. This was his Club; he the member, Golich the guest. He had no need to knock. If there was knocking to be done it should be Golich who should be doing the bloody knocking. 'Useless, Hemmings. Simply useless,' he murmured beneath his breath.

Entering the room in a fluster, folder clasped deep within a sweaty palm, Derek was halted as he stepped over the threshold by a huge hand attached to a huge man, muscles straining inside a shiny, jet black suit. Further ignominy was endured through the intimate patting down of his bony, sixty-four-year-old body in the thorough search for a concealed weapon. The very notion of which was, of course, quite preposterous. Derek stood there limply with his arms outstretched, blushing and assiduously trying to avoid any eye contact whatsoever.

The large room was empty, save for one small square tea table at which sat a round-shouldered man whose age Derek would place somewhere between his late thirties and early forties. That is if his briefing file hadn't already informed that the man was in fact fifty-one years of age. His face was round. Cold, grey unblinking eyes were framed with thick black eyebrows. The eyes of a hardened criminal, Derek mused to himself with disdain. He studied the Russian at the table as he sipped mint tea from a delicate china teacup, fat fingers struggling to hold it with any sense of refinement. Derek wondered if the cup might fall as it wobbled its way to fleshy lips. It struck him, on examination, that Boris Golich had a perfectly wrinkle-free and lineless face. A baby face. It was bizarre. His smooth features were accented by a short cropped black beard flecked with silver. Hair was of exactly equal length and colour. An oversized diamond earring twinkled from his left ear. Derek was heartened at least that the man had made an effort to respect the opulent surroundings and rules of the club. He wore a light grey suit, stitched of the finest cloth, with neat, precise creases. It was set off by a black shirt and surprisingly tasteful tie of deep purple interwoven with fine gold thread. Much to his annoyance, the whole outfit came together rather well, emanating the impression of wealth and elegance. Well, what had he really expected? Trainers and a denim jacket? Perhaps Disney characters on the socks and tie?

'May I offer you some tea?' came the offer.

'Oh yes, very kind. English breakfast if you please.'

Unfailingly courteous to the last. *Actually*, thought Hemmings, *isn't he supposed to be my guest?*

Seizing the initiative, Derek began. 'So, Mr Golich, I understand that you wish to do a little business with Great Britain?'

'Well only if Great Britain wants me. And of course, the little business of my money.'

He laboured the word, clumsily attempting to draw every last grain of irony from his point. They locked eyes. And then the oligarch began to laugh. Loudly. Heartily. After a short period his mirth spread to the muscle in the unforgivable suit who chimed in with an obsequious snigger. He stopped laughing and straightened the knot in his tie. Cleared his throat.

'This little business, as you call it, is billions of pounds invested by MY Rublex Corporation into gas exploration in the international waters off YOUR British Falkland Islands, and the infrastructure for YOUR British workers living on them.' The emphasis of his words was used to make the crude point. Derek reciprocated.

'Yes indeed. OUR Falkland Islands. YOUR money in exchange for Britain's co-operation in transporting this gas for sale across the world under our protection and licence in the good name of British Petroleum. Joint enterprise, sharing in the proceeds, potentially one hundred billion pounds over the next ten years.' A stiff retort.

'Correct. I'm pleased you have an understanding of the arrangements, Mr Hemmings.' He tapped his fingernail crisply against the edge of the teacup. 'It seems your Prime Minister wishes to move ahead as soon as possible. He told me so himself when we played golf at Queenwood the other day. I love you British because of your famous justice, the sense of honour. Not like those bitch traitors in the US. You say you will make the deal. You make the deal.' Golich spat out the word 'bitch' with genuine venom, causing Derek to glance around to see if they had been overheard. *Well*, the old stager thought, *the rumours are true, they are golfing buddies after all*. Followed quickly by a second thought: *I wouldn't mind an invitation to play at Queenwood with the Prime Minister myself*.

'British Prime Minister has given me his word. He tells me this is stronger than the mighty British oak tree. Deal happens, okay.' Again, the hard stare. Unblinking eyes. No invitation to respond.

'With all due respect, Mr Golich, whilst I am indeed here to discuss and ratify the deal with yourself and Rublex Corporation, we do have due processes and procedures to follow. And I intend to satisfy myself with the full probity of this deal before we make a commitment to you or anyone else. Now, I have some questions regarding the origins of your investment stake for the gas development station. We need to be satisfied with regard to international money laundering rules and regulations.'

Boris Golich stood up from his seat, raising a hand to silence the civil servant in mid flow.

'The talking is over now, Mr Hemmings. The offer stands for one week only and then is off the table forever.' He waved his hand dismissively, curling his upper lip. 'We know plenty of governments who will make such a deal with Rublex during this period of, how do you say, "global economic uncertainty"? So, you have no business asking questions of my wealth. It will simply do no good for you.'

The word YOU appeared to be emphasised. These not-so-subtle messages were certainly being telegraphed. Golich stalked from the room followed closely by the gigantic minder; a disproportionate shadow. Derek was left feeling distinctly uneasy. He peered from the huge bay window out onto the square, partially hidden behind a long, elegantly embroidered drape. Watched as the Russian climbed into the back seat of a waiting Silver Fox Rolls Royce which purred away in the direction of Park Lane. 'Well, that went better than expected, Derek old boy,' he chided himself aloud with rueful condemnation and scuffed his foot deliberately against the leg of an antique table in self-disgust.

9

Daniel awoke fully clothed on top of his still made bed. The morning sun streamed through the window, stinging his eyes. He rubbed his face and coughed. The rancid taste in his mouth made him gag and, looking down gingerly, saw he had been sick over his once pristine black shirt. He clambered off the bed, made it into the bathroom and splashed cold water over his grimy face. The pathetic image reflected back in the mirror forced him to look away. Pulling off his soiled shirt made him wince. The stinging was from two deep parallel scratch marks that ran diagonally across the length of his torso. Alarmingly red and sore to the touch. Hunched under a hot shower the scratches throbbed and burned.

After, he stepped out into the room in just a towel and scoured the room for his wallet and watch. They weren't in his trousers and he couldn't see them lying anywhere in the room. He checked the wardrobe and under the bed. 'Stupid bastard,' he groaned to himself. 'Mum's going to kill me if I've gone and lost Granddad's gold watch.'

After five minutes he gave up, the exertions making his head thump in raw, uneven pulses. There was little doubt about it, he was in bad shape, probably still drunk. Doubts and questions flooded over him. If he was this bad now, how had he got back to the room last night? If he didn't have his wallet, how could he even get back in the room without the key card? How was he going to pay his hotel bill this week without his work credit card? He couldn't afford this place and he couldn't face the idea of explaining this mess to Silvio. Closing his eyes, Daniel tried to redact the intense throbbing inside his head.

An eternity later, the digital clock wobbled back into vision. The illuminated red digits blinked back at him, boring into his skull. 0928. It was the first day of the tournament and Aaron and Andy would be halfway through their round by now. *Damn it!* But hadn't Andy been with him up till the end last night? He struggled to remember as he dragged himself back over the preceding evening, fighting to recall any real detail from incoherent snatches of memory and a whirling carousel of faces. There's just no way that Andy could have been with him in this state if he had to be up before the birds to prepare the gear the way Aaron wanted it for tee off at 0645. The man wouldn't have made it to bed at all and he seemed to be drinking as hard as everyone else. The fragmented pattern of thoughts coursing through Daniel's head smoothed into a cohesive stream of consciousness. A deep sense of foreboding hit him with the realisation that he would be late out onto the golf course having promised that he would be there to walk the ropes and show support to his player on the first day of the tournament. The very least he could do. And this was the very first professional tournament of his new career as a golf agent. A cold sweat beaded across Daniel's face and neck.

He dressed hurriedly, pulling on a powder blue polo shirt

and neatly creased grey trousers from the hanger. What had Silvio said about looking the part? The imperative now was to move as quickly as he could without throwing up. The fresh air would clear his head and if Daniel still couldn't find his belongings when he got back to the room then he'd simply have to front up to the mess he'd got himself into, cancel the credit cards and file a report with the local police for insurance purposes. Frustration and anger bubbled up within him. He cursed himself. What a bloody fool for getting into a drunken mess on the first night. For jeopardising the one big chance he had at a new career. At that moment Daniel knew he wasn't exactly repaying the faith that Silvio had shown in him.

Out through the hotel and still in one piece; Daniel stalked his way past the practice range. His sole objective was to avoid any eye contact that might draw him into an unwanted conversation about this game that he really knew so very little about. Skirting the row of enormous black television trailers connected by an umbilical cord of endless thick black cable, he strode over to the imperious white scoreboard standing in splendid isolation. Squinting into the morning sun, Daniel scoured down the names alphabetically until he came to CROWER, A. With not half the players out on the course yet he could see that Aaron had begun the day well. In fact, four under par after nine holes was a blistering start and the stylish Australian was tied in second place at the turn. Daniel calculated that they must already be playing the tenth hole by now. He consulted his crumpled scorecard for its crude map of the course and headed directly to the eleventh hole to intercept the group.

The eleventh was a beautiful par four hole. It snaked around a rugged head of sublime Andalucían coastline. The tee consisted of a postage stamp of well-watered grass positioned on the edge of an exposed headland, surrounded on three sides by sheer rocky cliffs and the shimmering blue and green Mediterranean Sea. The coastline cut in dramatically to the clifftop leaving the tee precariously positioned and set apart from the rest of the course. Whilst lush fairway stretched up to the green on the right-hand side, the greatest reward and a seductive temptation for a glorious birdie or eagle chance was to aim your sights directly across the natural rocky cove which had been carved through centuries of attrition from the lapping of the unrelenting waves. To attempt to 'drive the green', those players who needed to score aggressively would fire their ball across the aqua swell aiming at the flag beyond. Watching intently, praying their projectile wouldn't get caught in a capricious swirling wind and drop down into a watery grave. The green itself was surrounded by deeply hollowed, perfectly raked bunkers of pure white sand. It was an epic hole, designed for risk and reward golf. Like a siren's beauty calling a ship's captain towards the rocks, the hole's allure was set to tempt even those players whose 'course management' mindset was of the most puritanical.

A small crowd had gathered behind the ropes surrounding the green and were facing back up to the players on the tee. The group ahead were putting out on the green and the body language of the caddy raking the bunker told the story of the hole which had just proved so costly to his boss. Daniel headed straight there, noting Aaron's group trooping up from the recently completed tenth hole. He claimed a place between an elderly couple and two women, ripe to the point of plumpness, in their late teens, both wearing rather short shorts and jostling each other whenever one of the handsome players walked near. Sweat dripped from his brow. It was starting to get hot and Daniel was still feeling decidedly ill.

'Mind if I join you?' came a voice from behind him. Daniel turned to face a tall, good-looking man dressed in black slacks and an immaculately embroidered white collarless shirt, buttoned up to the neck. His ashen blond hair was perfectly parted to the side, not a strand out of place. He enquired again, 'May I join you, Daniel?'

'Of course,' replied Daniel, anxious at how this man happened to know his name and if they had already met. 'I'm Aaron's manager,' he said as if in some justification for him being there and pointing to the silhouetted figure now crouching to insert a tee peg into the turf some distance away.

'Yes, Daniel, this much I already know. Good morning to you, I'm Sergei Krostanov, Head of Golf Sponsorship for the Rublex Oil and Gas Corporation.' He extended his hand in greeting and Daniel caught sight of a small crudely drawn star in blue ink tattooed on the flesh between thumb and forefinger. It reminded him of something a bored student might have doodled during an oppressive maths lesson. It seemed incongruous given the way the man was dressed. 'We support the Tour very much you know?' he said and continued without waiting for an answer, 'I also do a lot of business with Randy Hughes who owns Crown Sports.' Daniel thought of the huge sponsorship billboards he had seen around the course promoting Rublex Corporation, the Russian Oil & Gas conglomerate, and the title sponsorship they held for the race of champion golfer of the year.

'It's a pleasure to meet you,' Daniel replied, offering his hand and half turning to look Sergei in the eye just in time to miss Aaron's tee shot from across the cove.

'We all like to help each other out here on the circuit, Daniel. We look after our own so any problems, anything at all, you must please let me help.' Sergei purred. He moved to stand next to Daniel behind the roped off green, the unremitting stare from those lifeless pale blue eyes never wavering. Daniel shifted one foot to the other. Although his English was excellent there was still a noticeable undercutting Russian bite to Sergei's speech, an unmistakeable hard edge to the consonants in his diction. Feeling under interrogation, Daniel decided that the omnipresent beads of sweat bubbling up on his forehead were determined to visibly betray the hidden throbbing inside his skull. He wanted to crawl away and vomit. But there it was, once extended, incapable of being ignored. Just left hanging out there. A platitude. A kind but empty promise of future help. That was all surely. The last thing he wanted to do was further humiliate himself by admitting to this important cog in the machinery of the Tour that he had lost his watch and wallet, or had them stolen, after getting drunk on his first night on the job. But this was a big deal to Daniel. Nothing like this had ever happened to him before. Sergei seemed friendly and might know who could help, whom he could speak with about it. And so the awkward silence did its work and Daniel found himself drifting inexorably towards the point of confessing his predicament. After a long uncomfortable period of time had elapsed between them Daniel cracked and practically blurted out loud:

'Sergei, my wallet and watch were lost or stolen last night. It was my grandfather's watch and the wallet had my company credit cards in it and I thought you might know the best way to register this with the local police or with the Tour. Or if there was a lost property department or something?' He inhaled sharply.

Sergei chuckled. 'Lost property? This isn't a nursery school, Daniel.' The young man's face turned a fierce shade of burning crimson in response. 'It's serious if you have lost those things. Okay, I will ask some questions and try to help you. I too know what it is like to treasure a gift handed down through the family.

The family is the only thing in life with any true meaning.' His voice seemed serious, hard edged. But then he continued with a smile, 'And golf as well, of course. Few things are more important than golf.'

'Thank you so much. I feel like such an idiot.'

'Not as much of an idiot as when my friend Randy Hughes finds out that you lost his company credit card! Your boss, the owner of Crown Sports is not, shall we say, a patient man where money is involved.'

'I'm not looking forward to telling him to be honest. I haven't had the chance yet.' Daniel looked crestfallen.

'I tell you what. Let's not make a drama out of all this.' Sergei reached inside his trouser pocket and pulled out a neat shiny black leather wallet. 'Take this credit card. It belongs to Rublex. Use it for expenses while you find your wallet. If you don't find it then you should cancel the card and you may hold on to this one for the week of this tournament in Spain. Give it back to me at the next event. Okay?'

'I don't know what to say. That's incredibly generous. Thank you.'

'Please, Daniel, Rublex does what it can to support golf in every way. We have a strong working relationship with Crown Sports and I'm sure you will find a way to make it up to me. Besides I can't let you get on the wrong side of our Mr Hughes already, not when you have just started out in your career on the Tour.'

Daniel shook his head and regretted it. Sergei pointed with his chin beyond the ropes as Aaron skilfully skimmed the ball out of the bunker, plopped it onto the green, and watched it roll past the hole to within two feet. 'He's got a fierce talent, that one. I've been speaking to Andy Sharples, the caddy, about Aaron's aptitude and he thought you might like to enrol him in the Rublex Corporation player sponsorship programme?'

~

Daniel brightened up at once. Sponsorship was one of the key facets of his job and a measurable element of how well agents are looking after their players. Silvio had warned him that it was also a lever which rival player managers used to pry star golfers away from other management stables. In golf, money spoke and it spoke loudly.

'That sounds most interesting, Mr Krostanov. I really would be delighted to discuss terms,' answered Daniel, trying to sound as professional as he could under the spectre of his debilitating hangover.

'It's Sergei, please, if we are to be working together. Everybody just knows me as Sergei.' He ran his fingers through his hair, continuing, 'I'll have my secretary draw up the papers specifying the terms and send them to your hotel room. It's a confidential program for a select few out here so please don't disclose any details.'

'Yes of course, thank you. I really appreciate it,' answered Daniel. This man was turning out to be quite the saviour of his disastrous morning.

Aaron drilled his two-foot putt and followed up with the obligatory fist pump. Applause rippled through the gallery. Sergei slapped Daniel once on the back, hard and firm, before turning to head back through the trees towards the hotel.

Stepping under the ropes, eleventh hole now complete, Aaron approached Daniel who stood smiling gently to himself. 'Good to see you made it out here, mate,' he drawled pointedly as he made his way down a short dirt path that led to the twelfth hole tee box. 'Andy didn't seem to think you'd be getting out of bed today for some reason. Sloppy stuff on your first day I reckon, we've been up since the crack of dawn.' Andy smirked in the background.

Daniel trotted to keep up and immediately wished he hadn't. His skull rattled. 'Actually, I've been busy working on a new sponsorship deal for you with Rublex Corporation this morning,' he countered with as much false enthusiasm as he could muster. 'It's all looking pretty rosy.'

'On yer, mate,' came the lazy unenthused response and a fist offered in congratulation for Daniel to bump with his own.

'The greens are like putting on a glass table this morning, mate. Lightning quick.' And with that Aaron Crower was back in the zone, standing to the side on the twelfth tee, swishing his driver back and forth like a fly-fishing rod. His stocky Italian playing partner stared doggedly down the fairway, executing his pre-shot routine with assiduous focus.

Pleased with the way the morning was shaping up after its disastrous start, Daniel watched the golfers stride off down the tree-lined fairway after their pair of booming drives. *If I'm going to survive today without fainting, I'd better try and get some breakfast down*, he thought, and began the long slow loop back towards the hotel.

10

At the appointed time and place, or near enough, I found Mickey leaning on the bonnet of a Jeep, tinkering with a tiny screwdriver in the back of a two-way transistor radio. He was a wiry man of about five foot seven, always clean shaven, with a thick brush of spiky black hair. His angular inquisitive face, protruding nose and furtive dark eyes generated the perpetual impression of a badger in the wild poking his snout out from the inside of a hedgerow. I don't think anyone really knew Mickey's surname. Perhaps it was long forgotten, perhaps never been shared. He'd been working with Charles Hand for many years prior to the set-up of the Unit. A talented engineer and communications expert, he was also resourceful and loyal. Calibrated to be unquestionably dependable and I liked it that way. You can't afford to be left wondering if you've got a bullseye on your back during a job because your gear is going to let you down at the wrong moment.

He glanced up at me and grinned.

'What blinkin' time d'ya call this then, Hunter?' he cried out in mock exasperation, with a dramatic show of checking his watch.

'Tommy Time, baby,' came my response. 'Been here long then, have you, Mickey?' I laughed.

'You'll be late for your own funeral, Hunter,' he flashed back. 'Now, I've got something to show you Tommy-boy. And I think you're gonna like it too.' The words sang out over his shoulder in that rasping cockney lilt. I scooted round to the back of the Jeep and he slid back a green tarpaulin under which sat an array of equipment that we would require for the job. I scanned the neatly compiled arsenal, noting everything in its place. The gear was strapped onto a square cut piece of thick green material. This would fold up tightly, wrapping the weaponry to be stowed into one or other of the two grey and sandy brown camouflaged rucksacks sitting to the side. The equipment was set up with the precision that a heart surgeon might lay out their life-saving equipment prior to a major operation. Tools of the trade. There were two Berettas, both with attachable silencers. Mickey knew it was my favourite handgun because the model came without a safety catch to hamper a quick draw, the double squeeze trigger preventing accidental fire. Next, there were two stub-nosed Mack 10 machine guns, a sickening bull of a weapon which could extinguish the occupants of a room in mere moments at close range, its roaring clatter of thirty bullets a second pronouncing death on arrival whenever it was called into play. There were boxes of ammunition clips and both stun and flash grenades. Handier and less volatile than their destructive TNT-based cousins, these grenades could be used to cause a distraction or temporarily blind assailants without the risk of collateral damage. In addition, Mickey had stocked a water bottle, energy bars, a field medical kit, a magnetised GPS tracker button and three razor-sharp knives.

Long ago, Mickey had told me a tall tale of how, back in the mob, a Sergeant Major in the Marines had requisitioned one of these same trackers from Mickey's munitions store. He'd affixed it on the underside of his buxom wife's car, as he suspected she was having an affair. Given his fearsome reputation and violent temper, the attractive blonde had always been extremely careful that she wasn't being followed when she left the base, doubling back on herself and constantly checking in the rear-view mirror.

The tracker had located her. The Sergeant Major waited until she entered the cheap motel and was deep in the throes of passion with a strapping chef from the military base when he stormed inside. The story went that he'd made the chef watch as he forced his wife to swallow both her engagement and wedding rings on her knees. As she sat sobbing on the floor he pulled out a set of knives that he'd taken from the young chef's kitchen. He sharpened them right there in front of the petrified couple and then proceeded to slowly remove the skin from the lovers' arms and legs before slitting their throats. Rough justice indeed.

Completing the kit were two-way radios, binoculars, and a slim box of industrial cable ties. I had always found these plastic ties the most efficient method of securing necessary captives on a job with the least hassle. I wasn't surprised that he'd been so thorough, but it was good to know we were well prepared.

'You don't do things by halves, do you, Mick?' I laughed, punching him on the shoulder. 'D'you know something about this job that I don't yet, mate? You've pushed the boat out. How come we're so tooled up on this one?'

'The Hand of God says that fella, Bob Wallace, is on the level and he's a man to be trusted. They served together and Hand doesn't forget a man he's shed blood with. Now he needs help. We talked this job over whilst you were in the air catching up on your beauty sleep. It's not straight forward. Wallace can't go to the police and he blames himself for the boy's disappearance.'

'The weapons are untraceable I take it?'

'I tapped up a contact who deals hardware to some of the more unpleasant elements of Spanish criminality. He's very good. This lot has never even existed, my friend.' Mickey waved his hand with a regal twist of the wrist over the weapon haul before him, beaming like a proud father.

'Nice. Thanks for sorting things, Mick. I appreciate it.'

'The pleasure is all yours,' he retorted smugly, accompanied with an overplayed sardonic look.

'I'm heading to the golf resort where Daniel Ratchet was last seen so I can find out what I can about the situation. With a bit of luck Daniel will pop up nursing a hangover and a sore dick before we're even required. In the meantime, if there are leads on the ground, we'll turn them up. If he doesn't make an appearance sharpish, we'll have to figure out if he's still alive, who's got him, where the hell he's been taken and make the intervention.'

'Good luck, Hunter. The clock's ticking hard on this one.'

I loaded the new gear onto the back seat of the Range Rover. Stamped down on the gas causing the wheels to squeal and a dust cloud to swirl behind me. The motor pulled sharply out onto the smooth tarmac. Heavy downward pressure to the accelerator urged the metallic beast onwards, seeking out the angular horizon. Rugged red mountains filled the bottom inch of the windscreen. Sharp, clean lines jutting harshly against the soft aqua sky. Sun dazzling as it presided over a beautiful morning.

Keeping one eye on the empty road ahead, I rapidly scanned through the mobile phone for any new alerts from base. I'd barely averted my attention for more than a brief moment when, from out of nowhere, a battered articulated lorry swerving wildly on the wrong side of the road came careering right at me. Bloody typical that practically the first other traffic I'd encountered on the quiet Spanish roads early that morning and the driver must be asleep at the wheel. I slammed my fist into the horn, blasting it loudly, and swerved a defensive manoeuvre to avoid a smash. Pulled the wheel sharply down, skidding over to the other side of the road where the lorry should be driving. Closing in on a tight corner just ahead. A heavily laden family hatchback turned into view on the road, heading straight towards me, oblivious of the carnage that had just ensued. Instinctively I heaved at the wheel and pulled the Range Rover back across the face of the road and slammed nose-first into a sandy verge beyond. The truck, avoided by mere inches, skidded on two wheels as it struggled and fought to grip the tarmac. I'd swerved a clean side-on figure of eight and just missed crashing into the oncoming traffic, avoiding a certain collision. The startled face of the driver in the truck cab was gripped in a mask of fear as he grappled with the unwieldy heavy machine. He finally managed to pull it back across the dotted white lines, the lorry rocking capriciously from side to side until it settled squarely back upon its rows of huge spinning wheels, slowing to a crawl.

Cursing under my breath from my stationary position on the roadside, I watched as the meat wagon, with side-panelling livery detailing its cargo of succulent looking pigs, continued on its journey past me. The image of the truck driver's horrified face close-up through the windshield stuck firm in my mind.

A green, open-top army jeep flies out from nowhere, bouncing off a dirt mound and taking a clean two meters of air. The machine gun affixed to the back rattles a menacing timbre. Our car swerves sharply on the dirt road leading into the village, hits a pothole, flips onto its side. Screams fill my ears from behind me. Stu, injured in the crash, is speared through the torso by a twisted metal shard from the damaged vehicle. Blood spewing everywhere, thick and sticky. I struggle with the impacted passenger door and crawl forward furiously, wriggling

on my front. Dirt and grit in my eyes and filling my mouth. Now jeeps, armoured vehicles, surround us from every angle. Guns shooting, indiscriminate bullets fired into the sky. Shouts and howls of excitement reverberating in the thin air. An ambush. An angry brown face thrust down at me, huge yellow bloodshot eyes, inches above me, shouting loud, flecks of snow-white spittle spraying from his mouth. 'Where is Mahood? Where is Mahood? You come to the village for the munitions cache but instead you will die a hostage. This is our trap. We will trade you soldiers for Islamic prisoners or you will die a painful death.'

Then the butt of a rifle descending hard toward my face. Shooting pain. And nothing.

The incessant tapping on the window grew louder, more insistent. Woken from the haunting flashback I turned my head to face the pristine starched uniform of a local Spanish traffic cop standing beside the Range Rover. He peered inside, speaking loudly at the glass. The response to the descending electric window was a further torrent of rapid agitated Spanish. I held out my British driving licence and after careful examination he shook his head.

'No sleep here. Very dangerous. Trucks. All come very, very fast here.' He pointed at the road shaking his head again as another truck ploughed past us, smashing a wall of hot compressed air up against the passenger window. I couldn't be bothered to struggle with the explanation of what had just happened, instead placating him with a lopsided grin and a goofy thumbs up. He stepped backwards as I fired the engine and after making an exaggerated show of checking the mirrors, swung back out onto the dusty road and continued on my way at speed, still shaken by visions of the past.

11

Daniel sauntered back towards the hotel, weaving his way past the crowded practice putting green which was speckled with players and scattered with gleaming white balls. The old Scottish golf coach he'd met the previous day hovered, hawkish, at the scene. He greeted the affable manager with a nodded salute. Still wearing his navy-blue flat cap, with cigarette stub gripped firmly in mouth, the old boy leaned on a seven iron directing his lanky charge who stood captive inside a neat semicircle of balls. Bob Wallace, whose name had been discussed in disparaging terms last night, was by all accounts quite a character. Sean, the ginger haired Glaswegian caddy and self-anointed Master of Ceremonies for the previous night's debacle, had recounted various nefarious tales about his fellow Scot. Clashes with the establishment, flared tempers and one legend back from the 1980s when on falling into disagreement with a celebrated Hollywood actor concerning his tuition style he'd chased the star brandishing a nine iron straight off the range and into a nearby pond. These stories always got distorted and built up over time but Daniel chuckled to himself, picturing the scene as he tracked the pathway back towards the side entrance of the hotel.

'Hey, hotshot,' called out a voice from behind him. He turned to see Matilda, sitting in the sun on the steps of the physio truck, clutching a well-thumbed paperback. Daniel waved in response. 'Got time for a coffee?' she cooed.

'Absolutely,' he replied, regretting sounding so keen. By the time he reached the truck, Matilda was inside filling a cheap plastic kettle with bottled water. He bounded up the tightly spaced metal steps like an energetic puppy, only to trip on the frame of the truck as he entered, stumbling over his feet. Feet followed torso as he lurched forward clumsily, chest first into the angular corner of the glassed-off office space which dominated one side of the truck.

'Hey, steady there, hotshot.' Matilda laughed as Daniel, looking sheepish, rubbed the painful point of impact. 'You okay?' she asked, concerned, a cute furrow appearing on her brow just at the top of her button nose.

'Yeah, no, I'm fine, really,' he said. 'Just caught myself there. It's cool,' he said before offering, 'Sorry,' as an afterthought and then wondering why.

'Really, are you sure, Daniel?' Matilda replied. 'Because that looks pretty sore,' motioning to the dots of blood soaking through his powder blue polo shirt.

'Ah, crap. I got scratched somehow last night and I must have knocked it again when I fell back there.'

'Here, show me,' she said, patting the massage table next to her, encouraging Daniel to sit.

'Matilda, it's really fine, honestly. Nothing to worry about.'

'Listen to me,' she retorted, her accent more pronounced, vowels drawn longer, 'I may only be a physiotherapist and not a real doctor but I know that if you got scratched it needs to be sterilised properly.'

Daniel carefully peeled off his shirt, wincing a little as he did so. Matilda soaked a ball of cotton wool in iodine and dabbed his chest with care. 'So, how did this happen to you then, hotshot? You have to tell me. It was another woman, wasn't it?' she teased and tutted, shaking her head. 'I knew you sports agents were all the same!' she continued in mock horror.

'I don't think so, unfortunately. Not one I'd want to meet again at any rate,' Daniel replied, scrunching up his face as the iodine stung into him.

'Oh well! I guess she can't have been that memorable then anyway!'

'Rough night, I'm afraid,' offered Daniel by way of explanation. 'I went out with some of the caddies on the lash. Lost my wallet. My watch. Everything. Pretty sure they were stolen. It's a major bloody disaster.'

'You poor thing. You don't deserve such bad luck just when you start a new job.'

'Well not all bad, fortunately,' he said, brightening. 'An important Russian guy out here on the Tour who works for one of the big sponsors came and found me this morning and has offered to sponsor one of my players. Could be great news and sets me up well in the eyes of the new boss.'

'Sergei Krostanov, by any chance?'

'Yes, how did you know?'

'Because he's involved in everything round here.' Matilda gave a weary sigh. 'I'm not surprised that he spotted the chance of a deal to be done. He always ingratiates himself with the new player managers the second they arrive. Especially if their guys have game.'

Daniel pulled a face.

That infectious giggle again. 'Okay. Sorry. I guess you deserve some credit and for something good to happen after all those issues. But let's just say I'm not surprised. Somehow Sergei even gets to set the budget of the physio truck each season and decides that it's a prerequisite that he needs to discuss it personally with me over dinner. People talk and say we must be close but business is business.'

'What does Michael say about that?'

'Michael? Nothing, Michael does what he's told.'

'But I thought you guys were together?' Daniel tried to make it appear like a casual enquiry as he fished for information. He needn't have fretted.

'No, no. I'm a very independent woman, Daniel. Michael takes it on himself to protect me from some of the slimeballs out here on Tour perhaps, but we aren't together. I prefer a man with a bit more of an edge to him. Besides, he's got a family; a wife and a baby daughter back in Hanover. He works every hour he possibly can to send money back home to them, but they always want for more. And I'm more than capable of looking after myself, I can assure you. I have done so for a very long time indeed and that isn't about to change.'

'I have no doubt about that. I'm sure you are very capable,' Daniel said, grinning in admiration at her, then suddenly aware that this may not have been an appropriate response to verbalise. After a little while he asked thoughtfully, 'If you aren't with Michael, what's with the engagement ring?'

'Oh, the ring,' Matilda replied coolly, avoiding eye contact. 'It was my mother's. I feel that it keeps me safe.' A pained and distant look held in those enchanting pale blue eyes and Daniel decided that this avenue of conversation was better now closed.

'Just leave that to breathe,' Matilda instructed, regaining control. She turned to pack away the iodine and threw the damp ball of used cotton wool into a small metallic wastepaper basket under the sink. Daniel pulled on his shirt and fished out his mobile. He switched on the company-owned phone and INSERT SIM flashed up on the screen. *Oh come on*, he thought, *where's the damn SIM card gone?* An instant later he was hit by a sinking feeling in his stomach as it occurred to him that the SIM had been pre-programmed with a record of many of Crown Sports' key golf business contacts. The phone was also useless without it.

He discarded it with contempt, letting it spin over to one side of the massage table as his mind turned to his missing wallet and cash card. He considered ruefully how any more than only very modest spending on his cash card at this point would obliterate his overdraft and that he might be left liable for any theft on the company account.

'Matilda, listen, thanks for the patch-up,' Daniel called out as he bounced off the soft, padded therapy table. He was starting to feel an urgent need to get back in control of things. 'I've got to get back to my room and sort a few things out.'

'Okay,' she replied, hugging the corner of the medicinal storage cabinet and in the process exposing a perfectly toned, sun-kissed leg. 'Will I see you later?'

He gambled.

'Well, if you aren't busy we could maybe meet for dinner tonight? If you're free that is?'

Matilda hesitated, smiling. 'Sure, why not?'

'Great. Come to my room in the hotel, 503, for about seven thirty?'

And with that Daniel was gone, spirit restored, grinning from ear to ear and trotting back down the steps of the physio truck towards the hotel. Energised and resolved to sort the grief he was in and get his new life back on track.

12

Derek Hemmings sat alone in the secluded gardens of St James's Square in the gathering gloom. Across all corners of the Square, people were heading home from their day jobs, rushing to get back to their families. These days, Derek had only his wife, Alice, to go home to, with his two children, Robin and Samantha, both having flown the nest many years ago now. Their visits were becoming less and less frequent and he felt he barely recognised them as the bright inquisitive little people he had helped bring into the world, raised with his own impeccable values and manners. No, these days as they navigated themselves through the onset of middle age, their own bustling social lives, demanding partners, and burgeoning careers took unrivalled precedence above their ageing and unfashionable parents.

Derek cast his mind back to when he himself had been a vigorous young man. He might be weary of all the political games now but when he'd first joined the Foreign and Commonwealth Office as a sharp, intelligent and dedicated twenty-one-year-old Cambridge graduate, he'd been intent on changing the world. Selected by MI6 as potential Intelligence

Unit material and fast-tracked through the training set up, Derek had thought of himself as very much in the mould of Ian Fleming's James Bond in the secret service. Equipped with sharp suits, boundless confidence and high aspirations, everything had seemed possible. So, he put himself about, volunteered for assignments and cut a dash with army commanders and politicians alike. His patriotism and unstinting sense of honour made him determined to make a difference to that which he cherished most, his beloved Great Britain. For Queen and Country: Do the right thing. The mantra by which he had lived all these years.

And as quickly as it had begun, it was over. He'd met Alice, a secretary in the typing pool at Whitehall, introduced by his sister, Mary, with whom she was friends. They'd shared cocktails and theatre visits on the Strand and romantic walks through Covent Garden entwined arm in arm. Within two months, Alice was pregnant with Robin and Derek couldn't bring himself to take the posting to Cairo. He'd done the honourable thing, followed his immutable moral compass. With a young family to raise and a burdensome mortgage to pay, his fanciful ambitions of secret spying missions and glamorous foreign travel would simply have to wait. And wait they did, as his work and the family settled into a comfortable routine all together. The wee baby grew into a toddler and Derek was handed greater responsibility within the department. Alice fell pregnant again with Samantha and Derek's ambitions were pushed further into oblivion, curtailed by the administrative quicksand of a civil service position, albeit with a slow-moving rise toward seniority and respectability. Too slow moving for Alice, perhaps, but by appointment of The Queen no less. The eventual nominal promotion was in reality on paper only but it still caused Alice to weep tears of pride and fetch out the best china for an extended family celebration. Derek was nonplussed. He had known it was dead man's shoes right from the very beginning.

And here he was, forty-odd years later, sitting outside in a cold St James's Square, contemplating the course of his life, decisions taken and choices made. And too stubborn to go home yet again and drink tea and finish the crossword and listen to the pick pick pick of Alice's knitting needles.

His mobile phone rang. The jaunty whistling theme tune to *The Great Escape*. Robin had changed it for a joke when 'the old man' was out of the room on one occasion, presumably to poke fun at his old-fashioned sense of patriotism. Derek had never changed it back. It was a standing joke around the office that Derek was too out of date and inept to understand how these gadgets worked. The truth was that Derek liked the tune and what it stood for. It flared up some of the old bulldog spirit somewhere still inside him. The ring tone remained unchanged.

He answered the phone and listened as Andy Bartholomew oozed his rich, unctuous Celtic tones down the line. This was the particular tone reserved only for when he either needed something very important indeed or on returning from a lavish booze-fuelled lunch spent entertaining an enthusiastic and comely young researcher looking to climb the greasy pole. With junior female researchers of this type it was an open secret that in order to properly progress their careers it would need to be Andy's very own greasy pole that they would have to climb first.

'So, Derek my fine sir, how did it all go today?'

'How did what go, Andy?' Derek sighed.

'That would be your little tête-à-tête with our new friend Mr Golich, Derek,' came the smarmy reply.

Derek Hemmings considered the state of play. Something didn't sit well with him. He was being rushed and he didn't like it. For Queen and Country: Do the right thing. He was tired of being pushed around by Bartholomew... by Golich... by Alice...

'Ah yes, Andy. Everything went very well with our little friend, thank you. He just wants to move some cash around before he signs and we need further clarification on one or two small things. There's no problem. But he says it should be about a week or so. Leave it all with me and we'll have everything wrapped up pronto.'

'Sounds fine and dandy, Hemmings. Just keep me informed and be sure to bring me a signed copy of the agreement personally.'

Andy hung up.

'He's bought it,' said Derek aloud to himself in disbelief, standing to his feet. Then a little louder, 'I've just lied to a senior government official and he's only gone and bloody bought it.'

The Great Escape.

13

The soft bed linen billowed as he flopped back onto the mattress, letting the cool of the air-conditioned hotel room wash over him. Not much by way of exertion had taken place, but Daniel still felt drained from his short time under the baking heat of the demanding Spanish sun. He grabbed an ice-cold can of lemonade from the minibar, soaking wet from precipitation as if it could have been perspiring itself. He pressed the hard, cold metal against his neck.

Refreshed, Daniel dialled down to reception and asked for the number to International Direct Enquiries. In an efficient sequence of activity, punctuated by slugs of the refreshing drink, he spoke first with his mobile provider, requesting an alternative SIM to be couriered to the hotel, and then to his bank to put a stop on the cash card and check the account balance. Just as he'd feared, the damage had already been done. The bastards had drained his account to its maximum overdraft limit taking him two thousand pounds into the red. Worse than this he was still missing his grandfather's gold watch. Come home without that after chasing some 'Flash-Harry dream with a bunch of foreigners' and it would not go down well. Not one little bit.

Listless and despondent he stared out of the window. In blissful contrast to his sombre mood, two colourful rotund little birds danced and hopped outside on the terrace.

Sitting up on the edge of the bed now, trying to breathe steadier, Daniel spotted a slim tan file lying upon the coffee table at the side of the room. He didn't recall seeing it before. Couldn't be his. Something from housekeeping perhaps?

He hauled himself off the bed, head spinning, and steadied himself before dragging himself over to the table to examine it. The outside of the folder was blank. He opened it to find several neatly bound pages of stiff, crisp document inside. The first page was adorned solely with the large imposing logo of the Rublex Oil & Gas Corporation. *When did this arrive in my room?* he wondered. He scanned the following twelve pages quickly, unable to absorb too much detail or comprehend the legalese which framed it. Daniel gathered it was a private and confidential proposal outlining some type of financial option scheme. Rublex Corporation was offering to make a series of significant upfront payments to Aaron Crower, care of Crown Sports, in exchange for a percentage of his winnings throughout the year. Accompanying pages outlined a schedule of bonuses, some of which appeared markedly discretionary on meeting 'required expectations' and payable to him on achieving specific positions in a number of listed events. Daniel gawped at the figures, counting out the zeros with his fingers twice to be certain. There were enormous sums of money involved. They dwarfed the sums that the major equipment manufacturers paid the higher profile players on Tour to represent their clubs, shoes, clothing and balls. There was no reference to Aaron overtly representing the brand or wearing logoed apparel. This was usually the heart of any standard player agreement; branding at Tournaments and player appearances at corporate golf days, in the media or at certain specified occasions. Instead, it was written as if Aaron was a company and Rublex would become a silent investor, calling the shots behind the scenes. Daniel couldn't make sense of the bonus schedule. The ones that Silvio had emailed to him by way of example all grew in denomination as the player achieved a higher position in the tournament, with an emphasis on the Majors. That's why they were called 'win bonuses' as the better you did in an event, the more time on TV the sponsors got and more exposure could be derived in media value and brand awareness from association with that player. The difference with this agreement was that these bonuses seemed to reward failure in certain events above victory itself.

It makes no sense, Daniel thought to himself, tossing the folder back onto the table in front of him. It was the first agreement of its kind that he had read and with a combination of his fuzzy head and bleary eyes, he was convinced that the document was littered with mistakes and missing pages. *I'll run it past Silvio and see what he thinks*, he thought. *Perhaps I can make it sound like I've delivered a serious coup in my first week, prove that I'm worth my salt after all. That will overshadow all these teething problems when they hear about the money I've brought in, as long as we can iron out the errors in there regarding the performance bonus. Silvio will know what to do.*

It didn't stop the uneasy feeling in his stomach that was beginning to pervade.

He flicked on the TV to check the player scores of the tournament which, ironically, was playing out on a golf course only metres away from him. Aaron had finished his round on three under par after a difficult back nine. François, whom he'd also met briefly in London at a Crown Sports summit but hadn't caught up with so far this week, was fairing much worse. A later tee-time had left him combating the worst of the blustery afternoon wind and he was two over par after three holes.

Daniel hoped he would be able to keep his head out there and battle round in a decent score to make it to the weekend. He'd been warned that François had a fiery temper and a tendency to get disconsolate if his game wasn't producing the results he felt his talent was capable of delivering. Missing the cut wouldn't help at all. Jeppe Ossgren was leader in the clubhouse at six under par. Daniel smiled to himself. *Well, that's worked out just like I said it would! After all, he was swinging it just lovely on the range.*

He leaned back in his chair, hoping his luck was truly starting to change. Daniel felt his head loll to one side as he willingly succumbed to the seduction of sleep.

He awoke at six that evening, refreshed and invigorated. Next, he showered and shaved, liberally applying aftershave and cleaning his teeth with new-found zeal. He dressed in a red and white checked short-sleeved shirt and faded blue jeans, going for the casual look. Someone had once told him: where women are concerned, never make it look like you're trying too hard. He didn't know if that was good advice or not, but it was certainly easier to follow. But fighting the desire to try and impress was, of course, impossible. He could already feel the butterflies whirling in his stomach. Although this could also be attributable to the remnants of the lingering hangover that he had so far survived. And things were looking up again. There was no denying he was excited by the prospect of dinner with this sexy worldly woman; an available woman who was displaying a genuine interest in him. And in this testosterone-rich environment with so much wealth, talent, and the very essence of competition on display, she would certainly have her fair share of suitors. She'd practically alluded to as much herself. That thought lingered and annoyed Daniel, unsettling him more than he quite expected. Yes, he wanted her for himself. There was also something else about her that intrigued him too. She was confident, certainly aware of her own self-worth and possibly the devastating mind-numbing effect that she could have on men. That was if his own reaction were anything to go by. Yet she remained vulnerable. She was grounded and down to earth and seemed to shield a secret hurt. But she enjoyed teasing him and could establish her superiority with just a look. Above all else, Daniel loved a challenge.

He was, however, getting ahead of himself. He'd overslept and hadn't made dinner reservations. With no access to money, except for the Rublex corporate credit card which Mr Krostanov had so kindly extended to him, impressing Matilda was going to be a tough job. And he could hardly ask her to pay. He toyed with the idea that Sergei would consider that buying dinner for the Tour physiotherapist a fit and proper use of his generosity when the time came for expense reconciliation. It was, after all, a favoured activity of his own apparently. Thinking on his feet, Daniel figured that at least he might be able to arrange for his hotel bill to be covered by Crown Sports HQ at the end of the week, buying him some time. He grabbed the room phone quickly and dialled to order room service.

As a lad growing up, Daniel had been told that he displayed an easy manner, a relaxed charm. Perhaps it was the natural antidote to being the only child of a neurotic mother and uptight father who calculated and affixed a risk assessment to each of life's everyday decisions. To say that they had been shocked and concerned when he'd taken the job with an American company at such short notice, without the usual period of intense and expected due diligence, was an understatement. This was compounded when they learned that he would be travelling abroad for his job, a different country week on week, living out of hotels. His father was naturally suspicious of the type of money that a man of twenty-one would be earning in these endeavours. Was Daniel quite sure of what would be expected of him by these foreigners? His mother repeatedly warned of impending doom with so many flights to be taken during the year across the busy international golf schedule. Above all, they didn't consider sport to be a serious, sustainable career, nor the best use of a university education. A bunch of show-offs, dressed up like clowns, trying to hit a little white ball into a hole was, to them, a frivolous affair.

Daniel gently persuaded the friendly, female voice on the end of the phone to open up the full restaurant menu to him for room service, rather than the limited listing on offer in the room. He ordered with gusto, a classic trap for anyone who has chosen food whilst gripped with pangs of hunger. Hoping Matilda would be pleased with his choices, he added a couple of bottles of champagne and hung up the receiver. It was 1915.

He briefly considered phoning François to touch base and offer some words of encouragement. On balance it was probably safer to let him stew in his own juices on the range, beating out his frustrations on dozens of innocent inanimate objects instead. He opted to leave a simple, upbeat message of support for him to be collected at reception. Boxes ticked, he sprang off the bed and sauntered out onto the balcony, gazing below at bronzed couples in light evening dresses and linen shirts, smoking cigarettes and sharing pre-dinner drinks by the pool. He hadn't really registered it when Silvio explained that he would be staying in five-star hotels on his trips with the players, all paid for by his new employer. When he'd queried the itinerary, Silvio had explained that the beautiful golf courses on which the tournaments were played often had hotels affixed to them or situated close by to form a resort. Staying at these made access to the players, whether your own stable or perhaps those of another agent if you were seeking to establish an opportunity to poach, much easier. The caddies take care of themselves, sharing in whatever cheap fleapit they can find between them during the week to keep costs down. But it simply wouldn't do for a player manager not to be close at hand for his stars.

Daniel was woken from his thoughts by a rap on the door. He scampered across the room, opening it to allow two smartly dressed waiters to bluster inside wheeling long metal trollies adorned with white tablecloths, ice buckets and several large silver salvers stacked up together. They looked with concern first at the room's small coffee table, and then in turn at the writing desk and patio furniture, calculating the lack of furniture surface space versus the volume of dishes steaming patiently on the trollies. The waiters enquired politely in heavily accented English where 'sir' would like dinner to be presented. Daniel considered the balcony for a moment but then pulling one of the folded white tablecloths from a trolley, he shook it free and laid it on the floor at the foot of the bed. 'I think we're going to have ourselves a picnic.' He grinned.

At 2003, the door knocked twice. The minutes had ticked by. He checked himself in the mirror one last time before taking a deep breath. Peeked through the tiny fisheye security peephole out into the corridor. Matilda was standing there holding a single flower in both hands; a large drooping yellow and white daisy. He sprang the door open.

'For you.' She giggled, offering Daniel the flower, kissing him on the cheek and stepping into the room in a single motion. He turned to see a vision standing before him, her shoulders swaying slightly, hands clasped in front across her lap. Matilda's long, straight-cut, platinum blonde hair cascaded down her shoulders. Her dress was made of white embroidered lace, cut an inch before the knee to reveal two long, shapely, tanned legs in a pair of strappy black heels. Her look was natural, with simple and sparing make-up, highlighting strong Nordic cheekbones and those big blue eyes. Full, lightly glossed lips glistened at him. Soft and inviting. Daniel hadn't realised quite how hungry he really was.

Gesturing behind them to the generous picnic spread which adorned the tablecloth that stretched over the carpet he mumbled aloud, 'I was going to take you to a restaurant but...'

'Daniel, you did all this just for me? It's wonderful. I can't believe it.'

'Oh, it's no problem. Really. I just figured it might be fun. I hope you brought your appetite,' he said, fumbling to open a cold bottle of champagne from the bucket and fill two glasses but spilling half of the spurting bubbles and losing the cork somewhere behind an armchair in the process.

They toasted each other, 'To new friends,' and stepped out onto the balcony to enjoy the view.

'You are so lucky to be staying here, Daniel,' said Matilda, looking around. 'You realise I have to share a room with some old dragon in a cheap downtown apartment. Michael prefers to sleep in the truck.' Daniel wondered if the old dragon might be the efficient, line-faced matron he has seen registering players on the first day. He couldn't help but envy her being able to share a room with the sumptuous woman standing in front of him.

'I know,' he answered, 'I can't believe it myself. I think I could just about get used to living the life of a golf agent.'

'Don't you dare change on me though,' said Matilda, placing her hand on Daniel's shoulder. 'There are enough assholes around here already.' The Swedish accent was coming through stronger again.

'Who d'you mean exactly? Although I think I've already met a few to be honest,' replied Daniel, draining his glass and then refilling Matilda's.

'Well, some of the caddies you already know, I believe? Your new drinking buddies? They give me the creeps, always hanging around, staring, whispering, making lewd remarks. It can be a bit menacing really sometimes. Most of the agents are just slimeballs, always making innuendoes with me and ordering Michael around.'

'No one ever taken your fancy then?' asked Daniel.

Matilda fixed an enigmatic expression on her face. 'Well a girl's got to have some fun sometime, right? I've been on a few dates, got to know a few of the agents out here. But they're all so boring. I went out with one guy in particular, Ollie. His daddy started the company managing sports stars years ago and now Ollie runs around on Tour sucking up to the players and pretending he's very important to everyone else. I guess you could say we had some fun. He really made it big though when he got his whole stable to be sponsored by Rublex on their player programme. You should think about that too, I guess, if that's an opportunity with Sergei. That's life-changing money.'

Daniel thought back to the slick looking guys he'd seen on the range, gelling with the players and their teams. Making it all appear so natural. *Was Ollie one of those guys?* he wondered. He found himself bristling with jealousy.

'Righto,' he tried to brush it off. 'So, what do you know about Sergei, the Russian guy? He's such a nice bloke. He's already been so kind to me but from what you've said there seems to be more to him?' fished Daniel.

'You're just all business, you hotshot agents, aren't you?' answered Matilda, smiling at him. Daniel sensed she was also trying to change the subject. Perhaps he should have settled for safer ground but persisted instead.

'Sorry. It's just I'm new here and any information is a help. I've got one chance and I'm determined to make my mark.'

'He's the face of the Russian Rublex Corporation in golf.

They did this massive deal with the Tour a while back, supporting tournament infrastructure and building up the big prize funds to attract the best international players. Sergei delivers it all and ensures they get what they want. Not everyone approves though. Some of the traditionalists like Bob Wallace, that tough old Scottish swing coach with the cap and the cigarettes, one of the longest serving guys out here, he says the Tour has "sold its soul" to compete with the US Tour.'

'Surely that's a good thing for the game, a bit of competition. Must be good for the players too,' Daniel mused.

'Rublex has certainly divided opinion but they're the future. The game of golf is changing and Sergei gets that. He's a clever guy. He has an eye for a deal and knows the right levers to pull at the right time. He's worth getting on the right side of. Bob seems to think that Sergei is somehow resentful of the game's exclusivity and traditions but he's actually very committed to golf. He understands the importance of family and loyalty and I think his heart is in the right place.'

'Sounds like a bit of an enigma,' scoffed Daniel. 'But he's certainly helped me out this week, that's for sure.' And then, 'Look, our food's getting cold. Shall we eat?'

Leading Matilda by the hand back into the bedroom they sat facing each other on the corners of the tablecloth which served as their makeshift picnic blanket. He busied himself removing the numerous lids that covered the delicious-smelling food, unpacking baskets of warm bread rolls and small jars of exotic looking sauces. Since the aborted restaurant plan, he'd decided against choosing a specific meal on behalf of his date, equipped with little prior knowledge of her tastes. Instead, he'd decided on ordering an array of tapas dishes.

'It could get messy,' joked Daniel. 'Please, just get stuck in. There's no order to it really.' He reached across the spread to spoon paprika-rich chorizo, a slice of tortilla and some folded pieces of thick-sliced rustic ham onto his plate. Matilda helped herself in turn to a modest portion of thick lamb stew with a side of lush green salad leaves. With glasses replenished and second helpings served, Daniel leant back, content, and sighed.

'I really don't know much about you,' Matilda commented, peering over the rim of her glass and holding his gaze.

'Not much to tell really,' he replied. Which was met with a disappointed look. 'Okay. I'm a straight-forward bloke I suppose. Guess I'm just running scared from my boring life back in England. I want to do well in life but I'm not sure I fancy having to cut corners and compete with the supposed sharks out here that are doing this job.'

'A man with principles! That can be very sexy, you know,' Matilda teased. Daniel felt his cheeks blush red. *Steady on with the champagne*, he chided himself, *you're getting a bit loose here, and that's not a good idea on the back of last night's effort.*

'I suppose I'm trying to escape from my background, my parents, my life as it was all mapped out for me. I only got this job through luck. You know, right place, right time. I feel like a bit of a fraud most of the time. Like I don't fit in.'

'Oh, Daniel, of course you fit in. You fit in because you're real. A real person. You don't find that too often. You're not someone pretending to be something that you're not. I really appreciate your honesty in sharing with me.' She clasped her hands against her heart as if to show the depth of feeling. 'There's not much genuine conversation or guys brave enough to show their true feelings and make themselves vulnerable out here. Thank you.' She reached out and held his hand in hers, keeping eye contact.

'What about you?' Daniel asked, softening his voice, head cocked slightly to the side.

'Me? I'm a bit of a mess too, I guess. Only in my case I wish I had parents to run from.'

'Seriously? What happened?' said Daniel, not releasing her delicate hand from his grip.

'They were killed in a car crash outside Stockholm when I was nineteen. I lost the plot after that for a while. I didn't know where to turn, Daniel.' She held up her other hand and offered it to him. 'I wear this ring you noticed because it's all that I have left of my mother, she gave it to me on my eighteenth birthday, it had been her mother's too you see, and it's always protected me.' She pulled back, retreating a little. 'I should have been on that trip with them that day. I only wish she'd been wearing it instead of me, you know?' She looked at her hand and twisted the small stone around on her finger. A moment of silence passed between them and she continued, 'After a while I managed to get it together and I just threw myself back into my studies. My brother, Nils, he took it harder, he went off the rails, got in with a bad group, turned to heroin to escape. It's a dirty, horrible drug, Daniel,' she spat. 'He damaged himself permanently. Now, he's trapped in a state clinic in Malmö. Lost. Alone.'

She looked up at Daniel and he could see her eyes brimming with tears. He reached behind and tucked a strand of fine blonde hair behind her ear.

'It's okay,' was all he could manage.

Matilda reached forward and traced her finger down his shirt over the scratch on Daniel's chest which she had treated some hours earlier. He let her nearly finish before grabbing her and pulling her towards him. Wiping the tears from her cheeks Daniel found himself suddenly kissing her tentatively on the mouth. He cupped the back of her head and, feeling her yield, he kissed her soft lips again harder.

He pulled back, holding her face in his hands, and gazed for an age into those pretty blue eyes. With an impish grin escaping across his face, Daniel Ratchet couldn't contain himself any longer. Still kissing her at delighted, random intervals, he asked, 'So why me, Matilda? A girl like you could have anyone she wanted out here. I'm curious to know because I get the impression you don't do this sort of thing very often?'

'Right place, right time! Didn't you say that yourself, hotshot?' She giggled, pushing him away and easing herself up and onto the edge of the bed. 'Okay, you want to know what I like in you? You're sincere. Honest, vulnerable, even. You didn't act all cool and in control like most of the other guys out here when we met and I really liked that. Besides, despite all the people out here performing with this travelling circus, it can be a pretty lonely way to live and although I'm with Michael in the truck all the time, he's married and treats me like a kid sister. Can you blame a girl for getting excited when some fresh meat arrives on the scene?' Daniel blushed again. 'Besides, I need an escape plan to get off this merry-go-round at some point. So, play your cards right and make sure you sign your players up to lots of juicy sponsorship deals out here and make it big. Aaron's some of the hottest young international talent on the Tour right now and you're his manager, so as far as escape plans go, you might just be it.'

Daniel grinned and, standing directly in front of her, pushed Matilda onto her back. She squealed with laughter, thrashing around playfully as Daniel kneeled on the bed, pinning her by the arms and planting quick playful kisses all over her face as she snorted and squirmed.

14

ENGLAND. LONDON. WHITEHALL.

B y the time Derek strode back into his office, chest thrust
out, the blood coursing through his veins, there were only
a few lights left on in the building. He marched down the
corridor with a spring in his step he'd not felt for many a year. A
lone chink of light emanated from under a single door. The
small office of his diligent assistant, Alexander Gontlemoon. A
double first in languages from Oxford, the immaculately
groomed young man was tipped as a rising star of the
department and, Hemmings had noted to himself at the
interview, was cut from the right cloth. That didn't hurt one jot
around the corridors of power. Tall, expensive suits, perfectly
parted hair, and always prepared to go the extra mile. *Not like his
own son, Robin, or the rest of this self-entitled 'snowflake' generation,*
he mused.

He rapped twice on the door and cleared his throat as he
pushed it open. 'Alexander, dear boy. Would you be so kind as to
come to my office? I could use your help with looking into
something important, something of grave sensitivity to the
interests of our great nation.' Derek straightened his back,

drawing out the words so as to labour their significance. 'And I do hope you don't have plans. It may be a long night.'

'I'm at your disposal, sir,' came the reassuring reply. 'It all sounds rather intriguing. Is it by any chance concerning the Russian Gas deal you were looking at today?'

'I need to know I can depend on you, Alexander.' Hemmings' voice choked thick with emotion.

'Of course, sir, rest assured you can trust me with anything.' An earnest reply, sure enough. 'I will be the very soul of integrity in the matter.'

'Well, you should be made aware that there are factions right here within our esteemed governmental departments, Alexander, that would wish for this commercial agreement with a certain Russian businessman to be signed, sealed and committed to without the proper and correct due diligence it warrants.' He laboured the word 'businessman', lacing it with heavy irony as he stared resolutely into the handsome face of his young aide. 'I can't allow that to happen I'm afraid, Alexander. No, not on Derek Hemmings' watch.'

Over the next thirty minutes, Alexander was fully apprised of the situation at hand. They ran through the stringent timelines imposed upon them and the dire implications of getting this decision wrong. The UK could be entering into an imminent legally binding commercial agreement with an international criminal organisation. This would de facto mean that Great Britain became little more than a conduit for money laundering on an epic scale and a reseller of dirty energy. By sanitising it with Britain's good name and transporting it for sale in the western open market, there would be a significant risk of damaging carefully fostered international relations and crucial trading partners. It could take decades to repair the fallout. If such misuse of the Falklands Islands was seized upon by Argentina, with all their usual sabre rattling, the result could possibly prompt another war or having to cede the territory once and for all under pressure from the United Nations on the basis of illegal occupation for financial gain. The desperate alternative meant pulling out of this deal at the last moment and sacrificing seven thousand British jobs. It would mean passing up on a huge industrial infrastructure investment and a boost to the economy of nearly seven billion pounds, plus the share of a projected hundred billion in sales over the next decade. All this whilst in the teeth of record national debt and facing spending cuts, tax rises, increasing unemployment, refugees and a contracting European economy amidst the threat of a volatile geopolitical outlook. It also meant potentially handing a prime opportunity with the Russians over to an aggressive Chinese-Argentinian axis intent on exploiting the natural resources for themselves. Derek's hands began to sweat. Get this one wrong and he'd be assured of a legacy in the annals of history all right.

For Queen and Country: Do the right thing. Do the bloody right thing.

They worked through the night, fuelled by endless rounds of coffee and packets of custard creams raided from the office tea trolley. Derek worked like a man possessed. His heart soared; energy abounded. A man on a mission once more. Under his close direction, Alexander scoured reams of intelligence data and financial records, seeking to understand the complex financial ownership of Rublex Corporation and its meteoric rise from such humble beginnings. By sunrise, they were both agitated and exhausted in equal measure. Some of the individual elements of what they sought to expose had been identified but they had been unable to pull the pieces together to make any sense. Without that golden thread tying facts together, the information would be as potent as the other unsubstantiated and unpleasant conjecture surrounding Golich. Nothing had stuck. Derek was in despair. He tugged intermittently at his forelock as he worked, brow creased deeply in concentration. Gut instinct told him under no circumstances to trust the Rublex Corporation; despite the fact that he couldn't prove a thing. *Innocent until proven guilty, old boy*, he chided himself. The deal would be on the table for only a few more days. And the clock was ticking.

15

A shard of warm sunlight streamed across the bed. Daniel stirred and stretched. He rubbed his eyes, blinking at Matilda as she stooped at the foot of the bed pulling on her crumpled white dress.

'Morning.' He smiled, pulling his pillow behind him and scooting up to lean back against the headboard.

'Morning, sexy,' cooed the womanly silhouette framed by a backdrop of fragmented sunbeams. 'Last night was amazing, darling. But I'm so sorry, I've really got to run. I need to shower and change in time for a really early appointment this morning.'

'What's the time?' mumbled Daniel.

'It's five-fifteen, sleepyhead,' Matilda replied, moving to the bed and ruffling his hair. 'Thank you for a beautiful evening,' she murmured, kissing him full on the mouth. 'But I'm so late. Come and find me at the truck later, will you?'

'Sure thing,' Daniel replied, and shuffled back down the bed, yawning. 'Have fun.'

The door pulled shut and Daniel, with the sunlight causing vibrant colours to bubble and dance across his eyelids, slipped back into a dreamlike state, peppered with snapshots and memories from a night of passion with an intoxicating Swedish siren. Ratchet was in freefall and he was falling hard.

Rising at just past seven, he dragged himself out of bed before forcing himself to stand under the powerful jets of the walk-in shower. Revitalised, he dressed in a hurry, leaving the room with his hair still damp. The elevator doors pinged open. He trotted out, whistling down the hotel steps and out through reception.

'Excuse me. Mr Ratchet?' an over-groomed man at the front desk called out as he passed. 'We have a package for you, sir.'

Daniel signed for a neat square box, tightly wrapped in plain brown paper. Ripping it open and lifting the lid of the navy-blue cardboard box, Daniel pulled out a gleaming new gold watch coiled around a Perspex cuff. It was adorned with smart lettering which announced it as a Rolex Datejust Oyster, no less. Daniel fished out a stiff black business card stuffed into the side of the box, turning it the right way up. The bold logo of the Rublex Corporation filled the centre of the space. Beneath it in gold leaf: Sergei Krostanov / President / Golf, complete with phone number, email, and an office address in Perm, Russia, on the reverse. Daniel felt his jaw go slack. 'Are you sure this is for me?' he enquired of the receptionist, eyebrows raised.

'Yes, sir. It was left by Mr Krostanov's assistant this morning. He was very insistent that you received it personally. We were about to send it up with this letter to your room.'

Daniel thanked the receptionist and tore open the note. It was handwritten in spidery blue ink. Ink from a traditional fountain pen, he noted. Somehow the old-fashioned touch added deeper cadence to the sentiment of the gift. It read:

Dearest Daniel,
    I was saddened to hear of the loss of your treasured watch. A

memory of your grandfather. This modest gift could never replace such a thing but I hope it will go some way to showing that we are all one family on the Tour and as our newest member I feel great responsibility for your well-being. Enjoy the Rolex.

I look forward to working closely with you and to completing many deals together in the near future.

Yours, Sergei.

Daniel shook his head. Whistled through his teeth as he walked away cradling the box in both hands. This really was a different world.

By the time he reached the practice green the new Rolex was snugly on his wrist with the accompanying guarantee and documentation stuffed into a back pocket. Bob Wallace was kneeling on one knee holding a Stimpmeter in place to record the ball speed of a certain patch of green. A row of balls were neatly lined up in preparation of the pre-round warm-up session he would be giving to one of the players later that morning. 'You surviving out here, are you, laddie?' he chirped without glancing up from underneath the tattered flat cap.

'You could say that,' replied Daniel, beaming. 'In fact, so far, I think it's coming together quite nicely.' He glanced down again at his new watch and waggled his wrist.

Wallace struggled to his feet with an overt display of effort. 'That new then, is it, m'boy? Mighty fine timepiece you got there.'

'Yeah. Thanks. It's great, isn't it? New this morning. It's a gift from the Rublex Corporation. I had my watch stolen the other night. It was my granddad's and all I had left of him since he passed. I'm gutted it's gone, to be fair. So nice of them to get me this one though!'

'I see, laddie. I thought it looked like the sort that some vulgar Ruski might wear to show off their bloody money. Just don't trade your soul away,' the old dog sniffed, turning away with contempt.

'I'm not quite sure what you're saying?' replied a brooding Daniel, stuffing his left hand deep into his pocket to conceal the watch which now felt rather too conspicuous on his wrist.

Wallace looked back towards him. 'There's a lot more going on out here than meets the eye. Some unsavoury characters who don't have the game's best interests at heart.'

'Who do you mean? I can't really imagine that's true, Bob.'

'I've long been of the belief that these celebrated Russian benefactors of ours, with their ostentatious display of wealth and showboating, actually resent the British game deep down. I think they hate our history, our rules and exclusive clubs because they dragged themselves up from the dirt. They could never be part of it and now that some of them have made a fortune from raping their own people, they want to own it and lord it over us. Well, it's our bloody game, laddie, and this Scotsman isn't giving it up without a fight!'

Daniel stood quietly, uncertain what he should say in response to this quite unsolicited rant. It sounded like the racist ramblings of a deranged old man.

Red-faced and worked up into something of a sweat, Bob continued, 'Have they approached you about your players shaving shots yet? I know that damn well goes on out there.' He nodded darkly towards the lush green golf course stretching out behind them.

'What are you talking about?'

'They always start with some sort of a sweetener.'

'What are you saying, Bob?'

'Some of the caddies. They like to get the agents onside all right. They work a system out here, I'm sure of it. There's secret gambling and players' results not matching up to their form and all sorts. I've raised it with the Tour's top brass at the AGM before now but the ideas of an angry old man are just laughed away. I've got a bit of history with those fuddy-duddies who run the game. No one takes a blind bit of notice of anything that doesn't toe the party line. Not one bit.' He took a hard drag on his tatty cigarette end.

'Are you suggesting that they're really fixing tournaments then? That's all a bit too Moon Landings, Area 51 conspiracy stuff for me. Besides you can't fix golf because the rules are so strict and the best guys stand to win too much money, don't they?'

Bob ignored the attempt to lighten the mood. Puffing himself up, like a wizened minister readying to deliver a scathing sermon down to a chastened congregation, he began.

'It breaks my heart, Danny, it truly does, but it is only about the money now, and there's too much of it out here for sure. You can forget about the love of the game. The honour and tradition. Proud and honourable gentlemen founded this fine Tour and grew it from nothing but an impoverished sideshow into a genuine rival for the US Tour. They made it so that there was no longer one show on the world stage and the cream of European golfing talent had bigger and better tournaments and fatter purses to compete for right on their doorstep.'

Daniel offered a sage nod.

'Ay, that indeed built some confidence,' Bob muttered to himself. 'We started beating them in the Ryder Cup, filling the top spots in the world rankings and winning more and more Majors. That attracted the best international players to our events and in turn the commitment of the sponsors and TV.' He picked at the dirt under his thumbnail with a metal pitching fork.

'Europe doesn't mean Europe anymore. We play in any country that is willing to foot the bill. The cycle self-perpetuates. You see, laddie, money attracts talent. But time moves on as they say and I think the new guard at the Tour got greedy with the success and wanted even more.' Bob shook his head.

'It wasn't good enough to simply compete anymore, they wanted to outgun the US PGA altogether and stick it up them after all the noise they make about the huge money available in the FedEx Cup. So, in came Rublex with all their dirty energy money, and how things have changed!'

'You're pretty passionate about this.'

'I still know a thing or two about this ancient game of ours. But it's always been fair. The best golfer won out. It doesn't feel like that anymore,' said Bob, pawing at the turf with his spikes. 'Maybe some of them are just happy to take a cheque. To do what they're told and forget about the winner's circle.'

Daniel nodded. 'I want to keep away from all that if it's going on. I wouldn't want to lead any of our guys down the wrong path or get Crown Sports into any bother either.'

'You might want to catch up with that big lump, Michael Hausen, from the physio truck for his take on all this then. He told me that last month a player leading an event came to him in tears on the Saturday night asking for a medical exemption to withdraw from the tournament. Daniel, there was nothing wrong with him. Michael didn't want to sign anything but apparently he had a little visit afterwards from the player's bag man which helped him to change his mind. He was left with no option.'

'I don't get it,' said Daniel, shaking his head again. 'Golf 's always been beyond reproach. It's so skilful that drugs can't really enhance performance and the huge prize funds available mean it will always be a meritocracy with the best talent winning out on the course.'

'Like I've said, it just seems to me that a certain element doesn't want the best guys to win out here at all.'

'Right. Thanks then,' mumbled Daniel, feeling like he'd been punched hard in the gut and keen to get away. The old man gave a solemn salute then casually swung the trusty seven iron in his hand, swishing it across the top surface of the grass in front of him. He turned back in silence to the arrangement of balls and practice drills on the green. Daniel scuttled away. He had some thinking to do.

The rest of the morning was spent following a brooding François as he moped his way around the golf course. Each hole appeared to deepen the darkness of his mood as a succession of errant drives and lipped-out putts forced the South African farther and farther from the cut mark and the chance of making it into the weekend money. Daniel welcomed the silence and anonymity amongst the galleries as an opportunity to clear his head. It had been a hectic few days. He needed space to reflect on the enormity of what he'd learned about the dark workings of the golf Tour. He felt vulnerable and exposed. There was no way he could act on any of this until he knew more and was sure of the facts. He couldn't do anything simply on the hearsay of one bitter old man. He'd be risking his job too. A job he was beginning to love. Although he figured he'd already been on the receiving end of how some of the caddies, that Bob had mentioned, operated out here. What if he got drawn in deeper? How would it play out if his own players were asked to co-operate in any kind of results fixing? Suppose there was actual proof showing guys in the field cheating on the Order of Merit.

By ignoring it, wouldn't he be tacitly assisting a dishonourable practice to thrive, conning the sponsors and the fans who adored the sport and supported the stars? Perhaps it wasn't even Daniel's choice anymore. Even if he wanted to keep his head down, hold a low profile, and stay away from trouble; it seemed apparent that certain people out here were determined to get him involved one way or another. Daniel made up his mind. He needed to know the state of play, to understand how far this went for himself.

François splashed his beleaguered ball out of a bunker and straight into a patch of thick penal rough. Daniel made eye contact for the final time, pumping his fist in solidarity and willing the erratic streak to rescind. He splintered away from the throng of fans scurrying between hole and tee, vying with each other for the premium vantage points along the fairway. He headed back towards the hotel complex, deciding to pay a quick visit to Matilda before getting to grips with Aaron's Rublex sponsorship agreement.

He stole a shortcut through a grassy parking area, closed to the public this week and used for housing the wealth of trailers and trucks required to service the infrastructure of the event. Daniel's eye was drawn to two figures in a heated discussion, partially hidden behind a massive generator. He didn't approach but instead, intrigued to get a better view, sidled up between two black articulated lorries, edging closer until he was within earshot.

He recognised the men in the throes of a vociferous argument. Sean, the ginger Glaswegian caddy, whom on the balance of probabilities Daniel blamed as at least one of the authors of his first night drunken ignominy, had hold of the hulking frame of Michael Hausen, Matilda's co-worker, by the scruff of his T-shirt. He was shouting into his face at point-blank range. Sean's face was screwed up into a hateful snarl, a grotesque spray of saliva emanating from his mouth as he berated and admonished the German. From the shadow between the trucks, Daniel tried to make some meaning out of the ranting. He had trouble understanding Sean in casual conversation, let alone when he was screaming and swearing uncontrollably. Michael owed some money. He had gambling debts that needed to be repaid and it sounded serious. The sight was somewhat farcical. The muscular German dwarfed the pugnacious Scot in height and bulk yet he was being totally dominated in the exchange. He seemed genuinely scared. Daniel was transported back to school where, one hot afternoon, his geography teacher had yet again decided that actually teaching something would be too much bother and instead switched on a video about cattle ranching in Australia. The enduring comic image was of a small, yet acutely aggressive and determined cattle-dog perched on the back of a huge dumb cow nipping and yapping away until the beast bent to its will and returned to the ranching station.

But there was nothing funny about this interaction. It was heavy. Michael was pleading for more time to pay and it was falling on deaf ears. What happened next shocked Daniel to his core. Uncontested, the Glaswegian grabbed a fistful of Michael's hair, dragged him forward and slammed his face into the hot metal grate of the generator, twisting and grinding it against the scalding hot grill. Daniel's instinct was to intervene. To take on the bully. To get the victim away from his torturer and this nightmare situation. Gripping the side of the Callaway equipment trailer that was shielding him from sight he suddenly paused, checking himself. Something was wrong about this situation. Michael could easily overpower the little thug tormenting him. He wasn't even resisting, instead he was allowing it to happen. When Sean pulled Michael free from the grill he was moaning in pain. The entire side of his face scorched with raw welts and burns. Next, Sean opened a can of Red Bull, casually taking a swig as he admired his handiwork, before emptying the rest over the pitiful German's head. 'Fockin' pay up this time, Sausage Meat, or you're a dead man. You know all about our connections, Sauerkraut. The Russians have always despised you Germans. Things could start to get very nasty for you indeed, pal,' he hissed, patting Michael on the face.

Daniel watched the casual turn. The lazy stroll away. Felt cold sweat streaming down the back of his neck. He didn't stop running until he reached the hotel.

16

Sergei Krostanov shook the hand of the tanned young Australian and handed across the glittering oversized trophy. Applause resounded in the winner's circle on the 18th green. Aaron Crower raised the cup aloft and beamed his pearly whites towards the bank of flashing camera bulbs. His maiden victory was evidence that his much-vaunted attributes as a strong front runner during a promising amateur career could translate into the big money Pro Tournaments. It was one thing being able to shoot the lights out and get on a hot streak by drilling a run of birdies. It was quite another having to sleep on a lead in the first professional golf event you were in contention for, with a hungry chasing pack snapping at your heels ready to prey on the first sign of weakness. Only the purest of swings and those players endowed with genuine self-belief and mental toughness would be able to make a habit of it. He was now an official winner on Tour, recipient of a large winner's cheque, a one-year playing card exemption and, perhaps most significantly, he'd become 'the one to watch'.

Aaron scanned the crowd gathered behind the ropes as they showed their appreciation with polite applause and searched for

Daniel. It annoyed him that the new manager Rudy had assigned hadn't bothered to show up on the biggest day of his career to date. He turned to Sergei standing beside him and asked if he'd seen anyone from Crown Sports.

'I hear a rumour that Daniel Ratchet has returned to England, I'm afraid. I don't think he was quite up to the job. Didn't seem to have what it takes to make it out here. I take it he didn't discuss your new sponsorship contract from the Rublex Corporation with you either, Aaron? It's a sixteen-million-dollar contract so it seems a little remiss of him if he didn't raise this with you. After such a fine display on the course today, now seems like the perfect time to have that conversation, don't you agree?'

He ushered the lean athletic golfer through a roped off pathway, dismissing requests for interviews with a wave of his hand. They weaved through the temporary cabins serving as Tour offices, which were assembled at every scheduled event, and entered one of the private meeting rooms together. Aaron sat at the table. Sergei laid paper and pen before him and stood hovering behind like a hungry buzzard studying a mouse. 'Let's get down to business,' he said drily.

Andy Sharples was counting money. It was his favourite thing to do and he liked to take his time doing it. Stacks of crumpled notes sat piled beside his little black notebook as he tapped away on a tablet, calculating sums and accessing accounts. The other caddies sat around him in a semicircle drinking bottles of beer, rolling dice, and discussing the golf round that day. A dark-skinned Spaniard named Salvatore was lazily tipping ash on the back of an Asian girl as she moved between him and Sean on all fours, ready for his turn to receive the soft attentions of her mouth. They'd 'borrowed' her from behind the counter of a Chinese takeaway in the town which hadn't been able to contribute adequately to their protection fund. It was in their own best interests. A kind of business protection insurance it had been explained. The group had found the 'payment in kind' on offer to be more than adequate. Sometimes it just worked out like that.

'Great numbers, boys! We've earned our trip to The Pussy Palace this time I can tell you,' exclaimed Andy, cracking the knuckles of one hand inside the palm of the other.

'With the wire transfers from Macau and Gibraltar we're nudging two and a half million euros in takings this week.' Razor, who'd been holding a lighter flame to the charred bowl of a ceramic hashish pipe, spluttered out a lungful of silver smoke in response.

Sharples smirked in satisfaction. In one swift motion he used his foot to deftly flip the Asian girl from her crouched position to flat onto her back. Then he slowly poured the remainder of his beer bottle over her small pointed breasts, drawing howls of laughter and derision from the room. They had earned the celebration.

17

Daniel Ratchet bolted the chain across the hotel door before slumping onto the bed, head in hands. He was sweating hard, mind racing over and over with what he'd just witnessed. He took a Coke from the minibar, hoping to rapidly increase his blood sugar levels and help to regain some control. He reconsidered. Removed a miniature bottle of Jack Daniels from the door-rack of the fridge, emptying it into his glass in one motion. Took a deep swallow.

After a few minutes had passed, settling himself somewhat, Daniel reached for the room telephone. He punched in the international dialling code followed by the familiar digits of the family home number in England. He yearned for the reassuring voices of his parents, hoping for solace and comfort. Something to cling to, far from the storm of this escalating dangerous situation that he felt like he was inexorably gravitating towards.

'Seven two four double nine eight, Ratchet residence,' came his mother's shrill voice down the line.

He smiled, answering enthusiastically, 'Mum, it's Daniel.'

'Oh Danny, how are you, love? Are you well? Wait, hold on I must just get your father.' In the background frenetic squawking, 'Malcolm, Malcolm, it's your son on the telephone. Malcolm, come quick, it's our Danny.'

Daniel waited. Heavy, measured footsteps grew louder through the hallway.

'Hello, Daniel. We'd thought you'd forgotten us back in Sheffield. How are you, son? Are you enjoying the big swanky job? You are being careful, aren't you, Danny?'

'Yes, Dad. The job's great. Better than expected even,' he lied. 'How's Scruff? I hope that rascal pup is keeping out of mischief without me?' He was trying his best to sound cheery. And by the time his mother had joined them on the other line and they had discussed the rain, an unmarried neighbour from number sixty-three who was starting to show as pregnant, and his dad had warned him twice about rising foreign exchange rates, Daniel simply couldn't bring himself to ask for the help and advice he needed. He couldn't disappoint and worry his parents further by confirming their worst fears about the job. He played out the call with a raft of insipid promises to call more often and hung up.

A renewed sense of purpose surged through him. Yes, Danny Ratchet was ready to understand things better for himself and take some firm decisions for himself now. He flicked on the tablet. He searched through his old university files, finally settling on a localised version of a unique statistical analysis programme that he'd created with three of his fellow students for their dissertation. It uncovered patterns in data flows. They'd hoped it would become an acceptable application for the medical industry, spotting patterns in drug trials. Now Daniel wondered if it would make some sense of the mass of information which accompanied the performance of every player currently participating on the European Tour, both before and after Rublex's involvement. He set out the parameters of his analysis, cross-referencing the ranking of top performers in separate elements of the game: driving distance and accuracy, greens in regulation, sand saves, putting, lowest rounds in sequence, scoring patterns, missed cuts. Next, he matched these statistics against the players who won out at the end of the events.

The findings were astonishing. Final round scores increased significantly for a specific set of otherwise high performing players going against the run of form from their preceding three rounds in any given event. It seemed to show that these particular players, with a track record of shooting very low scores and a history of winning multiple tournaments, would always do worse than would have been expected of them going into the final crucial round of key events; albeit never at the same time. It might have been barely perceptible to the galleries and Tour officials, but when charted out using a timeline of in-depth performance data, the trends were clear. There was no doubt that this was the tournament fixing that Bob Wallace's intuition had known was happening. A sickness at the heart of the game.

Next Daniel carefully reread Aaron's sponsorship proposal from Rublex. The Russian conglomerate was paying a premium for the best up-and-coming international stars of the game yet were incentivising them, it seemed, to underperform. The question was why?

Message alerts for new emails flashed up on the corner of the screen. Daniel dragged a new window open and watched four new messages drop into his inbox in orderly fashion. A Tour memo advising of travel arrangements for the tournament the following week, an update on the Order of Merit standings now that last week's Money List had been updated, an email from a very earnest sounding African lawyer bequeathing him the lost fortune of one of his newly deceased clients if only Daniel would part with his bank account details – how the hell his new work email had already fallen into the hands of the internet scamerati he had no idea. And, lastly, an email from Sergei Krostanov with a copy of the contract as an attachment, enquiring if Daniel had managed to progress the matter with Aaron yet and that with keen interest from other managers and their players on the table, he sincerely hoped he could expect a signature very soon. Daniel got up and paced around the room, exhaling hard. This was all getting a bit heavy. He didn't know how he'd been drawn into all this so fast and he couldn't yet fathom the implications. But it did now all appear to be unequivocal. You might get some anomalies through the beautiful quirks of sport, the psychology of pressure, luck, or through human error; but time after time for the top players to throw away events on the final day against the run of form was untenable. They were taking it in turns and over a long timeframe to hide the true extent of the malaise. It may have been buried deep, but once unravelled the data painted a clear picture. And it didn't lie. Given that he'd already experienced and witnessed how the caddies rolled out here with their gambling, drinking, petty crime, extortion and intimidation, this actual tournament fixing didn't seem so far out of the question. There had to be a connection with the gambling ring he'd stumbled upon. He hadn't warmed to Andy from the beginning, with his little book of numbers, the dominant display of aggression shown towards Razor on the night out, and for mocking him the next day for being late out onto the course when he clearly had something to do with getting him into that mess. Now with the pieces appearing to fit into place, the implications were unnerving.

With the SIM card of the company mobile still missing, obviously taken by the same bastards who had his grandfather's watch, Daniel grabbed the room phone again and dialled the mobile number that Matilda had scrawled upon the back of a napkin at their romantic dinner. It bounced straight to voicemail and Daniel left a long rambling message, which he started to regret even as he was garbling his way through it. He hoped it didn't come across as if he was blowing her off. He vaguely drawled on about wanting to meet up but needing to do further research on some data tonight. Now was not the moment to expose his insecurity and paranoia to this sexy new woman that he was really starting to like. It would probably make her run a mile. Besides, he'd share everything with her later once things were somewhat clearer. And when he'd worked out what the hell he was going to do next.

Outside the window, a thick black storm cloud emanated across the darkening sky. Daniel picked at the scratches that were starting to scab across his chest, his brow furrowed in deep thought. Having been steered by the old Scottish golf coach to make connections between the key protagonists in this sordid tableau, there were some hard choices to be made. Aaron was in contention to win the event at tomorrow's final round. Was his caddy, Andy Sharples, a threat to possible victory given the new information? He might influence the outcome of the tournament. It was impossible to know whether presenting the massive Rublex contract to Aaron was the right thing to do now, given that he better understood the implications. He had a duty of care to the player, both in looking after his commercial interests and in protecting his career. He also had a duty to Crown Sports who were expecting him to drive sponsorship value for his stable and yield some juicy commissions. Either way he felt uneasy about being pressured into getting the agreement signed. Perhaps this was just the way that business got done around here, he wondered, before taking a deep breath and punching in the digits to Silvio's mobile back in England.

'This is Silvio,' the silky voice purred down the line.

'Hello, Silvio, it's Daniel out in Spain.'

'How's the big time my friend? Have you settled into the life of a high-flying sports agent yet with all its, how shall we say, attractive benefits?' An earthy chuckle followed before Daniel had the chance to speak.

'It's good thanks, Silvio. But to be honest I'm not too sure what's really going on out here. I'm a bit confused on a few things really and wanted some advice. Have you heard of the Rublex Corporation?'

'Rublex? Don't be silly. Obviously, Rublex are one of the biggest sponsors in golf. They headline the Order of Merit. That's the equivalent of asking me if I've heard of an equipment manufacturer like say a Callaway, Nike or a TaylorMade, isn't it, Daniel? They're huge in golf. Please. What's the point of all this?'

'I wanted your opinion really. I've found some information which seems to show that players out here are cheating on the Tour. Sergei Krostanov, the Rublex Director of Golf, has offered a sixteen-million-dollar sponsorship contract for Aaron. Which is great but it's drafted like they would prefer him not to win all the time. Why would they sponsor someone and incentivise them to underperform? He's really pushing me to get Aaron to sign it quickly. And to cap it all off I'm feeling pretty uneasy about the fact he gave me a Rolex to keep as well. It feels very strange.'

'That's a great deal, Daniel. Fantastico! Well done. Don't concern yourself with these trivial details. It's just the way the Russians do business, you understand. Are you in possession of the paperwork?'

'Er, yeah. I've got a contract. But it doesn't make any sense?'

'What the hell are you talking about, boy? We've just made twenty per cent on sixteen American large. Has Aaron seen the contract yet?'

'Um, no. Not yet. Have you heard of Bob Wallace? He's a coach out here for some of the players, seems to have been around for years?'

'Sure, I know of the man. Wallace is a troublemaker, a firebrand, he got drunk at the PGA dinner last year and made a big scene. He publicly accused the Tour of being in conspiracy to bring down the game of golf from within. Such a ridiculous man. He spoilt a good dinner. Sergei was the most indignant. Bear in mind that this is the civilised world of golf, Daniel, not some dangerous shadowy cult from a Dan Brown novel.'

'Silvio, the data shows a group of top players getting into contention to win tournaments and then dropping away on the final day. They don't finish the way their statistics and tee-to-green form suggest they should. I think it's got something to do with gambling as well. A group of caddies out here seem to be running a book and shaking people down for money.'

Silvio raised his voice with unbridled, caustic anger. 'For Christ's sake, will you listen to yourself, Daniel? These things are none of your concern. You've been in this job for five minutes only. If Randy knew you were sitting on an agreement of this size he would skin your knackers, cut them off and feed them to you himself. Daniel, please, what's wrong with you? You disappoint me, boy. You were nothing when I scraped you off the floor at that dead-end job. Are you telling me that this is the way you repay me for setting you up in a new life? Your job is to do what you're told. Crown Sports have worked with Rublex for years. They helped broker the original deal with the European Tour in the first place. The way it works? You have to give them what they want. Keep your nose clean and don't call me back until you get that contract signed.' Without another word uttered, he cut the call.

Daniel cursed and cracked the back of the receiver against the bedside cabinet. His neck flushed red in uneven blotchy patches. He paced around the room for several minutes, throat dry and palms sweating. His head was swimming. He stepped onto the balcony, breathed slowly and cooled down. Relaxing a little, he allowed himself to be temporarily distracted by an energetic water-aerobics instructor leading a lacklustre gabble of flabby hotel guests splashing through their late afternoon activity.

Daniel was starting to get a sense of himself again. Here he was in a luxury foreign hotel, the like of which he'd never set foot in before, doing his dream job, dating a super-hot Swedish chick he'd just met, and holding in his hands a multi-million-dollar sponsorship agreement for one of the talented golfers he managed. And all in the first week. So, who cares what was happening out here on the Tour? Like Silvio had said, it was none of his concern. Besides, by all accounts, this Bob Wallace character was a bit of a nutter, and certainly an outcast from the close inner sanctum on Tour, which is where Daniel felt he needed to be if he wanted to make a real success out of this career.

With his dinner fixed for eight o'clock, he took his tablet out onto the balcony to refresh himself with the finer details of the agreement. The sun melted away over the red mountains, dissolving through an unsettled sky. Daniel soon lost himself in the nuances of the contract, memorising terms and clauses so he could create an erudite impression and deliver the illusion of control to his young Australian client. It was important to reassure the rising star that his manager was on top of his game, a safe pair of hands to represent him in these complex commercial matters so that he could just continue to focus on delivering results on the course. It might just serve as the boost he needed to go on to win the tournament in the final round tomorrow.

Order somewhat restored, Daniel decided that he would head out for a stroll to clear his head, study the agreement terms further and build on this new sense of perspective. He would swing via reception where he'd leave a message for Aaron to meet him for dinner to discuss the contract before the final round in the morning. If Silvio wanted a contract, then Daniel would make sure he bloody delivered one and hang the consequences. It wasn't up to him if they wanted to cheat on this stupid Tour. He'd go along for the ride.

He followed the pathway away from the hotel. He studied the tablet screen as he ambled, reading and rereading the sponsorship clauses and terms, whispering some of the more complex ones aloud to himself, as if studying for an exam. Daniel was determined to get this right after all of the early teething problems experienced in his new job. He wandered past the practice green, a number of players still grinding out their drills before tomorrow's final round. The neatly kept pathway led round to a cluster of Portakabins where equipment was stored, officials were briefed prior to the day's play and scores were collated and signed off following it. Daniel squatted on a set of cabin steps and scrolled through the document. He needed to appear confident in front of Aaron so the contract signing would go smoothly. Silvio was counting on him.

The sound of voices cut through the peace of the evening. Two men were walking together on the other side of the cabins, in animated discussion. They moved within earshot of Daniel, unaware that he was sitting only metres away out of view.

'Aaron hasn't signed the contract yet. He won't be on board before tomorrow's final round.'

'That useless new agent, Ratchet, hasn't delivered then? I tried playing nice. I don't know if the boy is simply stupid, doesn't understand how these things work or if he knows more than he lets on. He has after all been spending quite a lot of time with that agitator Bob Wallace.' The hairs rose on the back of Daniel's neck. He recognised the voices at once. Sergei Krostanov and Andy Sharples. And they were discussing him in very disparaging tones. He rose on impulse with the intention of interrupting them. He would bloody put them straight if they were going to be rude enough to talk about him behind his back. But he checked himself. Instead, Daniel avoided the confrontation and decided to let them talk. To hear what else they might say about him, what else they might reveal. He dropped to the ground. Crawled forward into the space under the raised cabin and edged across to the corner where the men were standing on the intersecting path. He manoeuvred himself a little way down and on instinct flicked the tablet onto video record mode. Angled the screen upward and without daring to so much as breathe he began to film the two men as they continued in their private discussion.

'This is a problem, Sergei. Aaron's looking strong. He's leading the event and I don't think there's anyone playing nearly as well in the field this week. There's a weight of money on him from Macau and this is one event we could do with having him throw to allow us to clean up.'

'I understand, Andy, but there's nothing I can do at this time. He hasn't signed the contract. He doesn't understand yet that the Rublex incentive scheme will be compensated to lose certain events on the final day rather than win them. We can't rig the book this time and take our high rolling sports betting clients to the cleaners. We'll have to find a way to make up the shortfall somehow. How have the local shakedowns gone?'

'Not the best in terms of producing cash, Sergei. But me and the boys secured ourselves a tasty little Chinese takeaway in part exchange though, if you catch my drift?'

'Not another girl, Andy.'

'This one is very compliant. There won't be any trouble like before.'

'I should hope not. Keep Billy Boy well away from her then.'

'You want a turn, Sergei?'

'No, Andy. Thank you. I have business to attend to.'

Daniel froze. Pulled the tablet back under the cabin unnoticed and watched as two sets of legs walked away from the cabins and where he was lying.

His breathing was still ragged by the time he returned to the room, shaken. Things were getting serious. There was clearly a conspiracy taking place right under the oblivious noses of the European Tour officials. Had he really overheard what he thought he had between Sergei and Andy just now? He might have been mistaken or taken it out of context and be jumping to a wild assumption. He double-checked the video recording saved on the tablet to be sure; to listen to it again.

The video clip ended for the second time. Daniel dropped his head into his hands. It was crystal clear. The angle had captured both Andy and Sergei's faces. There was no doubt about it. This was incriminating evidence. He swiped back onto the spreadsheets to re-examine them. There it was, as plain as day, a statistically provable positive correlation in the data that indicated cheating on a grand scale. Now backed up with a videoed admission of guilt straight from the Head of Sponsorship of Rublex Corporation, the Tour's title sponsor. Daniel swore under his breath.

A new email alert blinked onto the screen catching his eye. He opened it. Sent from physio-truck@europeantour.com. A single line read:

DANIEL, PLEASE BE VERY CAREFUL

Why would Matilda be emailing him this? Attached to the email was a scanned newspaper obituary of a veteran Russian investigative journalist. She had published a series of articles in the mid-nineteen nineties about a vast corporation named

Rublucon and its links to both serious organised crime and the upper reaches of the post-Soviet Russian government. The huge energy deals brokered had apparently provided a convenient cover and a conduit to launder money for the notoriously violent Russian crime families who had originated in the Gulags of the oppressive Stalin regime decades before. They'd been formed as a secret society living an alternative, strongly structured and codified way of life. Known as the Vory, they lived by a thieves' code, rejecting all work or acknowledgement of state and religion. They'd thrived over the years and, as capitalism had spread, many of the more charismatic leaders had seized considerable power and wealth. The journalist had dedicated her life and career to uncovering corruption and the obituary was posted defiantly on the front page of the newspaper she'd represented. She had apparently taken her own life, jumping from a bridge in St Petersburg. She had no record of depression and the authenticity of her suicide had been questioned with calls for an investigation into her death. No action had ever been taken.

Sweat dripped off his forehead, a droplet splashing onto the screen of his device. Daniel punched in a hurried text message to Matilda.

Thanks for the warning. Russians do seem dangerous! You have to see the video I just took of Sergei admitting cheating out here on Tour! It proves that Bob was right!! Let's meet up. XXX

His intense concentration was broken by the sound of a card clicking in the door. The maid had been in hours before. He swivelled in the chair and peered through the glass door of the balcony to see two men step inside the room, throwing furtive glances around them He recognised Razor in an instant, flashing back to Sharples throwing 'the mongrel', as he'd called him, off his chair at the bar. He didn't recognise the other guy. But he was simply huge, probably standing around six foot five. Massive muscular thighs bulging through tight jeans, supported a towering frame. He sported a thick leather belt with a large metal buckle in the shape of a hissing cobra's head. Two evil looking fangs protruded with menace from the serpent's open mouth. Daniel's hand ran across the tender scratches on his torso. *Could that belt have caused the cuts on my chest?* The beast stooped to avoid the frame as he entered the door behind Razor, who by now was quickly tugging at drawers and opening cupboards to rifle through Daniel's bags and clothing.

Frozen where he sat outside on the balcony, his natural instinct would have been to challenge the men breaking into his room. Given the recent severe violence he'd witnessed, coupled with the menacing presence of this monobrowed giant accompanying Razor, Daniel held himself back. He edged to the side of the balcony further out of sight and peeked through a corner of the window back into the room. By now, Razor was in a frenzy, emptying Daniel's briefcase, strewing papers over the floor. He was hell-bent on finding something very specific, it seemed. The 'monobrow' twisted his neck to the side, cracking vertebrae with a sickening, audible crunch. He bent down to lift the bed with a single paw, peering underneath. They'd be coming out on the balcony soon, no doubt about it. Daniel was sweating again. He scurried back to the table and snatched up the tablet. Sticking it under his arm he looked around for a way of escape, knowing he'd never make it out through the room and past the uninvited guests. It was too far to jump onto the concrete below. Besides he seriously hated heights, with just the act of looking straight down over the railings making him reel back and his head spin. There was about a four-foot gap between his and the next balcony, which was deserted except for a pair of brightly coloured swimming shorts, frilly black bikini bottoms and an enormous beach towel drying over the back of the chairs. No time to waste. Steadying himself against the wall and hoisting his foot onto the balcony rail Daniel strained to pull himself up so that he was standing balanced on the top edge. Puffing out his cheeks, he bent his knees and sprang frog-like as far as he could towards the adjacent balcony just as the glass doors clicked and slid open behind him.

It was an impressive leap and Daniel cleared the metal railings of the adjacent balcony with inches to spare, landing on his toes in a squat. The force of the jump banged his knees upward into his chin. He grunted and his mouth filled with the bitter iron taste of blood, as teeth bit into tongue. The tablet remained tightly clenched into his chest.

'The computer's not here, is it, Razor?' came a deep Russian voice above him, words spat out like bullets from a machine gun. Staccato. Cold. Stone on stone.

Daniel held his breath and, twisting his neck uncomfortably for a better view, peered upwards through the crack in the railing. Razor stood on the balcony just a few feet away, wiping sweat from his forehead in the heat. On his wrist glistened a slim gold watch with a cracked old black leather strap. Daniel swallowed hard. His granddad's watch. No doubt about it. The bastard must have stolen it on the night out at the Irish bar. The night when he'd passed out. Had he been drugged? He'd certainly been robbed. And sliced up, he now presumed, with the snake's teeth on that monster's belt buckle as he was probably dragged back and dumped in his room. He wanted to scream, to fight, to exact some form of retribution. But it wasn't going to happen. Closing his eyes tightly instead, Daniel waited. Frozen still with fear, sweat dripping off his nose and onto his shirt, desperately trying not to breathe. To make no sound whatsoever.

The door slid closed and after another few minutes had passed with no sounds or movements Daniel figured he could finally dare to move. Crawling across the concrete floor of his neighbour's balcony he tugged on the door handle. His only chance of escape. The handle crunched with the downward pressure, the heavy door opening first time into a smooth glide across its well-oiled mechanism. Stolen glances inside the room revealed it to be empty and Daniel slithered inside. Steam swirled, billowing around the floor. The sound of the shower and a woman humming a lazy, sweet melodic tune emanated from the bathroom. Without waiting to be announced Daniel covered the floor of the bedroom in just a few short strides. He exited out into the hotel corridor, heart pulsing urgently inside his chest.

He had no idea where the room invaders had gone but he knew he needed to get out of the corridor. Fast. Rather than take the elevator down into the main lobby Daniel took a strategic decision to bolt in the opposite direction. He darted down a maze of eery deserted corridors, past endless rows of identical rooms until a heavy door marked with the green sign for an emergency exit came into view. He ripped it open, lunging into the back stairway panting hard. In stark contrast to the opulence of the hotel rooms and elegant wallpapered corridors, the stairs had been left cold and bare; an unloved functional afterthought. But they were empty and Daniel needed to escape the hotel without being seen. His footsteps clattered a noisy echo, reverberating around the concrete stairwell. Each step filling him with fear, unable to separate his own noise from the sound of pursuers. He knew now he was embroiled in something dangerous and no matter what Silvio had ordered him to do, this was now about survival. Daniel had to look after himself.

He cleared the stairs in just over two minutes, keeping a consistent rhythm as he galloped down through the floors, twisting and turning down towards the ground. On arriving at the ground floor Daniel dropped his shoulder and slammed into the metal bar of the fire escape at the end of the stairwell, not caring if it triggered an alarm. He burst out into the peaceful evening dusk. Night was closing in.

He scoured the immediate surroundings for Razor and the monobrowed giant. Nothing. Gripping the tablet tight in his hand he adopted a natural brisk walk away from the hotel in the direction of the only person he felt he could trust out here. Matilda. A pair of well-nourished middle-aged women in pastel-coloured tailored shorts chatted together as he passed by keeping his head down. An assiduous avoidance of any eye contact as he scurried along the winding cobbled path towards the service truck park.

Daniel rapped his knuckles on the door of the physio truck. The door was unlocked but no one was inside. He tested the locker with Matilda's name stencilled on it. It was locked shut. Considering the empty space, he wondered what the best course of action might be. It was clear that he needed to find a safe, discreet place to hide the tablet which was the focus of so much apparent unwanted attention. At least until this was all sorted out. Remembering how he'd watched Michael store some equipment in the space beneath the bench seats at the side of the truck, Daniel flipped the cushions up and placed it in the cavity inside, covering it with some discarded towels. He'd let Matilda know later.

Now it was urgent that he speak with Bob Wallace. He found the gnarly old coach at the practice green, sitting crumpled over on an upturned bucket of balls. He was cleaning a sand wedge with a damp rag, chain-smoking a yellow-stained, hand-rolled cigarette. Daniel cleared his throat to announce his arrival and the old man met his eyes and nodded. It all poured out after that. In a single continuous stream of consciousness Daniel recounted the nefarious happenings of that afternoon. The break-in. His granddad's stolen watch on Razor's wrist. The data verifying Bob's tournament fixing theory. Underpinning it all was the video that Daniel had recorded on his tablet of Sergei and Andy discussing their illegal gambling ring and method of fixing tournament results by paying off and influencing players to drop shots. It was a cathartic experience and, by the time he'd finished, Daniel felt emotionally drained. He waited, expecting a profound response. Instead, Wallace coughed up a dose of mucous from the recesses of his beleaguered lungs and spat it quivering onto the grass at his feet. Finally, he spoke.

'I bloody knew it,' he snorted, taking a final drag of his dying tab before stubbing it out on the side of his golf shoe. 'I've got some thinking to do, son. If we're gonna get these guys out of the game for good, we've got to make sure we do it the right way. I've been laughed at and dismissed as a crazy old fool for bringing this to the PGA's attention before. I don't expect them to listen again after the fuss I've made. We need to take your proof and nail them once and for all. That's for damn sure. Meet me at Muldoon's in town at ten tonight, laddie, and we'll make a battle plan.'

Tired and aching as the adrenaline depleted from his bloodstream, Daniel trod a slow mooch back towards the hotel complex in the fading light. Dusk was falling and the fireflies danced together in chaotic spirals. As he passed the monolithic Tour equipment trucks, well-secured for the night, Daniel's eye was drawn to an attractive woman with bright red lipstick and heels, pink hot pants and a snugly filled white T-shirt. She stood alone in the shadows of the trucks fiddling with a large, wide-lens camera.

'Excuse me there,' she called to him as he passed by. 'Excuse me, sir, you don't by any chance know how to get this to work do you? My husband will be so cross.' She was smiling now and holding out the camera towards Daniel as he made to pass by, imploring him to take it with big, sad, heavily made-up eyes.

'Technology's not my thing, I'm afraid,' he lied, holding his hand aloft in apology as he continued on his way.

'Oh, please take a look, I'm sure you're much better at it than me,' she continued, batting those long eyelids and stepping towards him. Daniel paused and softened. Perhaps she'd just left the lens cap on. He took the camera from her, wondering what she was doing out here and where she was from. What was that undercurrent of an accent? European? Slavic? Surely not Russian.

Suddenly a sharp blow to the back of his head sent him sagging down onto his knees. A second clinical strike followed in succession. And Daniel Ratchet disintegrated into a sickening, velvety darkness. Floundering. Helpless. He was falling in slow motion. Towards a thick black silence. And then... nothing.

18

I'd bought fresh clothes and underwear on the way from the airport. Looking and feeling a lot less like an extra from a 'Die Hard' movie now and something closer to a semi-respectable member of society, I moved amongst the golf fans leaving the presentation ceremony. Avoiding eye contact, head down, studying my phone. People tend to remember a big man with a long nasty scar across his face staring at them. Besides, I was reading the updated intelligence that Ella had sent through to my device. Even serious messages and highly detailed encrypted data packets were signed off with kisses or some emoji or other depending on her mood. I found it plain kooky at first, but after a while it had begun to really tickle and I started to look out for them. It showed that someone cared. Here and now the intel was a steer from HQ noting a second interview with Bob Wallace taken over the phone. And a detail previously unavailable: he'd recalled that Daniel was upset regarding the behaviour of some of the golf caddies. His grandfather's watch had gone missing, presumed stolen by the same. It wasn't much to run with, but it was the start that I needed. Hunter was in the game.

I neared the 18th green and caught sight of a gangly Spanish teenager polishing the blades on a set of irons and setting them back into an empty golf bag. I sidled up to him and explained I was the brother of a caddy involved in the tournament and asked where they might be found after an event. Steered in the right direction, I soon reached a sprawling cluster of oversized trailers and trucks parked to the rear of the hotel, casting oblique shadows in the late afternoon sun. Voices rumbled from behind one of the trucks. I flipped onto my stomach and commando-crawled under the supports of the massive trailer. Manoeuvred to a vantage point where I had eyes on the scene playing out in front of me whilst remaining completely out of sight. A fat man in long blue shorts and white socks was sitting on a red plastic chair which looked as if it might collapse at any point under the strain. He was leafing through a ledger with freshly-licked fingers whilst a slighter man with a head of cropped ginger hair peered from behind like a parrot on a pirate's shoulder. A third man with olive skin and a thick glossy mane sat disinterested on an upturned crate. He smoked a cigarette.

'I see Michael paid up this week then?' the fat man chirped in an unexpectedly high-pitched Liverpudlian accent, an incongruous fit with the vast bulk of his body.

'Aye, paid up in full. The big German sausage won't make that mistake again in a hurry. Account closed, shall we say,' the ginger rat sniggered in a guttural Scottish patter.

'Good to see we're on track, Sean. Sharples will be pleased to see we've made up the lost ground from shakedowns in town this week too.'

'Aye. No bother at all big man,' came the casual response.

The two men left together. Their remaining companion finished his smoke before removing a handgun from a clip on his belt. He took his time stripping it down to its constituent parts on his lap and began the delicate business of oiling the mechanism with slick droplets from a miniature pipette. With the way the crate was positioned and how he whiled away his time I surmised that he was guarding the door to the truck behind him. It would be good to take a look inside and find out more about these 'shakedowns' that the caddies were making. It seemed that Daniel's instincts had been correct all along. Right now, I didn't have much time though. I needed to make contact with a number of key individuals on site who Ella had identified could be holding vital information on the background to the agent's disappearance. First and foremost, I needed to locate Matilda Axgren, Ratchet's girlfriend, and Bob Wallace himself, the coach who'd initially contacted The Hand of God about this escalating situation.

I wriggled back out of the hiding place and pushed myself up to my feet, wiping the palms of my hands across my trousers. As I turned to leave, I noticed two blonde women walking through the car park together, one older than the other. The first wore a tight ponytail scraped back to reveal a sour scowl on a face as brown and lined as dry cracked earth. Her taller companion glided alongside. Beautiful blue eyes were framed with long platinum blonde hair, falling in loose curls around her shoulders. I recognised her at once from the photograph downloaded from the research file. This was Matilda Axgren. And in real life she was some hot piece.

I let the women pass by a short way, following at a discreet distance. The older of the two turned and headed towards a green sign which pointed in the direction of the hotel spa complex. Matilda continued further into the car park, finally stopping to unlock the boot of a black Nissan Micra. As she fished for something inside, I approached. She spun round startled, incapable of disguising the cocktail of surprise and anger splashed across her face. 'Who are you? Get away from me,' she snapped, recoiling as I outstretched my hand to reassure her.

'Relax, Matilda, I'm a friend of Daniel Ratchet. I'm trying to find him.'

'Get away from me. Daniel's got nothing to do with me anymore. Leave me alone.'

'Please. I just need to ask you some questions, Matilda. I'm here to find Daniel.'

Matilda slid round the side of the car and fumbled with the keys in the lock. She was obviously not in a talkative mood. I followed round the vehicle, reaching her as she pulled open the car door and clambered inside. I forced my knee into the gap to prevent her from locking herself in and driving away. She slammed the door against my thigh with more than a degree of petulance. 'Hold still,' I ordered, one hand gripping the door frame, the other drawing my gun.

Matilda froze, her pale blue eyes widening as she looked up at me. She flicked her hair, jutting her chin forward in defiance. She composed herself, paused a thick five seconds and then spat back at me, 'What the hell d'you want? I suppose you're going to try and rape me now like a big tough man? Right here in the car park?'

The words hit me like a sucker punch to the gut. Bad thoughts. Too many haunting memories. The brutal weapon of war. I steadied myself against the car window, head reeling. *Maria... please... don't hurt her... it's me you want to punish...*

I breathed in hard. Exhaled.

'Calm down. That's not going to happen. Give me the keys. Put your seat belt on and the gun goes away. Now please. Just do it.' I struggled to bring control and measure to my voice. Matilda reluctantly buckled up. I put the gun away and walked around to the empty passenger seat, climbing into the car beside her.

Locked the car doors and looked at her in silence. She began to sob; whimpering, shaking.

'Matilda, listen to me. I'm not going to hurt you. I just need some information about Daniel Ratchet. We believe that he's been kidnapped and I'm here to bring him back.'

She looked through me with haunting tear-stained eyes.

'Who's taken him, Matilda, and where? Do you know? If you know you must tell me and now. We haven't much time.'

'I don't know much about it. He left me a voicemail saying there was a problem with a contract. He was studying some strange data patterns or something. I think his room in the hotel had been burgled. He needed my help and now he's gone. Hasn't been in contact since. They're saying things didn't work out for him on Tour and he went home. I thought we had something special.'

'Okay. Do you have any idea where he's gone or why? I need to get the facts here, and fast.'

'Try asking one of the coaches called Bob Wallace. He's been peddling some theory about how the winners on Tour are all fixed. It seems totally far-fetched. Everyone knows Bob has an axe to grind but Daniel was the new boy out here. Bob got him sucked into these crazy ideas and now he's gone. Perhaps he got disillusioned with it all. Couldn't hack it. I know that feeling too sometimes.' She looked so sad.

'Do you know any more about this tournament fixing theory? If it's for real and Daniel was poking about where his nose didn't belong, it could be a reason for someone to want him out of the picture, don't you think?'

Matilda turned and held my eye, a coolness revealing itself behind those watery blue eyes, somehow cutting her off from the pain. 'I already told you I don't know anything about it. We all have to survive and make our living out here. Now just leave me the hell alone, will you?'

It wasn't going the way I had hoped.

'Thank you,' I replied with as much sincerity as I could muster. 'You've been helpful. I know it's difficult. I only want to bring Daniel back to you and his family.'

I left Matilda sitting in the car, defiant. People react in a variety of ways following the disappearance of a loved one and being defensive was a common characteristic. She was hurting right now but something told me that she'd pull through. I figured that she was tougher than her looks suggested. I'd learn more from Bob Wallace, when I located him. Perhaps he'd know more about the complex relationship between Daniel Ratchet and the group of caddies that I'd overheard before. One thing was for sure, I needed to get on the Target's trail fast or when we did find him there might be nothing more than a cold stiff corpse waiting.

19

Throbbing. A dull, deafening pulse. A relentless beat drumming inside his brain. He opened his eyes to darkness and struggled onto his side. Hands and feet tightly bound. A coarse, thick prickly rope bit into his skin. He groaned against the rancid gag, mouth full of the taste of stale blood. Ribs felt like they had been smashed in on his left side. As the ear drum shattering sound continued unabated. He worked hard to get a better sense of his surroundings. A vast, cavernous, pitch-black space. The room felt empty. Cold. His thoughts were stifled by the imposing clatter of clunky old machinery. He wondered if he was in some sort of malevolent factory. He wondered what the hell had happened. The very last thing Daniel could recall was talking to an attractive woman outside the hotel. Something about a camera? A stabbing jolt jarred through his back as he was bumped up into the air like a rag doll and smashed back down hard onto his throbbing ribs. He emitted a pitiful groan. This was no old-fashioned factory. He was inside a moving vehicle.

The articulated lorry junketed, bumped and swerved wildly across the white lines of the road on two side wheels. Tyres screeched and smoked as they skidded to avoid a collision with a white Range Rover travelling fast in the opposite direction. Up front in the hot cramped cab, the agitated driver grappled with the wheel and then slapped his face hard to clear his head from its dreamlike trance. He'd driven all night, barely passing another vehicle, lost within the seductive trails of his own wandering thoughts as the mesmeric sound of turning wheels and empty tarmac stretched endlessly ahead. He'd woken from his daze to find his lorry driving on the wrong side of the road. It had been everything he could do to prevent a head on collision with the other vehicle. Too close. He shook his head in disbelief. His shirt drenched with cold sweat.

And after what seemed like endless hours of blackened hell to Daniel's aching limbs and battered ribs, feeling each imperfection in the road surface beneath as his helpless carcass banged and buffeted against the unforgiving wooden trailer bed, the sun began to rise. Shards of fractured sunbeams prised themselves into the lorry through the cracks and chinks in the side panelling. The temperature of the morning rose steadily with the sun, as did the unmistakable stench of rotting meat, ascending to an unbearable peak. Daniel retched as his body reacted. The sunlight stung his eyes. He couldn't remember when he'd last had anything to drink. Mouth and throat were so dry that it hurt to swallow.

Huge sharp metal hooks, like menacing inverted question marks, creaked in the gloom above. Some of the hooks held the enormous carcasses of skinned, untreated pigs fixed upon them, presumably unfit for refrigeration or human consumption. The stench of death, of flesh and smoke, was everywhere. Daniel Ratchet was imprisoned in some kind of moving abattoir.

'I'm telling ya, he was supposed to meet me at the Irish bar, lassie. Daniel had figured it all out. He'd made connections in the stats showing the inexplicable decline in certain players' form at specific times in events. He was onto those miserable cheating bastards and I think they knew. We were going to draw up the battle plan on how to get the Tour cleaned up and rid of this scourge of corruption.' They were sitting closely together in the busy, brightly lit hotel atrium. Safe. Drawing comfort from each other.

'I can't understand it. He wouldn't just up and leave the Tour. Not without saying goodbye. This was his dream job. And we'd only just met, Bob. He told me he loved me. I know it sounds strange but until I met Daniel I've always felt so alone out here. He was the only one to ever really understand me. Not just wanting to get me into bed. He really wanted to get to know the real me.' She pulled earnestly on the old man's shirtsleeve as if to emphasise the point.

'I figured he was sweet on you, princess. Suppose there's not a man out here that ain't. I wasn't buying that little ring you wear. It never kept Krostanov away from you either, what with all those fancy dinners and the like.' Bob always played a straight bat, whatever the wicket.

'That was business, Bob. I didn't have a choice. And I never said I was with Michael or anyone else, I let people make their own assumptions. They can think what they want. I just want the creeps to stay away. I was so happy I'd found Daniel.' She twisted the lace of the tablecloth between tense fingers.

'And I'm telling you, sweetheart,' Bob reiterated grimly, 'he never left. He didn't bottle it. Danny wasn't like that. That's just some official nonsense that the public relations people have put out so that no one will make a fuss, so he wouldn't be missed. Nobody will care one jot out here if some upstart agent decides he can't hack the pace and ups and leaves the Tour to head home, tail between his legs. People are always coming and going. And as you well know there are always plenty of young bucks ready to grab their chance with both hands when they get it. He'll be replaced without missing a beat.' He banged his fist on the tabletop as he spoke the word. 'What those bastards couldn't sanction would be some salacious crime or story about missing a person. Oh no, that would be picked up by the media and besmirch the precious name of the Tour. Reflect directly on their golden goose sponsors and the like. This is a fix up, Matilda.' They leant together, faces only a few inches from one another. He spoke in a low voice, cracking with emotion. 'They've taken Danny because he knew something about the dark forces at work out here and he told me he finally had the proof to make it stick.'

'What's going to happen? Who do you think is responsible, Bob? Do you have any real evidence that you can take to the police?'

'I've long held the belief that a certain criminal element amongst the caddies out here run a black-market gambling ring. I know they've bullied certain players to miss putts during rounds and manipulate the scoring to meet their own ends.' Bob scoured the hotel, as if he was expecting to be overheard. 'They even go so far as to get some of the coaches and managers in on the act when it serves them to score a big payday. I don't know how high up this goes but I wouldn't be surprised if the bloody sponsors were in on it too, for all I know.'

'But you don't have any proof of this?'

'Danny was going to show me the stats he'd uncovered showing the best players throwing tournaments away at the last minute against the run of form. Very convenient for a bookie if you have a lot of money piled on the favourite I'd say. I was going to ask him to use his position dealing with sponsors to see how they felt about it.'

'The sponsors?'

'I know you have to work with Krostanov, sweetheart, seeing as the company he works for sponsors the physio truck along with everything else around here. Lord knows I've seen him sniffing around you like a dog on heat, but I've a bad feeling about that mob from Rublex too. Why would a man of his position spend so much time with those lowly bag men? Especially cretins like Razor and Sean? My guess is that they are up to their necks in this too somehow.' Bob's face stony and resolute met the girl's eyes.

'Bob, that's crazy! Sergei talks to the caddies because Rublex sponsor the players they work with. And they would only want their players to do the very best when they play. That's surely the whole point of sponsorship after all? You've no evidence of any impropriety whatsoever, Bob.' Matilda shifted a little distance between them. Bob's conspiracy theories had been known to become contagious over the years.

'Listen, I've called in a favour,' the old coach growled in his gravelly Scottish drawl, eyes narrowing to hardened slits. 'I've brought in some help from the best I know, from my time back in the Services. They'll get the evidence if it's there. We're going to have to fight to get Danny back and figure out this mess. These are the fellas you want on your side and no mistake.' He looked down at the floor and spoke in a softer voice, the passion drained. 'Matilda, it's my fault the wee lad got dragged into this. I'm so sorry for that. I need to make it right.'

The old man sat back in his seat, a single tear snaking its way down his wrinkled cheek. He buried his head in his hands. Matilda gazed back at him, numb, again lost to a familiar world of hurt. After a prolonged moment she regained her composure, straightened up and without another word she walked away.

20

SPAIN. EUROPEAN TOUR. DAY FIVE. 1445 HRS.

The meat truck pulled up to the side of the road and finally came to a slow grinding stop. Daniel waited. Held his breath, listening for the faintest sound, anything to provide a clue as to what was happening. Everything was still now, even the creaking of the metal hooks straining under the weight of the heavy carcasses had stopped. He pulled against the ropes, burning his wrists as he twisted and writhed. Struggling was hopeless. He was tightly gagged and expertly hog-tied in the foetal position making movement barely possible. The idea taunted him that he was no better off than one of the stinking slabs of meat hanging above. The cab door slammed shut and Daniel could hear the sound of a man's heavy footsteps rounding the side of the lorry, moving away from the occasional traffic on the road. Whomever they belonged to, they must have been standing not more than a couple of yards away from him now, as he lay helpless inside the lorry. The driver cleared his throat and spat on the ground before repeatedly scratching at a lighter flint. The waft of bitter cigarette smoke, rich with tar, pronounced reward for his industry. Daniel could make out the faint sound of birdsong. *Where the hell am I and why is this happening to me?*

And then the crunch of gravel told of a car pulling to a stop. The double clunk of its slamming doors indicated to Daniel that his driver had now been joined by two new people. He heard footsteps walking away from the lorry and then gruff voices conversing at a short distance. *Boy, my head hurts. Can't think. This is it. I'm going to die. I'm going to die. God help me. Please. Please.*

The men were arguing. Voices raised and angry. Daniel couldn't make out any specific words nor even the gist of what was being said, but one thing was for sure, they were not happy people. Brisk footsteps moving towards the lorry now. Daniel shut his eyes tight and prayed. A button was pressed and Daniel could hear the incessant high-pitched whirring of electric gearing being worked at the rear of the vehicle. He could hear the grating of metal steps being set into place. Suddenly he felt super alert. Bristling with fear, nerves on edge. The door was flung open and blistering sunlight flooded the inside. Daniel winced, peering through sore eyelids towards the end of the tunnel of light making out the black silhouetted outlines of two bulky men framed at the entrance to the lorry. *They're going to kill me. They're going to kill me. They're going to kill me.*

One of the men clambered up into the back of the truck. He coughed and cursed under his breath as the stench hit him. Daniel gagged again as the man peeled his way through the hanging carcasses which wreaked a putrid stench in the heat. He paused, slamming his heavy fist against one of the dead pigs in his way forcing it to lash wildly from side to side and the metal hook to creak. Punishing the carcass for the unpleasant odour. Daniel heard chuckling. The shadow stepped closer, hunkering down onto its haunches to assess its bound captive. Suddenly Daniel's head was jerked upward by a fistful of his hair. The man stared directly into his victim's fearful bloodshot eyes and returned no hint of human compassion. So close that his warm moist odious breath bathed Daniel's face.

And then, upon satisfying himself with the sorry looking mess within his grip, he issued a cold smirk, then spat directly into Daniel's swollen eye. The grip on his hair was suddenly released, the body discarded like an unloved child's toy clattering to the floor. The shadow turned, weaved back through the lorry out of the heavy funk and into fresh air.

Daniel lay motionless, heart beating out of his chest. He could feel the gradual slither of the thick globule of saliva making its way down his cheek and onto his cracked bloodied lips. He was grateful of the moisture. It was pitiful. He breathed deeply. The paralysing fear which had overcome him was beginning to pass.

If they wanted to kill me then I'd already be dead. Somehow that bastard had seemed pleased to see me. They must need me alive.

21

A rusted tugboat blasted its horn in pugnacious warning at nearby vessels as it jostled for position on the river approaching Westminster Bridge. The sound caused Derek Hemmings to look up from his newspaper and check along the towpath for the twelfth time that morning. He relished crisp, bright, spring mornings such as these and invariably looked forward to his regular walk to work alongside the shimmering River Thames. Observing the bustle of the boats; marvelling at the industry of a city at work. But today was different. Derek was ill at ease and agitated. He was waiting for a clandestine appointment at the secluded riverside bench which he occupied. And his counterpart was late. Another furtive glance at his watch left him tutting to himself and shaking his head.

'Still impatient I see, Derek,' admonished the velvety smooth voice of Simon Prentice from behind him.

'Ah. I'm so glad you made it, Simon. I'm afraid I don't know who else to turn to, who could possibly be able to assist.'

'It must be serious, old boy. It's been forty odd years since you turned your back on us spooks in MI6. Defected to the

Foreign Office. Embraced the Dark Side.' He smiled the same slow calculated smile which had hung long in the memory.

'Come now. It was never like that Simon and you know it. I loved the job, truly. But when Robin came along so unexpectedly, well, there was just no choice. Alice needed me at home. She insisted that I had to put family first, and rightly so I suppose.' Derek stood, somewhat animated.

'We always understood that you were a good egg, Hemmings. And it's formally acknowledged and appreciated that you've kept our chaps informed on what's really going on from inside "the bubble" over the years. Insight into the Foreign Office's real agenda has certainly been useful, particularly given some of the peculiar sensitivities of interdepartmental rivalry. In many ways, you've really been spying for us internally to help the machine work better. I suppose one might say, Hemmings, that you've become the spy you never were.' Chortling to himself, he continued, 'Good title for a Bond film that, don't you say?'

'Oh, very droll, Simon. Very droll,' fired back, acerbic, laced with heavy sarcasm. 'Well now it's me that needs you. And I don't just mean a good lunch and a clandestine tour of the field armoury. I'm a desperate man.'

'Go ahead, old boy. I'm all ears.' Prentice raised his eyebrows quizzically.

'Ever come across a Russian businessman and erstwhile gangster named Boris Golich?' It was a rhetorical question. 'Well, I need to find out everything I can about him, his money and the dealings of his privately owned energy company, Rublex Corporation. I have two days to ratify a massive commercial deal for the government to the tune of a seven-billion-pound investment in the Falkland Islands with a purported hundred billion return and the creation of over seven thousand British jobs to support the exploration, extraction, and deployment of natural gas around the world.'

Simon whistled.

'Personally, I think the whole thing could be a ploy to launder vast sums of Mafia money and that Great Britain should stay well clear of it. But the bloody PM himself seems hell-bent on driving it through and has now got his pet Scottish pit bull, Andy Bartholomew, on my case; ensuring it all goes ahead for signature on time without any proper due diligence being conducted whatsoever. They're pushing for the positive headlines it will generate in the short term before the election and I'm afraid my conscience is taking a bloody battering.'

He cast his eyes to the sky. Paused for dramatic effect. 'Imagine the gross contamination of the UK's trade portfolio and our international relations if this deal is proved a sham and the selling of Golich's energy nothing but a front for organised crime. The deal goes live at the end of the week and I've looked into it as far as I can. Something is deeply wrong about this agreement. Every instinct and fibre of my very being is screaming out that we have to protect British interests. I have to do the right thing. Help me to do the right thing here, Simon.' Derek looked down and noticed for the first time that whilst he'd been talking he had been unpicking a thread from a button on his suit jacket, worrying it loose. Alice would certainly not be pleased at having to stitch it back on. He turned to face the river, shoulders drooped. 'We can't find anything substantial enough to halt this deal and I'm beginning to think that perhaps we never will.' His words hung in the air, desperation palpable, until his companion cut through the silence.

'All right, old boy. I can confirm that we do indeed know Golich. Have done since the little thug first popped up, illegally seizing oil wells in Uzbekistan with his own private army. Set about displacing ordinary folk from their homes to make way for infrastructure development. Corrupt politicians looking the other way in exchange for his hired muscle conjuring up the right number of votes in their local elections. Fast forward twenty-five years and he's still doing the same thing, only on a far grander global scale. He's a billionaire now who dines and plays golf with world leaders including, I may add, our very own PM. He entertains and influences the great and the good. Has even ploughed millions into the European Golf Tour in order to broaden his reach and legitimise his brand.'

'What else is he into other than oil and gas?'

'Our chaps on the ground in Moscow inform us that he has strong ties to the historic network of Russian Mafia gangs. We'll do some proper digging on his activities now he has become a person of significant interest. I tend to agree with you. This seems like a critical situation.'

'Thank you, Simon. I'm sure I don't need to tell you that this matter is under the strictest departmental security classification. Very few people know about it. The government wants to steal a march on the opposition and on our foreign rivals. We've apparently lifted this investment from the table of a state-run Chinese energy company and the PM is delighted with the coup. The good news announcement in Parliament will be the first sign that this government has cemented the progression into sustained positive fiscal growth with the shackles of the pandemic far behind us. And it couldn't come at a better time to influence the voters.'

'You have my word on behaving with the utmost of discretion, old boy. I'll be in touch.'

Derek blinked back the emotion. The two old stagers stood together in the quiet for a short while on the bank of the Thames, the morning sun resting on their time-worn faces.

They let the moment resonate. A final handshake. Turned and left in opposite directions, each in their own ways resolute to seize the day.

22

The breeze had dropped the temperature by five degrees at least. It sucked into the back of the open lorry, brushing Daniel's face, stirring him awake again as he oscillated in and out of consciousness. It also served to accentuate the sticky, pungent stench in which he lay baking. Daniel wretched as he came round. He worked his blistered lips over the tight gag and listened hard for sounds outside the truck. It felt like they had been stationary for hours but the truth was that all sense of time had become distorted.

A single voice spoke now. Talking in rapid bursts, punctuated by equal periods of silence. The urgent rising inflection at the end of his sentences indicated that he was asking a rapid series of questions. Then nothing; a period of protracted silence. A sudden scuffle. A muffled shout. And in quick succession the snap of a single gunshot shattering the air, the sound of a body crumpling to the ground. Daniel winced and held his eyes tight shut.

Moments later, two men in black leather jackets, one of them the vicious man with bad breath who'd spat into his face, sprang into the back of the lorry. They grabbed his feet without warning and dragged him fast and rough over the wooden truck floor, ripping his shirt and tearing the skin on his back over the jagged splinters. Above his head the bloodied pig carcasses twirled from the roof like a gruesome oversized infant mobile within some macabre nursery. Hoisted to the ground and slung over a broad shoulder, the limp hostage was now transferred to the open boot of a gleaming black Mercedes. Lying dumped helpless on his back. Still bound and sucking in what air he could, Daniel stared up at the colossal expanse of azure blue sky strewn with wispy strips of cotton-wool cloud suspended high above. The view was destroyed by the unceremonious dumping into the boot of a body directly on top of him. A splatter of blood wet his face, sharp particles of grit stung his eyes. The boot slammed shut descending them at once into pitch darkness. The cold forehead of the dead man nestled against Daniel's cheek causing him to twist furiously to free himself of its touch. His mind filled with a single thought. *This surely must be Hell itself.*

How long the car drove for or in which direction he had no idea. Daniel was utterly disorientated with no anchor to fix him in time nor space. He was pinned and squashed by the stout, heavy body on top of him. Running low on oxygen in the cramped boot of the car, intermittent dripping from the dead man's mouth was forming a syrupy pool of blood in the nape of his neck. By the time the Mercedes pulled to a final halt and its human cargo, both dead and barely alive, were unloaded, it was dark and cooler outside. Both bodies were dragged inside, up a set of broad tiled steps, on which the back of Daniel's head bounced in near-comedic rhythmic succession. They were laid out onto the stark marble floor of an opulent entrance hall. Only here were the two travelling companions separated from their haunting entwinement. A period during which Daniel had felt the slow tightening of the dead body on him to the point of rigid inflexibility.

~

A full bottle of cold water was poured over the hostage's head. He opened his eyes and realised the splendour of their surroundings. The palatial Hacienda-style entrance hall was encased entirely in white marble. Heavy gold-framed mirrors lined the walls and tall potted palm trees flanked a yawning white spiral staircase stretching up to the solid wooden minstrel gallery and beyond.

'You awake, lazy boy? Yes, lazy boy, you wake up now,' taunted one of the black-leather-jacket-men in heavily accented English. He issued a callous slap across his blood-smeared victim's face. Daniel was pulled upright, his feet and thighs at last freed from the bite of their tight bonds. As the blood flooded back into his legs he collapsed to the floor. A hand, now gripping his throat, pulled him to a standing position again. 'Get up, little bitch. You are a guest here with us now, Daniel.' And then he was shoved hard in the back from behind and Bad Breath Man dragged him away by the upper arm through a blurred series of doors and rooms and finally into a cold back passageway at the rear of the villa. A thick metal-studded door, a small bare windowless cell, paint peeling from the interior walls. The grind of a key turning inside a heavy lock.

23

I'd noted practice areas pocketed around the golf course like blots of ink split on paper: putting greens, chipping areas, practice bunkers, driving ranges. I headed on one now, following the basic logic that I'd likely find Bob Wallace, a swing coach, probably located in the areas where golf was taught. At the very least it would be a good place to start. I dialled into HQ as I moved and Ella picked up on the first ring. 'Hunter, how's it going? What's happening on the ground? Everything okay? You haven't had any more flashbacks, have you? I get so worried about that.' She didn't draw a breath.

'All good, Babydoll. You missing me then, are you? I think I promised you dinner back in London when we got through the last job. Sorry it had to be postponed. I'll try to make it up to you.'

'Dinner? Mmm. Okay. Sounds lovely. You do appreciate that I'm not some cheap date though, don't you, Hunter? It takes quite a lot to impress a girl like me.' It was a sassy reply. 'Anyway, what can I do you for, soldier?'

'Patch me through to Bob Wallace, can you? You guys have his mobile on record, right? I want to ask him a few questions about the Target and a few of the rats out here that I've already encountered. The pieces are starting to make some sense. I need to assess the level of threat before I squeeze some information out of a few people to help me figure out what's happened to Ratchet.'

'Patching through now, Hunter. Be careful, okay?'

The long international dial tone played out down the line. Although I was probably within less than a kilometre of Bob Wallace in person, the untraceable call was routed via our Unit's headquarters out of a little Victorian cottage in Barnes, South West London, England. Its size and quaint old-fashioned frontage, replete with little red bricks and creeping ivy façade, belied the high spec interior. Charles Hand had decked the base out with the very latest satellite equipment and military technology. To our knowledge they didn't even possess some of this kit at the Pentagon yet. There was little doubt that being able to access feeds from a massive range of multi-national and private enterprise global satellite communications enabled us to keep one step ahead, enhancing efficiency on the ground. Hand always maintained that it fuelled our ferocious success rate on jobs and was an investment worth making.

The call hitting Bob Wallace's British mobile phone was now being bounced across international exchanges and European time zones. The tone rang out and finally an answerphone message tripped into play. A gruff Scottish voice said, 'Leave your message for Bob after the tone. And remember: always keep your head dead still and eyes down after you strike a putt. If you haven't heard your ball drop in twenty minutes, then I'm afraid you've missed.' Beep.

I hung up. Leaving a message wasn't a good idea. Who's to say that Bob would want to speak to me right now anyway? And besides, if his phone fell into the wrong hands it would just alert them to my presence and compromise any advantage of surprise. I was contemplating my next move when a text message from Ella buzzed through:

Honour is what no man can give you and none can take away. Honour is a man's gift to himself. (Robert the Bruce)

I shrugged. *You can't argue with that, Ella.*

I needed to move fast, avoiding contact with other people as far as I could. An Indian guy in his mid-thirties was working on a series of drills on the practice green. He was wiggling his putter back and forth like a pendulum set between square shoulders. I approached from behind. 'Know where I can find Bob Wallace round here, mate?' I called across from outside the ropes.

'Yeah, I believe so. We finished our session together here not more than an hour ago. Mr Wallace can usually be found in the Halfway House hut off the ninth green about this time. He likes to be alone, save only for his whisky and his thoughts.'

'Much obliged, my friend,' I replied but by the time I'd finished thanking him, the head was bowed in fixed concentration again with golf balls firing off the blade in snappy order, sinking into a cup some six feet away. I continued my way down the paved pathway, following signs towards the ninth green.

The Halfway House was a smallish box of a hut fashioned from timber of the local cedar trees. It was staffed during the main part of the day by a team from the hotel, serving refreshments to golfers as they plotted their way around the course, offering welcome replenishment after their hours under the sun. Bob had presumably claimed it as his own when the golf course emptied. It was easy to see why a man who wanted to be alone with his thoughts would pick it as a hideaway. Out here in the middle of the deserted golf course, set back among a tangled cluster of gnarly olive trees, the hut sat squat in defiant isolation. The thick wooden door was ajar, but I rapped on it anyway out of courtesy. No response. I opened it with caution and stepped inside.

What I encountered hit me like a cross to the temple. I reeled from the savagery. In total juxtaposition to the tranquillity of its setting, a man, only partially recognisable as Bob Wallace from his mugshot in the briefing file, was slumped in the corner tied to a chair. His bloodied face had been smashed in entirely on one side revealing the hollow remains of cheek and jaw. Discarded on the floor next to him lay a pitching wedge, the blade stuck with shreds of flesh and splinters of bone. His throat had been cut. The clean gaping wound told of a swift single, well-practised motion. Wallace's head lolled to the side, exposing the inside of his neck from ear to ear. Flies hovered around the body, dizzy from their feast of sweet, sticky blood. I studied the room. A small square table, age-worn with the chips and scars of a purposeful existence, was set in front of the body littered with playing cards and an overflowing ashtray crammed with the scorched ends of extinguished blackened roll-ups. A half empty bottle of Johnnie Walker Black Label was accompanied by a single glass. Next to it lay a square of coarse sandpaper and a wet rag. I grimaced. Searched for the telltale patches of worn skin and exposed bone on the underside of elbows, knees, knuckles and fingertips and was bitterly rewarded. Whoever had done this knew what they were doing. Had taken their time to sand away the skin on particularly sensitive portions of the anatomy, using the alcohol to increase the suffering. I wondered at what stage of the ordeal they'd broken him. What the old soldier had finally told them. I hoped, for his sake, that he'd been able to retain his personal sense of honour and integrity before he gave them what they wanted. I'd never forget the haunted look of shame and realisation in the eyes of the men that I'd watched betray their friends.

I held the grubby glass aloft and swallowed the remaining inch of amber liquor. A risk of contaminating the crime scene perhaps, but the dead man, one of The Hand of God's fallen comrades, deserved a final toast. With the glass wiped free of my prints, I moved out of the hut. This was someone else's mess to clean up now and whoever was responsible might still be lingering and preparing an ambush. Plus, I figured that if anyone else happened upon the scene right now then a big, armed, uninvited trespasser chancing on a bloody murder might not be easy to explain.

I needed time to think. There was no further information available and the figure central to explaining Daniel Ratchet's disappearance was dead. The who and why usually didn't matter as much as the where in this job. Time is an inversely proportional factor in finding a Target still alive. The more time elapsed after they've been taken, the less likely we are to get them back safe. I urgently needed more context to the disappearance. From the moment that even the motivation to a kidnap is germinated the perpetrator starts leaving trails of evidence and information. Tiny packets of data will always exist that can be assessed and interpreted as clues to help unravel the details of their plan. The technology deployed back at HQ can tap into real-time transactions made with bank and credit cards, access vehicle GPS systems, toll booths and has even been known to lock onto IP addresses which can identify the whereabouts and data storage of computerised devices and smartphones when they connect online via public access wifi. We can start to understand a suspect and assess their movements to build up a profile.

That's for the gumshoes. The smart way to do it. And if you

have time on your side, of course. Boil it down and my job is to find the Target. Recapture them if they're still alive. Document the body if they're dead. We get paid either way for reaching the Target but there's a sweet financial incentive for getting them back still breathing. I don't ask questions about who they are or why they're in whatever predicament they're in. And I don't need to bother myself with the fallout. Not all of the victims we save could be considered innocent people either. Solving crimes is for cops and if there's collateral damage from my work, then so be it. The Unit operates off-radar and I take my orders straight from The Hand of God. Nothing else matters. The other method for getting the information you need when you need it most is a little gentle persuasion of the 'Tom Hunter School of Charm' variety. And of the two there's no doubt which I find more my speed.

Even so, experience has taught me a number of unsavoury lessons. The need to pause for a little strategic thought before a tear up is one of them. According to an evaluation report given by The Hand of God to army top brass: 'Hunter possesses a positive predilection for preproperation'. Whatever that actually meant. However, I do know that getting the right intelligence at the right moment is a finely balanced art. Extracting answers the hard way on the Target's whereabouts from the suspects on Ella's list of caddies like Razor, Sharples, Sean, or Billy Boy was simply no guarantee of reliability. Even if interrogation is conducted at gunpoint or through a waterboarding technique we've learnt that the perpetrators of a kidnapping rarely give it all up when confronted. The crime has too many psychological factors such as leverage and punishment of a victim at play for them to roll over. Interrogation can take hours, sometimes days. Besides, a caddy is also a recognised and respected role within the fabric of the European Golf Tour, which might serve as insulation against suggestions of impropriety. The resort security team would handle the fallout from any immediate disturbance and if the local police were on the payroll as suggested, they'd look the other way should matters escalate. If the authorities got involved, I was most likely to be the one who'd end up in the clink.

If a suspect deploys a strategy of misdirection to feed us false intel it can cost vital time. There's no doubt that if you put the squeeze hard enough on someone for information they'll eventually talk. I don't care how tough you are the world over, it's a rare man who won't sing given enough time and attention with the right toolkit. It's the veracity of the information provided that you need to be careful with. Right now, there were still some options to explore before I rolled the dice.

24

'Mr Flavini? It's Daniel Ratchet's father here.' The broad Sheffield accent, firm and true down the telephone.

'Yes, good morning, Mr Ratchet. And please do call me Silvio,' oozed the warm response given between sips of rich Italian coffee.

'Right-oh. Er, Silvio then. Yes well, sorry to telephone you at the office, we did promise that we wouldn't use the number except in emergencies, but I'm ringing because, well, to be frank, the boy's mother is agitating. She's concerned that we haven't heard from him for a few days and we were expecting to hear all about the tournament and the ceremony of last week. We read in the paper that the golfer that he's working with won that big tournament and with that being such a big deal to the lad and the like, it just seems rather odd that we can't reach him. The mobile number he gave us doesn't work and we called the hotel who say that he's up and checked out.' A pause for breath.

'Mr Ratchet, I'm sure that there's nothing to be concerned about. Daniel is working hard for us to put a contract in place and I expect that's what he's focusing on at the moment. I haven't heard from him myself but I'm sure it's all perfectly normal. We all know that mothers like to fuss, Mr Ratchet. And I can certainly testify to that, being a good Italian boy myself.'

'Yes, well, that's true enough. You'll let us know when you hear from him, won't you?'

'Of course, Mr Ratchet, of course,' came the silken platitude. 'Now, please, do try not to worry. Daniel's a big boy. Working on the road as we do, there are many days when we lose the communication. It's really no problem.' He replaced the receiver in its cradle and smoothed the soft silver hairs of his beard around the creases of his mouth as he considered matters. His next call was transatlantic, placed to the direct line of Randy Hughes, founder and autocratic owner of the Crown Sports Empire.

'Randy, we have a problem. Our new agent, Daniel Ratchet, has been missing for a few days now. There's the outstanding Aaron Crower agreement to be finalised with Rublex Corporation, part of the incentive programme. I think we may need to get someone else out there on the ground in Europe.'

'You screwed up, Silvio,' came the booming American baritone. 'You hired the wrong guy. A guy who couldn't get the job done and you didn't even have the balls to tell me that the agreement wasn't signed. What's wrong with you people? Can't you manage to do what you're told?'

'Randy, please. The boy had some concerns about the terms of the agreement and I put him straight. It was due to be signed imminently.'

'That's sixteen goddam million dollars, Silvio,' he shouted. 'Crown Sports doesn't tolerate playing fast and loose with that kind of green.'

'I know, Randy. I'm sorry, I truly am.'

'It's a good thing that one of us is on the ball, you greasy Italian waste of space. I've been speaking with Sergei and Rublex directly. I've been through the agreement and it's the usual format, same as all the others. I've authorised him to deal with Aaron and sign the paperwork in Spain. We can't afford to leave the door open for some other agent to present him with another offer and snatch him away from right under our beaks. Crower is hot property after that win and those sharks will be circling.'

'Okay, great news, Randy. Thank you. What about Daniel, what should we do? Have you heard any word on where he might be?'

'The hell do I care about that little limey bastard? He was sticking his nose in where it wasn't wanted, Silvio, and from what I hear he was starting to piss off our wealthy Ruski friends. I'm just pleased that he's out the way and not obstructing the course of good business being done no more.' The phone went dead. The conversation was very over.

Daniel lay on his side. He'd been staring for hours at a single patch of flaking paint on the cell wall. His body ached. The throbbing in his head had abated but it was still tender and sore to the touch. If he turned his neck suddenly, he was overcome by a sickening dizziness. The cell was empty except for a split and stained pink child's mattress partially spewing its yellow foam innards. A green cracked plastic bucket, presumably for use as a toilet, stood unloved in the corner.

Each day he'd been there so far, a small plastic bottle of lukewarm water for him to drink had been lobbed into the cell. Nothing to eat for the first two days. On the third day, with his strength all but faded, a squashed service station sandwich of warm limp lettuce, rancid tomato and processed cheese was thrown inside. Daniel gagged as he crammed the food gratefully into his mouth. The stench of the dark heavy urine to which he had grown accustomed was brought vividly alive to his senses again. The meagre sustenance he was attempting to swallow had a sudden vile impact on his olfactory system, reacting in a painful explosion of dormant taste buds awakened after the long period of neglect. He'd been left untied in the cell, presumably considered be no threat given he was so weak. The cell was thoroughly secured under lock and key.

Daniel had neither spoken to nor seen any of his captors since first arriving. Alone with nothing but his thoughts he was driving himself to the brink of despair. *What do they want with me? It must have something to do with what I'd discovered about the cheating on Tour. If they wanted to kill me, I'd already be dead like that truck driver. There has to be a reason that I'm still alive. For now. Why am I here?*

He was awoken from a fitful slumber by the crunch of a key rattling in the metal grate. Bad Breath Man stooped and entered the tiny room, watching Daniel as he sat up and rubbed his eyes. He loped to the corner and then, in a sudden and aggressive motion, scooped up the plastic bucket, hurling both it and its foul contents at Daniel's head. There was no time to roll to his side. The bucket caught him on the corner of the temple, cutting him above the eyebrow and covering him, the bed and the wall, with an ugly slop of rancid excrement. Daniel reeled back in shock as the assailant stepped forward and screamed into his face, 'Where is computer tablet? Where is tablet, you stupid boy?'

The door banged open on its hinges. A second man, whom Daniel also recognised from his capture, grabbed Bad Breath Man and forced him against the wall, jabbing a thick finger towards his face. 'No questions yet. Not until Avtorityet arrives.

These are his rules. Can't you understand. Are you stupid like pig?' He pointed towards the door and they filed out again, leaving Daniel sitting on the mattress in soiled disbelief, choking on a torrent of frightened tears. Sorrowful, bleeding and dripping in piss.

25

The two men spotted each other from afar and made a guarded approach towards the lock. It was a narrow and picturesque stretch of the River Thames. Today, choppy grey waters swirled against the sluice gates.

'Simon, it's been a very long time.'

'Good of you to come, dear boy.'

'I don't recall having much choice in the matter,' came the stiff reply.

'From what I remember of you, Charles, there was apparently always a choice.' The words were punctuated with a deliberate and humourless chuckle.

'Not a choice when the safety of my people is involved, Simon, or perhaps you've forgotten that?'

The two men held each other's eyes. Hand's glare unbreakable, unflinching. The aura still surrounded him. The man who'd transcended into army folklore. Some men didn't just deserve respect, it was a natural reaction commanded upon entering their orbit. Simon Prentice finally cast his eyes downward and scratched instead at a dull mark on the sleeve of his smart, navy overcoat.

'Please, there's no need to dredge up the past. No one will ever forget what happened, Charles. I was compelled to think of the greater good. There was more at stake than just the lives of three British soldiers left back in Pakistan.'

'My greater good was saving those boys. It was my command. I sent them into that village to reconnoitre. MI6 deliberately withheld vital information regarding insurgent activity in the vicinity.'

'Charles, you were operating under the radar. Officially deniable. We couldn't share intelligence with you or we'd have risked exposing the whole operation in a highly sensitive political climate. We were risking an all-out war if the Pakistani government had rumbled what we were up to.'

'The simple fact is that you cut a deal behind our backs, Simon. You left those boys there to die in exchange for the freedom of some low-level turncoat informant, bartering information on a non-existent weapons dump for his life.'

'We didn't know it was non-existent at the time, did we? How were we to know that the local intel had been inaccurate?'

Hand glowered, fists clenched by his side. 'When our team went in deep behind enemy lines to capture Mahood in his brother-in-law's village, you'd already bloody cut a deal and spirited him away. It was a deathtrap and you let us walk right into it.'

'We couldn't have known that they would lay such a heinous ambush. That they intended to trade those soldiers' lives for Islamic prisoners. It was a very difficult time for us all.'

'My boys nearly died. I lost my career, Simon.' Again came the stare.

'Hardly, old boy. An honourable discharge. A very healthy Army pension. More medals than you can shake a stick at. It was your time to go anyway. And regardless, my people tell me that you've created a highly lucrative enterprise freeing kidnap victims on the black market whilst leveraging a pretty powerful network to boot. Doing well for yourself it seems, Charles, and probably only thanks to the top brass sweeping the fact that you went rogue under the carpet. An MI6 recommendation, I may add.' Prentice looked pleased with himself.

'I did what needed to be done and I'd do the same again in a heartbeat.' Voice raised. Stark.

'Charles. You commandeered a bloody US Apache helicopter at gunpoint and flew it into a burning enemy village.'

'We all know the story.'

'Yes. The Hand of God. The type of story some men's reputations are built upon.'

With both men now simmering on the edge of fury, Hand continued unapologetic.

'I saved three lives which you had put at unnecessary risk. Three of our finest men.'

'The ends justifying the means? You were lucky things worked out, Hand, or the blowback from a buggered-up rescue mission on an operation that didn't exist would have been totally catastrophic.'

'You should have told us what you knew!'

'Do I need to remind you that we were at war? Tough decisions have to be taken, Charles.'

Hand took a breath, checked his watch, turned to go. 'What do you know about Boris Golich?' Simon called after him.

Charles stopped and turned around. The question hung between them for an age.

Finally, a measured reply, 'He's a very dangerous man. Is that what this is about?'

'Walk with me.'

The two men walked along Shepperton Lock in silence for half a mile or so. It was a picture-postcard piece of river flanked on one side by a number of elegant houses with large glass frontages designed so owners could derive optimum pleasure from expansive and scenic views. Across the narrow stretch of river lay Pharaoh's Island. An unusual free-standing island in the Thames, it was home to a cluster of glorious houses, often of unique architectural design, and accessible only by boat. Moored in front of these properties bobbed a succession of powerful looking motorboats and lavish floating 'gin palaces'. On their side of the river, the two men passed a number of gaily painted houseboats and barges. They walked in silence along the grass until they reached two barges conjoined to each other. The first, a working functional houseboat, charming in springtime but, Simon noted, not particularly practical for an unrepentant British winter. Or indeed for those in need of plenty of standing closet space to hang their best Savile Row suits. The boat tethered to the port side of the river was sheathed in a heavy white tarpaulin. The men paused to read a sign which had been erected on the riverbank. It read:

The little boats of Dunkirk project. This boat is being renovated to its former glory. It is estimated that this boat served on over 350 missions and during the Dunkirk rescues saved an estimated 165 lives. Please give generously to help with the cost of this privately funded renovation project so that future generations can enjoy the majesty of our brave and historic boats.

Hand stuffed a crisp twenty-pound note into the plastic envelope stapled to the sign.

Prentice chose his moment. 'There will always be wars, Charles. It's incumbent on us as servants of the nation to pick the right battles and win them.' And then ensuring he caught his eye, 'We're on the same side you know, old boy. Men like us need to work together for the common good. So, I suppose you'd better tell me, Charles, why are you looking into Boris Golich?'

Hand arched an eyebrow, feigning a practised bafflement.

'Come, don't deny. Don't do me that disservice. We know you still have contacts. You've been using an encrypted security clearance traced back to your old job to find out everything you can about Golich and his Rublex Corporation. Then there's a certain inquisitive young lady named Ella Philips, tied to your operation, who's been putting herself around to find out everything she can.'

A gravid pause. 'Where's all this going, Simon? Why should you care who we look into? We're a private business and this is a private matter.'

'I was rather hoping we may be able to help each other out. I've had a favour pulled from an old colleague in government who needs help fast. He's trying to shine a light on uncovering the shady money trails stemming from Rublex and this Golich character before he binds the British government to an embarrassing commitment which might damage relations with some of our overseas trading partners and stain our good name in the international money markets.'

'You're talking about Russian Mafia money. The Vory.'

'So, you do know about this then. I was rather hoping you'd be able to help. What have your people been able to find out, Charles? We know Golich has become "Pakhan" now within the Vory hierarchy, a mastermind who pulls the strings of organised crime and a man whose reach is so far inside the Kremlin he only needs to sneeze and the Russian president gets haemorrhoids. If we leverage the usual channels to follow the money and Moscow gets so much as a sniff of it, we risk closing down our whole operation. We practically operate over there under licence these days anyway. We can't bet the farm and risk upsetting years of careful contact grooming and intelligence gathering on this one, Hand.'

'And if we choose to assist your colleague, to furnish him with what we've found?'

'Then I shall ensure that Her Majesty's Secret Service "misplaces" certain evidence accrued against one Tom Hunter following the siege at the Nigerian Embassy last October. I believe the two of you are still professionally acquainted, are you not?'

Charles Hand gripped his fist tightly. Fingernails turning white as they dug into his palm. He was backed into a corner, outflanked. Practically invited it on himself. Hand stepped away and after a few moments of composed consideration he turned and spoke in a calm measured voice. 'We'll trade information. Set up the meet.'

26

I moved fast. Bob Wallace's body wouldn't lie undiscovered for long and I didn't need heat from the Guardia Civil who would soon be crawling all over, examining the scene of the crime. I decided to go cross country in the twilight through this tract of once undulating rural land which had been carved out to produce such a beautiful and testing course. I'd approach the truck park from behind, to avoid any unnecessary contact.

The few kilometres back to the truck park soon vanished under foot. In the Regiment we'd undergone relentless training. Despite incessant cuts from the Ministry of Defence, the British Army still retains some of the latest technologies and an impressive array of multi-purpose vehicles designed to transport soldiers across inhospitable war zone terrain. Sometimes, however, a soldier has no choice but to travel for miles on foot, often in adverse weather conditions and under the constant threat of ambush or engagement with a hostile enemy. It's always been the same across the ages and remains the case today even with the advances of robot soldiers and spy drones. Covering vast distances in double-quick time was known as a 'yomp'. My feet had developed a hard leathery skin on them which prevented blisters and blocked out the pain. Muscle memory returned as I tracked over the immaculate lush greenery of the course. Solid legs and a brisk rhythm propelling me forward at pace, eating up the ground beneath. Whoever we were up against had shown no compunction in the violent murder of Bob Wallace. The Target was still missing and it stood to reason that the longer it took to locate him, the less chance there was in bringing him back alive. Time was slipping forward and I couldn't afford to wait on ceremony.

Taking up an offensive position, shielded by the unwieldy branches of an aged olive tree, I checked over the Beretta, examining it in my hands. Screwed on the silencer that Mickey had so kindly furnished. The greaseball guard remained on his crate whittling a piece of wood with a curved blade, stripping away the bark. The rest of the man-made clearing between the trucks was empty. The hut beyond sat dark and lifeless. Ghosting from my vantage point, I was able to slip up behind the guard unnoticed. It was only when almost upon him that he glanced round from his handiwork with startled eyes bulging wide. He rose fast, thrusting with the blade. I shifted my feet and leading with the butt of the gun, smashed down into his nose, shattering cartilage against the bones of his face. He squealed like a stuck pig. Snorted in pain as blood spurted freely before crumpling to the ground, squirming in agony. A sharp well-placed kick, steel toecap against temple, rendered him unconscious. Seconds later, his hands were secured together behind his back; cable ties biting tightly into fleshy wrists. I rolled him under an adjacent truck and after checking around me with muzzle primed, I pushed forward into the hut. I'd been expecting a golf equipment store or some kind of caddy shack but inside resembled something of an operations centre.

A large central table, strewn with maps and papers filled the main part of the room. The walls were encased in large cork noticeboards, pinned with charts and lists. A long shelf ran along the back of the hut where a kettle and several chipped tea-stained mugs were kept. Beneath it stood a fridge. I leafed through the papers on the table trying to find anything that might point to Daniel's whereabouts. There was nothing obvious to hand, but it didn't usually work out that easy. The extensive documentation did highlight significant gambling and extortion activity listing punter names with betting and payment account activity detailed. This was coupled with neatly presented tables holding the names and addresses of local businesses and their 'taxes' payable week by week. The European Golf Tour travelled to a different country every seven days. This group increasingly looked like a network of sophisticated criminals shaking-down businesses at every stop of the merry-go-round, raking in hundreds of thousands of euros at each event.

But I wasn't a cop. I didn't care what these scumbags did to make their money. All I cared about right now was getting a lock on Daniel Ratchet and with luck, getting him back alive. Like I said, if the Target is still breathing when they're recaptured, it delivers a bonus payment on top of the standard engagement fee. And that meant more to me than saving a life or putting the world to rights.

I entered the smaller room. It was done out as a personal office with desk and chair, smart metallic filing cabinets lining the walls. A bone dry pot plant gamely struggled to add life to the sterile environment. I tugged on the top drawer of the nearest cabinet. It was locked shut. From my boot I fetched out the Bowie knife from inside the hidden sheath. The cabinet drawer was tough and clearly reinforced. The spring lock resisted the tension of my blade with the stubbornness of a bridesmaid's knicker elastic at a catholic wedding. I gripped the handle tighter, leant my weight down onto it and twisted my wrist to prise open a gap between the drawer and sturdy metal frame. Still no dice.

Footsteps drummed into the hut, breaking my concentration. I dropped into an instinctive crouched position behind the partition wall of the small office. Hunkering down onto my haunches, balanced on my toes, primed to spring upwards and lead with shoulder at first contact. Thinking fast: no windows in the hut and only one entrance meant there were no natural escape routes. I had company and unless I was going to pump a volley of holes into a wall and kick my way through, and in the process alerting the entire Guardia Civil to my movements, then the only option was to fight my way out.

I'd experienced enemy conflicts going in as many different ways as you could think of. But even with the element of surprise on my side this time, I could feel in the pit of my stomach that this wasn't going to go the good way. I watched as the massive hulking form of a lumbering monobrowed thug filled the main room of the hut. He was shadowed by a skulking grey-hued figure, redolent of a sickly hyena looking for an easy meal. I recognised him to be the caddy labelled as 'Razor' in the briefing notes that Ella had compiled.

Given the size of this place, I'd surely be discovered in seconds. I checked the ammo clip in my piece was full and exhaled to steady my heart rate. A massive thigh waded across the floor towards the office, floorboards creaking under heavy boots. With my back to the partition, crouched on my haunches, I angled the barrel of the Beretta round the crack in the open door and fired two soft thuds, piercing just above the knee of that meaty leg. It was enough to bring the huge man crashing down, bouncing chairs out of his path as he fell.

'What the hell?' shouted the hyena as his powerful sidekick collapsed clutching his leg in agony. I moved. Blazing a volley of shots to create some cover, I rolled out of the office and pushed into the main room of the hut. Better a moving target than a sitting duck. In the close quarters of the hut I was caught by a slug to my shoulder tearing through the flesh and knocking me into the wall. The wounded giant had pulled a Glock from his belt and, from his sprawled floor position, was letting a succession of rounds rip in my general direction. Razor was backed up flush against the wall of the hut, keeping away from the gunfire. Figuring he wasn't packing a shooter, or it would have already been firing in the tear up, I rolled hard to my right and threw myself forward at him. Dived face first over the large table in front of me, sliding, scattering papers like a speedboat's wake cutting through a still pond. The move bought me vital seconds. The monobrowed beast was unable to twist his injured body to meet my new position and get a line of fire on me with the Glock. I landed shoulder first on the other side of the table. Turned in a single motion and emptied my clip, riddling the giant's back and ribs with a scorching of hot lead. Razor fled from the hut in a blind panic.

I'd learned the hard way, through losing the closest of mates, that in the heat of theatre you should never leave a threat alive which might serve to compromise you later. That threat could be a stash of live ammo or weaponry or it might be leaving an enemy alive who would recover sufficiently from their injuries to finally become the one to call out your number. At least that's how I justified it to myself. I crawled towards the slumped muscled torso of the beast. My shoulder was sopping in claret from the bullet wound. Pain thumped through me. Adrenaline surged around my body. *The blood was up.*

∽

The freak was slumped over moaning in pain. I kicked him onto his back on the floor. He wheezed. That thick muscular neck looked too thick to snap. I picked up a chair lying next to him, positioning one of the legs over his face. The look he gave me was confused and pitiful. I stamped down on the seat of the chair driving the leg into his eye socket and down through to the back of his skull.

What was it with me and using impromptu pieces of furniture to kill scumbags? First tables and now chairs! I guess if the hostage recovery game ever stopped paying so well I could always put my uncanny product familiarity to use working at an Ikea store.

I scrambled to my feet and piled down the steps of the hut. The hunt was on for a fleeing hyena.

And it didn't take long to spot him. In fact, he hadn't got far at all, making the strategic error of heading through the open car park to escape when he could have covered his movements by cutting through the trucks back onto the golf course. Gripping my shoulder to try and stem the flow of blood, I started after him hard. Gaining ground, I shouted for him to stop, threatening with the barrel of my empty gun. Razor wasn't to know that I hadn't been able to reload and I figured that a warning of impending violence may be sufficient to jolt him into compliance, given that he couldn't get away quick enough from the recent firefight. He stood panting next to a gleaming, red sports car, waiting for me to reach him with his hands raised. I greeted him by throwing a stiff right cross, catching him square on the jaw and knocking him backwards over the bonnet of the car. Picking him up by the lapels I shook him hard. Yelling into the contorted face before me, 'Tell me what you know about Daniel Ratchet, you worthless piece of crap? Where is he?'

'Nufink, man, I swear it. Please. Please don't kill me,' came the rasping reply. His hands feebly gripped my forearms in a vain attempt to free himself. The gleam of an old-fashioned gold watch on his wrist caught my eye. It was incongruous with the rest of the trendy sports casual gear he was wearing. I followed a hunch, recalling Bob Wallace's comments on Daniel's distress at having had his grandfather's watch stolen earlier that week.

Intense. Aggressive. Inches from his face. 'Tell me why you're wearing Ratchet's watch then, you pathetic little runt? You want me to shoot you in the face right now? Don't lie to me unless you want to take a bullet, Razor.'

I held my gun against his ear. Hot breath on his cheeks.

'Okay, okay. I'm sorry. Please just ease up man. It wasn't my idea, I swear. It was Andy what made me take it. Sergei wanted some leverage for a player deal, to get the new agent in our pocket. And Andy likes to play games, man. I just do what I'm told, innit.'

'Where is he now?'

'I swear I don't know nufink, man, for real.' I tightened the grip on his neck and squeezed. 'Look, I just hear bits and pieces all right. They don't tell me the plans,' he bleated.

I figured he was probably telling the truth. I wouldn't share secret information with this specimen either. I doubted he was part of some tight inner circle. He wasn't brains-trust material. 'Tell me what you know and don't hold back or you're dead meat like that giant-carnival-sideshow-freak back there. Understand?'

'Okay, okay. Daniel Ratchet was pissing off a bunch of people. He's been here five minutes and he's already sticking his nose in where it don't belong. He was asking the wrong questions about tournament fixing and dodgy contracts and the like. He got Andy's back up and was holding out on Sergei. All I know is that's a silly mistake, man, thems not to be messed with them guys.'

'So, where the hell is he now?' I shouted. Patience draining fast.

'He had some information about the player fixing that goes on out here on Tour. He was snooping about with that crazy coach Wallace. Had some kind of evidence on the scores and stats that prove a pattern apparently. Me and Sorlov had to find the device, give him a slap. We couldn't find it and we couldn't find him neither.' Razor was flustered. Babbling. 'Listen, mate, I swear, me and the caddies, we're just into a bit of gambling, making a few shakedowns from town to town, that's all. It turns a nice trade and the bosses keep things organised so it doesn't spill over and raise too much bother with the local roz. They all know it goes on but we're just an irritant, a nuisance that can be put up with. They don't want to cause a fuss or Rublex will pressure the Tour into ensuring that they don't stop at that town's golf course next time. That's a fortune lost to the local community from tourists and the like. They don't want to miss out so they don't go grumbling when we come knocking with a shakedown. Besides, we've gone and made sure that we got some of the senior local police in these places in real deep on the betting ledger. They like a flutter and then when we hold what they owe over their heads they tend to do what we tell 'em. But honest, I didn't know it was going to get heavy. I didn't know they were gonna take him.'

I leered down at the snivelling rat, giving up his mates as fast as he could spill it. As much as I needed the intel to find the Target quickly, I also hated squealers who'd grass given half a chance. If you didn't have the balls to even make a pretence of holding out for your boys, then that made me sick. I reached back and slapped Razor across the mouth with the back of my hand. It's called a bitch slap for a reason. I'm right-handed. The slug had hit my left shoulder, so I was able to give it some real purchase. The result was a whimper and then a trail of blood dribbling from the corner of his swollen mouth.

Shouting came from across the car park. I jerked my head backwards to see two uniformed security guards legging it towards where I held Razor over the bonnet of the car. They were obviously concerned at the altercation and intent on breaking up a fight in the grounds of this high-class establishment. That could mean possibly detaining us until the Guardia Civil arrived, which wasn't a chance I was prepared to take.

I met the first of the two uniforms with a scything right elbow to the side of his neck knocking him out cold. With my left hand still gripping Razor's collar I pivoted and kicked the second skinnier guard hard under the ribcage. A liver shot. I felt his ribs crack under the thick tread of my combat boot. The authority drained from his face and a moment later he was groaning, contorted in pain and fighting for breath as he squirmed on the tarmac.

I turned back to Razor. 'Who's got him? Where could they have taken him, rat?'

Razor was shaking. 'I'm not sure, really I'm not. The boys have talked about a villa outside Madrid. A fat place where they enjoy whores and piles of coke when we've had a good run. It's like a reward for us to let our hair down now and again.' He looked up at me, a nervous glance. 'I've not been allowed to go yet.'

'Where is it? Exactly where?' I repeated deliberately, bending him further over the motor with his back in an unnatural arch to accentuate the vulnerability of his position. 'There's an address inside the hut.'

I grabbed Razor by his hair and spun him so he was bent over the car bonnet face down. Roughly pinned his arms behind his back and looped his hands and then ankles in turn with cable ties from my pocket, pulling them tight to pinch off the circulation in his arms and legs. Slammed his face into the car metalwork with a single crack and let him slump unconscious to the asphalt, heaped between the two parked vehicles. Clutching my shoulder to apply pressure through the blood-soaked shirt I jogged back towards the hut.

There were answers waiting to be found.

27

Daniel Ratchet was broken. A hollowed shell. His confidence shattered and body taken beyond any level of pain and suffering he could have imagined. Beaten, tied up, starved and humiliated. No resolution offered itself. He couldn't reason with these men given they barely spoke English. Besides, they treated him no better than an animal. Nothing existed behind the cruel darkness of their eyes. He'd probably be dead now if Black Leather Jacket Man hadn't put Bad Breath Man on a leash when he did. His mind raced over the decisions he'd taken in the last few days. Questions to which there were no good answers. Why had he been drawn into looking for corruption on the Tour? What place was it of his? Why had he questioned the Aaron Crower contract and believed Bob Wallace when no one else had batted an eyelid about player fixing despite it probably going on right under their noses for years? He scratched at the walls in anguish. Couldn't he just be sodding happy for once? Why hadn't been able to take this life-changing career opportunity without screwing it up? He wondered if he would ever see his sweet vulnerable Matilda again.

Daniel languished in the dank, lonely wallows of despair for an indeterminable period. The once significant, finely calibrated increments of time blended together into a single, meaningless void. Bitter remorse licked at his soul as all hope seeped into the deep pit of abject despair mixed with the ashes of his dreams. Now just pitiful remnants of his life. In sorrowful tandem to the tight grip of his misery, a sticky pungent film formed and crusted on his skin; the drying remains of excrement, left unwashed from his face.

Alone with his thoughts. Deafened with silence. Daniel could hear the blood throbbing round his head and pulsating in his ears. Haunting kaleidoscopic images of his worried parents and life back home in Sheffield cascaded through his mind's eye. And then Matilda. His beautiful, brave Matilda who had somehow tried to warn him of the impending danger with that email. So close to happiness. How he yearned to see her again.

He awoke from a fitful sleep. Sat up, pulling cold knees close to his chest. The fact was that the choices he'd made had got him into this mess. He couldn't change that. He was here and in this nightmare situation whether he wanted to be or not. He either lived or he died. They wanted his computer and presumably the incriminating evidence about Rublex and the golf Tour on it. They'd made that clear. Wily old Bob Wallace had been right all along. If that was what they wanted he should just tell them where it was and, perhaps, they'd let him go?

Wise up, son. Men like this don't go to these extremes just to let me skip off into the sunset once they get what they want. Right now that tablet and the data and video stored on it is probably the only thing keeping me alive.

If they were determined to gain the tablet's whereabouts, however, Daniel knew in himself it wouldn't take long for them to extract it. He was weak. These guys knew what they were doing. It wouldn't take much pressure for him to spill his guts and that would be game over. They'd said to wait for somebody to arrive. Some Russian or Eastern European sounding name. They certainly wanted the tablet. If they were Russian, then it had to link to Rublex and the crooked agreement that he'd raised concerns about. Things had started going bad right after that. The video he'd recorded had proven that Sergei was involved in the tournament fixing. But surely, he couldn't be involved in kidnapping as well? The man who'd been so kind to him, so generous in lending him the credit card. Gifting him that amazing watch. It couldn't be so.

Daniel would reason with the man. Perhaps he could promise to keep quiet and this whole situation might disappear. But they'd murdered the driver of the meat truck. He'd heard the gunshots with his own ears and had a body dumped on him in the car. That was probably to eliminate any link to his disappearance from the golf course. These men were ruthless. He didn't know who was due to arrive but, Sergei or not, Daniel figured he didn't have much time. It was imperative that he try to take matters into his own hands if he wanted to stay alive. The only option was to escape.

Daniel braced before slapping his own face hard in an attempt to sharpen his focus. He surveyed the room afresh through tear-streaked eyes. It was practically bare. No windows. Flaking paint. The child's foam mattress. The cracked plastic bucket. The doors were locked and bolted from the outside; a heavy studded wooden door which was secured by an outer gate of iron bars. *Not a whole lot to work with then.* Daniel smiled weakly to himself at the helpless situation he faced. On closer examination of the plastic bucket he spotted that the crack had exposed a sharp edge. He listened at the door for signs of movement, for a presence outside. Nothing.

Applying pressure to the side of the bucket and working the crack deeper, he twisted and cajoled the weakness in the plastic with an urgent ripping motion. The cheap bucket splintered at its base and Daniel kept forcing it until he was able to break off a single shard of sharp green plastic. He placed the bucket back in its corner with the broken side facing the wall. Slipped the shard into a trouser pocket and felt his heart soar.

With no hatch in the door for interaction with prisoners, any bottles of water or what little food that Daniel had been provided had been thrown at him from round the corner of the opened door. This meant that if they wanted to see their captive then they needed to unlock and open both doors; his only way out. Daniel rose to his feet and, for the first time since his ordeal began, he started to stretch out his beleaguered body. His head was still sore and he had a fat lump of swelling across his right cheek with open lacerations inside his mouth from where he'd been struck. His neck and the top of his shoulders ached from lying cramped on his side. He tried to shake it out a little. The movement made him wince. It felt like he was carrying a full set of cracked ribs. He checked under his shirt and a smear of yellowish bruising, the colour of a rotting pear, covered the entire right-hand side of his torso. His legs were weak and stiff from the forced inactivity and he lacked in energy from the terrible nutrition of the previous few days. Besides all this, he was functioning and he was alive. And he was now also armed with a weapon, of sorts.

Daniel called out for water. Restrained at first before building to a wailing crescendo which left no room for doubt that the prisoner needed attention. The footsteps started down the hall. Daniel readied himself. Keys jangled in the lock; the crash of the metal grate flying against the wall.

'Shut your mouth, little bitch.' Gruff, staccato words like unoiled machine parts working against each other. Daniel waited behind the door crouched and coiled. Heart pounding. Bad Breath Man bowled through the door with a black leather belt in his hand, buckle swinging menacingly. Daniel didn't skip a beat. He pounced as soon as his jailor was a step inside the door, forcing the sharp plastic shard tight to his throat. He unwrapped the belt from the man's wrist, forcing his face against the wall of the dingy cell.

'Where are the keys for the door?' he demanded before shouting in desperation close to the thug's ear, 'Keys? Now!'

'In lock,' came the stifled, begrudging response. Daniel checked over his shoulder to verify. Placed a kick swift and hard into the back of the knee. Pushed the guard face first into the wall and down onto his shins. Darted through the open door, slamming it shut. The euphoric sound of the turning key signalled that the reversal of fortune was complete. Captor had become the captive. Trapped inside the cell which had served as Daniel's own cage of despair. He couldn't believe that the feeble plan had worked. The dizziness of freedom surged through his body.

Pocketing the key, he spun round to face a long dark corridor. He was alone, no sign yet of Black Leather Jacket Man. If the two of them had been summoned to the cell by his commotion there would have been no chance of getting through that door and the repercussions didn't bear thinking about. It had been worth the risk.

In one sweaty hand he gripped the plastic shard; the thick belt wound round his other palm with a foot or so of slack leather swinging pendulous from the weight of its metal buckle.

Inching forward in the dark, feeling like an armed gladiator about to enter the arena and meet his fate. The hammering on the cell door and angry shouts from behind echoed along the corridor, spurring Daniel forward with renewed intensity.

Scuttling through the darkness conjured a fear of entombment within an endless labyrinth. Panic abounded. Instead of being pursued by the mythical beast, the Minotaur, as had Theseus, Ratchet's paranoid imagination presented monstrous Russian guards at each and every turn. He arrived at the end of the corridor with great relief and found himself in a kitchen pantry and utility space replete with a large white porcelain sink, industrial-sized washing machine and dryer. Vast shelves, heaving under the weight of food tins, bottles of oil, dense packets of flour and dried meats, lined the walls. Industrial-sized bags of rice sat squat on the floor below. Out of one such sack, telltale grains spewed across the floor from a small hole chewed in its base; evidence of industrious rodents at work. Through the end of the pantry he spied a large Spanish-style kitchen. Edging closer, Daniel peeked through the saloon doors and found himself looking at the back of a uniformed maid standing over a sink of steaming water scrubbing a burnished pot. The kitchen was dominated by a sturdy range cooker. In front of this stood a beautiful, solid rectangular wooden table, the type perhaps sawn from a single piece of an ancient Spanish fig tree. To the side of the kitchen, painted patio doors led out towards extensive manicured grounds which surrounding the hacienda.

He tiptoed forward. The maid gently sang to herself in Spanish, swaying her backside in rhythm to her simple tune. Totally preoccupied with her chores, back facing the pantry. Daniel slid through the saloon doors, fearful that the slightest squeak from their hinges might alert her to his presence. He crept like a burglar across the stone floor, not even daring to breathe for fear that she might summon help and he'd be recaptured. At last, with hands reaching of the patio doors, a surge of electric panic flushed through him with the idea that they might well, in fact, be locked. This exit was his own real chance of escape. The guards would be on him soon.

He tried the handle of the door. Eased it down fully with it feeling like an age for the lever to engage with the mechanism of the door latch. He pushed against the frame and, to his total relief, it eased open. Daniel exhaled the breath he had been holding and stepped out into the dazzling sunshine.

28

Derek Hemmings shuffled forward in the queue as if heading for impending doom. He was ambivalent about the coming meeting, to say the least. On the one hand, he was anxious to learn what MI6 had discovered about Boris Golich. He hoped that the long overdue favour he'd exacted from Simon Prentice would yield results that his limited resources were just not capable of. On the other hand, he didn't possess a head for heights and the prospect of spending the next thirty odd minutes suspended high above the River Thames in a small glass capsule, buffeted with wind and rain, filled him with dread. Whomever he was meeting apparently had a flare for the dramatic, messaging a series of complex instructions for the meet, finally culminating in arrival here for 1400 precisely. The London Eye was a busy tourist attraction on the bank of the River Thames, resembling a fun fair big-wheel, providing stunning panoramic views across the city of London. When it wasn't overcast and tipping with rain, that was, grumbled Derek into the promotional pamphlet that had been thrust into his hand. Vertigo, meanwhile, didn't seem to be particularly bothered about the weather.

The pod continued the gradual descent on its unending vertical rotation. Doors slid open with a grand welcome. The capsule had been allocated as private. Derek swallowed and clambered inside. A low block bench filled the centre of the space. A man in a smart military-style overcoat already inside, stood gripping the rail which traced around the centre of the big transparent egg, as if transfixed by something on the horizon. The doors swung shut and the pod rattled and shunted forward.

'I gather we have a mutual friend,' said Derek, opting to sit well away from the glass and keeping his eyes fixed squarely into the middle distance.

'I'm afraid not,' flashed the curt retort.

'Pray tell, why am I here then?' sniffed Derek, beginning to feel his fragile patience wane. His stomach lurched and the pod began to climb the steep ascent on the wheel.

'Simple. You need information about Boris Golich. I'm here to provide some enlightenment,' answered Charles Hand, spinning to face Derek for the first time and taking a single step towards the seats rooted in the middle of the bubble.

'It's a matter of utmost gravity. I trust you've been given the background?' The distinctly unwell looking civil servant was beginning to turn green around the gills.

'I appreciate that you're being inculcated to commit the British government into a business deal with one Boris Golich and that you're rightly reticent to do so.'

'Yes. That would sum it up. Do you have information I can use to help put a stop to this madness then?' Derek just wasn't taking to this man.

The Hand of God stared out over the steeple of St Paul's Cathedral and across the City of London. He paused before answering. 'My organisation is currently engaged on a job that leads to the door of Boris Golich. There's been a crime. Kidnapping or murder of a young British man and in the course of our investigation we've been led to believe that several agents of the Rublex Corporation are involved.'

'I see,' said Hemmings, wringing his hands as furrows of concentration battled for pre-eminence across his brow. 'A grave affair... What else have you discovered? I'm of the volition that the whole organisation is a front to launder substantial sums of dirty Russian Mafia money. If we can tie this to Golich and validate the origins of the money trail then the government would have to abandon this cursed gas exploration deal off the Falklands. I need to prove it before it's too late. The repercussions of opening the gates of Europe to Golich's stolen energy and the flood of black Vory money will be catastrophic.'

Hand's expression remained unchanged. Derek continued with pressing urgency to force home his point.

'Britain will be complicit, sir, in legitimising a corrupt Russian organisation which will contaminate both our fine reputation in the world order and damage relations beyond repair with our hard-won international trading partners.' For some reason he flung his hands out as he said this, gesticulating towards the city over which they hung suspended. Derek's passion for the cause was transcending into the theatrical. 'We may create some jobs in the short term but I'm of the mind that British-sanctioned gas exploration in the waters surrounding the Falkland Islands, to which Rublex have acquired pre-emptive rights, would place us at risk of inciting a new war with Argentina and their South American partners who contend territorial ownership. Only they'd be better funded this time by their wealthy and insatiable Chinese paymasters who are avaricious for new natural energy assets.'

The Hand of God understood the implications of war and he didn't appreciate being lectured upon the subject. He probed in response. 'Have you considered what will happen if the deal gets derailed? It may be wise to be careful what you wish for.'

'Well, yes, I have in fact.' Derek sniffed. He considered himself somewhat of a political intellect and this was an opportunity to demonstrate that he understood both sides of the equation with a fair and balanced rationale. 'The counterargument, and a real danger that I think concerns the PM, is that if the British don't work with Rublex, then they may just work with the Chinese direct, build an offshore platform as a base for the workers and cut us out altogether. They wouldn't get a free ride for gas distribution into Europe, but I suppose the Chinese would open those doors themselves by leaning on the governments of the impoverished European nations like Serbia, Italy, Spain and Greece, whom they've been propping up financially since the great recession, via the purchase of government bonds as a backdoor policy veto. It all ties in with their great Belt and Road initiative to open up Africa and Europe along the old Silk Road.'

Hand had heard enough and was tiring of the meeting. For all the careful planning perhaps it wasn't such a good idea to have arranged it in a moving capsule which you couldn't leave until it had completed its orbit. 'It's a complex situation indeed. But one that can only be handled with true integrity, Mr Hemmings. If you've searched your heart, studied the facts, and made your decision for the right reasons and in the best interests of Great Britain, then you will have done the right thing.' Derek's cheeks flushed pink.

'I will turn the use of our gifted researcher, Ella Philips, over to you. She's already started to uncover trails of laundered money through a network of accounts feeding into Rublex. Vast totals paid in primarily small denominations appear to be filtered through a series of legitimate subsidiaries and recycled back into the corporation.' As he spoke, Hand splayed his fingers to depict an ever-expanding web. He continued, 'We believe that the kidnapping was instigated at a professional golf tournament in Spain and we have men on the ground at the scene right now. You may know that Rublex is the main sponsor of the European Tour and supports many of the leading players also, on an individual basis. When we were called in on this job, we looked into potential suspects and the murky past of their wealthy owner came to bear.' He stole a glance out over the Houses of Parliament unfolding beneath them. 'Seems he is keeping some pretty interesting company these days. Then MI6 got in touch and availed us of our support for the Foreign Office. We've joined the dots, so to speak.'

'Can any of this illegal financial activity be documented and proven beyond reasonable doubt?' Hemmings pressed for some proof.

The glass pod slowly continued its inexorable descent to the boarding platform on the bank of the river. Charles Hand turned to his companion and spoke firmly, his face expressionless.

'Our job at this moment, Mr Hemmings, is to find and to rescue a missing Briton. To bring him back safe. We're running out of time. Meetings such as these serve only as a distraction from this vital work. We're not tasked with investigating international organised crime, financial or otherwise. Not unless it helps to resolve our work faster and save the lives of those we're paid to rescue.'

'Sir, I implore you. I can't do this on my own. I need to be able to demonstrate the veracity of these unfounded claims, to prove to the world that Golich is not who he says he is. I need documentation to show the Prime Minister. This is about doing the right thing. This is about serving the best interests of our country.'

Hand stood staring through the rain splattered glass over the city, letting the words wash over him. 'As I've already said, we'll help you how we can, Mr Hemmings. Ella will pass over what we've found to date. She can alert you to the trail of accounts. I'm confident that you'll be able to follow it at your end to find the evidence you require to make your Boris Golich a persona non grata to the British government.'

'I understand. I'm indebted to you, sir. The sands of time have all but run out. This has to work or the deal will go through unchallenged.' He fell silent.

'Don't thank me. Save your thanks for Simon Prentice of MI6, Mr Hemmings. When it comes to doing the so-called right thing, to which you allude, MI6 never fails to disappoint. But, as you know yourself, leverage requires but a single point of pivot.' The statement was as cryptic as it was barbed. The cabin arrived at the docking station once more and the doors swung open. Derek was relieved to feel his feet standing again upon solid ground.

29

I reached the caddy shack again, nestled amongst the eerie shadows of the truck park, door hanging open upon its hinges. Everything was as it had been left following the tear up. My eye followed a succession of discarded papers and upturned furniture leading to the massive, unmoving carcass, spread out like some freakish shop dummy twisted into an action pose. The body occupied a large portion of the free floor space. A chair balanced unevenly on three legs, the fourth impaling the eye socket of the dead man and embedded firmly into his skull. A dark crimson puddle of viscous blood had seeped across the wooden floor, filling random cracks in the floorboards like spilt paint. Flies buzzed, circling the body in geometric oscillation. The pitiless scene would no doubt be discovered at some point soon. I needed to work fast. Gathering up pages of scattered documents and files from the floor I skim read through them scanning for clues to the venue that Razor had mentioned as I went. Records of bets, odds for players finishing in specific positions in certain tournaments; names and numbers mostly. I didn't have time for this and would need some heavy machinery to bust open those filing cabinets in the adjacent office to trawl through their contents. That could take an age and I needed to get going fast or I had a bad feeling that the body count was going to continue to grow. With Daniel Ratchet possibly the next name on that list.

I checked around the hut in case I'd missed anything obvious. Something not necessarily in my nature but that I'd drilled myself to try to do in the field. To take a step back before letting rip. So, this was it; empty coffee cups sat unwashed in the sink. Kitchen towels and drying up cloths lay folded, unused. A packet of biscuits spilled their contents across the counter at the back. The walls were bare except for a fat cork noticeboard hanging on the side wall. Scorecards, a detailed yardage map of the golf course, an extensive list of tournament tee times and a calendar were pinned to it. A topless blonde woman in a golf visor as white as her teeth, perched on the side of a yellow sports car cupping a pair of obscenely large breasts. The month of May was certainly not left wanting. To the left of the calendar a handwritten note was pinned to the board and caught my eye. I walked over to examine it. It read: **Pussy Palace! Carascalle, Mimbreras 4, 03201 ELCHE.**

This had to be it. The place Razor had mention where the crew went to celebrate a good streak on the take. Pussy Palace circled in red with a residential address. It was as good as I was going to get. I tore the note from the board using my good arm, the other now hanging by my side, an unseemly soggy, bloody mess. The pain scrambled my thoughts. I stuffed the paper into my pocket. Grabbed a wodge of kitchen towels from the counter. Dampened them under the warm tap and held the paper tight against the wound to stem the bleeding.

Noises now from outside. I piled out of the hut fearing I could be disturbed at the scene of a murder at any moment. Tipping down the steps, I clocked two burly television engineers with matching beer guts competing to spill out from under their sweat stained T-shirts. They were hauling heavy cables out from under one of the trucks. At the level they were stooped, if they happened to glance under the adjacent truck, they would spot the bound, gagged and unconscious body of the guard that I'd neutralised earlier. I turned and moved fast, heading in the other direction. Head down. The fewer people who could provide my description after the carnage was discovered, the better.

I covered some distance and redialled the latest encrypted contact number to reach HQ. Ella picked up right away as usual.

'Hey, soldier,' she purred in her well-to-do, throaty voice, 'are you making progress?'

Sex on a stick.

'Think so, Ella. Although I've gone and picked up some lead for my troubles.'

'Are you injured, Hunter? A bullet?' she pressed.

'I'll live. Although I need some space to get patched up before it properly slows me down. Don't worry about me. Just get me some intel, can you please? I've got an address and I need you to process it. I think they may be holding Daniel there. Find out what you can. How far it is from here? Whose name the deed of ownership is in. Try and get a visual on it, different routes in, points of access, that kind of thing. I'll check in with Mickey and boot down as soon as I can.'

'Give me a little time, Tom. I'll check Google Earth but doubt it's got the detail you need. If that's so, then I'll have to hack access to a Pentagon eye-in-the-sky. I'll come back to you when I can, but this stuff usually takes a little while. Use the time to get yourself patched-up, will you?'

'Sure. Thanks. Find me a way in. There's no point me just tearing off without preparing first. It won't help Daniel if I get taken out the moment I arrive on the scene, from what I've seen so far, these guys mean business. And Ella, you'd better tell The Hand of God that his mate is dead. They've killed Bob Wallace.'

The Range Rover was parked half a mile down the road from the golf course, hidden from view behind some rusting oil storage tanks for a quick getaway. I slumped into the front seat. Sweat poured off me as I sucked the air into my lungs. The throbbing hole in my shoulder clawed at my energy. I scrabbled inside the dash box to locate the medical kit, which Mickey had provided. Tore the sleeve of my shirt off and tended to the wound. First, I cleaned the coagulated blood and scorched skin with a sanitised wipe before taking a set of tiny metal tweezers to fish inside the cavity for any pieces of shrapnel and bullet. There had been trauma in the tissue and damage to the blood vessels, nerve endings and muscle as ripples of force from the bullet passed through the flesh after the impact. The pain was immense. But bittersweet. At once like revisiting an unhappy yet familiar place and being compelled to explore. I'd been here before and I knew the drill. Knew I needed to get the metal out of me fast, sanitise the wound, get stitched and bandaged before I lost any more blood; before I'd become no use to anyone. Not to myself and least of all the Target. Working through the pain, I clamped my teeth together with a pressure so tight I felt my jaw might shatter. A proper job done and I'd lived every second of it. I was confident that most of the particles were removed as best I could. Wiry, black butterfly stitches knotted in place. Only now could I risk numbing the pain. Before dressing the wound, I fired up a hit of morphine and injected the weeping needle into my damaged deltoid. Then padded and bandaged it tight.

The phone lay idle. Nothing back from Ella. She'd be a while yet getting me the information I needed. I sparked a Marlboro cigarette and smoked it down to the butt. Locked the doors of the motor. Eased back further in my seat, inclining it below the window line. Closed my eyes and allowed the deep flickering purple and yellow lights to wash over me like coloured dye spreading over water. I welcomed the colours as they clung to me, feeling myself falling away piece by piece, letting go of the pain. Slipping away. Letting go. Despite knowing that my dreams always ended in terror and death. And always, so much blood. Maria.

The lugubrious repetitive clack clacking of the oversized ceiling fan as it cycles above. The sash window held open by an army boot, balanced on its heel and jammed tight between frame and ledge. The tread of its furrowed sole caked in dried flaking mud. Shouts and yelps and laughter from children playing on the roadside below. An old-fashioned wooden cabinet. Drawers yawning open, crumpled clothing spilling out. The heavy framed mirror with its chipped corners. Flecks of shaving cream splattered on it sharing an unintended language of indecipherable hieroglyphics. The old-fashioned gramophone sits hissing and spitting as it sticks, scoring across the slither of vinyl held beneath its predatory needle.

Another drop of sweat scores its way down my forehead as if in slow motion, gliding over the contours of my cheek and jaw. It finally splashes onto my chest. Forgive me, Maria.

Making wild and uninhibited love in the hot sticky afternoon. The air thick and heavy. The undeniable smell pervading the room of raw sex. She should have been teaching local kids that day, part of the UN Aid programme. But I'd persuaded her to play hooky. Craved her every moment, every chance I could. This beautiful, intense, passionate woman consumed me. She'd helped me to heal, helped me to feel human again. Even after all of the horror and damage that I'd seen. That I'd created.

The fan spins. Relentless. Clack clack clack. The gramophone stuck on its baleful lament. The words of the song imploring, reaching for one more touch, one more interaction with a love long lost.

I see her tied with rope. I see the pain in her eyes, pleading, beseeching me to save her. But I do not. I do nothing. I don't help her because I'm bound helpless myself. Each of my limbs tied and secured with clinical precision. No movement possible. Then I'm hooded. And in the dark recess of Hell that becomes me, I strain to amplify every slightest sound. To feel it with her. I hear it all. The totality of each barbaric abuse. And I'm powerless to help her. Impotent. Maria.

And they delight in my suffering with each grain of her agony. No perception of depth or space. Just pitch blackness. I hear slow and purposeful movements. Steadied and practised as they take their time.

Then the sudden violence of a rapid SHINK, SHINK slicing through the heavy air right next to my ear. I recoil from the savagery of the sound. Steel blade honed on whetstone. Guttural laughter sickens my stomach.

Then scrabbling, clawing. Heavy blows as bone meets flesh. The sorrowful whimpers. An animal broken and in pain. My Maria.

Silence, pregnant with meaning. Waiting, hoping for an eternity in the pitted darkness that envelops me. Until hope is shattered with shards of screaming so primal that I may never quieten the sound again.

And I listen to the soundtrack to my nightmare as I strain with all the force I can muster against my bonds until at last, defeated and exhausted, I collapse. Maria's screaming and begging has now stopped too, replaced only by a low imperceptible moan. Her suffering, the result of a series of sadistic cuts and intrusive insertions designed to administer the utmost pain possible to bear.

And I cannot escape the reverberations of this endless torture even as the door closes behind them and stillness is sucked back into the room. The clack clacking of the oversized fan above us. The hiss and spit of the old gramophone as it pours out its doleful lyrics. No noise from the street below now. And one sound cutting through it all. The persistent PAT, PAT, PAT that's hardly noticeable at first but that builds into a deafening waterfall as comprehension washes over me. Maria bleeding out onto the wooden floor of the apartment. I bind myself forever to that haunting sound, as each splash takes her further away from me.

30

A wall of heat hit Daniel in the face. The bright sunlight stung his eyes as he stepped through the kitchen doors onto the patio. He had to put distance between himself and the house. It wouldn't be long before he was discovered missing and the two thugs, who had been doing such a princely job babysitting him, came to take their retribution. He shivered in the sun, as he remembered the beatings. Running his hand tenderly across his throbbing ribs, Daniel prayed he wouldn't have to take any more.

The winding pathway which led away from the back of the house was made of smooth white pebbles, adorned on either side by a lush green lawn, well-watered by a pulsating sprinkler system. Conscious of the loud crunches his footsteps were making on the stones, Daniel stepped onto the damp springy Bermuda grass and broke into a lumbering jog. The garden was exquisite. Vibrant flowers of exotic reds, yellows and purples splattered across large green bushes. Bendy fronds and stooping palms swayed together to an unheard rhythm of their own making. Lemon trees dazzled with ripe yellow fruit nestled amongst a mess of dark green foliage. It was a wondrous garden but Daniel was in no mood to appreciate it. He was scared. Dirty. Out of breath and racked in pain from the punishment absorbed in the preceding days. The aching in his ribs made it hard to pull oxygen into his lungs.

Head down, Dan. Keep moving forward.

The snap of a gunshot fired from the house cut through the sky, running through Ratchet like he'd been struck by a bull whip. He ducked on instinct, although from the distance of the sound he knew the gun couldn't have been aimed directly at him. It was a warning shot. The escape had been discovered and he was now being hunted. Pressing on, not daring to look behind, branches tore at his skin as tangles of undergrowth were hastily brushed aside in the desperate attempt to make distance from the hacienda. That distance wouldn't hold for long though. Dogs barked, shouts and fractious voices filled the air. A group had been rounded up to recapture him and he was sure that soon he'd be surrounded from different sides.

Adrenaline pumped around Daniel's ragged body as he set into a small cluster of fruit trees, each encircled with a neat border of hay on freshly turned soil. He ducked and weaved through a tangle of caustic branches and pulled up clear in the shadow of an imposing drystone wall at the back of the property. It encircled the grounds of the villa and had obviously been there for many years; a hand-built monument to privacy and protection from outsiders. At this moment, however, with the bitter irony not lost on him, Daniel was on the inside and desperate to get out. The baying of dogs beyond the fruit trees grew louder. There was no gate in the wall and nothing immediately visible to help scale it. But the wall was constructed in the old Spanish artesian method of laying heavy stones over and on top of each other with no cement or binding agent.

Secured in place by only their collective mass and the steadfast yoke of gravity, that most irrefutable of masters.

Daniel jammed his foot into a space between the stones and leveraged himself up using fingertips to claw at the vertical mass of rock above. Next step upwards he scraped his cheek on the rough wall and by the time he was able to haul his arms over the top, some fifteen feet from the ground, his fingertips were bloodied and his kneecaps swollen and split from scraping against the jutting chips of rock.

'Freeze or I shoot!' The shout came from below. Daniel looked back into the garden to see a muscular, brown-skinned man with a shaved head standing on the grass below, waving a semi-automatic machine gun in his hands. Two spiteful looking dogs snapped and scrabbled up at the base of the wall snapping at his dangling legs. Daniel hung there motionless. Heart pounding inside his throat.

'Capture him, you idiot,' came a barked order beyond, as the rest of the search party caught up. As the muscled skinhead turned to look, Daniel took advantage of that brief moment with the gun barrel lowered. Hauled his knee onto the top of the wall and without pause to look at what lay below, hurled himself straight over the edge and into the unknown.

Suspended in time, stomach in mouth, the beleaguered body dropped through the air like a stone. The landing was hard, first clattering with his shoulder and then jolting the side of his hip onto the solid ground below. He rolled into a crumpled heap and moaned. Spat the dirt from inside his mouth. He could hear an argument ensuing behind the wall. Pulling himself to his feet and brushing himself down, Daniel looked cautiously up and down the dirt track. It was deserted, except for what looked like farm machinery parked behind several dishevelled outbuildings. A little girl in a long dirty pink T-shirt and flip-flops several sizes too big, was playing with a hoop about a hundred yards away. She was totally absorbed in what she was doing, hadn't looked up. The drop had hit him hard, knocked the stuffing out sideways. Daniel didn't feel he had it in him to set off running again. But he had to get away and now. His captors would scale the wall in no time and, if he was caught again at this point, he was dead meat. Thinking on his feet, he limped across the road and, checking that he was unobserved, pulled open the rotted wooden door to a looming farm storage building. The dry boarding splintered in Daniel's hands, flaking away from the door and he squeezed through the gap into a dark spacious void.

Inside and safely out of sight, the prey breathed easy, feeling the tension fall from his shoulders for the first time in days. He rubbed the goose pimples off his arms, noticing that the space he now occupied was several degrees lower than the outside temperature, far away from the baking sun. With his eyes adjusting slowly to the gloom, Daniel groped his way forward. Then he froze, before grunting in disgust, spitting and scrabbling at his face to remove the sticky tangle of cobwebs that had enveloped him. A bat flustered and flapped, swooping from one corner of the dusty grain store to the other causing him to drop to the floor in fright. Straightening up and squinting around to get his bearings, Daniel could make out that the farm building was little more than a utility barn which had seen better days. It was now ostensibly being used for storing discarded old equipment and some rotting harvest produce. The floor consisted of dirty, cracked poured concrete coated with discarded kernels of grain and dust. A rusted combine harvester, emasculated by the removal of its two front wheels, lay abandoned to one side of the space. A collection of ancient scythes, hoes, and a burly wooden ladder lay piled against a large wooden water barrel. One corner of the barn was dominated by bales of straw stacked up high. Daniel nodded in appreciation. *That's got to be the perfect hiding place.*

31

ENGLAND. LONDON. WESTMINSTER.

'Alexander, please could you come through to the office? I'd like to bring you up to speed with certain developments.' Hemmings switched off the intercom, leant back in the crimson leather chair and allowed a smile of quiet satisfaction to spread across his face. A pigeon strutted along the frame to the window through which the morning's gentle light poured into the room. His uncomfortable meeting with Charles Hand had led to new avenues of enquiry providing access to compelling information which had previously been inaccessible. For the first time since meeting with Boris Golich at the club Derek felt like he had the upper hand, that his instincts were about to be justified.

He'd stuck his neck out, at significant risk to his long and established career, in order to best serve and protect his beloved nation. *Done the right thing indeed, old boy*, he gloated. And now he could feel, nay practically taste, that he was soon to be vindicated. On reflection, Derek admitted to himself that there was probably more to it and that he'd secretly always accepted that this whole escapade was to some extent the daring mission which he'd always longed to undertake for MI6; previously forsaken on account of the sacrifices made for Alice and their nascent family. He fantasised that the resulting fallout from saving the country from this poisoned Russian chalice would provide the perfect swansong to an industrious albeit less than glittering career. Recognition. Perhaps some minor honour or other and the chance to finally get one over on that supercilious Scottish shit, Andy Bartholomew. Derek Hemmings considered that he had every right to smile and enjoy his moment of impending victory.

'You wanted to see me, sir?' his smart young assistant purred as he stepped into the office, snapping the door into place.

'Yes, Alex. I wanted to share some good news with you, given all the recent late nights and help you've provided in researching the Boris Golich situation.'

'Really, sir? That does sound exciting. I should say, sir, that it's absolutely no bother at all. I'm always at your service. Privileged, in fact, to simply be able to aid you in your important work.' Gushing. Even by Alex Gontlemoon's very own levels, forged in the machinations of an expensive public school education where prefects dished out bare-bottom canings on a whim to those who hadn't displayed requisite levels of idolatry, he was plumbing new depths of gratuitous obsequence.

Derek continued unabashed, relishing the moment. Beckoned Alex closer. He was rather fond of his assistant, considered himself something of a mentor. 'I've pulled some favours from the top. I'm being sent classified data imminently which will conclusively prove that Boris Golich is a notable crook and that the gas exploration deal with Great Britain must be halted at all costs.'

'That won't be happening any time soon, Hemmings,' boomed a brash Scottish voice from the doorway. Derek spun in his chair to find a red-faced Andy Bartholomew striding into his office, a slim manila file clutched in his hands. He was sweating profusely, an angry blue vein throbbed on the side of his blotchy neck. 'How dare you cross me, you useless old prick,' he seethed.

Derek rose slowly from the chair to meet him, only for a fat sweaty palm to slam into his chest, forcing him backwards into the seat. 'What the devil,' he blustered.

'You're finished, pal. Your career is toast. You're out. As of today, Hemmings. Sans pension too, Old Boy.' Andy spat the last two words with pure disgust, mere centimetres from Derek's face, expelling his diction with the vehemence of a motocross rider splattering a muddy trail. He continued, 'Our mutual friend here, Mr Gontlemoon, has been most enlightening regarding your undercover detective work, you sad old goat.' Andy gloated with an ostentatious fanning of the loose sheaf folder in his hand whilst nodding towards Alex. 'You certainly are an ambitious young man, aren't you, Gontlemoon?'

'Alexander?' croaked Derek, his gaze unreturned as the young civil servant fixed a dogged stare at the thick carpet which nestled around his well-polished shoes.

'Yes indeedy,' chortled the ebullient Scot, savouring his moment of triumph, 'and a damn good judge of character too it seems. Shown that he knows how to back a winner, wouldn't you say, Double-O Nothing?' The attempt at an exaggerated Sean Connery impersonation was designed to heap further humiliation on his older colleague. 'Alex here needed to back the winning horse to further his career prospects in Whitehall. Guess what? It turns out that was me, pal.'

'I don't know what on earth you are banging on about, Andy,' Derek retorted, his poker face devoid of emotion. *I'll see your stake and raise you double, to hell if my hand consists of nothing but a bag of spanners, I'll bluff this out.* 'Have you been drinking at lunch again? I'm afraid I don't have time for your petty shenanigans. Now, I really do need to get on with some proper work, so if you'll excuse me.'

'Everything's right here in this file, you slippery old bastard. The unauthorised activities. Refusing to sign the trade agreement and putting thousands of British jobs at risk. Disrespecting a powerful new ally of the United Kingdom and, to add injury to insult, making clumsy enquiries into Boris Golich's past to try and stymie what's already been agreed at the highest levels of Government.'

Derek sat stony-faced, listening, calculating his next move.

'I have your freshly typed letter of resignation inside this file, Hemmings. It's already been accepted. It just needs your signature. Sign it by the end of the day or I'll personally make sure you're escorted from the building under a dark cloud of dishonour and a wave of unpleasant negative publicity. How would little Alice like that then, d'you think?' he snorted.

Derek winced at the cruel mention of his wife's name. But by then Andy had already turned and flounced out of the office, shadowed by a smartly dressed traitor. His evidence file deposited behind him on the desktop, innocuous amongst the other papers and understated in its deadly purpose.

32

I awoke with a rancid taste in my mouth and a pervasive sense of regret. Rubbed my milky eyes and pulled the knife from the inside of my boot. Gritted my teeth before tearing the blade against the back of my hand, slow and deliberate. Blood bubbled to the surface of the skin and snaked its way back towards my cocked wrist. The body's reaction to the cut fired instant pain receptors to my spinal cord, releasing chemicals which stimulated the hypothalamus in my brain. The signal to the adrenal glands released adrenaline and noradrenaline hormones to raise my heart rate, increase respiration, and slow down digestion in readiness for a situation of either fight or flight. I found the technique always worked for me. And in this instance, the standard biological response to pain served a more powerful personal purpose. To cleanse my thoughts and flush away the violent memories which haunted me. Besides, I needed to function effectively if I was taking on this group of savage criminals who'd snatched the Target. I checked my shoulder wound, which seemed to be a little less tender already, not bleeding overtly. I redressed the burnt fissure scarring, padded it with extensive wads of cotton wool, strapped it tight and then rolled an Elastoplast tube over my arm to keep everything in place. Overall movement was slightly restricted, but it would have to do. I popped a couple of painkillers into my mouth and swallowed them dry. It was time to get moving.

I gunned the engine of the Range Rover, squealing back out onto the bricks, heading in the direction of the mountains towards this place known as the Pussy Palace. I'd cover some ground and check in with Ella for intel on the way.

I drove for two hours straight, locking onto the tarmac in my eyeline. A parade of bodies from the last few days danced through my mind. The stark images played out to a backdrop of throbbing pain which continued to lick at my strength. Pangs of hunger finally roused me. I needed to reach the Target but The Hand of God was forever imploring me to slow down, prepare, wait for the right intelligence before busting a move. That meant refuelling when I had the chance, so I pulled off the dusty highway to the back of a single-pump gas station, following signposts towards a restaurant. Pulled in next to a rusted pickup truck, sporting muscular winching gear on its flatbed. The structure of the restaurant was that of a rudimentary corrugated iron box on the outside. Inside, however, it was beautifully appointed. Instead of the cheap, uncomfortable fast-food joint I had been expecting, the whole restaurant was panelled with wood and framed with lush hanging baskets. Bright green vines appeared to spring from the ceilings and walls. A pretty, brunette waitress smiled a greeting at me as I entered. She led me to a table in the corner and presented an extensive triple folding menu of delicious sounding tapas dishes. Too many options to pick from.

I scanned the dishes listed as I reflected on my situation. On the choices I'd taken in getting to where I now sat. War had made me selfish. I often felt as if the normal rules of a civilised world somehow weren't applicable to me. I'd become desensitised to emotion and empathy, as if the nerve endings of my soul might have been burnt away during my excursions to the edges of hell. My time seemed to be divided between a situation reality of danger, fear, and adrenaline; and the traumatic, inescapable flashbacks which brought memories of pain and cruelty so powerful that I would taste the gunpowder in the air, hear the screams. The scent of Maria's perfume consuming me. Surprising me at the most unexpected moments. Blurred lines. To avoid confronting this entwined confusion of states I'd settled on a strategy of pushing on the accelerator of sensory experience. Not so much as to hide, but in order to simply feel more. And to grip onto what I could of real life to stop it slipping from my grasp. But like a wet beer bottle, sometimes the harder I gripped, the faster it squeezed from my hands. I'd rebuilt my life only to have it smashed from under me. I remembered when the pain was at its worst, with only the consumption of increasing amounts of narcotics to shut it out. That is until The Hand of God had found me and dragged me free. I still drank too much and popped pain pills for fun. When alcohol was ruled out for operational purposes, I drank coffee like it was going out of fashion. And when one addiction had abated, I merely substituted it for the next. Killing had at first become normalised to me and only later had I appreciated its gratifying impact. The thrill.

There were others who understood. Who appreciated that a man like me, with certain skills and experiences, a man prepared to go to the darkest of places, who would hold his hand to the flame longer than the rest, had his specific uses. Hunter got the dirty jobs done.

My period of reflection ignited a fresh sense of self-loathing.

I ordered a beer. Slugged it down on arrival, immediately ordering a second. I was ravenous. My body needed fuel and I was certain that where I was headed I would be seeing some serious action.

I ordered with gusto and leant back in my chair, taking pleasure from observing the waitress sashaying around in her tight jeans, moving her hips between the tables as she tended to the patrons. The food duly arrived. A plethora of small circular terracotta dishes filled the table. I helped myself to liberal servings of succulent lamb, plump beans, and crispy calamari heaped together on my plate. Simple hearty food. I swallowed down the other beer, aware that the local police turned a blind eye to driving slightly under the influence, something that was still deemed to be part of the local dining culture. The waitress took her time cleaning the table. She paused, ensuring she caught my eye. 'You're British, no?' she cooed, her head tilted to one side as she dabbed a cloth at a smear of split sauce.

'Yeah. British,' I responded, noticing the cute dimples set into the soft skin of her rounded cheeks.

She continued, 'I like British. I study the language. I want to go there.' I grinned up at her and she blushed, looking down at the table before returning my gaze, eyelashes fluttering. 'British are polite. Nice. Not like Russians. They are rough in here, you know. Always causing trouble. Problems for us. For my family.'

'You get Russians in here?' I asked.

'Yes. Often, they stop here. Get drunk. Break things. Every month.'

'I see,' I muttered, eyes narrowing to slits. 'Well, that's just no good, is it? I'm on my way to find some Russian tough guys myself. Maybe the same ones if they come through this way. There's some business that needs to be attended to.'

She leant towards me and traced her fingers across my

bandaged shoulder. 'I like the sound of that. I think you're a good man.' I held her gaze for a long moment, feeling the connection. Pushed back the chair as I stood to my full height and made my way to the back of the restaurant towards the restrooms. When I reappeared, shaking my hands dry from the basin, I found her standing right there waiting, hands clasped together in front of her. She smiled, stepped towards me with hand outstretched and, in a single motion, I grabbed her wrist, pulling her back into the men's toilet, closing the door behind me with the heel of my boot.

I kissed her hard, tongue swirling inside her mouth whilst she backed up flat against the wall. Her fingers played in my hair. I responded, running a big, callused hand over her elegant throat and down over her T-shirt, holding her pert breasts. She gasped. Raised her knee upward and wrapped her leg around me as I pawed at that tight ass. She was panting ragged now and I was in no mood to take my time with this seductive señorita. Entwining my fingers into the back of her hair I tugged her head back. Kissed along the elongated neck presented to me, running my teeth along the soft flesh and inducing involuntarily whimpers and moans as she writhed again, thrusting her body hard against me. I forced her forward, so she was bent leaning against the washbasin, her pretty face, already jewelled with beads of perspiration just inches from the stained cracked mirror. Holding one arm twisted loosely behind her back I tore her jeans and black lace panties down over her smooth hips in a single movement. She groaned and arched her back, causing those curvaceous buttocks to thrust out towards me. I growled and forced myself inside her with a single, primitive thrust. 'Oh yes. Give it to me, baby,' she pleaded as I banged into her, grunting as she lifted off her feet with each individual thrust. Relished the savage intensity of our coupling for several delicious minutes before finally exploding inside her. With one arm wrapped around her waist and her feet dangling below I pulled her pelvis back onto me and ground my hips against her. Exhausted, I collapsed over the back of my little Spanish conquest, crushing her with my weight and pushing her pretty face squashed against the cold mirror.

'You are delicious,' I panted as she wriggled from underneath, turning to face me as she wriggled her jeans up from around her knees.

She stood up on tiptoes and kissed me, running her fingertips across my face and down the scar on my neck. 'Thank you, baby,' she purred in that glossy Spanish accent. 'I want you come back and visit me when you return this way. You promise me, no?' Her face was open and earnest. Challenging. 'Only after you find your Russians. I want that you make them pay for me and my family.'

I cupped her face in my hands and kissed her full, succulent lips before pushing the door to the washroom open. Tossed a wad of bills onto the table, covering the cost of the meal and a more than generous tip. *The service had been sensational.*

I stepped out into the car park, adjusting my eyes to the natural light. Noticed that the pickup was gone. I climbed into the motor, stretching out my muscles in the car seat like a spoiled house cat. Checked the phone. A location map had been sent and a red dot blinked on the screen, highlighting the location requested with links to detailed access plans from the surrounding area. The party house where the hostage had been taken was still a good few hours' drive towards Madrid from my current location. Daniel would have to sit tight for now. I sent a signal back to the team in London so that Ella could track progress and keep Mickey informed of my movements in case backup or an escape route out of there was needed. In response, a sonorous tone announced the delivery of a new message nagging for attention. Another of Ella's quasi-poignant military history quotes:

A good battle plan that you act on today can be better than a perfect one tomorrow.
   – Gen George S. Patton

I grinned and stuffed the device back into my pocket.

33

ENGLAND. LONDON. BELGRAVIA.

Boris Golich grunted as he climbed off the bony porcelain skinned whore beneath him. He wiped the sweat from his hairy belly and rolled onto his side. He fumbled for the mobile phone resting on the cabinet adjacent to the vast circular bed. Smoothed away the crumples in the black satin sheets, as if a restorative process in returning order to his thoughts. Then he scrolled pensively through a long list of messages waiting for attention on the device. The young girl groped at a puddle of skimpy clothing not long since discarded on the wooden floor. Humiliated by the brevity and general disinterest she dressed and stood awaiting instruction. The oligarch didn't look up, instead he sighed aloud, a solitary line crinkling across the bridge of his nose.

He read the message a second time. Progress had been hindered with the UK gas deal and one man at the Foreign Office in particular didn't appear to subscribe to the very British sense of fair play which Boris regarded with such alien admiration. His men on the inside had assured him that everything was in hand but, irrespective, Golich reasoned that not only had his crucial deal schedule been placed at risk but he'd also been deceived and disrespected. Which was not an acceptable situation. After all, he had the word of the British Prime Minister himself agreeing the deal. He punched in a curt reply before tossing the phone idly aside. With a wave of his hand the casually dispensed-with whore slipped from the bedroom, head bowed, without a backward glance.

He had sent an SMS; Short Message Service. The radio frequency signal instantly transmitted a micro packet of code from the handset over the ether to the nearest base station. This, in turn, forwarded the incoming signal carrying the data onto the network of the receiver's mobile phone at a slightly different frequency. The message was received only an instant later. The device in question was held by an Anglo-Russian sleeper cell deep inside the reaches of the British government.

The text read: **The old man must die.**

Derek Hemmings tapped with reticence on the shiny black door belonging to the Secretary of State for Foreign and Commonwealth Affairs at the top of the grand old building in Whitehall. Inside sat Brian Weston, Member of Parliament, Cabinet Minister, Head of Department. A man more accustomed to bringing a metaphoric cutlass to the diplomatic negotiation table than a quill and ink. Brian was Derek's ultimate boss, known ubiquitously throughout this building as the Minister. He was also the man who was about to bring Derek's career to a premature end, mere months before he was eligible for the full pension and gold watch following years of devoted service to his country. It was a painful situation but one which Hemmings had recognised was unavoidable. *Outplayed this time, old boy*, Derek thought to himself. What hurt the most was that he'd been shafted by the very bugger he detested above all.

'Come.' The solitary bark from inside the sweeping oak panelled office summoned Derek into the lion's den. He turned the door handle, wiped clammy hands onto stiff suit trousers, and entered. His throat was dry and coarse.

Shuffling inside, the slim sealed envelope quivered in his bony fingers. It contained the letter of resignation so kindly crafted by Andy Bartholomew on his behalf. He hadn't bothered reading it, knowing it would be as blunt and inelegant as the author himself. *No finesse. No class*, Derek mused with disdain. The same skills and guile were just not required like they used to be in order to forge a career within the great halls. Now it was all self-promotion and crude attempts at power base alignment. Still, if that's what's required, perhaps he should have moved with the times and he might not be in the bloody mess he was in now; and all over a principle: to do the right thing. What was the use if it didn't end up making one blind jot of difference?

The room was dark, lit only by the glow of a single lamp emanating from under an oversized shade. He could make out two figures in easy chairs positioned to one side of the spacious, richly appointed room. A tall cabinet, polished doors yawning open, displayed a copiously stocked bar and the glint of cut glass. 'Do come in, Derek. I'm told you have something for me.'

'Well yes, sir, I'm afraid I do.'

'Not your day, is it.' A flat statement. No response required.

'Can't say that it is,' Derek sniffed anyway. He stepped forward towards the cluster of chesterfields, extending his arm, offering the envelope to the Minister. 'I don't believe that any introduction is necessary?' Weston nodded towards the occupant of the chair with the back facing Derek. Charles Hand sat stony-faced, nursing a cut-glass tumbler of neat Scotch whisky partially submerging jagged splinters of ice. He turned and directed his eyes to the empty chair without breaking his scowl.

'It seems you are in grave danger, old boy,' the Minister intoned conspiratorially as he thrust a tumbler of amber liquid and chipped ice towards Derek, offering him the chair. He continued, 'This is real James bloody Bond stuff, Hemmings, and I don't know how you of all people have wound up in the middle of it. Hand will fill you in, but it doesn't make a pretty picnic. What we're about to share with you is classified, and some way above your pay grade, I may add. We're only obliged to share it because somehow you've got yourself right in the bloody centre of the whole affair and have apparently just become a target.'

Derek stiffened; he felt the blood draining from his face. 'A target?' he stammered.

Now Hand took control. 'Our team have intercepted intelligence which indicates that you are to be murdered on the direct orders of Boris Golich at some point in the next few days.'

'Murdered? This must be some sort of mistake. How?'

'Probably a staged car accident, perhaps a hit and run. Maybe a fake suicide, or perhaps the latest favourite, a bungled mugging after work somewhere.' It was a factual unemotive response.

'Christ,' Hemmings mumbled to himself. 'I suppose I didn't actually mean how... more like how come? Why me?' and his voice trailed off.

'Listen, Derek,' chimed in the Minister, 'you've put yourself in harm's way for the sake of the country. You've risked your career and you've pissed off some very serious individuals in high places in the process. It hasn't gone unnoticed.'

'I was trying to do the right thing,' came the doleful reply.

'And you bloody well have done, sir! That's why I'm refusing to accept that phoney resignation of yours.' Weston leant forward and clamped his hand onto Derek's bony knee. 'Tell him what you know, Hand.'

'Well, after our most pleasant of meetings on the London Eye, I encouraged my team to undertake an additional forensic accountancy investigation into the money trail. Ella really went the extra mile on this one. It seems that your gut feeling was correct, Golich's business empire is fuelled by dirty money via a series of Vory criminal networks and all of it gets washed clean in plain sight. The money streams come from six separate strands of Russian Mafia families, or "Bratva", which literally means "brotherhood".' Derek noted that Hand used the same splayed finger motion when he said this as at their previous meeting. 'In years gone by, Golich used to be the nominated "Obshchak" for these families, the man responsible for collecting the money from their feared brigadiers in the field and tasked with bribing the government and any other officials that got in the way. He used this position of influence to get, shall we say, a little too close to that arch-ruthless-bastard-in-chief who has occupied the office of the Russian Primacy for far too long for anyone's good. He leveraged that relationship to remove the heads of the Bratva families, literally in some cases and exile in others, and seize a stranglehold of control for himself. He now holds the position of "Pakhan", or overall head of the united family. It's the Russian equivalent of the Godfather. Boris Golich is omnipotent. And their crime money is now sanitised across the globe through a network of genuine business deals with established and respected organisations.' A glance was thrown in the direction of the Minister.

Was that a sneer? thought Derek.

Hand continued, 'And, of course, the high profile sponsorship deals in golf and motor racing. All gilded with a halo effect from the endorsement of irreproachable friends in high places and insidious political influence.'

'The PM?' proffered a guarded Derek from beneath a pair of arched silver eyebrows.

'I'm afraid so.'

'I thought playing golf at Queenwood together sounded just a little too cosy! I take it all this can be proved then. Unequivocally, I mean?'

'Before this major gas exploration deal cropped up, Golich had selected the benign environs of the European Golf Tour to funnel his dirty money through. As you know I have men on the ground right now searching for a sports agent who appears to have uncovered corruption in the sport at a high level through overt sponsor influence on players, illegal gambling and tournament fixing. We're working on the premise that this sports agent has since been kidnapped or murdered to prevent the information being exposed.' Derek listened, chewing off an errant hang nail from a much-beleaguered thumb. 'As a body hasn't surfaced, we're working on the assumption that the Target must be withholding access to this information. The alternative that they've disposed of the body is not one that we can bring ourselves to consider right now when there's a chance that he's still alive. Especially given the Vory have never been shy about leaving their victims on display to perpetuate their terrible reputation.' Hand gave a solemn shake of his head to emphasise the point. 'It's apparent that they're ruthless in achieving their own ends and will stop at nothing to meet them. The Pakhan won't deviate course. Money talks and, given his immense reserves of capital, when Boris Golich has something to say people listen very carefully indeed. Infiltrating the governing body of a sport to sanitise his company's image and launder some petty cash is, however, small potatoes compared to this Falklands gas deal, as you well know.' Hand nodded towards Derek. 'That deal impacts real people's lives, their jobs and their families. He's literally played world governments off against each other in their bid to woo him. And once you have entered the spider's web, it appears that there's no going back, regardless of who you may be.' The men let this hang there for a while as they considered the implications.

'He sounds capable of anything,' spluttered Derek in despair, shifting uncomfortably in the armchair from buttock to buttock.

'Indeed so. The local mayors in regions where Golich's organisation owns assets, Russia, Kurdistan and Ukraine, are replaced at will or simply vanish if they don't play ball. It's the same with dissenting journalists. Anyone who crosses the little bastard. We have evidence surrounding a protest group of eight Uzbekistani wives from blue collar families, angry at the poor treatment of their husbands following an accident at a refinery that left people maimed. They pursued one of his companies through the courts. Each woman was found beaten and raped in their own homes on the same night. It was no coincidence.'

'Son of a bitch,' snorted the Minister, before draining his glass.

'It gets worse,' continued Hand, voice unwavering. 'It was hard to find but there's a certain company located in the Cayman Islands, one Hamilton Advisory, of which the sole director and employee attended Eton with our very own upstanding Prime Minister. It turns over seventy million a year and serves as principal advisor to a group of luxury developments situated on the Caspian Sea. These are "black holes", vast chasms for Mafia to pour dirty money into and remove again freshly laundered. The residencies and casino resorts are supposedly constructed with the highest quality materials to the finest specifications, fit for the most demanding Emirate Sheik, but they never see a single visitor. The companies that build them for Golich use local work gangs, forced labour and cheap materials. If they even get built at all, that is. They're protected by local government from tax implications and inspection. A torrent of fee capital is directed from Hamilton Advisory via two numbered bank accounts, both which are attributable back to the PM.'

'I'm afraid, Derek,' growled the Minister with censorious intent, 'that it's become clear the PM is up to his neck in this for personal gain and he's intent on committing Great Britain to a shotgun wedding with a notorious gangster. All under the noble subterfuge of creating countless jobs that will forge his legacy.'

'I bloody knew something was amiss,' said Derek, stunned at the news. 'And Golich wants to bump me off, I suppose, because I've been a thorn in his side and delayed the timings of the deal?'

'And challenged his authority, don't forget that,' chimed in the Minister. 'He has an impatient intolerance for insubordination it seems.' He looked pleased with himself for the spontaneous alliteration. 'And you've gone and pissed the little thug off, Hemmings. Not the done thing really.'

Hand levelled things out again. 'We've uncovered a few others in Whitehall on Golich's payroll as well, including your friend, Andy Bartholomew.'

'I always knew he was a toad!' the old civil servant crowed in triumph, brightening up for the first time. 'What happens now then?'

'Well, for starters, it's imperative that you lie low,' said Hand issuing a directive. 'We've arranged for you to stay in the building tonight, in the executive suite. Call Alice and tell her you'll be pulling an all-nighter. Make it convincing, the less she knows about this the better.'

'She's not in any danger, is she?'

'Nothing immediate that we've detected. The sleeper cell has orders to eliminate you alone for now, although we know the Vory have a history of using family members as leverage and to exact revenge. The Minister has authorised a plain-clothes officer to be placed outside your home as a precaution, Derek.

I've requested that he be joined undercover by Phil Manning, one of the guys from the Unit who's been working the Golich connection in London. Alice will be safe, I can promise you that.'

'This is all rather unpalatable,' murmured Hemmings, wringing his hands.

'We need to wait and let this play out a little further, so we won't be disrupting Bartholomew in situ just yet. We need further firm evidence of collusion and corruption before arrests can be made.'

'Indeed,' added in the Minister, 'the PM is a powerful man. Many have underestimated him at their peril. I'm going to bloody-well make sure he swings for this. We'll take the whole sordid matter to the press before Britain commits to a deal with that devious Russian crook.'

'Oh, I'm certain that you will, Minister,' Derek replied from the corner of his mouth, 'and in the process take the plaudits for preventing such a debacle on the international stage. A move that will no doubt reflect well on someone with aspirations for the top job.'

'Why of course,' came the dry response. 'Someone's got to show some leadership to get us out of this mess. But your part won't be forgotten either, Hemmings. You'll have your pick of where you want to go next, Commander Hemmings of MI6, is it? If you've still got the fight left in you, old man.' He flashed a wolfish smile and settled back into the chesterfield, glowing with overt satisfaction. The Minister had never apologised for being ambitious.

The Hand of God got to his feet. He didn't hide his scowl. 'Gentlemen, when you've quite finished congratulating yourselves, there's much work remaining to be done. There are lives still hanging in the balance.'

34

The afternoon tranquillity shattered with the sound of the wooden door being kicked open. The barn flooded with light; a myriad of falling dust particles floating captive within the sunbeams. 'Find him,' barked the order over the snarl of straining dogs. Men spread out across the floor kicking over equipment and rifling through grain bins, heaping armfuls of produce onto the floor. Black Leather Jacket Man cut an imposing figure fixed stationary before the stack of hay bales. Shoulders back, legs apart, he brandished his weapon of choice nestling within his hairy muscular arms like a sleeping baby. The Uzi. Blowback-operated, select-fire and closed-bolt. The modern version has its grip recalibrated from Israeli engineer Uziel Gal's original 1948 design so it can be operated with both hands to deliver greater control during full automatic fire given it's such a lightweight firearm. The gun has a cyclic rate of fire of twelve hundred rounds per minute with minimum recoil and kickback. It's capable of delivering punishing volleys of bullets at subsonic speed, which can rip any living thing apart within a deployment of fifty metres. To its Russian master the gun was simply an old friend with shared memories of putting the hammer down on the streets of St Petersburg in the aftermath of Perestroika where he had served as one of the Bratva's most feared Boyeviks. The term whose literal meaning was 'warrior' was hard earned amongst the Vory as a family enforcer. The Russian letters 'МИР' tattooed on the back of his hand denoted the pride taken in a violent and murderous past.

He now held that same hand aloft to command silence. The group responded, halting their frenzied activity where they stood. Black Leather Jacket Man grinned. 'I know you in there, little bitch,' he called out, mimicking a child in song. 'Come out and say hello, Daniel, or you going to eat my gun right now.' The group waited for a reaction. Nothing stirred. The enforcer wiped the corner of his mouth, spat onto the floor and in a sudden movement jerked the barrel of the Uzi upward spraying a rapid burst of bullets scorching into the haystack. He unleashed the entire clip; finger tense and white from the pressure on the trigger long after the magazine had extinguished itself. He ran forward, a maniacal grin fixed on his face and using the butt of the gun began to smash into the dishevelled hay pile, conducting a frantic search. Two others joined and, within a minute, the entire stack had been torn apart. Loose hay was strewn everywhere across the concrete floor with dust and errant scraps descending all around. There was no sign of the escaped prisoner.

Ten feet away, Daniel Ratchet had witnessed the drama through a crack in the wooden barrel within which he crouched, submerged to his nose in stagnant water spread thick with a film of algae. He'd considered the haystack to be the perfect hiding spot. With his heart pounding inside his chest he'd been transported back to frenetic childhood games of hide and seek as packs of energetic cousins sought him out. Realising that if a hiding place was obvious to him it might also be to his pursuers, he'd changed his mind and squeezed into the water butt, soaking himself to the skin in the process. Cold, frightened and trapped, Daniel didn't dare to move a sinew.

From within the darkness he watched transfixed as the little girl in oversized T-shirt and flip-flops, who'd been playing on the dirt track outside, was frogmarched into the barn. She was shoved to the floor at the feet of Black Leather Jacket Man, who reached down and hoisted the child up by a fistful of hair. He watched her amused as she squirmed and screeched like a scolded cat. 'You see man in barn? Did you see man go in barn or no, little pig?' he shouted. Unable to form the words, perhaps unable to understand, the child kept shaking her head as tears streamed down her grubby face. He called out into the open space of the barn. 'Daniel, listen to me good. You come out and say hello or I gut this little pig right here.' He pulled a blade from a sheath on his belt and held it tight against the girl's throat as she struggled for breath through uneven gasps and sobs. He called out again, louder this time. 'This is your fault, Daniel. You can save her if you come say hello. Don't cause this problem for little pig. Come out and talk.'

Exhausted. Defeated. No move left to make and no energy or will to make it. Trapped. This was finally, at last, the very end. Daniel emerged from the barrel at the side of the farm building. Water poured off him from every angle onto the floor. He was a total mess. The putrid water stung his eyes. The men rushed towards him as one. His bedraggled frame was hauled up and thrown onto the unforgiving floor. Shaking his head to clear it, he struggled to his knees, opening his eyes in time to find a meaty fist closing in at prodigious speed. It smashed into the bridge of his nose and Daniel felt the cartilage splintering, blood spurting. He reached up to his face, a reaction to the pain. As he did so another blow rained in, forcing his palm to bang hard against his lips, knocking teeth back into his mouth in the process. He grunted in agony. A swinging boot to the groin put him down again. Gasping for breath on the cold stone floor, he watched the girl's skinny brown legs scurrying away as she escaped to freedom through the open barn door.

35

SPAIN. CARASCALLE, MIMBRERAS 4, 03201 ELCHE. 2124 HRS.

The Range Rover came to a stop alongside a tall metal fence obscured with conifer trees which lined straight as far as the eye could see. The back of my thumbnail traced along the groove of my scar as I popped a soft pack of cigarettes, catching a Marlboro between my teeth. Sparked it alight, pleased with the trick. I hadn't passed another car for almost half an hour or so since pulling off the main road. I'd been circling the grounds of the venue that the caddies used to decompress, where Daniel had been taken. Checking several possible discreet entry points, identified by Ella at base, which I could use to launch an assault on the party house.

I allowed dusk to start drawing in before making a move. Grabbed the canvas bag of assorted toys that Mickey had put together; namely stun grenades, ammo clips, and a couple of spare pieces. I was tooled up and itching to get inside to spring the Target.

We'd identified a vulnerable section of mesh on the metal fence at the side of the property, out of view from the main house. It swayed and folded awkwardly under my bulk as I scaled it, making it hard to control. I flipped over the top, landing on my feet in a crouching position. An automatic video camera rotated through an arching sweep of the perimeter along either side of the grounds. Ella had calculated that each sweep took twelve seconds before it would return to cover my entry point. I commando-crawled forward into a clump of bushes a couple of metres beyond the range of visibility. I'd cleared the first hurdle. Allowed my heart rate to settle before my habitual double-check that the Beretta was loaded. I regarded most guns as aesthetically pleasing and this piece was a thing of simple beauty. Produced by the oldest active manufacturer of firearms in the world, with over fifteen family generations of Italian craftsmanship dating back to the sixteenth century. They'd supplied weapons for every major European war for the last four hundred years and I found that provenance reassuring. If the guys inside were anything near as mean and ugly as the giant I'd tangled with back at the caddy shack, then this was going to be a war to remember. I scanned the grounds for signs of guards or dogs. I knew they were out there but saw nothing. Darkness was descending and remaining stationary wasn't a smart option unless I wanted to take a bullet in the back of my skull.

Comrades had often told me that they were bewildered by my ability to recall minute details from the heat of battle, things that they'd missed in the fight for survival. It was a useful skill for debriefing after a skirmish but I'm not someone gifted with photographic memory recall. Like the sportsman who can still smell the grass from a match they played twenty years ago, when in a heightened state of arousal, deep in the thick of the fight, everything just seemed to seep into me. To drink in the detail, to feel the energy, to experience enhanced colours and smells. The merry-go-round slowed down. It was my music.

Edging closer, I took in more of the property. Built on several tiers, it sprawled out in an ungainly design, almost embarrassed by its own vulgarity. Rather than retaining the beautiful traditions of classic Spanish architecture, the house and outbuildings were a mix of extravagant modern opulence and overdone kitsch. The marbled drive was dominated by a water feature which would have been out of place at a palace three times the size of the main house. Sculptures of five life-sized stone stallions reared up out of foaming jet streams which shot twenty feet into the air. The front of the house boasted pillars fit for a Roman emperor's mausoleum, framing a door which looked as if it might hold an army at bay for weeks. The unmistakeable pulse of bad Eurotrash dance beats made its way towards me over the grounds. I kept moving forward. Crouched low. Finger comforted by the torque of trigger pressure.

The rear of the property was a similar grotesque marriage of bad taste and ostentation. A massive swimming pool, in the shape of a palm tree, took up the majority of the space. It came complete with jacuzzi, plus a deserted bar in the centre of the main pool surrounded with stone columns for stools. A number of brightly coloured lilos, rubber rings, and what appeared to be an inflatable sex doll floating face down, occupied the still water. The music was louder from the back, patio doors wide open. From my vantage point in the shrubbery, I studied a tableau of figures on the deck and inside the house through the glass doors. A woman sporting a skimpy hot pink bikini was dancing with her hands in the air between two men, one of whom slugged from a square shouldered bottle of spirits. Three serious looking guys, competing for the accolade of heaviest stubble, played cards round a table with piles of notes and coins set before them. Fat cigars rested in a crowded ashtray, a magnum revolver had been discarded without a thought upon the glass top.

The house seemed crowded. I considered the options. If I was to spring the Target with the minimum of grief, then I'd need surprise on my side and that wasn't going to be achieved by announcing myself with a blazing gun battle upfront. I'd revisit the access points to the building which Ella had identified and uploaded to my phone. At that moment, a fat man in long shorts and socks, protruding stomach slung low over his belt, staggered out of the double doors. Wrapped within the grasp of his thick arm was the squirming skinny body of a teenage girl dressed in heels and a yellow bikini. His other hand clasped a bottle of tequila by the neck. Clearly in a party mood, he was trying to encourage the others to join in the revelry. Swearing loudly in a Liverpudlian accent I clocked him as Billy Boy, the caddy. An unpleasant character and holder of a sizeable arrest record, mainly for bar fights and vandalism. One charge was for indecent assault on a German tourist who'd rebuked his incessant attentions only to be lifted off her chair, laid on top of the bar and held down with one arm whilst he buried his face under her skirt in front of a baying crowd. She'd fled in tears to the police station, whilst afterwards Billy would claim to all and sundry that she'd loved every second. The bite marks and months of victim counselling which followed, told of a very different story. His identification at least verified I was in the right place.

Unnoticed, I doubled back in the direction I'd started out from. Try as I might, I'd worked out a long time ago that I really wasn't cut out for stealth. With my build and mindset, I was more of an agent of brute force, not cut out for reconnaissance detail. Some of my buddies in the mob had been perfect at it. Small wiry guys who would run all day carrying bergens packed with three times their body weight. Men and women who could fit into tight awkward spaces and sit camouflaged for hours, sometimes days, patient and invisible. Tough as nails those soldiers. But I was under no illusion that Tom Hunter was more the proverbial sledgehammer which the top brass would use to crack a walnut. It was well documented in dispatches that I relished a tear up, something borne out by the rows of tin which had been slapped across my chest. That was before I got myself kicked out for being a naughty boy though. Even The Hand of God couldn't protect me when matters of so-called national security had apparently been compromised.

I tracked around the side of property, keeping low. The darkness was drawing in and, from what I'd seen, these guys weren't treating security as their number one priority. I was confident that I'd remained undetected, or I figured I'd have known something about it by now. I located the ground floor window which had been identified as a potential entry point. It was open on the inside for ventilation, with a metal screen in place for rudimentary protection. Behind the window lay a storage room; a graveyard for sun loungers and parasols, a washing line contraption and a number of standard household appliances. I confirmed that I was unobserved with a quick scan of the area before drawing the hunting knife from my boot and jacking it between the window frame and screen. With the slightest leverage it pinged out and flipped back into the room with an angry rattle over the concrete floor. This was clearly just a cursory effort at security, one designed more to keep out stray cats than trained killers.

Resting my forearms on the window ledge I heaved myself up so that my torso was half-wedged through the open space, legs dangling below against the wall of the house. It was a tight squeeze but by twisting and wriggling my shoulders so that I fitted through the frame I could use my hands out in front to take my weight on the floor. I walked forward on my palms in a wheelbarrow motion, legs following behind. Pain shot through my shoulder. I ground my teeth and completed the untidy dismount in a tangle of limbs. There were no points for style, all that mattered was that I was inside.

The corridor leading from the storage room was empty. I would work from the ground up, checking and clearing each room as I went. Hunting the Target and neutralising threats. Aside from the storage room, which was little more than a drab concrete box, the rest of the house had seen some serious money thrown at the décor and furnishings. It was a colour scheme predominantly consisting of reds and golds. The floors were laid with polished black wood. Delicate ornamental tables stood in splendid isolation displaying individual artefacts, statues or sculptures. Huge canvases of modern art, splashed with eccentric swirls of paint, adorned the walls at every turn. For a guy like me with few material possessions, who'd lived in the clothes on his back from job to job, country to country, over the last few years, it seemed a little overblown to say the least.

Checked the first two rooms and found them empty. The first, a spacious gym with hard plastic flooring, was littered with oversized weight bars and dumbbells. A token exercise bike had been pushed to the corner. Plasma screens on each wall blared out music videos to an invisible audience. The second room was dominated by an imposing oval dining table anchored at its centre by a foursome of chunky silver candlesticks. Formal upholstered chairs tucked underneath. An oil painting of Moscow's Red Square, with the historic Saint Basil's cathedral captured like an enchanted castle, hung at one end. A spectacular picture window looked out across the brown hills to the east.

The corridor's third door had been left ajar. Without needing to check, a succession of animalistic grunts emanating from inside left no doubt that it was occupied. A voluptuous black woman was kneeling on the couch facing towards the door, sandwiched between two men. She was being hammered at one end by a guy covered in spindly tattoos, ink over his arms and torso like the doodles on a bored schoolkid's desk. All stars and crosses and sickles and scythes. Jeans untidy around his ankles, a black T-shirt was rolled halfway up revealing his matted hairy stomach. At her front, another equally unpleasant character was attending to her mouth with remorseless aggression. He tugged at the nipples of her huge chocolate-coloured breasts, which were flopped over the edge of the couch, using them to pull her plump lips closer. He had his back to the door. The three of them were absorbed in their feverish joint enterprise.

One of the men called to the other. 'Next time we come back here, we stop off again at the roadside restaurant and take our sweet time with that hot little waitress. I want to tie her father up and make him watch as we tag team her too. Remember how we laughed when Sorlov made the bitch dance for us?' It was a Russian accent.

'Nice idea. She'll take some punishment and then serve us beer all night long.' They laughed and slapped hands in the air, pleased with themselves. *Russians, golf caddies, party in full swing – just like Razor had said*. It was all I needed to know.

I reached round the door frame and fired over the left shoulder of the blow job recipient into the forehead of the man facing me as he took the surprised girl from behind. His eyes remained open for the short journey it took the .22 calibre bullet to bore through his skull, demolishing the frontal lobes, penetrating the cortex and exiting through the cerebellum at the back of his brain. The devastating damage was delivered in just a fraction of a second. He collapsed backwards, a look of ecstasy still frozen across his face. Time now hung in glorious suspension as everything happening thereafter seemed to have slowed right down. His partner in crime spun as I moved forward into the room to engage him. A burst of short steps before slicing his throat in a single rapid motion. Blood glugged and spurted from the artery in his neck like a can of beer shaken before opening. The girl looked up, shrieking unintelligibly, her face and naked torso now drenched in claret. I reached across, slapping her with the back of my hand off the couch and onto the floor in order to shut her up. I bounded over the bleeding man as he scrabbled on the polished floor creating frantic patterns in his own voluminous bloodletting. Stepped around the couch to prevent the girl from crawling away for help. Behind me the splutter and gurgling of a man's life draining away as he clutched in vain at his throat.

'Quiet, unless you want to get smoked too,' I growled into her terrified face. Tears seeped through thick false eyelashes. Her glossy lips trembled. The message was clear but, in case she didn't speak English, I held the gun to her head and put my finger to my lips demonstrating that silence was required or there'd be consequences. I pulled out my phone and tapped a photograph of Daniel that Ella had provided. 'Where is this man?' I asked slow and clear, holding the screen in front of her. The woman was sobbing. She looked at the picture and shook her head. I asked again, softening my voice. 'Is this man here? Is he in this house?'

Still trembling, she shook her head again. 'No man. Not here,' was all she said.

~

Shouts from the garden made it clear that I'd been compromised. I hadn't used the silencer on the Beretta. Given the number of guests in this place, I figured that I wouldn't be ghosting in and out unnoticed anyway. Might as well make an entrance. And from what I'd seen about the way that these guys partied, it wouldn't be a problem if there was a little noise and a little mess whilst we got to know each other.

Leaving the room in carnage behind me, I pulled back into the corridor and then entered the main hall. A barrage of sub-machine gun fire poured down at me from the first-floor landing, atop a broad staircase. I wasn't hit but the marble floor at my feet was chewed up badly enough for me not to ponder the merits of holding my position whilst he readjusted his aim. I rolled forward and took cover behind a potted palm tree growing inside a huge terracotta jar. The machine gun rattled again, pouring relentless swathes of bullets into the walls all around me. I returned fire, pumping three rounds out in the general direction that the shooting was coming from, buying some time. Sprang a stun grenade and tossed it up onto the first-floor balcony. The explosion is designed to elicit sensory deprivation to those within the blast vicinity using the combination of a huge sudden noise impact and white light flashes. It's quick, unexpected, and highly effective. I tossed the bomb as I broke from my tropical cover point covering my ears. The distraction had its desired effect and I made it directly under the balcony unchallenged, escaping the sweeping range of the machine gun. The impact of the stun grenade soon faded and I heard movement again above my head; a regrouping. I strained my ears, adjusted my position and then, holding the Beretta upwards, emptied the remains of my clip into the plaster ceiling. A heavy thud and shouts of pain told me that I'd hit the unsuspecting shooter standing directly above.

These guys were packing real heat. I was outnumbered and outgunned. At this point checking room by room throughout this mansion wasn't going to deliver the rapid results needed. A hostage would take me to Daniel, though, and provide some bargaining power to get us out alive.

I pushed against a closed door and found myself inside a games room boasting an empty drinks bar and full-sized pool table with a scatter of balls across its immaculate blue baize. On one wall hung an eight-by-eight-foot square mirror with a thick wooden frame. The other supported a cinema-sized plasma screen, showing a pornographic movie. The feeling was like boarding a ghost ship, cast adrift on the ocean without her crew. I had turned to back out the way I'd come when an in-built cupboard sprang open. Two burly assailants burst forward wielding pool cues. Seems they'd been shooting a game together and enjoying the flick when the gun fight in the hallway alerted them to an intruder and they'd holed up until now. The choice of pool cues in their hands told me they weren't packing heat. Raised my gun with cold detachment and squeezed the trigger.

It clicked. No shot. The clip was spent, and the timing couldn't be worse. My complacency melted as the first guy reached me a second later, using the thick end of the pool cue to smash at my wrist, causing me to drop my piece. Much use that it was anyway. I pivoted, turning to stamp down on the inside of his knee, making him buckle. As he slumped, I caught him with a powerful uppercut, the crunch of teeth against my fist. Caught his shoulders as he went down and slammed his face into the edge of the pool table rendering him out cold. Three moves. Three seconds. Punishing and precise. His mate came at me with a vengeance. He was a big solid lump, probably six foot four and heavyset with it. At a blind guess I would have placed him at nineteen stones of fat and muscle. *Too much weightlifting without the speed-work keeps you slow*, I observed to myself, remembering the words of a fearsome Maori hand-to-hand combat instructor who The Hand of God had used to drill us. Size and strength mean less than the precision of action and taking the right combat decisions at the right times. Hit first and hit hard. And do whatever it takes to get out alive.

But he was in at close quarters now, real close, and speed wasn't a factor. He was able to force me over the pool table, choking me from behind with the cue. He pinned me down squeezing the wood against my neck for all he was worth. This was tight. I was using all of my strength to counter the choke, to just about keep the cue from crushing my windpipe. It was an even match. If I couldn't wriggle free somehow before I blacked-out then this was going to end very badly. I kicked out but he used his massive thighs to pin my legs under the table, leaning every ounce of bulk over and on top of me. Snarling face inches from mine; close enough to smell the stench of tobacco on his breath. Managed to wedge my right hand between the cue and my throat. I used my left to blindly grope around on the table for a ball. Checked myself. Given the position my body was trapped in, trying to smash a pool ball against his head wouldn't do much damage and might only serve to piss this animal off even more. So, I gambled. Recoiling my left arm to generate leverage, I flung the ball as hard and fast as I could up and into the mirror hanging behind us. It shattered with the impact, crashing showers of razor-sharp shards flying down onto the back of my assailant. The shock loosened his grip for just an instant. The heavy mirror frame followed seconds later collapsing from its hook onto the Russian's neck. Pieces of mirror had lanced my face and I could feel trails of blood snaking their way down my cheeks. I heaved the brute up, rolling to one side. He shook the mirror from his back and lumbered at me again. I wasn't going to let myself get into a bear hug with fatty again, so I reached across him diagonally and grabbed the wrist of his right arm as he flung out a fist. Bent at the knee to grab at the handle of my knife, left hand to left boot. Rose fast, pivoting in an arch on my toes.

Hurled a left hook, stabbing the blade inside my attacker's right ear. He howled and I thrust forward, twisting and driving the knife deeper, working to bore it into his head. Slammed my right fist into his solar plexus and watched him sag to the floor like a sack of wet cement. There was no way these guys were all simple golf caddies. They knew how to shoot and they knew how to fight dirty. My guess was ex-Soviet military. A dangerous breed.

I reloaded a fresh magazine clip; wiped the blade clean on the shirt of my recently deceased pool partner. I needed to get out of this place before I was overwhelmed but as yet there was no sign of the Target.

The pounding of feet alerted me to new company. Perhaps the guys from the card game, perhaps more guards. I exited the games room and decided to break for the stairs. Daniel was surely being held captive on the upper floor. Three guys packing an assortment of small arms entered my line of vision. I crouched to one knee, exhaled to steady myself as they ran, and banged off a round, catching one of the group flush in the thigh. He flew backwards like a cigarette tossed from the window of a speeding car. I rolled a stun grenade towards the others and, using the flash as cover, bounded across to the stairs, firing at intervals in their general direction. Checked for contact around the stairwell but found it to be clear. I took the steps three at a time, firing continuously ahead to ensure a clear path and pin back any ambush in waiting. Reached the top deck with a dive flat onto my stomach, rolling to the side and away from the expected position of arrival. A burning sensation like the stab of a red-hot poker flushed through my injured shoulder as I landed. The pain had been masked until now by the rush of so much adrenaline. I shrugged it off, growling. There was a more urgent matter at hand.

I scoped the surroundings. The centre of the upstairs landing was occupied by a figure slouched against the wall in a pool of blood, head resting upon chest, a redundant AK-47 machine gun upon his thighs. My welcoming committee in the hallway had bled out from the bullets I'd hit him with from below. Judging by the puddle of blood spooling around his inner thighs, death would have been as slow and painful as much as it would've been unexpected.

I took to my feet. Pressing on, ignoring the emphatic dull ache in my shoulder, I fired a volley of bullets into the base of the closed door of the nearest room to drive any inhabitants back. Kicked it open and entered behind the Beretta. Beyond the bed, handcuffed to a thin metal pipe that ran the length of the skirting board, two women sat huddled together on the floor. I say women but these were little more than emaciated teenagers, heavily made-up and wearing tawdry see-through nightdresses of the sort that might be hanging in the window of a grubby backstreet sex shop. I recalled the name that the caddies gave this place: 'Pussy Palace'. From what I'd seen so far, this fine establishment was doing its best to rigorously comply with the Trade Descriptions Act. It was clear that these girls were being kept locked up like this until their talents were required again by the guests of the house. It made me sick.

'It's okay. I'm not here to hurt you. Don't worry. Do you speak English?' I soothed.

'Yes. Oh Lord. Thank you,' one of the girls replied behind pretty tear-stained eyes. 'I'm American. She's Russian. You've got to help us. These monsters tricked us into coming here weeks ago from Puerto Banus. They had a yacht. Told us there was a party, told us there would be modelling scouts there.' She scrambled to her knees.

Moving fast and keeping one eye out on the door behind me I ushered the girls to scoot to the side before putting a single bullet through the pipe; shredding it. A heavy stamp with a size fourteen combat boot broke it apart and I helped the girls to slide their cuffs off between the two broken pieces. They'd have to figure out how to get them off their wrists later for themselves but at least they could run and make a break for freedom now. 'Are you okay?' I asked.

'I don't know,' she replied shaking her head as the tears flowed. She looked pretty broken. The Russian girl kept her eyes to the floor. I pulled out the phone and tapped on the picture of Daniel. 'Have you seen this man in the house? He's been kidnapped. Do you know if they're keeping him here too?'

'There's no one else here. This is a party house. We've been raped in every room of this shithole. The guests come and go. So do the whores. The guards aren't sober enough to hold a prisoner here that isn't for their own entertainment.' Her face was contorted with disgust as she spoke, her hands covered her body in an involuntary movement as if to offer some kind of protection from the memory.

'You've got to be kidding me,' I hissed under my breath. 'This is the wrong place. I've got to move out and move now. You girls make sure you get the hell out of here too. Run and don't look back. You sure don't want to be here when those animals come looking for you.'

I'm not paid to be a hero. I'm paid to spring hostages and bring them back. Dead or alive. I need to focus on the job in hand and do whatever it takes to make that happen. I didn't look back. Didn't give a second thought to leaving those girls behind to fend for themselves. Perhaps I'm wired up the wrong way.

Perhaps my sense of morality is distorted. Not all of the Targets we rescue necessarily deserve to be saved, nor are they all wanted free for the right reasons either. It's not for me to make those calls. The only thing that can be counted on is money. In that sense I'm no more than a mechanical toy soldier moving forward in the direction in which I'm pointed. And I sure as shit don't consider myself to be a good person. I ducked back onto the landing and made it across to a first-floor window to peer out across the grass. A well-muscled man in a black tank top and jeans clutched a pump action shotgun to his chest. Standing with his back to a garden wall, illuminated by the light from the house and the brilliant silver crescent moon, he was a picture of nervous energy as he cast anxious glances to all angles. My best guess was that he'd heard the commotion, seen the litany of dead bodies and was now well and truly spooked. I didn't know how many more of these guys there were here, but my priority was getting out in one piece, finding the Range Rover, and finding a new lock on the Target's whereabouts without wasting any more precious time. I just had to hope that this wild goose chase hadn't made me too late to get to the Target alive. Right now, Tank Top Boy was standing in the way of my rapid exit.

I eased open the window and, crouching at the corner, nuzzled the barrel of the Beretta through the open gap. I whistled once. Loud and shrill. Tank Top Boy couldn't help but turn to look and as he presented his torso to me square on, I double-squeezed out slugs in quick succession, tearing two adjacent holes into his stomach. He dropped the shotgun, fumbling his hands across the gaping wounds in a desperate attempt to stem the blood which was already beginning to seep down the paving cracks in the direction of the swimming pool. The dying man sat, a twisted look of bewilderment across his face. For all his caution, he'd seen neither the gun nor the shooter who'd sealed his fate.

I flipped open the window and assessed the drop. Twelve, maybe fifteen feet to the ground. I arched my body, levering through the gap onto the window ledge, so that my legs hung dangling below like an oversized child perched on a playground swing. The gardens were deserted. I pushed myself off and landed on the soft grass below, rolling into a textbook parachute drop landing. More pain. I hauled myself up and set out sprinting across the well-tended lawn, until I found the section of bent metal fencing that I had entered over. It was harder doing it in reverse with the metal grill bending towards me. With no toeholds to power off, I had to jump up vertical and grab the very top of the fence, using brute strength to pull my body up and eventually to swing a leg over the top in the most graceless of efforts. Gravity did the rest. I landed on the other side of the fence, banging my heels into the deck. I took a moment to steady myself on my feet. Checked all directions for pursuers, with my senses prickling with the anticipation of dangers in the darkness. All clear and time to move out.

36

'Please relax. May I offer you a glass of cold water to refresh yourself?' Sergei Krostanov stood over Daniel Ratchet, bathing him in the warmth of his most benevolent of smiles. The disenfranchised body was upright on a hard-backed chair bound with rope across feet, thighs and upper torso. Hands were trussed behind back. The exhausted amalgam of flesh, bone and muscle was limp save for the tight support of its bonds.

'It's good to see you again, Daniel. My colleagues tell me you have been on a little, how shall we say, excursion? What is it, Daniel? You want to leave us, is that it? Don't you like our hospitality? It's a little rude to repay such generous hosting in this way, don't you think? To leave, without even so much as a goodbye.' The face remained impassive. A succession of noises were being received by the ears, but they were incomprehensible as words, washing over him, like waves lapping at the seashore. The brain didn't know if it could induce the vocal cords to respond, for the lips to form words.

'Dan-i-el,' Sergei cooed his name like it was a verse from a nursery rhyme; a lullaby in his ear. 'Daniel, you have something that I need and I'm afraid I will have to insist you tell me where it is.' The mouth opened. Throat straining to speak. The biological mechanisms attempted to respond to the command issued from deep inside the brain. But the mouth was dry. No sounds came out. He tried again. Until finally his throat croaked. Words were formed. 'I don't know what you mean.'

'Daniel, I know that you and the incorrigible Mr Wallace have been spreading dreadful lies about me.' Sergei spoke with a calm, measured voice. Impeccable English with that irrefutable thread of hard-boned Russian accent cutting through it. He locked onto Daniel with a cold unblinking stare. Piercing blue eyes so pale they could be mistaken for grey. Shark's eyes. It was an innate recognition by the prey from deep within his primitive reptilian brainstem. No window to the soul. *Perhaps he has no soul.*

'I haven't, Sergei. I promise.'

'Liar.' The retort was sharp and followed by a swift, crisp slap striking Daniel across the cheek. His face stung hot with a crimson flush of shame. 'You have been seeking to implicate me in the corruption of players and the manipulation of tournament outcomes. I'm sure you appreciate that this cannot be tolerated.'

'It was Bob's idea. I wasn't sure. I just wanted to check. Things didn't add up.'

'You have some documents and a video I believe, purporting to substantiate this, Daniel. They are stored remotely on your personal tablet device. We cannot find this. I want you to tell me where it is. I don't wish to be forced to hurt you.' The words remained even, measured in tone.

The eyes staring back towards the pacing figure before them were vacant. It seemed to infuriate his interrogator. 'Daniel, your parents have been calling and calling. They're very worried, Daniel. They are also very annoying. They have been upsetting my friend, Mr Randy Hughes, wanting to know what's going on.

Have you been found yet? What are we doing to help? Boo hoo. Do you think we should give them some news, Daniel? Good news perhaps? Or maybe some bad news? Maybe send them an appendage from your worthless broken body to shut them up? Do you think that might work?' The torso twisted and strained on the chair.

Sergei's face suddenly softened. His tone no longer taunting and cruel. 'Come now. I merely wish to clear my name, Daniel. You can understand this, can you not, my friend? I need to see what information you have in this respect so that I may simply defend my honour and prove that I'm a worthy ambassador for our great game of golf. Do you remember how kind, how generous I was towards you when you needed help?'

'You've kidnapped me, half killed me to get that tablet. You're a freaking psycho.'

'Give it to me!' Sergei flashed with a sudden surge of anger, his immaculate diction slipping.

'I can't tell you,' Daniel said, half pleading.

'Stubborn boy,' he murmured, shaking his head. And then, almost as a throwaway afterthought, 'You'll pay for your insolence and then you will tell us.' He casually lit a cigarette, inhaling as he surveyed the captive like a predator looming over a burrow of helpless newborns. He circled around the back of the chair and bent down until his face was so close that Daniel could feel the warm breath on the hairs of his neck. He held the glowing tip of the lit cigarette aloft, moving it to within a centimetre of Ratchet's left eye. The smoke spiralled into the eyeball. Panicking, blinking furiously as he struggled against the ropes, tears trickled freely down Daniel's cheek.

'Is this so important that it is worth losing an eye for, Daniel?' Sergei enquired, with genuine interest.

I can't betray you, Matilda. My dear, beautiful Matilda. I just can't.

'Please. I don't know where it is. I gave it to Michael. He has it. I swear.'

'Michael Hausen? The physiotherapist at the training centre?'

'Yes, yes. I gave it to him to look after.'

'We will check for this. If you're lying to me, I shall be most displeased, I can assure you.' Sergei straightened up to leave, before reconsidering. He leant back in towards Daniel. With a casual snap of the wrist he stubbed the cigarette onto the side of the captive's neck, extinguishing it fully before tossing the charred butt onto the floor. He exited without another word, the cell behind him resounding with rabid screams.

37

I punched the contact number into the new burner phone. The morning sun had roused me from my slumber, stretched out in the Range Rover, pulled up in a lay-by in some unremarkable dusty Spanish town; the kind littered with empty high-rise blocks that no one wanted to live in.

'Where the bloody hell have you been, Hunter?' Ella exclaimed with a well-practised tone of injured innocence. 'We've been trying to reach you.'

'I've been a little busy. Had to find out the hard way that the Target wasn't at the address we found.'

'Sorry to hear it, Tom. We checked it out. It's a viable location for us to assume the Target was being held at. Worth the effort. Things have changed though. We've got fresh intelligence from tracking the movements of one of the key protagonists in this shake-up. Mickey's getting a lock on the Target. We need you there right now.'

'I could probably have done with knowing about this before I crashed the wrong party. Not sure I'll be invited back any time soon.'

'Well, if you answered your phone sometimes, it might make communication a little easier!' she teased.

'Okay, okay,' I grinned into the handset. 'Guess I was just eager to crack on.'

'What went down?'

'It was a connected property for sure. Like we thought, a venue used for rest and relaxation by the caddie crew. Plus a few well-drilled Russian mercenaries. It did get a little messy in there.'

'Not more bloody body count? You'll have the police forces from all over Europe looking for us now as well as the whole of the African continent. You're clearly feeling all right though and back to your charming self, Hunter.'

'It's only for you, Ella. You know that.'

'Enough!' She giggled. 'I've been doing some research for Charles. This whole gig runs deeper than just a few rogue caddies, Tom. Read the whole report this time and I'll get back to you when I receive the latest location co-ordinates from the tracker Mickey placed on Sergei Krostanov's car. We're closing in on Daniel's real whereabouts at last and we're going to need you there sharpish. And please, Hunter, be careful.'

I hung up and scanned through the report. Originally founded as an entity named Rublucon, Rublex Corporation had its murky origins from inception in 1986 during the transition of the USSR at the time of perestroika. An aggressive, and they suspected, unauthorised takeover of previously state-owned oil and gas fields in Siberia had turned the prodigiously youthful and ruthlessly ambitious owners into billionaires overnight. Rublucon had a rapid expansion into new markets and territories enriching those officials who enabled its growth whilst building a morass of enemies along the way. Growth seemed to be always at the expense of the common man, with thousands of homeowners and farmers displaced to make way for new infrastructure in specific territories. After the land grab, the business ostensibly cleaned itself up and was renamed as Rublex. There wasn't much information on the ownership of the organisation.

By the turn of the millennium, Rublex's operation had sanitised itself further. Reach had spread internationally and there were photographs on the internet of Boris Golich, one of the original founders, socialising with world leaders. The conglomerate would now withstand all scrutiny and was considered beyond reproach. A massive pipeline had been constructed through Kurdistan and down through Turkey, providing access into Europe. The latest news was of a gas exploration in the international waters off the Falkland Islands with several national governments interested in partnerships to develop the resources. The sanitisation of this once dubious organisation seemed complete.

The report also contained details of the fifty-million-pound sponsorship deal with the European Tour, now in the second year of five. They supported the overall Order of Merit sponsorship and end of season championship, something of a big money bonus shoot-out which replaced the successful and long-standing Race to Dubai. In addition to this, they funded provision of the physiotherapy truck and a fleet of personal trainers available to those players without one already in their team. There were pictures of Krostanov everywhere: with players, at dinners, with the Tour committee. Ella had updated her cast of characters and mugshots too. The 'usual suspects', as she referred to them, with tongue in cheek, each time she pulled profiles together regardless of the job. She'd been thorough with the catalogue of caddies and officials who could possibly be linked to Daniel's disappearance. Using state of the art image recognition software, she'd searched for further images documented around the world to link them to those under suspicion in the kidnapping. She'd found some of Sergei in an American investment prospectus for oil exploration in Uzbekistan. A strapping man in his thirties. In one grainy image, he was standing in front of a corrugated iron hut, framed by a rugged mountain range in the background, wearing a hard hat and smiling. He held a clipboard, his arm clamped around a mine worker. Tough beginnings. A world away from the refined environment of the golf Tour where he now seemed so at home. There was a caption accompanying the photograph.

Site manager Sergei Krostanov with engineer Andrei Sharplov at the Uzbek oil refinery pumping station, 10 September 1999.

Ella had highlighted the name in red to make a point. Andrei Sharplov. I zoomed in and focused on the face of the other man in the picture. Compared with the updated list of 'usual suspects'. He was also wearing a hard hat and the photograph wasn't the best, but the bone structure and those eyes, even early traces of that sculpted beard, were all the same. There was little doubt. Soviet mining engineer Andrei Sharplov and former colleague of Sergei Krostanov was now Aaron Crower's caddy on the European Golf Tour, Andy Sharples.

Two old men, skin leathered from years of living under a burning sun, played cards over tiny cups of coffee. They sat outside the rundown café opposite and looked up in unison, startled for a moment by the thrust of the engine as it roared to life. Then resumed their early morning ritual. A shared, unspoken distraction from the gradual slippage of time, their lives winding down like a full moon setting over water. Nothing else stirred in town as I sped through the dirty deserted streets and back out onto the motorway; invigorated by news of Daniel's location.

~

SESEÑA. OUTSKIRTS OF FRANCISCO HERNANDO VILLAGE

'Get lost again, did we, Tommy Boy?' Mickey called out as I pulled off the road about thirty miles south of Madrid. We were sheltered under a large shady fig tree which cast long shadows over a cluster of disused farm buildings. 'I hope she was worth it mate. I've only been 'ere for four blinking hours!'

'Is the Target inside?' I nodded towards the large hacienda style property at the back of which we were parked, ignoring his well-meaning jibe.

'It's well-protected. I've clocked at least six different heavies coming and going so far but there's bound to be more inside the compound we don't yet know of.'

'And Krostanov?'

'Yep. All parked up. If our sources are correct, he's probably attending to some business with Daniel in there right now. Assuming the kid's still alive.'

'I'd usually wait for nightfall to lead a strike but I reckon we're running out of time now that Krostanov is getting personally involved. Is Hand sending us anyone else to assist? Where's Phil Manning when you need him?'

'Phil's in London, mate. He's working the Golich angle in

town. It's getting serious at that end too with an assassination order made on some government official or other so it's just you and me on this one pal.' He slapped me on the back displaying something near to genuine affection.

'What have we got in the way of heavy artillery, Mick?' I enquired.

'How did I know you'd bloody ask that? You do love your toys, Tommy,' he chuckled. I followed the wiry little character for about fifty yards to a clump of dry thorny bushes nestled behind a masonry shed, which had probably housed livestock at some time or other. Partly covered in the undergrowth, an old Spanish bakery van lay concealed. Mickey had clearly swapped vehicles at some point. He unlatched the back of the van and I peered inside. An assortment of weapons were neatly strapped against the internal metal sides of the van. I selected a snub nose combat Kalashnikov machine gun. A superior beast, it fired an armour piercing round with greater range, accuracy and penetrating capability than sub-machine guns which loaded pistol-calibre cartridges. I smirked at the irony that this fine personal defence weapon, as they were known, was in fact a product of the Russian Motherland. The 'PDW' label was cooked up to justify their existence, in my view, by the powerful American gun lobbies. They'd flooded the black market since the early nineteen nineties, when they became a trusted favourite of the notorious Jamaican Yardie drug gangs. But this was Russian weapon technology through and through and now I'd be turning it on some of their own. I strapped it over my shoulders. 'Big guns too, Mick?' I nodded inside the van.

'Quite proud of myself on this score, mate.' He straightened a little, appearing pleased as punch. 'I have only managed to acquire our very own M9A1. Yeah, a bloody bazooka, Tom! I didn't like doing it, mind, but The Hand of God set me up with a meet with them ETA Basque fellas and they were happy to trade. Seems they bought a load off the Portuguese Defence Forces after they'd finished fighting them Marxist guerrillas in Africa during their colonial wars in the mid-seventies and they just had 'em lying around. Hand figured that if it's just you going in there on your tod then you'd want me to at least clear you some space.'

'A bloody antique then?'

'I've done some testing and trust me, mate, the rocket launcher has still got some grunt in her. You all good for small arms too?'

'Need some mags for the Beretta, but otherwise I'm good to go. You're on point for this one, Mickey. I'm gonna need you to smash the gaff up a bit with that bad boy.' I nodded to the big metallic tube that Mickey was caressing like a six-year-old with a new favourite Christmas present. 'Draw their fire whilst I bust in. Keep hidden and be ready to get us the hell out of Dodge when I break out with the Target. That van's good cover. It's slower than the Range Rover but it won't get picked up as easily.'

'Sounds like a plan, mate. Make it happen, Tom.'

This was going to be an in and out job. Crude but effective. And just my style. Mickey was tasked with blasting holes out of the east side whilst I penetrated the kitchen door on the patio at the rear from the west. Once I was inside, I'd be taking out anyone in my way who didn't resemble the picture of Daniel Ratchet from the phone. Not particularly scientific, I know, but there was no time to get fancy and I wasn't here to be making new pen pals.

The message that buzzed through from Ella didn't improve matters.

The graveyards are full of indispensable men.
    – Charles de Gaulle

. . .

Funny thing. That girl had an unnerving sense of pertinence and timing with her quirky military quotations. Not particularly helpful given that more often than not they had a knack of turning out to ring true to the situation. My stomach churned. I'm not sure it was what I needed to read moments before heading into theatre.

38

The stage was dark. A screen curved across its back, displaying a montage of uplifting and iconic images. Oil fields. Gushers. Mountains. Sunrises. Teams of smiling workers. Gas tankers in rapid convoy on otherwise empty roads. Bustling offices. Graphs depicting positive growth spikes. The Union Jack fluttering in slow motion. The legend which ran across the top of these pixelated images read:

A UNION FOR GROWTH. DELIVERING ECONOMIC SECURITY, SUSTAINABILITY AND NEW BRITISH JOBS.

Rows of journalists and especially invited delegates from government and the ranks the Ministry of Trade & Investment and the Department for International Trade sat facing the stage waiting for the activity to begin.

Andy Bartholomew strode with purpose onto the centre of the stage. He cleared his throat and took a moment to survey the audience who now fixated on his every move. 'Welcome, ladies and gentlemen. Thank you all for coming. I know that today has been somewhat shrouded in secrecy but until now the government hasn't been in a position to release details of the historic deal which my department has been working on tirelessly. A deal that we've now agreed in order to generate and guarantee seven thousand British jobs over the next ten years!'

The audience erupted into spontaneous applause. Bartholomew looked really rather pleased with himself. He continued. 'As you well know, ladies and gentlemen, there hasn't been much real cheer for the economy in Britain since we cast off from a toxic Europe and survived a record national debt inducing global pandemic over the last wee while. Well, this government has bucked that trend at last! We've beaten off fierce international competition for this deal and created a union that delivers fiscal growth and safeguards more British jobs!'

More applause. Andy savoured every last morsel, not deeming to commence his next sentence until the very last sound of striking of hands had completed. 'Therefore without further ado,' he rolled his R's like a bugler trilling the arrival of the regimental goat, 'I am honoured to introduce the Prime Minister to share the full details on this momentous day.'

The Prime Minister swaggered onto the stage, tracked by a spotlight. Announcements of this type usually took place in Westminster, not amidst this poor imitation of American-style political razzmatazz. It had been Bartholomew himself who had choreographed the slick stage-managed announcement, in order to generate maximum media interest and impact around the globe.

'Thank you. Ladies and gentlemen, you've no need for me to remind you of the torrid economic and political climes through which we have lived and served and although, over the last couple of years, there has been something of a modest upturn, due to this government's prudent careful plans, we know that many parts of the European Union continue to wallow in the swamps of financial despair. During this sorry chapter of our time, trading partners have collapsed, currencies have fallen, banks have gone bust, businesses have failed, jobs have been lost, lives have been ruined.' He paused for the implications to settle before continuing with gusto to announce the steps taken to consign these bitter memories to history once and for all. The speech detailed how, in the face of stiff international competition, the government had secured a trading alliance with Rublex Corporation, one of the most prodigious and fastest growing oil and gas distributors in the world. The historic deal, partially funded by the UK, would create a minimum of seven thousand jobs for British workers over the next ten years and was worth an estimated seven billion pounds to the UK economy with a share of the hundred billion generated in revenues from the venture over the next decade. It was, he hoped, a defining moment. He turned, half-facing the vast screen stretched behind him as the lights dimmed again and a video vignette, offering more statistics on the deal, danced into life. As the audience settled, following the images playing out in front of their eyes, a figure emerged from a throng at the back of the room. Calling out as he approached the stage, a thick sheaf of papers waving in his hand, the Minister, Brian Weston, shattered the silence within the room.

'Prime Minister! Stop this charade. You have left me with no choice.'

A hundred heads swivelled in unison to watch as he sprang onto the stage. 'Stop this nonsense, Prime Minister. I beseech you. Stop this at once.'

'Take a hold of yourself, man,' warned the Prime Minister, stepping towards him.

'Prime Minister. I cannot allow this to proceed. You have

chosen to consort with Boris Golich, a man whom we have now unequivocal proof of involvement in the most audacious of criminal activities.' He faced the audience, urgency in his voice. 'You have opted to commit Great Britain to a commercial relationship with a Russian Mafia overlord via the veiled guise of gas exploration which is merely a front for laundering the criminal gains of drugs, extortion and people smuggling. You risk tarnishing our standing on the international stage by support of this nefarious criminal activity and costing us millions in the unwarranted joint venture infrastructure fees negotiated to facilitate this cursed deal.'

'Have you lost your mind, Minister? You simply have no grounding for these quite absurd and unsubstantiated allegations. I won't tolerate such insubordination.'

'Stand aside,' the Minister admonished. He depressed a button on a clicker which, until now, had been concealed within the pocket of his suit jacket. The visuals on the screen changed. Now a series of enlarged scanned documents were presented. Interpol warrants for the arrest of Boris Golich on the charges of conspiracy for the acts of murder, extortion, embezzlement, organised crime and various other criminal atrocities committed in several of the old Eastern Bloc countries. Additionally, a number of bank statements were shown, highlighting a series of large offshore payments made to numbered accounts purported to link the Prime Minister to Hamilton Advisory, a consultancy advising Rublex on the marketing of incomplete or non-existent casinos and resorts. The PM held a fixed smile on his face, conjuring mock laughter as his head rocked from side to side in faux disbelief. Gasps of horror and howls of derision from the audience followed. Displayed on the screen next came photographs of abandoned building sites at the locations of these ghost developments, followed by screen grabs of sexy marketing material featuring endorsements in the name of the

UK Prime Minister. He was quoted as saying that the resorts had 'strong investment potential, impressive sustained occupancy rates and unparalleled facilities'.

The audience, beginning to comprehend the gravity of the facts presented, grew as one in audible discontent. Camera bulbs flashed, smartphones were held aloft to capture the action. Within moments those journalists who were streaming live at the launch on social media had alerted the world to the sensational turn of events. #PoliticalAmbush and #PrimeMafia was already trending. The President of the United States of America, without a hint of irony, had himself just weighed in with a tweet regarding the importance of commercial transparency, the need for probity in politics and high moral standards across public life. A frenzy of responses had begun. Journalists and MPs jostled for position, crowding the stage in a menacing cluster, intent on exacting answers. It was nothing short of an unedifying scrum which soon overwhelmed the event security.

Sensing the moment was at hand, the Minister signalled to the side of the stage, summoning a grey-haired man in a donkey jacket accompanied by a ruddy-faced police constable buttoned to bursting inside his uniform. 'Prime Minister, you'll need to accompany these fine gentlemen of the establishment to answer a few questions.' He looked across at the Special Branch officers at the side of the stage who were detailed to protect the Prime Minister in public. Shaking his head and raising his voice to issue the directive. 'Stand down please. There's a warrant in place.' He continued, speaking both to his opponent and for the benefit of the audience. 'Prime Minister, in the next few days I shall be tabling a vote of No Confidence in the House of Commons surrounding your leadership of both Party and country. We'll submit our letters demanding your resignation to the 1922 committee as part of due process. You're in no position to carry on given these errors of judgement and obvious lapses in moral fibre. I'm challenging for the leadership at once!' Chaos ensued. Chairs were knocked backwards as reporters and staff alike rushed forward jostling for position, reaching over each other for photographs and answers.

Hidden in the shadows at the edge of the auditorium, Andy Bartholomew, with head down and heart racing, scurried away through the back door.

39

The deafening explosion shattered the surrounding peace of the Spanish countryside. A gaping wound had been torn into the side of the hacienda building like a screaming mouth displaying her broken teeth. Rubble was strewn everywhere. Billows of brick dust swirled in the baking sun.

Mickey followed up the bazooka's first strike with a well-placed and equally damaging second just above it into the first floor, taking out the entire corner of the building. Within a matter of seconds, the elegant architecture of this fine old building had been decimated. The unmistakable sounds of warfare and panic filled the air. Even though this was a sparsely populated rural region, some distance from the main conurbations, there was no way that these huge explosions weren't going to draw official attention to the hacienda at some point. I didn't have the impression that Mickey had factored in an engagement with the Spanish military when he sourced our gear for the mission. That was something we could well do without if we were to execute a clean and successful mission. I couldn't imagine the Russians wanting that kind of attention either.

Using the noise cover from the explosions, I smashed the glass to the patio door with my elbow. Leaning in and fiddling with the handle on the inside, I found that it was already unlocked. 'Good start, Einstein,' I muttered to myself and walked inside, scanning left and right behind the pugnacious snout of the Kalashnikov. The kitchen was clear.

Footsteps clattering on the stone floor somewhere from inside the house. I crossed the kitchen and reached the door. Dropped to one knee. In my experience, an enemy running at speed into contact will be expecting to hit a target standing at a height of around two metres. Adjusting your muzzle on the move to half that, or the height of a man kneeling, takes a vital extra second; leaving ample time for me to get my rounds off and bring them down.

I waited, kneeling just behind the frame to the open kitchen door. Eye fixed to the target-scope. Shooter cocked and primed. Forefinger resting a light tension on the trigger. Two heavyset men, revolvers waving out front as they ran, cantered around the corner of the staircase. The death rattle of my magazine emptying itself echoed round the vast hallway; a spiteful rage of bullets spraying. They didn't even see me crouching as they sped towards the sound of the assault on the building. They died where they fell, with bloody holes torn through chests and necks and thighs, sending the pair of useless carcasses tumbling to the cold floor. I reloaded and tracked the empty corridor round to an opulent marble atrium leaving a trail of dark sticky footprints behind from the gathering pool of glossy crimson.

A bullet whizzed past my head, thudding into the frame of a large painting hanging on the wall. I ducked and moved; bobbing and weaving away from the direction of fire. I returned shots in short random bursts, pinning back the shooter so I could hold a new position. Bullets hailed down on me from the top of the sweeping staircase, leaving me trapped in the crosshairs between two deadly angles. To my left, the gunman resumed and intensified his firing. Sharp fragments of wall plaster chips cut into my skin as I worked my big frame into the tiny space presented beneath a table displaying a large ornamental vase. I was taking some serious heat and, if it carried on like this, it wouldn't be long before one of these stingers had my number on it. Cold sweat soaked the back of my shirt. Angling my barrel upwards, I took aim above the shooter who was peppering me with shrapnel from his nest at the top of the staircase. I squeezed the trigger and let the beast rip into the ceiling directly over him. It was like a hammer being taken to a wedding cake. Vast chunks of plaster cascaded down onto the top tier of the staircase, crushing the sniper under a deluge of heavy debris; blunt trauma dialled in.

The other shooter held their fire, temporarily distracted by the recent architectural adjustments. I commando-crawled out from under the table, moving steadily towards the direction of attack. The gunman had withdrawn behind a door and I managed to hold him at bay with repeated shots into the wood and surrounding walls. With no return fire coming back my way, I scampered a retreat back into the corridor from where I'd first emerged.

Another crash into the roof of the building. Mickey was doing his bit to cause chaos all right, but if he kept on like this, there wouldn't be much of the property left standing by the time I located the Target. This was a big house and I needed to reach Daniel in double-quick time. I wasn't going door to door searching him out this time if I could help it. In and out as rapid as possible was the plan.

From out of nowhere, the butt of a revolver smashed into the side of my head, splitting it open; the force of the blow knocking me sideways into the wall. A bull of a man in a black leather jacket, sporting a face not even a mother could love, grabbed me by the shoulders before throwing me head-first back into the wall. *Where were they breeding these monsters? He should have just shot me in the head when he had the chance. Done us all a favour.*

He grabbed my hair, pulling my head back, and thrust a revolver into my face. I winced up at him through blood-encrusted eyelids. Thinking fast and hedging that his gun could be out of bullets as he hadn't already used it, I feigned collapse. I dropped like a stone leaving him to take the full weight of my body in his fist supported only by my hair. It stung like hell as thick clumps ripped out of my scalp by the root. But the surprise action, submission as opposed to expected aggression, delayed my would-be execution for just long enough to grab the handle of my Beretta and, with it still secured to my belt, I managed to angle it away from my thigh and squeeze off a couple of rounds into the foot of the thug looming over me. He bellowed, releasing my hair as he hopped in agony. Falling to the floor in a heap, I scrambled to my feet and kicked off from the corridor wall to slam into the wounded Russian beast. I hit him with power in the midriff. Hard. Uncompromising. Cut him in two with my shoulder, forcing him to wretch as he doubled over. He might be huge but he didn't have much fight in him. As he straightened up to face me, I jabbed him with a swift left in the throat. Clean. Clinical. Not hard enough to smash his windpipe perhaps, but enough of a precise blow to cause instant swelling, to make it hard to breathe. He choked and spluttered, eyes watering uncontrollably. I pulled the Beretta loose and jammed it inside his mouth, pulling up the picture of Daniel from my phone and holding the screen to his face.

'Where is he?' I demanded. The goon shook his head, still gasping for breath. 'Where is this man?' I shouted again and pushed the barrel of my gun deeper into the recesses of his mouth, making him gag. He nodded in resignation and I pulled the gun free, keeping it trained on his head. 'Take me to him,' I ordered, shaking him by the collar of his leather jacket like a disobedient dog. Even if this lump didn't understand English, he'd got the message sure enough. I shoved him down the corridor, gun poking into the middle of his back. Blood smeared the exquisite stone floor as he dragged the injured foot after him. Every so often, to keep the hustle going and drive him on at a faster pace, I delivered a well-placed kick, steel toecap into calf muscle, to bounce the trailing leg ahead of him. We passed by a number of side rooms and passages, which offered new avenues of escape or threat like unexplored tributaries of a coursing river, until gradually the corridor grew colder, gloomier, undeserving of the need for decorative attention by the weak glow of the yellow sodium lighting. I drove my hostage forward until he came to a natural halt in front of an iron gate – bars in front of a studded wooden door.

He grunted to announce arrival. I shoved him forward so that his nose was touching the metal. With the menace of my gun still pressed into his back I pulled his arms up onto his head interlocking an inordinate set of fingers. The pat down brought the reassuring jangle of key chain inside his trouser pocket. I handed Daniel's jailor the keys and he unlocked the gate and door as I stood harrying from behind.

The door creaked open, heavy on its hinges. It unveiled a pathetic scene. There was no mistaking the Target. Daniel Ratchet sagged on a wooden chair, tied with rope, listless and unmoving. Blood caked his face, his sallow skin, his shirt. His trousers were wet, and his feet wallowed in a puddle of dark and odorous urine. On his neck, an inflamed burn, weeping pus, broke the smoothness of pale skin. I pushed the Russian inside the cell as I called out to Daniel checking he was still alive. The boy stirred. Eyes flickered with weak desperation. 'It's all right, mate. I'm here to get you out of this place,' I said, stepping towards him as I spoke. As I reached the chair, the black leather jacket took a stride towards us. I half-turned and, without warning, fired point-blank into his face. A splatter of blood and brain matter particles expelled onto the cell wall behind. It wasn't pretty, but with an incapacitated Target to now extract from the building I couldn't afford to mess about. Drew the hunting knife and cut Ratchet loose.

The boy slipped from the chair and onto the floor. I slapped his face, then shook him. I repeated the action over and over trying to rouse him. After a short time, he came to. 'Wake up! Pull yourself together, Daniel. We're getting the hell out of here. NOW!' He started to kick into gear; a slow start before visible engagement of waking functions one at a time. First salient consciousness, motor skills starting to fire, then gaining spatial awareness. He looked at me. Throat croaking as he attempted to speak. His mouth formed the sounds before they could be released. He struggled to enunciate the single audible word. 'Matilda,' was all he said.

I lifted him off the floor and hauled him over my shoulder; head draped over my back, legs dangling at the front of my chest. I hadn't any water to give him and even if I'd been carrying a full emergency first aid kit there was no time to administer treatment. We were in the field and needed to fall out sharpish. I pressed forward, supporting Daniel with my left arm wrapped over his lower back, gun gripped in my right. He was a tall, rangy kid which made him difficult to keep hold of, but he didn't weigh as much as some of the army kit we'd trained with on twenty mile yomps across the moors. Checking left and right, I exited the cell and set off at a steady pace back down the corridor; precious cargo stowed on board. I hoped the remainder of those still inside the building were being kept busy by the barrage of explosions assailing the mansion and grounds from Mickey's bazooka frenzy. The dingy corridor remained empty and we covered the distance fast.

Dripping with sweat and panting hard, I heaved the dead weight of Daniel's body onto a hardwood kitchen counter and stretched out my injured shoulder. It was numb from the bullet wound taken back at the golf course, with my deltoid muscle near shredded. I'd grown used to the dull throb of pain threading down my side, strangely savouring the familiar cruel sensation as it racked my body. The electric impulses between the damaged nerve endings and pain receptors in my brain told me that I was alive, not merely inhabiting some fragment of a disturbed dream sequence. I was feeling something for real; was not yet consigned to Hell.

The kitchen was empty. A large copper pot bubbled on the range, above which a set of ancient cow bells hung; a rustic trophy of yesteryear. The table in the centre of the room was typical of an archetypal Spanish country kitchen and I could picture a family spanning three generations gathered round it over a hearty meal, engrossed with the patriarch's rambling stories. My ruminations were interrupted by a long-haired, olive-skinned man in a white T-shirt banging through the saloon doors to our left holding a hunting rifle. He wore jeans with cowboy boots. A hand rolled cigarillo hung from lips which presented themselves in a perpetual sneer. The scene could have been lifted straight out of some dodgy Western.

I grabbed Daniel. Pulled his limp groaning body from off the countertop and down on top of me as we fell to the floor behind the kitchen table. I shunted forward and, grabbing the ankles of its front two wooden legs, heaved sharply backwards, flipping the heavy unit onto its side. The thick wooden front would serve as a shield for the two of us. Cowboy Boots unleashed a couple of cartridges whizzing into the tabletop. They stuck fast. The table was solid. Fig wood. Old school and built to last. Lucky it was a low calibre rifle, probably best suited for shooting rabbits and birds in the surrounding countryside. Even so, if whoever furnished this place had gone with some self-assembly flat-pack instead, the lad and I would be cashing in our chips right about now. I pointed the barrel of the Kalashnikov over the lip of our makeshift barricade and returned fire, lashing bullets around the kitchen. The tone of the gun, accompanied by the metallic notes of bullets bouncing into tiles, pans, and the cooking range generated a raucous musical cacophony around us. Cowboy Boots retreated behind the flapping swing gates. I waited, head down, forefinger caressing the trigger of my smouldering weapon. Counted fifteen seconds of silence in my head. Nothing. I jammed the barrel of the shooter over the top of the table and blasted another short burst of fire. With no response I peered around the side of the table. The kitchen was empty. Then I saw it. The pointed toe of that scuffed cowboy boot just visible an inch or so from under the saloon gates. I aimed low, knee height, to where I projected the shooter was standing and gritted my teeth. Squeezed on the trigger and let the gun do its work. Leapt over the table closing forward to ensure I had the best angle to make a hit. Gunfire blasting ahead of me, keeping him pinned back, I kept shooting until I could practically engage hand to hand, clip emptied in full. Crashed through the saloon gates and found Cowboy Boots just beyond, taken down in a bloody pile clutching at his legs. He reached for the rifle by his side with the last of the fight left in him. I leapt forward onto his chest. Slit his throat from ear to ear. Butcher work with cold steel in the kitchen somehow felt appropriate.

It was time to grab the Target and get the hell out. A slobbering thick-shouldered American pit bull bounded in from the corridor and launched itself at Daniel, who lay curled up at the base of the upended table. By the time I reached him, it had clamped its jaws into his leg and was shaking it furiously. Ratchet's resistance was limited to a low moan. I pulled out the Beretta and took aim at the devil dog. The mechanism jammed.

Damn. No shot. I flung the gun at its head missing and bouncing off its thick neck. The dog didn't even look up. I stepped in and kicked it square in the side as it ripped at the flesh on Daniel's leg like it was toying with a bone in the backyard. I felt ribs crumple under my boot. The mutt yelped. Turned its attention from the Target towards me. First job done. It snorted and set after its new prey. As the dog bounded at me I dropped my shoulder and hammered my fist down into its nose, knocking it sideways, sending it rolling. It righted itself and, in a slavering frenzy, came straight back at me, snapping and growling with the myopic purpose of pure animalistic fury. I'd succeeded in my objective of deflecting the dog's attention but, with no time to reload the mag on the Kalashnikov and the Beretta spent, I wasn't going to risk a scrap with this vicious animal. I scooted back onto the counter and flipped my legs onto the kitchen top. As the animal jumped up snarling, trying to bite me, I grabbed a round copper saucepan and fended it off, striking it in the mouth and skull. At last, the dog gave up and prowled instead, pacing in a tight circle below me, panting hard. I stood up on the counter, stooping my neck to keep my head from bouncing on the ceiling. There was just no way I could bring myself to finish off man's best friend down there if I could possibly help it. It wasn't the mutt's fault, even if that Hound of Hell was holding us up and giving me and the Target some serious problems to think about. I scanned the kitchen. A little further down above the counter was a spice rack hanging off the wall. Next to that hung a long string of onions, garlic and a thick dried Spanish sausage that was curved into a U-bend shape. I bundled across the countertop and grabbed the cured meat. Whistled down to the slathering frenzied pit bull to grab its attention and waved the charcuterie above its nose, just out of reach. It followed the hypnotic swaying of the sausage; malevolent intent evaporated in an instant. I hurled the chorizo stick around the kitchen door and out into the corridor, from where we'd entered. The dog bolted after it. In a single motion I bounded off the counter and across the tiled floor just in time to reach the door with my boot and slam it shut. The dog flung itself against it in frustration. I breathed out hard. The beast barked as it scrabbled against the wood in its feverish attempt to get inside the kitchen and back at us. I checked the spare pocket of my cargo pants then slotted the final magazine into the machine gun. Then hauled Daniel up by his shirt and out of the foetal position he'd adopted in the shadow of the table; our improvised barricade.

There was little doubt. This was now a serious situation. The Target was in a terrible state. Couldn't stand. Blood was soaking through his trousers. I crouched and using the fireman's lift technique flopped him again over my heavily strapped shoulder. We made it through the same kitchen door which I'd broken into earlier. *Still unlocked.* Over the patio at a trot. I made a vain attempt to check for contact as we ran but the truth is I was knackered from carrying a twelve stone deadweight on my back and from the intense fighting to get us outside. Plus, I was carrying a gunshot wound which was eating at my energy more than I'd reckoned on. There was no use pretending otherwise, if we were going to survive this we needed to make it out of the compound fast.

40

By the time we reached the drystone wall at the back of the garden the sweat was pouring off me. We'd threaded through lush vegetation and beds of vibrant flowers. Now and again, I'd needed to stop to readjust the Target's body, shifting the pressure on my shoulder; catching my breath. I kept talking to him as we went. After all, the kid was worth more to me alive. 'Keep it together, man. You're going be okay. Daniel, are you listening to me, mate?' The occasional grunts which came back at intermittent intervals told me that at least he was still breathing. That's all I needed. *Tom Hunter is seeing this job home.*

I fished the burner phone from my pocket and dialled Mickey from the list of previous calls. He answered on the second ring. 'Take your bloody time, why don't ya, Hunter? What you bloody doing, making new friends in there or something?'

'Something like that, Mick. Something like that.'

'I've been keeping 'em busy for ya, Tom. There's three or four of them up there returning fire whenever I punch holes in the gaff.'

'So I heard, Mick. Good job. Right now we're situated by the back wall in the compound. Target's incapacitated. Living, but he's in real bad shape. I can't get us both over this wall with him on my back, it's just too much weight with this wounded shoulder and what we've been through busting out of there.'

'I'd make a nice fat hole for you to walk out through, mate, but I've spent my wad on our little fireworks show. No rockets left I'm afraid.'

'What do you have, Mickey? They'll be down here any second now.'

Moments later, a thick length of rope lashed over the wall about twenty metres down from where we were crouched. I jogged over to it and shouted back, 'Got it, Mick. Is it secure?'

'It's on the front of the van. Tie the kid on and I'll winch him over.' It was a rudimentary plan, but it was all we had. I pulled the rope across the top of the wall and secured it around Daniel's waist. The engine revved from somewhere in front of us and I helped to push the limp body upwards, bent in half under the strain of the rope. It didn't look comfortable, but he hoisted up just before the top of the wall and I hollered. Mickey jammed on the handbrake keeping the van fixed. Our precious cargo hung precarious from the taught rope. A full minute later, Mickey's head popped up from the other side of the wall, the very image of a furtive meerkat surveying its territory. He reached over and grabbed hold of the dangling body. Began to haul him over.

Gunshots cracked into the stone. I hit the deck and rolled on instinct, finding cover beneath an orange tree. Daniel was a sitting duck. He couldn't have presented an easier shot. A slug caught him flush in the buttock as Mickey gave a frantic final heave to pull him over the wall. The screech of suffering might well have been made by a wounded animal.

'Tom, he's hit! He's hit!' came the urgent shout from beyond the wall.

'Get him out of here. Now,' I called back. 'I'll meet you in the town by that old casino. If I'm not there in fifteen, move out, soldier.'

'Gottcha. Oh, and Tommy, think you might be needing this.'

A spare ammo clip arched over the wall and landed on the grass before me.

Golden.

There were new voices, inside a minute. From my vantage point amidst the orange grove, I scoped four guys. One was dressed in an immaculate business suit. Judging by this and his body language towards the others in the group, he was clearly in charge. Of the other three, two looked like local lads. Hired muscle. T-shirts, jeans, trainers, sun-bronzed skin, slicked back hair. The fourth was cast in a mould that I'd encountered before. Bigger than the others by a head, his skin was a milky white with shoulders square as an aspirin bottle wrapped with a shiny black leather jacket. He was agitated, pawing at the ground with his feet. I guessed that he wouldn't be best pleased when he found out that I'd pasted his stunt double's face all over the cell wall. Or maybe he already had.

I assessed the available options. There was now one full magazine clip in the Kalashnikov, thanks to Mickey's spare. The Beretta was spent, lying back on the kitchen floor. And I had my knife. They'd shot Daniel when they saw him flip over the wall. Perhaps they thought I'd also managed to make it over and would divert all their efforts to outside the perimeter. However, the group were fanning out and that wasn't a chance I could take. They were checking the bushes and trees; clearly hunting for unwelcome guests. I figured that most people pinned back in my position would try to scale the wall or find a weakness in the fencing surrounding the compound. But I wasn't most people and I'd been in tighter scrapes. This was no time to panic. If that's what was expected, I was going to do the exact opposite. *Tom Hunter would breeze right out of the front gate, just like I owned the place.*

I skirted the orange grove and tracked back up towards the villa. Watched as the group split up, tracing the back wall. Spied one of the hired Spanish goons making a half-hearted attempt with the barrel of his rifle to prod and poke into the foliage. Felt my blood rising the way I often did before a kill. I locked onto him, revelling in the knowledge that these precious moments were the last he would experience, and he'd no idea how soon it would all be over. His life was in my hands and I'd decide to take it however I chose. Concealed by the lush greenery, I stalked him to within a few meters. I was so close now I could make out the sheen of perspiration covering his biceps and hairless forearms. Muscles sculpted by hours in the gym, not natural power; more show pony than shire horse. He'd need a few years yet to put a bit of man on him, but I wasn't going to allow him that privilege. Abandoning his efforts, he skulked round the side of the mansion to check out the gaping hole in the brick work left by Mickey's bombardment. It was redolent of a ripped stage curtain left unsewn, offering a peephole onto a fully dressed theatre set. I watched the casual way he scuffed through the rubble, blazing a cigarette alight. And I'm breathing hard. Heart thumping. The blood pumping, coursing through me. I can feel my nerve ends tingling. *I feel so alive.* And then I can't contain it any longer. Have to taste it. I pounce and I'm on him before he's exhaled his first drag, punching my blade into his stomach and twisting it as I lift him off his feet. He bends double and as his feet scrabble for the ground I catch him with a left hook crashing into his temple. Letting go of the knife handle, blade still embedded inside him, I follow up with a right uppercut, driving into the underside of his nose with speed and force. He crumples at my feet. Pathetic, bloodied, motionless.

Endorphins surging. Waves of serotonin flood my brain. For a brief moment, I am cleansed and all hurt is washed away.

I'd seen it happen once before in a street fight. A man killed by a single punch to the nose, death from internal bleeding. I'm passionate about 'the sweet science', as it's known. I'd trained myself to be a switch hitter in the boxing ring – unusual in being able to deliver equal force from both orthodox and southpaw stances. I wasn't ambidextrous, so it had taken considerable practise. Hours on the heavy bag, setting the correct balance, shifting weight to administer power from the body core, not just arm punches. I'd learned to avoid injury too as much as improve boxing technique. If, like most sluggers, your natural stance is conventional, it's far easier to break a hand in the heat of a tear up. You've thrown your hardest punch with spiteful intent, usually a straight right. If the feet aren't correctly placed, this moves the body out of alignment and off balance. Should that first punch connect, depending on what's thrown back, then oftentimes you'll want to follow up with a rapid second blow to drive home your dominance in the altercation. The new position now lends itself to you throwing an overhand left coming from the side. If you don't focus on locking the wrist and keeping your fist in the right position, driving through with the first two knuckles, keeping the fifth metacarpal bone out of the way, then breaking a knuckle will occur almost every time. There's a reason why hand injuries, amongst other fight damage, are such a regular occurrence on emergency wards on a Saturday night. They're a common result of booze-fuelled wild-swinging pub brawls; often just a lot of bluster followed by a few mistimed scrappy blows and all over inside a minute. A broken hand is an unnecessarily painful way to make your point, even if you do come out on top.

I looked down with disdain at the discarded sack of meat, lifeless amongst the rubble. As far as punches went, that one was a hall of fame peach and one I'd recall with relish from time to time in the dull moments of transit between jobs.

A radio handset, fixed to the belt on the body, crackled into life. An accented voice speaking in syrupy English was moving through the channels asking the group to report their activity. The stock response being echoed back over the airwaves in response was 'Clear'. Then the name 'Alejandro' was called, a pause and then twice again in irritable succession. I scooped up the handset and issued a muffled reply, same as the previous answers. Held my breath. Waiting, uncertain if my brief impersonation had done the job. The radio crackled again: 'Keep searching the grounds. Secure the area.'

They wouldn't be looking for anyone at the house for a while. Sticking close to the villa and slinking amongst the yawning pattern of hazy shadows, I soon made it around to the impressive frontage of the building. The driveway stretched out ahead of me. No sign of patrols left or right. I checked again before taking a deep breath and setting out straight ahead into open cover. Sprinting hard out across the drive, jinking as unpredictable a path as I could fathom towards the gate. I could almost feel a supersized luminous bullseye burning onto my back and was fully expecting to be taken down by a bullet at any moment. Any rudimentary marksman standing at a first-floor window at the front of the house would have an easy shot and plenty of time. It was an audacious yet calculated strategy. The team was distracted, focused on searching the grounds and beyond the perimeter wall. My move would be least expected, and I gambled against stacked odds that no one would bother to guard the front door.

I made it onto a road a few hundred meters beyond the main gate. It was only then that I finally stopped moving. Hands on knees. Panting for breath. Sucking hot heavy air into my lungs. Sweat dripped from every pore in my shaking body, stinging my eyes. The shoulder wound had opened up and was starting to bleed again. *Not what I needed right now.*

I set off, striding down the road, my breathing still ragged. A mile or so down, an unwashed red Fiat Punto chugged by, travelling at around twenty kilometres an hour. I let it pass before stepping out into the empty road behind and, crossing my arms above my head, waved and shouted at the driver to flag him down. It came to a gentle stop fifty meters ahead of me and I jogged up to it. In fairness to the anxious driver, the sight of my battered ugly mug looming scarred and bloodied in the car mirror would make most people uneasy. Smiling in through the mud-splattered window, best lopsided grin set in place, I could barely get a greeting out before the bespectacled head looked up with shock and began to deploy the central locking system to secure the car doors.

'Do you speak English?' I asked louder and slower than was really polite, battling to keep my cool.

'No Ingleses. Perdóname,' came the response, accompanied with an apologetic flapping of hands. The nervous man was clearly regretting having stopped at all.

'I need a lift please,' I shouted as I tried the door handle. The engine revved. Sensing that I was about to lose my ride I revealed the Kalashnikov, smashing it through the glass window. The driver froze, a mask of fear twisting over his face. I swiped out the jagged excess of glass around the door frame with the gun barrel and flipped up the plastic lock. Motioned to the driver to get out on his side, weapon kept trained upon him. I pointed for him to lie down on the road and as he moved, I sprang into the empty driver seat. Revved the high-pitched engine before burning rubber towards the local town.

I arrived at the old casino just a few minutes later. I'd miscalculated. On foot it would have taken at least twenty minutes to cover the ground plus there'd been action to contend with. Pulling into the deserted car park, I searched for signs of activity; for Mickey and the van. The old casino had fallen from grace since its heyday in the nineteen fifties when it must have been quite a grand affair. A tattered sign, with peeling paint and framed by a chain of bare circular light bulbs, depicted provocative silhouettes of girls in fishnet stockings, high heels and bodices bending with their hands on knees. Faded glory now, this would have been the epitome of high life in the area. Today it stood empty, boarded up with plain wooden planks and rusting nails. The car park was a dusty vacant lot, deserted by daylight but a regular haunt for whores and their clientele after dark; perhaps a fitting use given its somewhat racy past. I checked my watch a second time. It was seventeen minutes since I had seen Mickey disappear with Daniel over the wall and I'd instructed them to leave without me after fifteen. I was getting twitchy. Could I have been followed? Those guys were known to be connected. They probably had eyes on the payroll everywhere. A shadow moved in my peripheral vision. Startled, I jerked around to meet a face only inches from my own, staring back at me through the car window. 'You're always late, Hunter,' Mickey scolded me, shaking his head in exasperation. 'Get in the back of the van with the Target and stay out of sight. We've got to get the hell out of here.'

281

41

RURAL SPAIN. DIRECTION: BARCELONA, CATALONIA.

In the back of the old bakery van, Daniel was burning up. I poured water into his mouth from a plastic bottle and mopped the fever from his brow. He was murmuring something incomprehensible. Something about Matilda again. I was just happy for him to cling to whatever he could to get him through. He was in a bad way. Beaten, tortured, mauled by a savage dog and shot. I doubted that he'd had much in the way of food, water or sleep during his ordeal. If I wanted my money then I needed him to make it. He had to stay awake.

The van trundled through the rolling Spanish countryside, Mickey driving, a flat cap pulled down low on his head. Concealed in the back, Ratchet and I were keeping out of sight. We knew these guys were connected and that they'd be coming after us at high speed. Hiding in plain sight, we were gambling on the fact that they wouldn't figure on us trying to outrun them by pootling along in a battered bakery van with a top speed of fifty kilometres an hour. We passed golden fields knitted together like a patchwork quilt. Sturdy hedgerows and trees neatly lined the roads providing layers of never-ending symmetry. Mickey flicked on the radio and the whine of sickly bubble gum Europop filled the van. Twenty minutes or more passed without seeing another car.

'Hold on, boys. What's all this?' the alarm in Mikey's voice filtered back to us. 'It's a roadblock, Tommy. Look lively.' I peered through the front seats and out of the windscreen. We were held in a small queue of cars on a narrow country road. Ahead of us two police cars were parked at angles across from each other on either side of the road. Officers of the Guardia Civil, adorned in full uniform and hats, were walking up and down the row of cars with clipboards, making enquiries of the drivers through their windows. It was too late to pull a U-turn and take another route without drawing unwarranted attention to ourselves.

'You think this is for us, Mick?' I said.

'Couldn't say. Don't see how it could be, do you? How connected are those Ruskies anyway? Guess we're about to find out. Not sure how I'll explain that I can't speak Spanish driving a van like this without them wanting to look in the back. If it goes tits up, mate, we're going to have to fight our way out.'

I grabbed an M16 semi-automatic assault rifle from the rack and loaded a new clip in preparation. It had been a firm favourite of the US military since the early sixties, first adopted by the US Air Force and then the Army where it was used heavily in Vietnam. It's a lightweight shooter manufactured from a mix of steel, aluminium alloy, plastics and polymers so you can strap it to your back and go for miles without it dragging you down. It's gas-operated and air-cooled, with a rotating bolt. A lighter, simpler gun with fewer operating parts to worry about. That really flicks my switches. I checked Daniel over, he was looking comfortable enough for now. Traffic was starting to move up ahead. The expected knock on the glass window arrived. Mickey dutifully wound it down, smiling. The policeman stooped. 'Hola,' he said without expression. Mickey nodded. Up ahead another policeman was waving cars through with an impatient ferocity. He called down to his colleague and the message was relayed. A grunt. A tap of the clipboard on the bonnet of the van. Waved us through. Mickey half-turned, winked at me and weaved the old vehicle through the roadblock and out onto the open road. I shook my head, exhaled and placed the MI6 to one side. Turned back to Ratchet and changed the dressing on the weeping bullet wound in his buttock, keeping on the pressure to stem the bleeding. *A regular Florence Nightingale.*

Less than five minutes down the road, the whoop of a siren and the flicker of blue lights alerted us to a squad car closing on us fast from behind. With no ability to outrun them, we reluctantly pulled over. The same policeman as before came to the window, a stern uncompromising look upon his face. He fired something in rapid Spanish at Mickey. No response. He tried again. Mickey looked back at him, nonplussed, and said, 'Do you speak English, gov?'

'English? Si, I speak some English. Please get out,' he sniffed with a supercilious air of disdain. Mickey dutifully did as he was asked, and I strained to listen through the sides of the little van as they stood together on the hot tarmac.

'Do you own this vehicle please?'

'Um. No, it's a rental.'

'You rent this?' The response incredulous.

'Yes, from a friend. I work for him running errands.'

'We have reports of a vehicle with this description being stolen from Alicante this morning. Do you have papers?'

'Yes. Surely. I'll have to rummage around in the back for them though. That okay?'

Footsteps approached the back of the van and Mickey made a loud show of opening the back doors. I primed myself with the MI6 cocked as the doors swung open. Watched as the expression on the policeman's face melted from sudden shock to serious concern as he absorbed the tangible threat of a machine gun pointed at his heart. It was probably the most action he'd encountered in the whole of his pen pushing, traffic counting career to date. It certainly didn't look like he wanted to be there.

'Tie him up, Mickey. Leave him by the side of the road. If we smoke him, we'll only draw more heat. We're supposed to be on their side anyway.'

'We haven't worked out who we can trust on this one yet. Intelligence that Ella provided shows that these Russians have paid their way right up the establishment in a load of countries. Some local cop, who's probably on the take from half the neighbourhood already, can easily be bought. We can trust no one on this job, Hunter.'

'Agreed. But I'm not killing him for the hell of it when it'll cause problems later getting back to London. We leave him tied up out here in the sun to work on his tan and crack on.'

We dumped the policeman, gagged with one of his own socks, hands and feet bound with rope, sitting in his underwear in a dried-out ditch as we rumbled away towards the city. Our destination was the central hospital. During his wait for me to turn up at the old casino, Mickey had been on the phone to Ella back at HQ. Given Daniel's critical state of health, and the fact that he remained in a perilous situation until his kidnappers were either apprehended or neutralised, Charles Hand had secured private treatment in the city hospital at Barcelona. We weren't to stop under any circumstances until we got there, not even for the Spanish police.

We drove for an hour in near silence. The Target was slipping in and out of consciousness. There was little that could be done to ease his discomfort. Even so my fist gripped his clothing, willing him to hold on until we reached Barcelona. The heat was oppressive inside the van, choking already parched throats even drier. Every bump and pothole on the neglected road surface jolted through us like electricity, providing a merciless reminder of each painful niggle and injury carried by my broken body. The elixir of adrenaline which had previously surged through my veins was now dissipating. Conscious of Daniel's injuries, Mickey drove with solemnity as if steering a hearse at the head of a funeral cavalcade. Guiding us towards our destination, eyes steady upon the road.

The open countryside narrowed with the hills and the battered bakery van began its crawl up a winding road, swaying from side to side as it made the tight turns. We pulled into a village. Passed squat sandy coloured houses. An old woman, bowed with age and dressed head-to-toe in black lace, inched up the road with the aid of a homespun crooked stick. The centre of the village was built around an austere looking church. Its size and ornate architecture incongruous and disproportionate to the simple surrounding dwellings. Turning a corner, the van slowed. Mickey cursed under his breath. Ahead of us, police cars of the Guardia Civil stretched across the road. Uniformed policemen flanked their vehicles, guns drawn. A welcoming committee.

42

Michael stretched out his muscled body and rolled to get comfortable on the couch inside the physio truck. He was restless and unable to sleep. A lot had been going on around the Tour since Spain and, whilst gossip had been rife in the last few days, few of the facts had been substantiated. The circus had inevitably left town on schedule following the conclusion of the tournament and the players and their entourages were now starting to reappear in dribs and drabs at the course on the outskirts of Munich for the Mercedes Championship. It was cooler in Germany than the searing heat of Spain. Time never stood still on the Tour. There was always the next event, always another trophy to play for, always another cheque.

One of the old swing coaches was reported in the media as having passed away at the last event; natural causes. Talk amongst the players was that it may have been a robbery gone wrong, but the story had been managed with care by the European Tour Public Relations team. Police reports were obscured, and the media had played ball. The last thing the luxury resorts, hosting their prestigious events with high paying sponsors, wanted was any negativity through a perceived association with criminality. Matilda had taken some time off from travelling with the Tour. Michael had always been protective of the beautiful, vulnerable girl whom, in many ways, he regarded as a kind of younger sister. It had been an unspoken bond between them, and Matilda had often depended on him to deflect the multitude of testosterone-fuelled chancers who came sniffing around as she tried to do her job. The only time she'd trusted anyone, allowed anyone to really get close to her, was her new boyfriend, Daniel Ratchet; a rookie player manager to whom Michael had also taken a shine. Yet no sooner had he arrived on the scene he had gone missing. She was very upset and it had all got a bit too much for her to be around the events.

Michael squirmed and twisted, squashing his face deeper into the stiff cushioning of the couch. More worries danced through his mind. In the process of trying to bolster his meagre pay packet, to support his family, he'd lost a lot of money to a certain unpleasant group of caddies who ran a book gambling on tournaments. Following a few early wins, using inside knowledge of the players' physical conditions, he'd doubled-up by backing some nailed-on favourites only for the results to take an unexpected turn each time on the final day of action. Unheralded performances against the run of form and he'd lost large. Failure to pay up had seen him sink deeper into debt on the interest payments. Recently he'd been on the receiving end of some beatings and scare tactics. It frightened him. Things were getting out of hand and no one seemed to be in a position to do anything about it. The caddies were acting like a law unto themselves.

Trouble seemed to be escalating too. Apparently, some big tough guy with a nasty looking scar had stuck a gun in Matilda's face in the car park back in Spain, asking questions and scaring the life out of her. It had been the last straw and she had taken sick leave for the next couple of weeks. He couldn't help but worry about her. On top of all of this, right before Daniel had gone missing, he'd left his personal tablet for Matilda, stashed right here in the truck. Michael had discovered it whilst cleaning up at the end of the Spanish leg of the Tour and with all the recent goings on, he'd of course been curious, particularly given that the guy had then vanished into thin air. Michael liked Daniel. He was different to the other player managers they encountered who were brash and arrogant, treating them like the hired help or, in Matilda's case, some cheap whore they could paw and gawp at. Unable to give Matilda the tablet for safekeeping, seeing as she'd left in such a hurry, Michael had dutifully taken care of things. The way he always did, in his efficient and dependable way.

The dark can play tricks on the mind when you're sleeping alone in a truck in the middle of an empty field during Tournament Week set-up. No fancy, comfortable hotel for him. Over time one got conditioned to the sounds of the nocturnal wild animals calling to each other. The lonely lament of the wind.

This, though, was a different noise from somewhere outside the truck. It held the attention of the big German. A chill ran down his spine. Sitting bolt upright, rubbing his eyes. T-shirt clammy. Head groggy. There it was again. Almost imperceptible. Persistent. Deliberate. The sound of light yet aggressive filing at a level that wouldn't have woken him, had he already been asleep. Michael threw the blanket to one side and levered his chunky frame down onto his bare feet. The noise continued unabated. There could be no doubt anymore. Someone was trying to get in.

A nine-iron leaning at a jaunty angle against the table,

discarded by some player or other, was snatched up shakily as a ready weapon. Gripping the club in his meaty left hand, the sleepy giant padded across to the door. He waited in the stillness. Breath held tight, a silent prayer on his lips. Each thump of his heart was deafening. And the scraping just kept on and on, tormenting him until at last a solid clunk and a satisfying click as metal slotted against metal and the machine manufactured components of the lock worked into place. The handle turned.

Michael stammered, 'Wer ist dort bitter?' and then after a short time, 'Who's there please?'

Silence. He called out again. A split second later, the door was kicked open with violent intent and two masked men charged up the little metal steps in close succession. They piled into the truck interior amidst a clatter of noise and fury. Michael didn't even have time to swing the club. He jabbed it into the ribs of the first man, slowing him down but the second was on him an instant later, clawing at him, grappling round his broad chest and knocking him backwards. It was enough to keep him occupied whilst the lead assailant rallied. He caught Michael flush with a well-timed shoulder charge slamming against his legs and bringing him down.

The German was overwhelmed by the suddenness of the attack and sustained aggression from the two men. Working together, they pinned him to the floor. A black sack was roughly forced over his head, its cord pulled tight. Punches rained down on his face and ribcage to the point where Michael Hausen eventually gave up struggling, instead curling up his knees and using those big hands and solid forearms to shield himself. Within a further couple of minutes, a skipping rope, borrowed in haste from the truck's training kit, was secured around his wrists and ankles which were pulled behind his back. Hausen was bound immobile, left trussed up and writhing helpless upon the floor.

A voice. 'You've got something we want, Michael.' The ensuing swift boot to the ribs generated a muffled grunt by way of response. 'Where's the tablet, you Kraut bastard? Don't waste our time or you'll be in for some real trouble,' threatened a cockney sneer.

Michael said nothing. The kicking continued. Legs, torso, head. Finally, tired out from their exertions, the interrogation began again in earnest. 'Where's the fucking computer? We know you've got it, Sausage Meat, we've been told,' screamed the enraged Scottish tirade just inches away from the hooded head. This could only have been Sean.

Michael gritted his teeth, his eyes squeezed shut. He hated that voice with a passion. Sean had tormented him, burnt him. Now he was being beaten on again. He may have been helpless, but he had something that they wanted. And he knew how important it was, what it meant. He wouldn't betray Daniel. And he wouldn't betray himself again. Not to these bullies. There was clearly too much at stake. The German swallowed hard. And right there within the darkness of the hood and the restrictions of his bonds, shrouded in fear, Michael Hausen fought against the instincts of his natural disposition and in the horror of the moment he took his bravest decision.

Streams of sunlight cut through the branches of the proud canopy of overhanging trees. The field was contained, sealed off with ribbons of thick blue and white tape. Swarms of uniformed police clustered together writing notes and taking photographs, bagging evidence and interviewing passers-by. The physiotherapist's lifeless body, trussed like a sucking pig ready for roasting on the spit at a medieval banquet, had been discovered at mid-morning the next day. Except that when the policemen were able to untie and un-hood the victim, they'd been unable to make an immediate positive identification of the body. Every bone and tooth in its face was smashed and broken into a bruised and swollen pulp. The body was lacerated and smeared with a grotesque green and purple bruising. The ruptured skin and crushed ribcage, apparently jumped upon like a child's trampoline, depicted a swollen tapestry of torture.

In the face of such extreme duress, Michael had chosen not to utter another word. The coveted tablet had not been surrendered. He had neither betrayed Matilda nor broken Daniel's trust. Picked on for his prodigious size and exploited for a sorry lack of bravado since he was a boy, the lifelong victim had chosen his moment to display the true courage which always slumbered within. In the stoic acceptance of his death the man had at last found the strength which found him complete.

43

'Only seventy kilometres to Barcelona and this has to bloody 'appen. Another pissin' roadblock. We can't afford to sit here idling forever. I might have to even switch the engine off and push it through, mate, we're that low on blinkin' petrol. If we don't find a gas station soon, we're going nowhere fast, Tom.' Mickey slammed his hand against the steering wheel of the bakery van in frustration. 'Hold up,' he continued, 'this looks serious, Hunter. The roz have come mob-handed. How's the patient doing back there?' He twisted his neck birdlike to peer into the back.

'Target's not in good shape. We haven't got long, I reckon. He's still bleeding. We can't stop for this lark, we just haven't got the time. Besides, they've probably found that cop in the ditch by now. We're not getting through this one without a scrap.'

'Take it easy for now. Let's suss them out. They might be on the lookout for a lost cat for all we know. We're miles away from the Russians by now, it's probably not even related.'

'I'm telling you, Mickey, I don't like it,' I replied, grimacing as I picked up the assault rifle and yet again checking the magazine was fully stocked. Pure habit.

Mickey rolled the van up towards the three police cars blocking the road in zigzag formation, beaming a broad and unconvincing smile. A tall, caramel-skinned policeman, sporting a carefully fashioned moustache, was waving us forward with insistence. We coasted to a proximity of around fifteen feet in front of him when the powerful snap of machine gunfire tore through the windscreen of the van, pouring a shimmering waterfall of broken glass onto the front seats. Mickey was pinned back onto his seat, body shaking and contorting as it was riddled with bullets. He never had a chance. Torn full of holes. We'd been compromised; trapped in the jaws of a fatal ambush.

The gunfire swept over the body of the van and I launched myself at the back doors, flinging them wide open. With the M16 grasped tight in my left hand, I squeezed out a wide arching volley of indiscriminate fire to pin down our assailants and attempt to free up our position. Had to clear us a way out. Grabbed the Target by the scruff of his neck, pulling his languid body after me and down onto the road. Seconds later, bullets screamed through the sides of the van, stabbing perforations through the metal. Head down, I caught Daniel by the scruff and, pumping my legs hard, dragged him across the road at pace. Laid him on his back behind a low white stone wall which framed the neatly kept front garden of a small house on the roadside. Sweating. Blowing hard. Bullets spitting past my head with spite. The Guardia Civil were agitated, firing their pistols over at us in random bursts from behind their stationary vehicles. I returned shots with interest, keeping them more than occupied.

But something didn't add up. *Where had that machine gun come from? Police don't shoot first and ask questions later. They knew we were coming. This was a planned ambush. They murdered Mickey. And there was nothing I could do.*

The intensity of the gun fight slackened. The shootout wasn't taxing. It was apparent that the Spanish police were in desperate need of a firearms refresher course and, seizing the opportunity, I scoped around us for a safer place to decamp. The low wall provided cover for Daniel lying stretched out prone behind, but it did little to protect a target of my size. I clocked a tall, narrow, building some twenty-five yards beyond the roadblock. My eye was drawn to two men exiting and walking briskly up the road to join the officers behind their cars. One was considerably larger than the other, walking with a limp. He wore a black leather jacket. His companion was dressed in a smart tailored suit. They came closer into focus. Sergei Krostanov and the lumbering goon I'd tangled with earlier. I pumped out a volley of slugs in their direction with renewed venom. Everything slotted into place at once. The Guardia Civil were on the payroll of the Russians. They'd been tracking us and predicted that we would take this route. It had indeed been a trap all along, with the machine gun waiting for us in the tower. They were still hunting the Target.

I held my fire and waited a long minute. Thinking hard. *Mickey was dead.* We're outnumbered and outgunned with only a garden wall for cover. I needed to get the Target, who was dying of his injuries, to the hospital in Barcelona as soon as I could. And our only transport had been shot up into little pieces. If that wasn't enough, they now had reinforcements in the shape of two crazy Russians, who hated my guts, wielding a shit-packing machine gun; probably a mounted Browning from the sound of it. It all added up to the odds being stacked against us heavier than a weighted coconut shy at a travelling fair.

The pause in the action and arrival of their paymasters appeared to change up the energy. Two of the uniformed officers lost patience and, perhaps riding on the confidence of their superior numbers, crept forward towards the van. A rudimentary attempt at battle strategy – the basic plan designed to outflank us. The machine gun started up, covering their slow progress and leaving no option but to return shots as it swept all before it, tearing up plants and thumping slugs into the stone wall.

The policemen reached the van and moved around to our blind side, using the vehicle to shield their position. The plan to trap us in a pincer movement had been obvious, but that didn't mean there was much I could do about it. The hail of bullets kept coming. I recalled Mickey saying that we were almost out of petrol. *That might be a blessing in disguise.* With the barrel of the M16 resting on the top of the wall I trained the sights at the van's gas tank. Gave it all I could. A ferocious stream of bullets scorched into the side panel and up across to the engine.

Spontaneous explosions require three elements to occur: a fuel source mixed with oxygen in the right proportions, and an element of heat. The boat-tailed, streamlined, tapered projectiles, known ubiquitously as bullets, propelled through the air with a muzzle velocity of over three thousand feet per second, leaving the barrel of my shooter and into the near empty gas tank. I was gambling that the paucity of fuel inside, which had been the cause of Mickey's consternation, might mean that the ratio of oxygen to inflammable liquid could be close to the optimum ratio of one to fifteen. The epic explosions seen in the movies where the hero shoots up a car, creating huge noise and a monstrous ball of flame, are something of a fallacy. I got lucky. The van was old and inefficient, its fuel tank perhaps not totally vacuum sealed. The bullets sparked a reaction, just as I hoped. The tank blew, not Hollywood production style, but enough to fling the two policemen, pressed against the van, into the road unconscious. What was left of the limited petrol not burnt up in the muted explosion seeped onto the tarmac. Flames engulfed the bodies. I watched Krostanov signal to the men behind the roadblock to hold back from assisting their police colleagues. They stood watching the fire lick at the twitching bodies like they were sacrificial offerings on a pyre. *His card was well and truly marked.*

The flames provided all the distraction we needed. Grabbing the Target by his lapels I backtracked, dragging him up to the front of the house in whose garden we'd taken refuge. I fired a single shot into the lock and hoofed the door open with a kick that any overworked mule would have been proud of. We shuffled inside. A solid looking sideboard stood in the entrance hall. I heaved it forward, tipping it over right up against the front door, jamming it shut. They'd be up on us sharpish now that there was no return fire to keep them at bay. I dragged Ratchet's moaning body into the kitchen and left him stretched out underneath the kitchen table. The gunshot wound in his buttock left a bloody smear behind us across the tiled floor. That he was making any noise at all at this stage could only be a positive sign. I made it to the front window of the house in time to clock the remaining three officers approaching at speed. Two of them made the error of pausing to look over the charred, smouldering bodies of their fallen colleagues. I smashed through the windowpane with the barrel of the M16 and slotted them where they stood; their compassion serving as the agent of their fate. *Did that make me the same as Krostanov?* I wondered. I brushed the irritating thought away. I had no duty of care to these men. This wasn't my troop; they were an enemy with intent to kill, engaged in battle.

The third officer, watching the others drop, hesitated on his advance towards the house, uncertain whether he should opt for the sanctuary of retreat. He was trapped in a virtual no man's land, out in the open and vulnerable. Too far to turn back, not close enough to attack with real impact. The uninvited visitor of a long-discarded memory, jumped into my mind's eye. *The pleasant greenery of an English village cricket pitch on a competitive Saturday afternoon. The batsman caught between wickets, stumps readying to be smashed by an eager keeper as his playing partner pulls late out of a tight run scoring opportunity. Sheer desperation turning to discontented resignation. The bitter taste of injustice as the ineffectual confronts the inevitable.* I spared the officer no quarter for his indecision, slotting a hole between his eyes with cold detachment. Watched as he first came down to his knees before toppling forward, face first. His life taken. An inauspicious innings brought to a premature end.

The Browning took out the remainder of the downstairs windows as the Russians advanced towards us. The Guardia Civil had served their purpose in slowing us down and now these criminals were pursuing us themselves. The M16 was running low on ammo. Returning fire and wasting indiscriminate bullets wasn't a viable option. I needed to regroup and find us a way out. With fragments of broken glass crunching under foot, I back-pedalled out of the front room, fast. This unstoppable assault just kept on coming at us.

As I made it into the hallway, the noise of a crying child pierced the silence of the house. I hadn't even considered that the occupants of the place might be inside. This was a seriously unwelcome complication. Enemy contact any second now. No time to check on Ratchet in the kitchen. Had to work on the assumption he was still alive. The stairs creaked and groaned under my weight as I took them two at a time, bounding up to the first floor.

I found them cowering in a back bedroom. A family of five.

Three children under eight years old; two skinny gap-toothed brothers and their freckled older sister, with neat fringe and saucer-wide brown eyes. They huddled around the skirts of their leather-skinned mother. The father stood frozen as I entered the room, displaying a look of unmitigated terror. I held my free hand aloft in a calming motion and put my index finger to my lips gesturing for silence. The father slunk back deeper into the room, protective of his brood. I wouldn't allow these innocent people to fall into the crossfire of my bloody war with these Russian gangsters.

The repetitive beat of the front door being kicked, until its blockade crashed to the floor, told me that our guests had arrived downstairs. The rhythm of bullets thrashing around the hallway and the graceless tones of destruction announced their intentions. These visitors were not here for tea and sympathy.

I glanced around the bedroom, seeking inspiration. There was a single neatly made bed, adorned with white lace. A simple chest of drawers and a solid wooden wardrobe. A blue tasselled rug stretched over the sanded floorboards. A painting of a small fishing boat on the vast green sea hung on the plain plastered walls. The window was slightly ajar. I prowled across and peered out onto a small rectangle of yellowing Bermuda grass littered with a tricycle and water pistols some fifteen feet below. Beneath the window, roughly five foot down, was a tile ledge running the length of the house, through which a rain gutter was supported. I pushed the window open. Ushered the agitated mother towards it, picking her up under her arms and lowering her until wavering tiptoes found the tiles and she could steady herself below the window. The pandemonium of the situation didn't leave the family with much of a choice. In the end, they'd chosen to co-operate with the scar-faced big guy holding a machine gun, rather than chance their luck with the men downstairs shooting up their home. I couldn't explain the situation in Spanish even if I wanted to, but there wasn't time for that anyway and I was just glad that they were compliant. I lowered the children from the window one at a time by a succession of wriggling arms and legs down to their waiting mother. They edged along the tiled ledge holding hands, flat against the wall. Their father turned to follow them out, but I caught his arm, spinning him to look me in the eye. The beaten expression melted as I handed him the M16 and pointed at the stairs; a look of understanding and resignation forming in its place. Next, I moved to the wardrobe, tearing out its contents of cheap metal hangers, shirts and trousers, littering them over the floor. Rocked the empty wooden carcass back and forth until I found its pivot. Rested it on my good shoulder and heaved it upward with my head inside; the sickly marzipan stench of mothballs filling my nostrils as I breathed. I staggered blind towards the doorway until, guided by my willing friend, I edged out onto the landing. Measured footsteps trod the staircase below. I leveraged the wardrobe off my back, tipping it downward over the banisters and into the stairwell beneath. Crashing. Skidding. Sliding. It crunched to a definitive final halt as it wedged itself firmly between wall and stairs blocking the route up. An angry shout below told that the intervention had been just in time.

I pointed to the gun and gestured with a shooting motion, instructing my petrified accomplice. Gunfire rattled into the wardrobe. He looked up at me through nervous bushy eyebrows and I nodded. He squeezed the trigger in return, jolted backwards by the unexpected kick of the gun, the bullets stamping a messy pattern into the plastered walls of his hallway. No way near accurate, but the noise alone was enough to tell the Russians that the stairway was guarded.

Leaving the man of the house on sentry duty, I moved back into the bedroom. Looked out of the open window. Staring straight ahead onto the garden you couldn't see the petrified family gathered on the ledge below. I hoisted myself onto the window frame and jumped the fifteen feet to the grass, landing on my toes and falling into the automatic roll that we'd been drilled in at parachute school to distribute the landing shock along other parts of the body. The training always kicked-in, muscle memory still intact. It was the debilitating sting from my shoulder that was the problem as I made contact with the lawn. A searing spasm throbbed through me. Eyes watered. I remained face down, the thick grass, coarse against my face, as I waited for the screaming set off inside my brain to subside. My body ached. The energy depleted from my limbs. The seconds passed. *I'm a corpse waiting to happen, stretched out stationary on the lawn. Move out, soldier. Move out, NOW.* I hauled myself to my knees and, clutching at my sticky weeping shoulder, staggered up off the grass and back against the cover of the house wall. Racked with pain. No gun. A house full of innocents depending on me to protect them from the wolves inside.

There was only one chance for us now and that was to come up on these bastards where they didn't expect it. I steeled myself for the showdown. Clenching my jaw and shutting out the pain, I re-entered the house. I'd half expected a message from Ella by now with some quote or other from Henry V about the rounding on the opposition and seizing the upper hand. All very well for him, but I wasn't an army of long bows facing fifty thousand French soldiers, in heavy armour, funnelled together into an unmoveable position on a muddy field. This was a one-armed Tom Hunter facing hand-to-hand combat with a freakishly big Russian maniac and his psychotic boss; armed to the teeth and really pissed off.

～

I made it through the kitchen undisturbed. Daniel was lying very still under the table. He looked like he was lapsing in and out of consciousness. There was no time to check on him. From inside the downstairs hallway the robust exchange of fire told me that the owner of the house was starting to relish his promotion in the field.

Then the shooting from upstairs came to a sudden halt. The depleted magazine clip must have expended. Another minute passed without shots fired. I peeked round the kitchen door and could just make out the thick legs of the Russian as he reached above his head to pound the butt of his gun into the wardrobe. Splinters of wood cascaded as he scythed into the obstacle blocking his way. He'd be through there in no time. I drew my knife and crept into the hallway on my hands and knees, tracking the banisters as I attempted to keep out of sight. The Russian giant was preoccupied with his violent assault on the sturdy piece of old-fashioned furniture. The element of surprise was in my favour. The blood lust was up; senses heightened. My mind emptied itself as pure instinct took over. With his attention absorbed above his head I reached a chunky forearm through the banister battens behind him. A deft flick of the wrist twisted the blade, slicing across his Achilles tendon to severe it away from his ankle bone. The tendon flipped and rolled up into a tight little ball just below his calf. Howling, he crashed down the remaining stairs as he clutched at his leg. His gun sliding and spinning down behind. It was all I needed.

A second later I was on him. Knees pinning his arms and chest to the floor under my entire weight. Blade plunging into his face, neck, heart in an inhuman adrenaline fuelled frenzy. Not halting, long after he'd stopped writhing below me, until totally exhausted. I collapsed forward on top of the body, panting for air, shaking, unable to move. This had been my last throw of the dice. He was heavily armed and in my current physical state, with my shoulder the way it was, I'd be no match for an animal like that in a fist fight. I had nothing more to give. Gambled seven lives on one last play.

Rolling off the body, I could feel my arms and face bathed in a warm gooey coating of gore. The carcass to my side was a mess, like it had been caught in the gears of a combine harvester – chewed up and spat out. Detached from the process, I searched his clothing for weapons and removed a revolver, concealed in an inside pocket. Stared at my handiwork, butchered and mangled, on the floor. I felt no remorse. Nothing but pure animal exhilaration from the kill. I licked the salty splatter of blood from my lips and vowed to never speak of this to another living soul.

I returned to the kitchen, finding the Target unmoved. There was still no time to be lost. The village would surely be overrun with cops any moment now. Hoisting Ratchet out by his feet from under the kitchen table, I checked his pulse. Slapping and shaking until his eyes flickered awake, I urged, 'Come on, Daniel. Wake up! Get it together, man, we're getting the hell out of here now.' Then I dragged him upward over my knee before pulling his limp body across my back. We part-staggered, part-trotted out into the garden. The mother and children were still there, clinging to the side of the house, peering down from the ledge as we made our escape. *They'd have to keep for a while longer*, I thought as I pushed forward, ignoring their pleas for help.

We rounded the front of the house. The van was still smoking. Bodies lying dead at every turn. The scene stretching before us depicted a sorry massacre. An animated group of villagers had clustered across the road; some in tears, some gesticulating in shock at the carnage. Others made urgent phone calls or filmed on their mobiles. Ignoring them, we continued on, unfazed, intent only on getting away as fast we could to avoid the inevitable next wave of law enforcement. I laid the Target on the bonnet of a blue Fiat parked on the road. Untroubled by the gathering witnesses, I smashed my elbow against the window of the passenger seat, shattering glass fragments across the inside of the vehicle. Reached through to flip the lock. Pulled open the door and laid Daniel onto the back seat before locking all of the seat belts across him to hold his outstretched body in place. Sweeping most of the broken glass away, I clambered through the car and inserted myself into the driver seat. It took a little longer than expected of tinkering with the wires under the dashboard before they sparked a connection. The engine roared into life and we squealed away.

I spun the wheel and floored the accelerator, heading back the way we'd come through, the only route that wasn't blocked in the linear village. The way Mickey had driven us in. Only now Mickey wasn't leaving with us. He lay slumped in the burning wreckage of an old Spanish bakery van, riddled with treacherous bullets. The Russians had butchered my friend and I wouldn't rest until there was retribution in full.

I blinked back hot tears, as I drove, recalling the missions we'd worked, the scrapes he'd saved me from. I thought of the verse that I'd committed to memory which felt so powerful at this moment. Words which Ella had given to me following the painful losses we suffered on the infamous Nigerian Embassy job. It was from the Anglo-Saxon poem, *Beowulf*; depicting tales of a hero of the Geats, in Scandinavia, who battles and overcomes both a terrible monster and its fearsome mother whilst defending the King of the Danes:

. . .

'Then Beowulf spoke, son of Ecgtheow... "Bear your grief wise one! It is better for a man to avenge his friend than to refresh his sorrow."

'"As we must all expect to leave our life on this earth we must earn some renown, if we can, before death.

'"Daring is the thing for a fighting man to be remembered for." The Ancient arose and offered their thanks to God.

'To the Lord Almighty, for what this man had spoken.'

I swallowed. A lump stuck in my throat. The grief would be hard to bear. I swore to myself there and then that whatever monsters there were left to battle, nothing, not even the fires of hell, would keep me from avenging Mickey.

44

ENGLAND. LONDON. WESTMINSTER.

'I'm calling a motion of "No Confidence" in the Chamber, Alistair. I've written to the 1922 Committee. The process has begun. Other letters will soon be submitted to reach the minimum threshold and force the vote. There's no way that the PM can continue to lead the Party whilst he's being investigated for criminal activity and after this monumental Rublex farce.'

The Minister trod an impatient circle around the trusted Whip. Alistair Worrell was an impeccable dresser. His suits, cut of the finest cloth, were always immaculately pressed and offset by the ever-present splash of colour from one of any number of silken handkerchiefs which would peek from his top pocket; hinting at a rakish flair bubbling beneath the surface. He was an intelligent man and one of considerable discretion, a powerful attribute for a successful career in politics. He'd secured a double first in classics at Cambridge and entered politics young. His ferocious intelligence was combined with a reputation for tireless hard work and for simply getting the job done; whatever job that may be. He'd grown to become the trusted aide and confidante, the right-hand man even, of one of the genuine power brokers still remaining within government. So good had he become at influencing, cajoling, leveraging toxic snippets of information and massaging egos, that his boss, Big Beast as he was, had long since declared him indispensable. It meant that he wouldn't further progress through the ranks of the party, for the simple reason that he'd proven himself to be too good, too proficient in the dark arts. The Minister couldn't bear to be without such sought after skills for his own ends, and he wouldn't allow them to become available to any potential rival.

Alistair spoke, 'You were instrumental in uncovering the seedy underbelly of this deal with Golich, Minister. Instrumental in undermining the PM on the day of his big announcement. We orchestrated the public humiliation. It's an act of out and out rebellion and a dangerous path we tread, if I may say so, sir. The PM didn't get where he is today without being a calculating, ruthless bastard. He has many supporters who are capable of some pretty nasty and effective stuff, as you rightly know. You won't have an easy ride of it, I can assure you.'

'Alistair, I need to know you can generate the support required to table the motion for the change in the leadership. And to swing the vote our way.'

'I shall have the appropriate words in the appropriate ears, as ever, Minister. I can make no promises and even if we think that we have the commitment of the necessary votes, one can never be certain of the outcome on a matter such as this until the final ballots are cast.'

'Let the chips, then, fall where they may.'

Derek Hemmings sat hunched by the window in his office, from which, if he really strained his neck, he could just about see the corner of Whitehall all lit up by the street lamps. He fixated on a tiny chip in the corner of the thick glass pane. Pale and drawn, his legs danced an uncontrolled nervous jig beneath him. Bony fingers worried at a fraying corner of material on his suit jacket. Things had just got very real.

Six minutes earlier, he'd taken a brief phone call at his desk. And Lord God Almighty, whilst he, Derek Sinjon Hemmings, resided in the sanctity and security of his office, pretending to be working long hours on an intense project in adherence to the Minister's advice, there had been a break-in at his home. A back window smashed. His little Alice alone and vulnerable. Soaking in her regular pre-bed lavender bubble bath. Dear Alice, unaware of the danger that her own husband had selfishly placed her in. The danger that he'd been unable to warn her about.

Her blood-curdling screams had alerted Phil Manning to the situation. Charles Hand's man had been provided as an additional security measure to protect the property should the imminent threat come to fruition. What the dickens Her Majesty's 'Finest' constabulary were doing at the time, Heaven only knows. They were supposed to be guarding the family, so thank goodness for that acerbic man, Hand, after all. The Hand of God they called him. Now Derek knew why. And jolly good for Alice too. His wife, always so buttoned-up and fastidious. She could scream the bloody house down when it served her purpose.

A young man had been found roaming the house. The trained killer sent to remove Derek Hemmings, the thorn in Golich's paw. Manning had ordered him to stop. To surrender his weapon. Request ignored. Gun raised to shoot. Armed. Resisting. Civilian endangerment. No second warning. Shot down where he stood. Shot down inside the Hemmings's family home. Blood staining their new cream carpets at the top of the staircase; carpets that Alice hitherto had not permitted the sole of a single shoe to meet. And a body, lying there prostrate, lifeless where it had fallen. Alice screaming blue murder. *God help us.*

So, the order to suppress Derek Hemmings had been given after all. To maim and to murder. Boris Golich's traitorous sleeper cell inside the British government had been awakened.

And there inside his erstwhile mentor's home, Aleksandr Gontlemoon lay dead.

Pacing around the snug at Chequers, his Buckinghamshire country retreat, nursing a snifter of the finest Napoléon brandy, the Prime Minister was lost deep in thought. He was in a veritably atrocious mood. A fact to which one member of the household staff, at least, could attest. His interview at Scotland Yard had lasted for five straight hours. It had, of course, centred on the alleged impropriety of his relationship with Boris Golich, the Russian oligarch and international businessman. To his mind, the Prime Minister had been paraded like a common criminal, certainly not afforded the courtesies deserved by the leader of the country. His finest hour had been usurped, turned into a mockery in full view of the world's media who were now baying for his blood. He reflected on the precipice navigated between success and failure; how he'd just lost his chance to become immortalised as a national hero through the creation of thousands of jobs and well needed boost to the economy. He also lamented the missed opportunity to amass the great personal wealth which Golich had promised. The Russian's exotic incentive scheme which accompanied the, now defunct, gas exploration deal was certainly capable of holding one's attention. He drained his glass and hurled it in disgust, smashing it inside the wastepaper bin to the side of his desk. The bitter taste of betrayal still lingered in his mouth. They'd gone for the jugular all right. No holding back in their attempt to finish his long and distinguished political career. The Minister had sought to outmanoeuvre the arch political strategist himself and remove him from office once and for all. But this leader of men had clung to the rocks of power for far too long, and he wasn't finished yet. Not by a long shot.

Composing himself as he lifted the ornate bone-handled telephone receiver sitting upon his leather-topped writing bureau, the Prime Minister made a rapid succession of calls. He spoke with fluidity and animation, relishing the emergence of a new-found energy as he beseeched, bullied, and cajoled. By the time the telephone receiver was settled back in its cradle, cages had been rattled, loyalties divided, and a calculated plan had been set in motion.

45

S lowing as we turned a tight corner at the exit to the village, a figure stepped off the curb at the edge of my eyeline. The passenger door flew open and Sergei Krostanov hurled himself into the seat thrusting a revolver into my face. 'Keep your hands on the steering wheel and continue driving please. Retain a steady pace. These mountain roads can still be dangerous even at this time of year,' he said without a hint of humour, the gun hovering a few inches from my temple.

We drove in silence for a few miles, at one point passing a fleet of four police cars driving at speed, lights flashing and sirens blaring, in the direction of the village. Krostanov chose to speak first. Measured tones. 'Your ingenuity has impressed me. I also wished to avoid these new police, seeing as you have spoilt our plans. I appreciate the lift.' He smiled to himself, before glancing into the back of the car at Daniel. 'And, I'm still going to need that tablet, you devious lying rat,' he snapped, the mask of polished decorum slipping momentarily with the unexpected emotion.

'He's half-dead. He can't help you. He can't even speak. I'm taking him to hospital in Barcelona. If he makes it there you might get your precious tablet. You'll never get it if he doesn't.'

'Do you think you give the orders here? You're not the one holding the gun, are you, big man?' I ignored him and kept my eyes fixed on the road. Struggling to keep my cool, hands gripping the wheel. Knuckles white. And then the Russian began to roll the bottoms of his suit trousers up. 'Do you see these, big man?' he asked, drawing my eyes towards the large eight-pointed stars tattooed onto each of his knees. 'You know these? It means I am a boss. "Avtorityet". I kneel to no man. I am a brigadier of the family. It means respect. It means that a pig like you does as I say.'

'Vory,' I growled in response.

'Yes Vory. The Bratva. Mafia. Crime lords. Thief-in-Law. Whatever you want to call us. We are all powerful. We buy the police, so they do our bidding. They work for us now. We will never obey their laws. Even the governments of countries from around the world fear our wrath. We've always operated outside of society by our lifelong vow, but society now bends to our will. I have even made your quaint little game of golf dance like a puppet to our tune. A distraction so we can run Rublex oil and gas through Europe! This gives me the greatest of pleasures. The whole of Europe has always viewed mighty Russia as some feral mongrel cousin. We spoke French at court for three hundred years instead of our beautiful mother tongue, so ashamed was our disgusting nobility by our lack of sophistication in eyes of the world. I came from dirt. I saw how the privileged played this game of golf in summer. It was not for boys like me. I knew they played it in rich countries whilst we toiled and stole to have enough to eat. I hated those people, and I hated those countries. I wanted very much back then to destroy everything they stood for, to destroy this game of the rich. And now we are the game. I hope you understand, big man, that even you proud

Englishmen now bow to the might of the Vory.' He rattled the gun and his free hand against the dashboard in the attempt at a theatrical drum roll. An announcement of fact.

Something inside me snapped. The road ahead bled from single carriage way into a main road with multiple lanes. As we approached the turn I stepped down on the accelerator. 'What are you doing? Slow down now,' Krostanov screamed. We came up towards the apex fast and I slotted my seat belt into place. 'Stop now. I order it,' he shouted, the concern palpable in his voice. He held the gun at my head.

The threats meant nothing. I was resolute. Committed. Metres from the junction, I pulled down hard onto the steering wheel and swerved off the road. The scene played out as if in fragments of a dream. The bonnet of the Fiat crunched into the metal signpost at sixty kilometres an hour. It crumpled on impact. The inside of the car was filled with unintelligible shouts and cries. Daniel and I were thrown forward and jolted hard against the protective belts. But we remained in our seats. Shaken. Rattled. The force of the crash tearing the belt into my shoulder like I was being sawn in half. When I looked across I found the front windscreen had been smashed through by the flying body of my uninvited passenger.

Seconds felt like years as in its state of shock my brain stretched the elasticity of the linear temporal continuum on which perception exists by scrambling to compute millions of tiny pieces of information as to the state of my body, the external environment and the exposure to near and current danger following the crash. This biological response explains why trauma victims often hold and replay vivid recollections of minute and seemingly insignificant fragments of their experiences. Why I was still haunted by the flashbacks perhaps.

I unbuckled the seat belt with deliberate care. Managing to pivot my body, I kicked open the twisted door metal. Staggered from the car. Took a drawn-out moment to savour the feeling of my feet on the solid ground as I lumbered away from the concertinaed motor. Two cars had pulled over some way behind us and the drivers were getting out to see how they could try and help. They called out to me as they jogged over but there was only one thought in my mind. My first consideration was not for my injuries nor even to rescue the Target from the wreckage. I was myopic in my dreadful purpose. At the front of the crash site lay the man responsible for Mickey's death, prone on his back upon the grass verge. His forehead was sliced open to the skull. The contours of his face were mapped with a network of tiny lacerations. By the odd angle his body was positioned, it looked as if he had broken both arms, shoulder blade, and collarbone. A pained scowl was wrenched across his face. The Vory was conscious.

I stood over him, staring down with unblinking eyes, as he writhed in agony beneath me. 'Help me. Help me please,' he rasped. I held his gaze, then stamped my boot heel down onto his kneecap shattering the patella bone and rupturing the conjoined cartilage; administered with vicious precision. The quiet moan of torment emanated from deep inside him. I shifted my weight and brought the boot down again, this time onto his second kneecap, smashing it beyond all repair. That noise again. He tried to twist away in pathetic desperation.

'Now you couldn't kneel again if you wanted to, you worthless thief.' I hocked up a globule of phlegm from the back of my throat and spat it into Sergei Krostanov's lacerated face. 'That's for Mickey.'

His eyes flashed with indignation, a futile last act of defiance. I knelt beside him on the grass. Our stares collided, an unflinching channel of emotional intensity between us as I placed my hand over his mouth and nose. He wheezed, twisted hard and then spluttered as he fought desperately for oxygen under my firm grip. A protruding blue vein pulsed prominently down the centre of his forehead, his face red and blotchy. At last, the fight left him and, submitting to the inevitable, his eyes once again locked onto mine, only now in a sad embrace of human fragility. I watched without remorse as his life faded in my hands.

One of the passers-by who'd stopped his car at the roadside to help with the accident was picking at pieces of metal and trying to reach inside. He looked very stressed. The other man had reached me as I finished with the Vory.

'Tú lo mataste,' he said in disbelief. He was shaking. I ignored it and kept walking. 'You kill him,' he said louder after me in English. I stopped in my tracks and fixed the good Samaritan with a steely glare, eyes narrowed to slits. I pointed directly at him.

'The crash killed him. You saw nothing.' The man dropped his eyes to the ground, nodded and said nothing.

I returned to the vehicle and motioned for the do-gooder, who was now leaning inside the car, to move aside. He looked relieved to be given permission to stand clear of the wreckage and a possible impending explosion. The Target had survived the crash. He was clearly in a terrible state but was somehow managing to cling onto life. Daniel was proving to be quite a fighter. I respected his stubborn refusal to submit to the welcome seduction of death after everything that he'd gone through. I unbuckled the seat belts, his bruised and swollen form like meat cooking on the grill. Reached in and pulled him from the car. Cradling the limp body, draped across both of my outstretched arms, we turned away from the contorted metal and staggered towards the motorway intersection.

A blur of vehicles raced past us as we stood, steadfast, on the edge of the road. There's no doubt that we would have made an unusual and alarming sight; one that many of the rubberneckers felt best to avoid. It wasn't too long, however, before a huge juggernaut pulled to a halt on the hard shoulder just in front of us. The driver wound down the window and in a strong Dutch accent shouted down at us, 'Are you guys all right? Is he injured? Can I help you?'

'He's in a bad way. We need to get to the hospital in Barcelona. Are you headed that way, mate?'

'Sure. I can take you. There's a turning off the motorway which heads straight there. It's not far from my route. But don't you think you should get an ambulance to take you there? I have a phone if you need one.'

'There's no time to waste. Thanks, though. Can I bring him up to the cab?'

'Sure. Come on up. There's a little day cot back here where he can rest.' The driver swung open the heavy door to his cab and scampered down a couple of short metal steps. He helped me to carry Daniel's limp body up into the cab of the huge eighteen-wheeler, protecting his head as we manoeuvred him through the door and into the back.

'What happened to him? He looks in a pretty bad way, no?' he asked and then, after running his eye over my bloodstained face and shirt, 'Come to mention it, so do you. You guys been in an accident or something? You look like you've been in the wars.'

'If I told you, mate, you really wouldn't believe me. Just put it down to a car accident.'

'That car that also fires bullets, does it?' he said from the corner of his mouth.

'Best you don't ask. Seriously. I'm sorry but we need to get going. He's fading fast.'

The driver, whose name I established was Joost, handed me a large bottle of water which I tried to get Daniel to drink from in vain. I left him alone to rest.

We drove in silence for the next thirty or so minutes, eating up miles of tarmac. With Ratchet secured in the cot at the back and as safe as he could be for now, I was able to relax for the first time in days. I closed my eyes for a few seconds, seeking some much-needed respite; having run on a high octane mix of anger and adrenaline for far too long. I fell into an instant deep sleep, enveloped by a comforting velvety shroud knitted of urgent images and dreamy fragments shooting through my unconscious. And time leapt forward until I was shaken awake.

'Hey, buddy. We're getting pretty close. It's the turn off at the next junction.'

I shook my head clear. 'Thanks. You've really helped us out here, Joost. Things were looking pretty dicey before you turned up.' The juggernaut swung off the motorway at the signs for the city of Barcelona. We followed a series of recently laid one-way roads connected by a complex pattern of roundabouts before arriving at a stark modern building on the outskirts of the city. They didn't make buildings look like buildings anymore. I wouldn't have recognised it as a hospital, it was so radical in design. We wheeled into a sparsely occupied car park and pulled to a halt. 'Well. This is it. I hope your friend will be all right.'

'Thank you. He might be now – because of you.' I offered my hand in a gesture of friendship. We both carried Daniel off the truck and, because our injuries might be in need of some explanation, I suggested that I carried him alone into the hospital. The trucker slapped me on the back and I cradled the Target in my arms through the automatic doors and into the air conditioned cool of the hospital reception.

From somewhere behind us a massive engine roared, a klaxon sounded a final farewell.

46

The brilliance of the early morning sun reflected on the windows of The East India Club and back over St James's Square. A pair of overfed pigeons squabbled on the Mayfair pavement over the grubby remains of a discarded hotdog bun. They ignored, with a practised nonchalance, the blacked-out Mercedes Benz as it pulled alongside them. The Minister stepped out first onto the pavement. Derek Hemmings piled out from the back seats after him, smoothing his suit. Decisions needed to be taken on the way forward. Late last evening they'd been summoned to a breakfast meeting with the Prime Minister. It was a curious thing given the battle lines had already very much been drawn. No explanations had been provided but, with curiosities peaked by a number of cryptic clues, there'd been little doubt that attendance would appear to be in best interests. Given the unpleasant altercation at the public unveiling of the gas exploration deal, leading to the PM being taken in for police questioning, the two men were not exactly looking forward to the engagement. Derek's stomach was a bubbling, twisting testimony to this very fact. So much so that he hadn't managed an attempt at breakfast, nor swallowed so much as a mouthful of

318

hot coffee. The truth was that he hadn't yet recovered from the enormity of what had occurred inside his own home. The mortal danger which Alice had been placed in, on his account. A point that was not lost on her either. She was requiring an inordinate amount of attention and fussing to keep frayed nerves at a settled peak. This was the first time since 'the incident', as it was now labelled, that Derek had been permitted to leave the house, a kindly neighbour sitting with her in his place. The spectre of the threat to his own life, and betrayal of the aide, for whom he'd fostered near-paternal affection, still lingered. Despite his enduring malaise however, Derek resolved that he'd come so far in his quest to do the right thing already, that he owed it to Queen and country to see things through.

The front door to the club was opened with aplomb by a portly man in smart red jacket and bowler hat. They entered a square room, usually reserved for card games, and were greeted by the welcoming aroma of freshly brewed coffee. The Prime Minister sat alone at the felt covered table, hands clasped as if in prayer. After a moment of staged silence, he gestured to the empty seats. Cleared his throat. He began, 'I want you to know that I've drawn a line.'

'How very generous of you,' the Minister replied. Derek noted the barbed spar and assiduously avoided any eye contact.

'You miscalculated, Minister. Played your hand too early.' The pertinence of the remark was not lost on the trio given they sat in a room designed for serious gambling.

'Pah! You've been caught with your grubby little paws in the till. End of story, sir!' the Minister snapped, smashing back his riposte. *Anyone for tennis?* thought Derek to himself miserably.

'I'm afraid that just won't wash. Better men than you have examined this matter in forensic detail. The only thing linking me to Golich appears to be a job taken by my old school pal in a foreign country. He's taken full culpability and I of course, shall, publicly distance myself from the little turd and maintain that any endorsements are fake. Nothing else is provable. This won't drag me down, not in the long term.'

'There is a vote of No Confidence to be scheduled in the House. Call it a long overdue coup, if you will. I'm running for the leadership.'

The Prime Minister offered an enigmatic smile and leaned backwards in his chair. Derek shifted in his seat and wondered if he might ask for a cup of the rich fragrant coffee that smelt so good. Or perhaps, he fretted, that moment had passed, in terms of polite etiquette, eclipsed by the overt sniping. He swallowed drily and kept his council.

'I take it you've canvassed for support on this one, Minister. Counted those votes home already, have you? Convinced that this stink is going to stick, aren't you?' A dismissive, derisory tone.

'Shouldn't I?' enquired the Minister, for the first time sounding a little less than sure.

'Well, I'm certain you've got your best men on it. How is Alistair anyway? I'm sure he'll be able to marshal at least fifteen per cent of the party to submit letters of support for the motion and then gain a majority to vote against me. Especially after all I've done for them. Bringing them back to power after so long. Rewarding so many with jobs, responsibility, purpose. Oh, by the way, is he still shagging that sixteen-year-old Filipino houseboy that he's got stashed away at his Fulham pied-à-terre? I don't expect he'd want a big scene made about that, now would he? The fallout of these things can be so unpleasant. It's the families in these situations that I always worry about.'

Derek gave an unexpected snort. Covered his face with both hands, humiliated. Stared down at the table. The Prime Minister looked directly at him for the first time and raised a hawkish eyebrow. 'You were the cause of this in the first place by all accounts, Hemmings. What's a no-mark civil servant on the verge of fading away into the obscurity of retirement doing prying into affairs that don't concern him anyway?'

Derek blushed. 'I was doing the right thing, sir.' The PM sniggered.

Hemmings rallied to his theme. 'I was looking out for the interests of this noble country at a time when, I'm sorry to say, our leader was displaying a spectacular dereliction of duty.' His face was flushed with anger. The Minister looked at him with pride. 'You've underestimated the depth of feeling surrounding this, Prime Minister.'

'And you've underestimated the power of national support for seven thousand jobs following years of economic wilderness. The country wants this. They don't give a monkey's red arse about Golich's past. They want a proactive leader, someone who'll stick their neck out for growth.' His diction was the immaculate epitome of self-assurance. Their eyes locked in an unflinching battle of wills. Neither man prepared to look away first. Finally, the Prime Minister spoke again. 'Humphrey has done the rounds. He's spoken to the troops. Some were a little nervous about yesterday and the Golich relationship, but on balance they're still with me. If you do manage to scrape enough letters for the motion to go ahead you'll only squeeze fifteen to twenty per cent of the vote. I've still got the whip, Minister. We'll smash you in a leadership contest and you know it.'

The Minister gripped the table with both sweaty palms as he absorbed the words. Derek exhaled and made eyes at the bubbling coffee jug. 'Why are we here?' he asked, his tone flat, deflated.

'I don't want a battle, Brian,' the PM oozed. 'I need you on my team. I'm not going to suffer for this, and I don't see the point in losing one of the biggest stars of the front bench in the process.' He gazed across the green felt at them both, riding his momentum. 'Is this really worth your career, Brian? Of course, I understand very well that after the rigmarole of yesterday and the public denouncement of the Rublex deal that some explanation is needed; some massage and management of the narrative. And yes, of course, someone will indeed need to take the fall.' With that the Prime Minister raised his eyebrows and chuckled, arms open in a magnanimous gesture of generosity. 'Who do you think that should be, Derek? How would you feel if I suggested that a certain Andrew Bartholomew could be lanced on the harpoon for this?'

Derek glanced sideways at the Minister and then back at the PM. 'I'm listening,' was all he said.

'Here's the trade, gentlemen. We'll continue the gas exploration but won't deal with Golich. He's off the menu for good. But we will try to find a partner that we can progress with to build infrastructure for those jobs. Minister, you'll call off the vote of No Confidence. Come out in support of me and I'll give you any tenure you desire. Your pick of the top jobs. Heck, I'll even endorse you to take over from me when my term is up. I'll recommend you as successor and won't stand for another re-election. So much cleaner than all this messy infighting which just serves to weaken the party, don't you say?' He waited whilst the rhetorical question settled between them. 'Hemmings, you'll get the bump up to MI6 your file shows you always wanted. A final hurrah. A kicker to the pension fund, something to impress upon the little lady. And best of all, old boy, you get to stick the knife right between Bartholomew's shoulder blades yourself. Whatdayasay, chaps?'

Derek looked at the Minister, who was looking right back at him. The Minister cleared his throat. He spoke with a quiet intensity. 'Well played, Prime Minister. It seems that you have yourself a deal.'

47

'Do you speak English?' I pressed the corpulent nurse,
squashed behind the hospital reception desk. She was
squeezed inside a baby pink uniform, brown eyes atop a pair of
pudgy cheeks and framed with a frizz of black curls. Completing
a complicated looking form she resembled a studious cuddly
toy. The look thrown back at me couldn't hide the alarm on her
face as I stood dangling a flopping body in my arms. She began
calling for help in Spanish, unbridled urgency in her voice. All
eyes in the waiting room were fixed upon us.

Two porters appeared from nowhere, dressed head to foot in
powder blue. They fussed around us, trying to ease the Target
from my arms. I stood steadfast. 'I need to see Doctor
Cavastendros. This is urgent.' The request elicited a series of
blank looks. I repeated the name back louder to the nurse as I
shrugged off the unwanted attentions of the hospital orderlies. A
brief phone call later and we were at last directed down a well-lit
corridor.

I tapped my steel toecaps twice against the base of the clinic
door to announce our arrival. Entered sideways, careful not to
bang Daniel's head on the frame. I smiled to myself. *It would be*

323

just my style to get this far and finish the Target off with a concussion on the way in to the hospital.

A small man in a white coat, horn-rimmed glasses and with a grey goatee beard rose from his chair, directing me towards a medical table. I laid the Target flat as the concerned doctor busied himself, checking for vital signs. 'Charles Hand sent me. He said you'd be expecting us.'

'Yes. Everything is arranged. There'll be no police record of the injuries, the gunshot wound. You guys weren't here. And, of course the treatment is already taken care of. Do you know what has happened to him?' he asked as he inserted a cannula into the vein, then attached a saline drip to the bung in order to feed the arm of the ailing patient. 'I need the truth.'

'What I know is this, Doc. He's in a bad way. He's lost quite a bit of blood. He was shot in the arse. Mauled by a dog. Think he took quite a beating before I sprang him.'

'Bad day at the office then,' the physician replied without cracking a smile.

'He's going to make it, right? You'll have to attest that I got him here alive.'

'He's very weak. Surprisingly stable given what he's been through. The bullet looks to be still inside him. However, you got him to me in the time frame in which surgery can still be performed and can make a difference. So, the good news is, once we've stabilised your friend, we can operate. We'll sanitise his wounds, replace the blood he's lost, and medicate him correctly. He needs fluids. I don't think he's eaten or drunk for some time.'

'What are the chances of him pulling through?'

'In my view he's got a better than fifty per cent chance of making it through this but that would have dropped by nearly ten per cent every hour that he didn't get the treatment he needs.'

A seriously close call.

It had been a rough ride, but we could handle those odds after what Daniel and I had been through together. I nodded. Backed up. Flopped into a plastic chair at the side of the room. Closed my eyes. Head spinning.

'We can't work with him until he's taken on the fluid. Your shoulder needs care too. It's seeping.'

'Yeah. I took a lump of lead a day or so back. Got the bullet fragments out myself. Tried to clean it up. It feels all wrong now though, Doc.'

'Let me see. It's not good that you haven't had treatment for so long. It hasn't been sanitised properly. You may have an infection by now.'

He moved across the room and peeled away the makeshift bandages and dressings to give the unfettered access he needed. He sterilised and cleaned the wound. Injected local anaesthetic into the shoulder. I watched as he took a set of metal tongs, resembling some form of medieval torture implement, and fished around inside the bullet hole for what seemed like an eternity. Gritted my teeth. A tiny metallic clatter inside the petri dish was reward for his industry and told that he'd removed the remaining shrapnel that my own primitive attempt had left behind. He dressed the shoulder tight, packed with clean gauze and wadding, and secured my arm in a sling. He smiled at me. 'No arm wrestling for you for a while, okay?'

'Sure thing, Doc,' I said, grinning back at him. I flicked my eyes towards Ratchet as a nurse tended to his medical requirements. 'Will he need to stay in overnight?' I asked, catching myself staring at her as she reached over the examination table, the hem of her uniform riding up a little.

Cavastendros smoothed the hairs on his beard. 'He'll be here for quite some time I should think. We'll determine the best course of treatment for his injuries. He'll need surgery as I've said, but first we have to check for signs of internal bleeding. He seems to have been beaten pretty badly. I have my instructions from Charles to look after him. You've done your bit. He's in safe hands.'

'Thank you. Take good care of him, Doc, you don't know how much it means to me,' I replied, holding his gaze before getting to my feet. I stepped over to where the Target lay stretched out, motionless. Placed my free hand on the back of Daniel Ratchet's head and held it there with tenderness for a moment. Then I nodded once at the doctor. About turned. Never looked back.

48

ENGLAND. HAMPSHIRE. FARNBOROUGH AIRPORT.

The Lear Jet sat idling on the runway strip at Farnborough Airport as the pilot completed his final checks. Inside the decadent cabin was a short martini bar, an unnecessarily large flat screen and two white leather swivel seats which faced each other across a faux marble table. Boris Golich sat expressionless in one of these seats, speaking on the phone. The blonde head of a young stewardess was just visible as it bobbed underneath the table.

'Boris Golich for Trade Minister Zhou,' he barked into the handset. He waited a beat for the familiar voice of the Chinese politician to answer. 'Zhou, it's Boris. I'm willing to resume our discussions. The British have got cold feet on the gas deal. There's a considerable opportunity for the People's Republic to secure this vast natural resource for yourselves and leverage the desperation of our naïve Argentinean friends. You know my terms. You have until close of business tonight.'

He ended the call with a single jab of his stubby forefinger, then took his time adjusting the angle of his seat. As the hum of the jet engines increased in pitch, Boris Golich produced an oversized Cuban cigar from his jacket pocket and blazed it alight. The wheels left the runway and folded neatly into the undercarriage of the plane. A look of contentment settled across his perfectly lineless face.

49

ENGLAND. SUSSEX. GATWICK AIRPORT.

The airport bar was quiet and dimly lit. An elderly couple sat together in wordless contentment, complete in each other's company. The impossibly young-looking bartender stood waiting, battling with the perennial boredom of the job. A man occupied the corner table with his back to the bar, a bottle of Scotch and two glasses set before him. I moved across the room and joined him. He filled the glasses.

'To Mickey,' he said as he raised his glass.

'To Mickey,' I repeated solemnly. Took a deep swallow of the golden liquid.

Charles Hand refilled the glasses. 'To fallen comrades,' he said draining his whisky.

'Fallen comrades.'

'It's good to see you, Thomas. You did well out there, in a difficult situation. You recovered the Target. Alive. Daniel Ratchet is now safe thanks to us. He'll recover from his injuries given time. We can get the lad back to his parents.'

'It was touch-and-go for a while, boss.'

'I know. They don't mess about, the Russian mob. They're a nasty, uncompromising group of savages who live by their own rules.' He paused. 'I trust that you made them pay for killing Mickey. I know that must have hurt you, Thomas. Badly. Watching as it all happened so fast in front of you and being powerless to help him. I hope it didn't stir up bad memories. Mickey was one of the best.'

I nodded. The lump back in my throat.

The Hand of God pushed back his chair. Rose. Pushed a brown padded envelope across the table towards me. 'Ten thousand pounds as usual. Plus, twenty for bringing him back alive. Take some time off, Thomas. I'll be in touch when we need you again. And for crying out loud, take Ella for some dinner or something, will you? That poor girl keeps asking after you.' I was still grinning as he walked away.

I sat alone with my thoughts for a while. The contents of the bottle were fast diminishing before me. I savoured the mellow, peaty flavour; the burning sensation on my tongue. I gathered myself and checked the phone for messages. An unopened text from Ella sat neglected.

So sorry about Mickey. We all loved him, Tom. xoxo

I blinked back a tear. Figured I might just listen to The Hand of God's dinner suggestion after all.

But no sooner had it entered my mind, the thought melted like snow on a hot chimney stack. Standing at the entrance to the bar was a curvaceous red-haired woman with white porcelain skin, hugging a man and pulling two tiny children close into her legs. They said their goodbyes and she stood as they walked away, waving after them. I watched her turn and, pulling a smart red case behind her, she wiggled into the bar. She deliberated for some time, just a couple of metres from me, and eventually ordered a drink. The skintight, three-quarter length crème trousers and red high heels she wore perfectly accentuated her physique. I felt the warm glow of the whisky in my stomach. She turned, clutching a bottle of beer, French tipped nails wrapped around its neck. She was deciding on a place to sit. I kicked the chair opposite me from out under the table and gestured to it. She smiled a polite acknowledgement and looked around for somewhere else.

'It's okay. I don't bite,' I said. And then, 'Please. Join me. I could use the company.'

She thought about it for a moment and then, with an imperceptible shrug, she stepped across and eased herself into the chair. 'That's quite the line,' she tossed back at me, manicured eyebrows issuing a challenge. 'What happened to your arm?' she said, running a glossy fingernail down the sling. I leaned forward, eyes narrowed as if pretending to offer a secret. 'I could tell you, but I don't think you'd believe me.'

'Try me. I might like it.'

'Really?'

'Sure, stud. Somehow I'm starting to think I might enjoy hearing about you getting badly injured.'

I laughed. 'Ah well. You know, it was just the usual crap. Saving kittens from trees. Rescuing damsels in distress, that kind of thing.'

'You must be some kind of regular hero, then,' she teased.

I flashed my best lopsided grin. 'I do my best.' Held her gaze for a second too long. 'So, listen. I'm only going to say it once. You can pretend you didn't hear me, finish your drink, and carry on with your life. But you look like the kind of girl who might just be crazy enough to want to step outside of the predictable boring bubble of this existence every now and then. Might realise that we're really only on this rock for a tiny amount of time. We all have to grab an adventure in life when one comes along. I like that. And I like you.'

She looked down at her drink, a coy smile playing round her lips. A few seconds later she flashed back up at me with those, big, bright eyes. 'Say it then,' she whispered.

'Your flight had better not leave anytime soon. My hotel's close by.' She emitted a moan. Then the smile flickered once more at the corners of her mouth.

'I hope that you have two rooms reserved, stud. One for you and one for your ego! Go to hell, big boy, and if I were you, I'd retire those chat-up lines for good.' My jaw slackened.

She pushed back her chair, took a swig of beer and walked away. I watched after her in disbelief, her hips rolling as she crossed the bar. She knew for damn sure I was following with my eyes. She reached the exit to the bar, half-turned her head back towards me and delivered a deep sultry wink. Then she was gone.

Golden.

50

F ive weeks had passed by since Tom Hunter had rescued him from his Vory kidnappers. Daniel Ratchet had felt strong enough to fly back to the UK. He'd healed well under the discreet supervision of Doctor Cavastendros in Barcelona. Charles Hand had facilitated Mr and Mrs Ratchet in visiting the Spanish hospital to see their son. The whole saga had been a blur. Draining. Daniel felt as if he had been caught up and spat out by a spiteful tornado. He wasn't quite sure what was actual memory anymore and what had twisted into cruel imagination.

He climbed the steps of the smart European Tour Headquarters in Wentworth, tucked away in an affluent and leafy part of the Surrey countryside. His stomach churned with apprehension. This was the chance to tell his side of the story. To seek some redress with the Tour and finally expose the tournament fixing in which the Rublex Corporation, principal sponsor of the European game, was so instrumental. He'd managed to speak briefly with Silvio by phone and agreed to meet him here as a representative of Crown Sports.

He entered the building and was shown into an empty room, bathed with natural sunlight. It was airy and oval shaped. The walls were adorned with paintings of various sizes, mostly depicting early Scottish golfing scenes, consisting predominantly, it seemed, of men in cloth caps swinging primitive looking wooden clubs at leather balls. Ratchet waited for both Francis Broome, Chief Executive of the European Tour, and Silvio to arrive. Fifteen minutes passed. Then thirty. Daniel paced the room, his stomach a fretful swirl of nerves. Perhaps he'd got the wrong time. Or had they forgotten about him? Surely the matters he'd come to discuss would be considered significant enough to warrant granting him an audience. He bristled.

When the double doors to the room swept opened, Francis Broome entered carrying a large leather-bound portfolio wallet. They shook hands and each chose seats around the antique table. 'I'm sorry to hear of your recent trials and tribulations, Daniel,' began Broome. 'We all are, I speak on behalf of the entire Tour. I know you had just joined us as an agent representing some of our players not so long ago, but we're a close-knit family in golf, and we were all so shocked. Especially coming at a time when we have had to contend with the terribly sad deaths of Rublex Corporation sponsorship director, Sergei Krostanov, long-standing coach, Bob Wallace, and physiotherapist, Michael Hausen. It's been a torrid time.'

'It's all connected. I was kidnapped by Sergei Krostanov,' said Daniel flatly.

'I've seen the police report,' Broome interrupted, cutting him short. Curt, direct.

'They kidnapped me because I found out about corruption on the Tour. Tournament fixing and unfair undue influence upon many of your key players is rife. The caddies are running an illegal gambling and enforcement ring. It's all bloody fixed. It's disgraceful.' Daniel was enraged. He rose from his seat clenched fists on the table, glaring.

'Daniel, please calm down. We appreciate that you've been through a lot, but I really can't sanction such overblown accusations. I won't permit you to besmirch the good name and reputation of the European Golf Tour and our major sponsor. You must be careful that you don't stray into the realms of slander with what you're saying. It's highly contentious.' Broome reprimanded him like he was a child. 'The truth of the matter is that you've been through quite an ordeal. It's known that this can affect someone emotionally. Distort their perceptions so to speak. Sergei kidnapped and tortured you, yes. That's been corroborated. And a dreadful situation that was.' He stepped towards the window and looked away from Daniel, unable to hold his eye. 'But whatever criminal actions he took, he did so in his own name. They're saying that he snapped. He's been overworked and under immense pressure to deliver the sponsorship programme for Rublex and it got too much for him. This "breakdown" he suffered manifested itself in the terrible criminal behaviour he inflicted upon you. It proves that he was in a disturbed state of mind in that he went on to take his own life shortly afterwards in a motor accident. He must have been feeling enormous guilt for his actions and the suffering caused. It's appalling what you've endured, Daniel, but I maintain that this can only be viewed as the individual and isolated criminal behaviour of a man with personal psychological issues. It's simply not relevant to call the probity of the European Golf Tour into question as an organisation. All this talk of cheating is complete and utter nonsense, I'm afraid. We have conducted an internal root and branch review for our own reassurance, and it's turned up nothing. We did find a little evidence of some unacceptable high jinks by some of the more boisterous caddies, which you mention, and since then a portion of these disaffected freelancers have moved themselves along and off the Tour, in the wake of so much sorrow.'

Daniel was exasperated. 'I have evidence. It's all documented. I can prove it. Rublex is ruining the Tour. Why won't you listen to me?'

'Daniel, Daniel, come now, this is pure fantasy. Rublex is the European game's greatest benefactor in our history. They've committed to invest over a hundred million pounds into our Tour through sponsorship and activation, to drive the development of the sport in countries all over Europe. I believe this relationship is one of their principal business engagement activities. They simply wouldn't do anything to endanger that. Where's this evidence you speak of?'

'It's all saved on a stats programme on my tablet. I've even got a video recording of Krostanov and Andy Sharples discussing the corruption at the highest level.'

'Show me.'

'I don't have it. I left it for Matilda Axgren to hold for safekeeping in the physio truck before I was taken.'

'I see. Well perhaps we'd better ask her ourselves then?'

Daniel felt the blood drain from his face at the mention of her name. *Matilda. Here. Right now.* He hadn't been able to contact her from the hospital. She hadn't been traceable. How he wanted to hold her in his arms again. 'Is Matilda here?' he stammered.

'Yes. And Silvio Flavini of Crown Sports, whom you also know.'

'I was wondering what had happened to Silvio, we agreed to meet here. He's fully aware of everything I've been saying. You must ask him yourself, he'll verify it.'

The older man stood up, ensuring the integrity of the crease in his trousers as he rose. He ambled across the room, opened the double doors, and disappeared for a brief moment. When he returned, he was accompanied by Matilda and Silvio. Daniel stood and feasted his eyes upon her. She looked so beautiful.

Somehow different to how he'd remembered. More grown up, perhaps. Aloof, distant somehow. She wore a black business suit, tailored to show off her striking figure, skirt cut just above the knee. No jewellery. Daniel had never seen her looking so professional. But there was something he couldn't place. Her long platinum blonde hair was worn in a tight bun, tied at the back of her head. She carried a smart new Louis Vuitton satchel. There was no eye contact as she entered the room. Silvio, in corduroy trousers and a casual open-neck shirt, sported a deep tan, as always. Daniel sensed that he was more uneasy than he recalled; the usual smooth demeanour appeared slightly ruffled. He greeted Daniel with a little wave and the hint of an awkward smile, choosing to keep the table between them.

'Daniel,' began Broome, 'I would like to introduce you to the new team at the head of Rublex European Tour golf sponsorship.'

Daniel felt his knees buckle. He gripped the table for support. 'What do you mean?' he asked.

'Matilda has replaced Sergei, following his breakdown and absence from the job due to overwork and stress. And, of course, the tragic road accident. Despite your personal situation, I'm sure you'll agree that it's also a difficult time for her to have lost her fiancé in such circumstances. She's still grieving. Silvio will be supporting her in implementing the sponsorship program across the Tour; on secondment from Crown Sports.'

Daniel had heard nothing after the word fiancé. His head spun. Then it landed. Hard. No jewellery. It was the first time that he'd seen her without her 'mother's' engagement ring, the ring that she claimed she wore to protect herself. That she claimed she wore to feel close to her lost family. All lies. The black suit seemed to show that she was in mourning for Krostanov.

Daniel looked at Matilda with disgust. 'Sergei? Your fiancé all along? How could you?'

Matilda said nothing. He flipped. 'Breakdown? Road accident? Is that what you are insisting on calling it?' Daniel Ratchet, ex-rookie agent, was screaming at Francis Broome, the Chief Executive of the European Tour; an unfathomable situation that would have been absurd to consider not more than three months ago. 'That bastard kidnapped me, beat me, nearly bloody killed me, and you call it a breakdown? At least I know his death was no accident. He got what he deserved, executed by the man who saved me. Someone with honour in his blood.' He looked across at Matilda as he said this, daring to meet her gaze for the first time. Pale watery blue eyes stared back with defiance. He continued, 'How the hell could you work for Rublex, Matilda? You know what's been going on. Didn't you find the tablet I hid for you? All the evidence is on it. The video recording of Sergei discussing fixing the events so they could manipulate the odds in their illegal gambling ring and cheat the big money Asian gamblers. My programme outputs, detailing the tournament fixing patterns and the player match statistics analysis, linked to the saved versions of sponsorship contracts for specific players incentivising them to throw places and drop shots.'

'You mean this tablet, Daniel?' Matilda answered, her voice cold and devoid of emotion as she produced the device from her satchel.

'Yes! Thank you. All the evidence is on there. Finally, you'll all see that everything I said is true.'

'There's nothing on here, Daniel. I don't know what you mean. I found the computer you left for me on the desk in the truck. I've been through everything and there's no data that you speak of. I discussed these matters at great length with Mr Golich, owner of Rublex. We needed to find a way forward between us, and he was most obliging. And, of course, regarding my future on the Tour with the advice of the kind Mr. Broome.' She beamed across at him. 'There's no evidence of this corruption. Somehow, Daniel, you are badly confused.'

She said that she found the tablet on the desk in the truck? I didn't leave my tablet on the desk, it was stashed in the cavity beneath the cushions on the bench seats. It can't be so. Is she lying to me again?

'Matilda, I trusted you. I loved you. How can you betray me like this?'

'Don't be silly, Daniel. What we had wasn't special. Sure, it was a little fun, but you need to get over it. I was merely playing my part in helping Sergei to secure the players for his sponsorship contracts. I need this job. I have to pay for my brother's treatment and care. Sergei was a mentor, a friend. We met when I was studying in Russia and later, when I needed work, he got me the physiotherapy job on the Tour. He knew my desperate family situation and we reached an understanding. Over time our relationship blossomed. There was always every aspiration for me to progress within Rublex, given my background of studying business. My degrees. You won't stop that from happening.'

'I think that settles it then, Daniel,' Francis Broome condescended. 'You're angry now, but in time you'll come to realise what really happened and you'll accept that Rublex will have a big part to play in golf for many years to come. The reputation of the Tour and our primary sponsor remains intact. Without the evidence you speak of, any claims you make to the contrary will, of course, be vigorously denied and contested in the law courts.'

Daniel looked around the room at each of them in turn. He shook his head and then, without uttering another word, he bolted from the room. Broken. Dejected. Confused.

He trailed down the steps, eyes brimming with the bitter

tears of shame. His parents, who hadn't let him out of their sight since their reunion by his hospital bed in Barcelona, were waiting where he'd left them. The front seats of their Vauxhall Vectra. They had driven him to the meeting in a show of familial support. Daniel climbed into the back seat.

'What happened, son?'

'Nothing. They wouldn't listen. I can't believe it after everything that I've gone through. I can't. It was all just a lie. I don't want to speak about it.'

'You need to accept it, Daniel. These aren't our sort of people, boy. You've aimed above your station and this is the result. You've tried your best to help people and you've been hurt. I've arranged a job for you with me back in Sheffield at the insurance firm. We can make the move back in with us at home permanent.'

Daniel placed his head into his hands. Head spinning. The desolation was absolute.

Their car pulled away and began cruising down the neat road that bisected the fairways of the exemplary Wentworth golf course. They tracked the winding tarmac through lush forest and out into the countryside. No one spoke. No one had anything to say. Daniel remained inconsolable.

Time passed. The motorway spread out before them. Inside the vehicle the emotion remained thick and heavy. What few innocent comments passed between them to lighten the mood were ignored or merely grunted at in response. Daniel sat in an unhappy trance, hypnotised by the blur of passing pylons, road signs and speeding cars. He felt as if he was now being transported towards his final terminus – a limited life without the possibilities and potential which he had so cruelly been permitted to taste.

The sound of a phone call cut through the tension inside the vehicle. Daniel fumbled around in his pocket for his mobile and, after what seemed an eternity, engaged the call. Mumbling in answer.

'Good afternoon. Is that Daniel Ratchet?'

'Yeah,' sniffed Daniel, half-expecting a pushy salesman at the other end.

'Daniel. It's Brooke Anderson from the Laureus World Sports Academy.'

'Oh. Hi,' Daniel said, brightening up moderately.

'I'll cut to the chase. I'm notifying you that we are publishing your article in our "Sport for Good" magazine.'

'Article?'

'Yeah. The one you submitted on corruption in golf and the undue influence of sponsors on top players, in order to further their own objectives. Particularly the Rublex Corporation. We're very impressed with the evidence you've compiled. The statistical patterns, the undercover video recording of the principal wrongdoers admitting their crimes, the background narrative. It's a compelling case you make regarding a very serious issue. Action needs to be taken.'

'Um. What article? I didn't write an article or submit one to Laureus.'

'Your representative spoke to us and posted a memory stick to us on your behalf. A German guy. One Michael Hausen?'

Michael. So, it was Michael who had found the tablet. He must have seen the evidence on there and in conjunction with his own brutal personal experiences made the connection between the caddy gambling ring and the Russian Vory. He took matters into his own hands – must have written the article to ensure that those who stood up for truth, for justice and for opportunity in sport would get the evidence to expose Rublex for what they really are. That bitch Matilda must have been in on it all from the start. Smoothing the way with her beauty and tantalising sexuality to encourage susceptible golf agents to sign Krostanov's dodgy sponsorship deals.

Once the man she'd used to get her leg up and over with on the Tour, her fiancé, had proven to be losing control of the situation she needed another means to achieve her ruthless ambitions. Krostanov went to extreme lengths to find and eradicate all traces of evidence linking Rublex to corruption. It seems that Matilda must have used that same evidence as a bargaining chip to replace him and secure his job with Boris Golich for herself, even before he was dead. No wonder he was driven to such desperate lengths. There's no honour amongst thieves, as they say.

Before he'd been murdered, Michael must have figured out that Matilda wasn't to be trusted and wouldn't use the evidence as hoped. He'd read the information contained on the tablet and understood the implications. He'd pieced together the connection to the gambling ring and the danger they posed. He realised that the Daniel Ratchet kidnapping and Bob Wallace murder were probably as a direct result of discovering the truth. Given such a serious situation, it had taken genuine, unprecedented bravery for Michael to act and to ultimately sacrifice his life. To do the right thing.

'Yes. Thank you, Brooke. That's fantastic.'

'Not only that, Daniel. We're so impressed by your efforts that we'd like to make you a job offer. On the strength of the Rublex exposé we are accelerating the launch of a new division at Laureus centred on corruption across sport worldwide, supported with a new endowment of five million dollars. It'll be run from a new Miami base. We think a young hungry guy like you, with significant experience in exposing major corporate sports corruption, would be perfect to head it up. We'll need you to come to London right away to discuss things. Can you make Monday morning at nine o'clock? What do you say?'

Daniel's heart soared. 'Thank you,' he stumbled. 'I'll be there!' He bounced on his seat, his father watching in the rear-view mirror as he rapped his knuckles in sheer delight on the car window.

He ended the phone call. Sat back in disbelief. Stunned into silence again.

'Who was that, love?' his mother enquired from the front seat. Daniel shook his head in disbelief.

'Who was that?' he replied. 'That was the voice of justice and the final deed of a man who, against the odds, found it within himself to do the right thing. A hero who I betrayed for the love of an undeserving woman and ultimately sent to his death. And in return I think he might very well have just saved my life.'

THE END

ACKNOWLEDGEMENTS

Thank you to the good folk at Bloodhound Books for inviting me into the kennel.

Also to the myriad of others who helped in ways great and small along the way. You know who you are and probably got name checked in the first cut; so that's your lot!

A NOTE FROM THE PUBLISHER

Thank you for reading this book. If you enjoyed it please do consider leaving a review on Amazon to help others find it too.

We hate typos. All of our books have been rigorously edited and proofread, but sometimes mistakes do slip through. If you have spotted a typo, please do let us know and we can get it amended within hours.

info@bloodhoundbooks.com

ABOUT THE AUTHOR

Author Ted Denton is recognised for his writing of intelligent, plot driven thrillers. Fascinated with the psychology of crime, the dynamics of power and complexities of the human condition, Denton brings the look-through of a cinematographer's eye to the written word; sharing close-up visceral intensity with the reader at every twist and turn.

Ted is a seasoned adventurer, having visited some of the world's most remote peoples and inaccessible countries. He is passionate about geopolitics, gastronomy, boxing and the shared responsibility to resist global cultural homogenisation.

He is a member of The Society of Authors and The Honorary Society of International Thriller Writers.

www.ted-denton.com

Printed in Great Britain
by Amazon

71234878R00213